Terror Australis

The Off-Worlder Chronicles
Book one

https://terror-australis.blog
https://kreative-droid.blog

First edition October 2018
Second edition February 2019
Changes include new cover artwork, adding a prologue, images, contextual corrections and note by the author.

Dedication

For Sandy in appreciation of her patience, understanding, encouragement, and above all else her belief. I should also thank my family and the "Slackers" a great bunch of eclectic people who also supported me on my writing path. Of course, there also are those who steered my word craft in a better direction.

The crew at Book Gremlins
Lorin from www.thewritething.com.au
Eeva from www.thebookkhaleesi.com
And Alice Lunsford.

Thank you to **Alex Gavrilas** for the front cover artwork

Contents

PROLOGUE

Lucius Neratius Marcellus roused from sleep, dressed in haste, and hurried to the town's hospital. The reason for his being woken in the early hours sat undisguised on his face.

"All of them?"

"Yes, governor," the Optio in charge of his Praetorian guard repeated.

The footsteps of the twelve men sounded dull and ominous. Around them, the mist and steady rain heralded the mood of Eboracum's governor.

Across the Empire, the location of Roman Hospitals differed little from town to town. The Milites Medici wanted them built away from the general populace and garrison barracks; other soldiers should never hear the cries and agonies of sick and wounded men lest it eats away at their courage.

Marcellus shrugged his cloak higher about his shoulders. Somewhere in his thoughts, he noted this visit to the northern province's capital heralded his third year as Legatus Augusti Pro Praetore in Britain.

He turned his head down when a gust of wind slapped the rain in his eyes and wondered if the weather and the night's news came only to spite those first three good years.

One week after Marcellus settled in as the new Governor of Roman Britain, he knew he despised the country's climate, and this night's miserable squall gave him no reason to change his mind.

The ice-filled rain, he decided, proved colder than the Emperor's decision to bleed troops from the armies in Britain to support the campaign in Gaul. An action which gave those Caledonian devils up north a chance to once more paint their faces blue and kill more Roman citizens.

Marcellus pulled his woollen cloak tighter about his and neck. By the gods, he hated the weather here.

When he stepped through the doorway of the hospital, Marcellus stopped to frown at the Augur who barred his way. The priest's sharp, nervous breaths and the soft spatter of water which dripped from Marcellus's cloak, and armour heightened the tension in the stone-walled foyer.

"Barrakus," Marcellus said, "why are you here?" Marcellus peered past the agitated old priest.

A meticulous man, Barrakus seldom appeared in any way other than well groomed. Now he stood in a dishevelled toga and robe. His silver-grey shoulder length hair hung off his head in wet, matted ringlets, and his eyes were held within red rings of weariness. Or was it something other than fatigue which dragged at the man's features.

Raised as a military man, Marcellus found his true comfort in battle strategies and action rather than the auspices of priests with their divinations of birds, foxes and the sacrifice of dogs. However, as a diplomat, he understood their political need as part of his entourage.

Barrakus massaged his Lituus, the small curved wand used for ritual divination, while he muttered litanies against the spirits.

"Governor..." Barrakus pointed skyward, and his hand holding the little staff twitched in fevered spasms above his head. "When I saw ravens and hawks pass as one..." Barrakus trailed off and shifted to look back over his shoulder along the shadowed blockwork and timber hall. "Governor, these men are now cursed and driven mad by the gods. Because of this, I instructed only the senior Medici and three of their aids to remain. The rest I sent away for fear they may catch the ravings of madmen." His words came in the rapid squeaks of a terrified man.

Marcellus held up a hand, the babble of the priest trailed off. With Barrakus quiet, Marcellus issued instructions for the Optio and his detail of Praetorians to shelter in an adjacent stable.

The Optio raised an eyebrow at his Governor.

Marcellus reassured the soldier with a pat on the shoulder before he rejoined Barrakus.

"Where are the wounded?" A taller officer beside Marcellus asked.

"Forgive me, Praetor Octavius; all but one are in the main treatment area. The separated soldier is in the storeroom to the left." Barrakus kowtowed and pointed down the corridor.

Marcellus motioned for Octavius to follow him and pushed past Barrakus who scampered after the two officers with fervent objections.

"Tell me again how many men returned?" Marcellus asked the Fort's commander.

"I am told only a handful, perhaps ten," replied Octavius.

They paused at the door to the storeroom from where a Medici's aid emerged, his back bent from the weight of woven baskets filled with blood-stained rags.

Marcellus raised an eyebrow when the young medic rushed past with the gruesome load.

The rooms only occupant lay on a cot made from wood and rope, his hands and feet tied to the four corners of the bed's frame. His face and arms, unrecognisable beneath layers of flax and cloth lathered in a waxen salve.

Marcellus and Octavius flashed a cautious look at each other. The wounded man's breath came and went in ragged gasps. His body shivered with convulsions.

At the foot of some shelves lay the legionnaires uniform. The metal armour scarred, pitted and scorched.

Inside the room, Marcellus balled the corner of his cloak to filter the smell of the oils, herbs, incense and burnt, gangrenous flesh. One large wound on the soldier's thigh wept puss as maggots feasted on the rotten muscle and skin.

They stepped back and bumped a table. An empty goblet tumbled to the floor where it rolled toward the discarded armour before it leapt through the air.

Marcellus and Octavius looked on in shock when the metal mug stuck fast against the burnt armour.

Octavius bent to retrieve the goblet and jumped back as the damaged armour slid and vibrated toward his own. Unlike his governor, Octavius was a superstitious man, and everything in the storeroom hinted at daemons or worse.

The shuffle of sandaled feet padding through the door distracted Octavius, who recomposed himself beside Marcellus.

The two men went over to the cot beside the young Marsi who inspected the wounded mans dressings. He then used fresh strips of cloth to wipe away the blood-stained spittle which dribbled from the dying man's mouth. The

Marsi flinched as a bubble of pink saliva burst when his patient coughed out his final mortal breath.

Marcellus knelt beside the dead man and released a mournful sigh. Although the face was blistered and scorched, he recognised the man who, for the last five seasons, carried the standard of the Ninth Legion with pride. Marcellus rose and saluted. "Rest well, Lucious Duccius Rufinus. Imaginer of Legio IX."

"You knew him?" Asked Octavius.

Marcellus gave a single nod. "Lucious had three years of subscription to serve after which, he said he would take a wife and become a shepherd."

Marcellus left the room with his Praetor walking beside him. "The Ninth Legion served in this country for almost two generations. They fought alongside Agricola to defeat the Caledonians and their usurper king Calgacus. They recovered from their near defeat against that slut Boadicea and for what? To lose against a horde of blue painted bastards from the north." Marcellus growled with bitter anger and loss.

"Forgive me, Governor," Barrakus interrupted. "The survivors claim a sky daemon took their Legion."

"What in the name of Mars does that mean?" Octavius asked.

"Dreams and misunderstandings from a wounded man." Marcellus sighed.

"Except every man, regardless of his wounds, tells of the same dream," Barrakus said. He steered the two officers out into the mist-shrouded courtyard.

The three men stood beside a torch which hissed and sputtered in the fog. Barrakus held his Lituus in both hands and repeated what he heard. "They spoke about how the heavens opened and breathed inwards with a maw of multicoloured lighting and fire which consumed the Legion and their baggage carts."

Governor Marcellus glanced skyward.

"Sir this is nonsense," Octavius scoffed. "The Caledonians simply used fire against them."

"Yes, they could have, but can you explain why the Imaginers armour beckoned other objects of metal." Marcellus sought the eyes of Barrakus for an explanation before turning back to face Octavius. "I knew the Tribune in command of the Ninth. He would have seen through a disguised attack."

"Governor," Barrakus insisted. "A surviving Frumentarii said, they were camped on open ground when the clear night turned foul and consumed the Legion before they moved into battle formations."

Marcellus dismissed Barrakus and paced a small circle, his face gripped in a mournful expression. The fingers of his left hand squeezed the hilt of his Gladius.

Barrakus waited for Marcellus to stop his agitated prowl. When he realised the Governor ignored both himself and Octavius, the old priest returned to the hospital.

When the priest left, Marcellus stopped in front of Octavius. "No one must learn about this. Not the stories, those injured survivors or about the heavens consuming the Legion."

"Do you believe the priest?"

"What I believe is of little consequence."

The light from the torch's fame twisted the shadows on Marcellus's face. A face fixed by a hard choice. The only choice. He watched a cabbage moth flutter around the fire of a torch. The insect dove and skirted the flames until a shift in the breeze blew the moth against the torch. In a

11

brief flare the winged insect ignited before plummeting to the ground.

"Octavius,' Marcellus said, "the Emperor and the people will only know the Ninth died in battle." Marcellus stared at the mud brick building which housed the last of the Ninth Legion. "Use only those you can trust. Section off the nearby houses and clear them of people and burn them and the hospital. Ensure the word spreads about a plague which the medici tried to control and purify with fire. An action in which they also sacrificed themselves. Once the ashes are cold, I want them all buried with dignity and honour."

"What of the Priest?"

Marcellus sighed. Nearby, the rain and mist hissed and steamed in the flames of the torch. "Barrakus will serve Rome and the Emperor." Marcellus gripped Octavius's arms, "I want no one to suffer. Can you do this, my old friend?"

"By your command Governor."

A fresh shower of rain parted the fog. Lucius Neratius Marcellus returned to his home. He wondered why some decisions, regardless of their need, still crushed the heart.

PART ONE

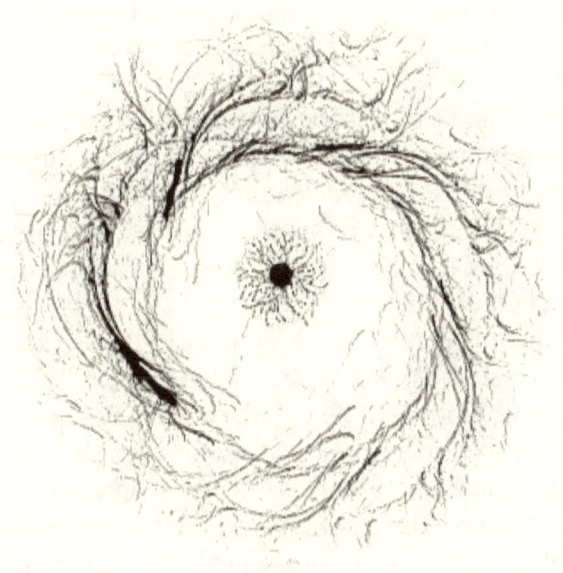

CHAPTER ONE

Marcus Civilis Emeritus enjoyed the comfort and air-conditioned air within his limousine. He did not enjoy reading the reports scattered across the seat next to him. With the northern region's profits and tributes down, Marcus wanted, no, needed the secret experiments to yield a result.

Both he and the Tribune in charge of the science auxiliaries promised the cabal success within three years. Now, six months past the deadline, Marcus is again travelling 160 kilometres southwest of Toowoomba, where he and the Senate ruled the Empire's northern state. Once known as Queensland.

For the thirteenth time, Marcus read the scribbled note in his journal; the twenty-third of January 2021. No more delays or all funds will be withdrawn. He flicked the diary closed and fixed his gaze on the point where the decaying highway blended with the heat diffused horizon.

The lead vehicle, a battery-powered, three-wheeled motorbike, veered onto a dirt access road in a plume of billowing dust. Behind the rider, mounted above the rear axle, and protected by a curved pale blue energy shield, sat an elevated D shaped platform. Mounted on the platform stood two Gatling-style machine guns and two Praetorian Guards.

Trailing the motorised chariot came two sleek plum coloured motorbikes whose high-gloss, aerodynamic, fairing flowed back over the front wheel and chassis forming a pair of matching panniers.

Marcus's six-door limousine followed the front escorts. Two small satin flags fluttered and snapped above the headlights. The gold fabric on the right side contrasted the jet-black silhouette of a bull above Roman numerals, and the opposite flag displayed a star within a red and green laurel wreath, above two, crossed Gladius swords, and the letters *S.P.Q.R.*

A kilometre down the arid dirt road, the cavalcade slowed to stop at a checkpoint. The driver of the limousine rolled down his window and issued instructions not to broadcast the proconsul's arrival.

A minute later the vehicles drove past a break in a perimeter fence. Dangling from the fence hung a faded sign; Gore Crop-dusting - Proprietor D.J. Grahams Est. 1973.

They crossed an abandoned runway stopping in front of a hangar. In the background, the pale dust from the processions passage floated northward on the sluggish, hot, dry air.

Running in one synchronised movement, each rider dismounted and formed a cordon as Marcus emerged into the harsh light.

The powder-dry dirt puffed out from under his polished, chocolate coloured, leather boots, and the dry heat pinched his exposed skin. After a furtive scan of the area surrounding the compound, Marcus leaned into the limousine retrieving his cloak.

In the distance, a grove of long-dead trees wavered in the baleful sun's heat haze. Phantom sentinels guarding the dead landscape.

Marcus draped the cloak over his shoulder and brought up his manicured hand, halting two of the bike riders marching his way.

"Stand at ease, Centurion." He glanced at the rusted security fence. The chain mesh holding back half a dozen small desiccated bushes. "There is a reason we call out here no-man's-land. Wait in the canteen. I will phone through when I am ready."

"By your command, Proconsul."

Marcus's chiselled face offered the smallest trace of a smile before he walked toward the structure. *May the gods and fortune favour me with a result.*

On entering the building, he paused, blinked, and squinted as his eyes adjusted to the lower light spectrum.

The air outside hovered in the mid-forty degrees centigrade, but inside, super-chilled air streamed through wall vents to sting his warm skin.

Blurred outlines and deep cast shadows coalesced to reveal a darkened room, not unlike a tactical operations centre on an orbital battle barge.

Against the two longer walls stood an assortment of computer cabinets and desks, attended by three Roman science auxiliaries dressed in bottle-green overalls.

Three of the men busied themselves in front of computers, typing codes on backlit keyboards. A fourth Roman paced up and down, scribbling notes on a luminescent green clipboard covered with papers.

"Lafrenius, why do you insist on keeping the lights so dim?" Marcus blinked and drew the mulberry hued velvet cloak across his shoulders and over his immaculate, ink-blue, two-piece linen suit. "And must you keep the temperature so cold?"

"Marcus?" An older man stepped out from behind a two-meter-high data bank. "When did you arrive?"

"An impromptu visit."

"You know my thoughts about such… visits."

Lafrenius needed no guessing on why Marcus was there. He and Marcus only spoke two days ago via a sub-ether unit about the progress of the experiment and the impatience of their benefactors. Lafrenius sighed. Yes, they were past the deadline, but he worked with recycled second-rate equipment and inexperienced technicians.

"Indeed. A point you have never failed to mention." Marcus wandered through the room, mesmerised with iridescent dials, gauges, and monitors filled with moving bar graphs and data streams.

"If you find the temperature too cold or the lighting too dark, you could wait back in my office," Lafrenius said in a dismissive tone, "We are about to begin the trial of the new targeting matrix, and the bright lights make certain gauges difficult to read."

"It would seem I came at the right time." Marcus smiled at the ageing Tribune. "Can I help?"

"Yes. You can ionise the mapping screen and then stay put."

Marcus tipped his head in acquiescence and moved across to the back wall where he activated a large rectangular screen. Charged particles between two plates of crystal glowed with a cloud of swirling blue, red, green, and grey.

17

Lafrenius continued his zigzagging between the consoles and the operators, making notes with his stylus and stopping beside a seated technician. Lafrenius referred to his scribbled formulas and adjusted the dials until a single red light pulsed on the technician's console.

With a grunt, Lafrenius shifted his attention to the mapping screen where a smaller green dot flashed. The scientist tapped his stylus on his nose and walked back to the bank of instruments to adjust more dials and type in added codes.

"No. No. No!" He trotted back to the technician with the first pulsing light. "You are not compensating for the spatial drift and phase variance. I have told you before; the two dimensions are not parallel," Lafrenius struck the younger man across the back of his head. "They are alternate. Now, rework the calculation for a…" he scribbled on his board, "… 6.536 variation. That should be enough to counter the drift vector."

He swivelled his head between the two out of sync red lights. "Quickly adjust the Z axis." He continued to tap the stylus against his nose until the console's red light turned green when both lights pulsed in a simultaneous rhythm. "Better." He called over his shoulder. "Tiberius bring the central console online."

A science auxiliary from across the room rose from his station and walked to the opposite end of the room to sit in a cockpit style console station.

Lafrenius made his way towards the mapping screen and tweaked several dials on a control panel. With each change, the cloud-like image changed until a spiral-arm galaxy filled the right side. On the edge of one of the spiral arms flashed a tiny green dot.

"All right, Tiberius. Are the solar capacitors charged?"

"Yes, Tribune."

"The backup batteries?"

"All at full capacity."

"Excellent. Proceed with initialising the power relays and then turn on the outside lights."

In front of Tiberius, the wall grew brighter revealing a one-way mirror.

Marcus made his way to the window accompanied by a growing hum. From his new vantage point, Marcus realised the control room stood on a raised platform within the hangar.

At the opposite end stood an octagonal ring carved from basalt. Embedded in the internal corners, contrasting the slate-grey rock, were eight tetrahedrons of quartz crystal set in place by brass straps.

Behind the ring, stood a circle of twelve magnets, each the size of a house brick and fastened to small, triangular columns interwoven by coiled cables. Once powered, the electromagnets pushed a bronze alloy gyroscope aloft on a cushion of air.

On the back side of the stone circle stood four steel tripods the height of a man, supporting drill-like arrays aimed at the crystals in the twelve, three, six and nine o'clock positions.

Dozens of leads from transformers against the back wall snaked across the floor to the six-meter-wide ring, the small towers, and the magnets.

Tiberius activated his console and slid his chair forward, so his hands rested on two rotating balls nestled amid an assortment of numeric keypads and toggles.

When he flipped a toggle, compressed air hissed, and hydraulics whined to lift his entire station. A second switch brought up a holographic target array. Tiberius rolled the balls under his palms until the centre ring of the targeting display sat over the gyroscope. Satisfied with the holograph's position, he thumbed two more toggles.

Transfixed, Marcus stood watching the middle of the gyroscope pulse blue-white, and then rotate with increasing speed until the apparatus resembled a golden ring around a white centre.

Lafrenius manipulated the crystal screens and called over his shoulder, "Bring the particle beams online." In front of him, the blurred image of the galaxy formed on the screen's left side. An exact mirror reversed duplicate of the first. Within seconds, another smaller red dot appeared on an outer arm of the new galactic spiral.

Hypnotised at the window, Marcus watched in awe as the pointed nose of the drill-like objects faded behind a purple glow.

"On my mark…" Lafrenius said. "One… two… three… mark."

Marcus leaned closer, his breath fogging the glass.

In unison, each emitter fired a pencil-thin mauve beam at a corresponding crystal. The quartz balls flared from deep within as twisting ribbons of lavender light crept outward and connected all eight crystals.

The quartz soon sparkled from the energy bolts, and in less than a minute, each turned into writhing balls of energy.

Without warning, a clap of thunder startled Marcus and sent vibrations through the glass wall. The lavender bolts of light met in the ring's middle exploding into a ball of chaotic energies.

"Status report?" Lafrenius asked.

"The portal is stable, but with only a half-meter dilation," replied Tiberius.

"Excellent. Commodus, start the carrier beam."

An assistant rolled his chair across the room and typed a command into a computer console. The instant he tapped the enter key, a bright white shaft of light shot from the spinning gyroscope and struck the pulsating sphere of energy.

Another sonic boom erupted from the ring.

The proconsul flinched and stepped back from the quivering window. The atmosphere beyond the glass turned into a white rain filled fog.

Behind him, Lafrenius's eyes darted between the two galaxies. He adjusted the dials to zoom in on the images, held his breath, and watched the screens. Within seconds, a thin orange line stretched from the green dot on the left connecting with the red dot on the right.

The air filled with static. The operations room shuddered. A small console fell off the wall in an eruption of sparks and trailing fused wire.

Beyond the window, the rain and fog funnelled into the basalt ring. Within a minute, the internal squall disappeared.

"Increase the particle beams' harmonics by a factor of 2.96."

The vibration within the room increased. A half-filled coffee cup slid off a table and shattered on the floor.

"Tribune Lafrenius." Tiberius called out, "the carrier beams are destabilising."

Lafrenius ran to Tiberius's console. He studied the readouts while massaging the back of his neck. Something on the third, left-hand monitor caught his attention.

"Tachyon particles are causing feedback. Something is creating a temporal loop." The old man's eyes clouded with concentration. "Hurry, re-modulate the frequency of the particle beam by a factor of seven."

"And the carrier waves?" A technician named Quintus enquired.

Weaving back to the mapping screen via several monitors, Lafrenius stopped at another console and adjusted the controls which increased the magnification of the right-hand image. "Twelve per cent added to the frequency output should compensate shift."

"Tribune," Quintus called over his shoulder. "I am picking up an image."

Marcus and Lafrenius joined Quintus as a black-and-white image formed on his screen.

"What is it?" Marcus squinted at the monitor.

"I believe we are looking at is the surface of another planet in an alternate dimension, and, if these readings are correct…" Lafrenius darted to the mapping screen and adjusted the image until a blue-green planet filled the crystal display. His fingers manipulated the dials in gentle caresses. Lafrenius proclaimed with a smug tone crossing his arms in triumph, "it is also the birthplace of our ancestors."

"Do you know what time or era?" Marcus asked.

"It is hard to say."

The scientist continued working the dials until the image zoomed in on hills covered in lush undergrowth, grass and trees, and the occasional village of stone houses and thatched roofs.

He collected a binder from a nearby shelf unit, rejecting it for another which he flipped open and leafed through the pages in a fevered search. He slapped his hand on a page and darted back to the crystal display. Lifting the folder against the screen and tapping the images on the page.

"Look. The images… They conform with those from the Novicus Patria scrolls."

"Well done, my friend." The proconsul patted the older man's back.

Superimposed over the topographical display hovered a transparent red disc rimmed with bright yellow. "The portal openings appear stable enough…" The old scientist frowned at the readout overlaying the time-lapsed video. "Tiberius re-modulate the beam by a factor of seven."

As Tiberius reached for the bank of dials, his console erupted. Green flames and arcing energy blasted outward. The entire console spasmed when its hydraulic base collapsed.

Tiberius screamed as his body turned into a writhing mass of burning flesh and clothes.

The mirrored window flexed before erupting into a horizontal hailstorm of glazed shrapnel. The atmosphere in the hanger below, danced with pulsing flames, sprouting from clouds of lavender and aqua.

A battering ram of air slammed through the control room in a pressure wave tipping tables, unfurling ribbons of perforated printing paper, and threatening to cast aside the four remaining Romans.

Twisting fingers of energy arced through the shattered window. Commodus dazed, and bleeding from a cut above his eye died from a bolt of energy grazing his chest.

The floor buckled as glass and sparks rained down from a bank of exploding ceiling lights. Charred spots peppered Marcus's cloak from the hot electrical cinders. Beyond the broken window, shadows fluctuated with the moving lights in the hanger.

The basalt ring now glowed an orange-red, and the quartz tetrahedrons burned white and, the eight emitters lay broken and scattered on the floor.

Above over the magnets, the gyroscope continued spinning amidst ribbons of arcing energy stretching toward each of the crystal balls.

When the last tendril and crystal connected, the gyroscope launched itself into the centre of the ring.

Inside the control room, the flow of the wild, howling wind reversed.

Marcus raised his head above the window frame peering at a single demonic eye glaring back from the chaos below.

A technician dragged himself back to his computer. "We've lost containment. The portal is drifting."

Lafrenius stood, bracing himself against the sucking atmospheric pressure.

The stone circle hovered above the floor; its orange glow haloed by a rainbow ring of light expanding inwards.

Lafrenius cast a quick glance at a monitor displaying an image from a camera behind the stone ring and equipment. What he saw made his heart race faster.

Facing them was a disc of swirling multi-hued energy with a white centre, yet, the image from the rear camera showed a circle of grey fog.

Inside the control room, Marcus watched as the ionised gasses and particle clouds rotated into a cyclonic whirlpool around the brilliant white ball of the transformed gyroscope.

The faster the energy and gas spun, the smaller the glowing ball became until it disappeared at the end of a reversed tornado.

Lafrenius pointed at the screen relaying the rear camera's image. "Do you see it, Quintus?" Lafrenius clutched the technician's shoulder for support. "The funnel extends back for hundreds of metres–"

"–Yet the rear of the portal still appears flat." Quintus toggled his head between the screen and Lafrenius. "By the gods… It's beautiful."

"A spectacular sight…" Lafrenius swallowed back his emotion.

Around them, the negative air pressure intensified.

Down in the hanger, loose items and broken equipment disappeared into the spinning vortex which bounced against the ceiling.

The outer edge of the vortex tore at the metal rafters, battens and sheeting before smashing through the roof with a sudden explosive scream.

"Track it!" Shouted Lafrenius.

Quintus ran back to the mapping screen where he spun dials and flicked switches. "It's heading northeast, travelling at forty-seven kilometres a minute."

Lafrenius helped the proconsul stand before he joined Quintus. Overlapping images replayed on the crystal plates.

In a translucent green circle, scenes of the local desert and salt-scrub terrain flashed by, washed out by torrential rain and lightning

"Is that a storm?" Asked Marcus.

"A possible by-product of the portal's ionised field," Lafrenius replied.

Quintus called out. "The images from the opposite opening... Something is different."

The red disc showed bitumen roads lined with headlights, pastoral lands, and townships illuminated by street lamps. In the green circle, static filled the screen before fading in on abandoned, ruined farms, and a broad undulating floodplain laced with gullies. All of which disappeared in a brief flash as the mapping screen went black.

Quintus and Lafrenius attacked the controls in a vain effort of re-establishing a connection.

"Sorry, sir," Quintus said, "by these readings, the portal has collapsed."

Lafrenius began a hushed conversation with himself and wondered from desk to desk.

A confused Marcus followed the old scientist around the room. "Lafrenius, what just happened?"

"Gravimetric distortions, solar winds, increased radiogenic disruptions, and electromagnetic fluctuations..." Lafrenius tore the paper from an overturned printer continuing his private conversation. "But what caused the temporal shifts? What did I miss?" His face contorted with internal calculations. "A passing space body? No... No, it would require one with a huge mass." Something on the printout stopped his musings, he ran across and rifled through readouts from another printer. "A simultaneous planetary alignment. How did I not see this?"

"In simpler terms."

"It means, Proconsul, the experiment was a failure." Lafrenius threw aside the paper in frustration.

"Sir," Quintus interrupted. He sat at his computer and re-ran the recorded images now superimposed with codes and formulas. "The last image we recorded."

"Just passing scenery," Lafrenius said. "We can analyse the data stream later."

"No, sir." Quintus faced both Marcus and Lafrenius.

"Explain." Marcus leaned closer frowning at the paused blurred picture.

"We pulled through Something from the other side," Quintus said.

Marcus fixed his gaze on Lafrenius. "Is that possible?"

"In theory," the grey-haired scientist shrugged. "Our aim is moving objects or people, but not at this stage of testing, and not from the other side."

"Are you certain of your findings?" Marcus continued to study the blurred image.

"Yes, sir, and…"

"And what?"

"By these readings, it is an artificial construct comprising metals, various hydrocarbons and synthetics," Quintus paused and highlighted a line of code on the screen, "and the object also contained at least one life sign."

"Lafrenius." Marcus tipped his head back, "where is your sub-ether Comms unit?"

"In the phone exchange beside the canteen building."

Marcus pulled the scientist aside. "Do you trust the men in this room?"

Lafrenius hesitated and gave his proconsul a worried frown. "They have kept our secret, thus far."

"Yes." Marcus smiled and patted the scientists back. "They have, indeed," he said on leaving the shattered control room. *And they shall continue to do so.*

CHAPTER TWO

On a Thursday afternoon in late August in 2014, Ex-Sergeant Benjamin James Ried sat silent and alone at a roadhouse café west of Brisbane.

He sat alone, because he preferred things that way, since his return from Afghanistan. It became a way of avoiding conversations about why Australian troops were over there or questions about fighting against the Taliban.

Why? Because those same questions and opinions brought back memories, he didn't want. They also became the reason he moved around and didn't hold a job for over two months.

By default, Ried became a drifter, never staying stationary for long and surviving off his army pension.

Ried glanced up as a cattle truck shuddered to a stop beside the twin set of diesel pumps. In less than a minute, the stale perfume of old manure mixed with bovine piss pervaded the air inside. The diner's only patron twitched his nose at the intruding odour.

The muffled sounds of the truck's cargo nudged Ried's sympathy. "Poor buggers. It's a good thing you lot don't know your future." He washed down the remaining sinewy piece of his steak sandwich with a mouthful of tepid percolated coffee.

The coffee, toast, meat, and salad fought against his stomach acids. Ried burped and swept his hand through his cocoa-dark hair.

The early dinner did not fall into the category of the worst food he'd ever consumed, but nor did the meal rate anywhere near the best. Still, it abated his hunger.

Behind and above his right shoulder, a wall-mounted TV depicted the decisive moments of a 1960s war movie where the hero defeats the hapless Germans, saves the damsel, jumps in a Jeep, and drives off on his next mission of glory.

Ried twisted in his seat with a lopsided smile creasing his cheek. "What a crock of shit. Where in the real world does a soldier save the day, defeat the enemy, and drive off with the girl?" He turned his attention away from the TV and picked up a two-day-old, dog-eared newspaper left abandoned on the chair beside him.

"Give me a break."

The bold typeset of the front page' headlines highlighted another football player's drug scandal. In the article, the journalist questioned the player's integrity, leading up to the September finals.

At the bottom of the page and taking up four lines was an article about another soldier killed over in the Middle East. Ried flipped the paper face down beside his plate and closed his green-flecked, hazel eyes and massaged his temples. *I suppose nobody gives a rat's arse about what we are doing anymore. Well, if the world doesn't care, maybe I shouldn't either.*

Ried rubbed his eyes. The weariness from his trip settled upon him. He nudged the empty plate aside, rested his head on crossed arms, and dozed off.

"What the hell are they playing at?" He tapped his throat mic. "Charlie Zero Two and Three, why have you dropped back?" Ried's earpiece crackled before a tiny voice vibrated through it.

"Sorry, skipper. A mob of goats and a farmer ran out on the road."

"Push your way through." Ried pulled out his briefing notes and scanned the coded page. "Shit." He turned to a soldier operating the twenty-five-millimetre cannon behind him. "Jimmy, swing around and have a gander at that hill on our nine." He fought the panic and worry rising in his throat. "Charlie Zero Two and Three, reverse your twenty. I say again, reverse your twenty."

"It's all good Charlie Zero One. We'll just go around the–"

"Negative! I repeat, negative! Do not go off-road." Ried flipped the safety of his Styr and tapped his driver's shoulder. "Simmo, spin us about." He thumbed the mike. "Two and three–" His earpiece erupted with a burst of static. "Fuck."

His ears popped when the vehicle's cannon fired at a small ridge. "Skipper! Tallies on our nine and six!" The gunner fired another shell. "Simmo, get us the fuck out of here."

Ried snatched up his satellite phone from the dash. "Sunray Minor. Charlie Zero one, two, and three under assault–"

A twisting train of smoke arced toward their LAV. The ground in front of the reversing armoured vehicle disappeared behind a ball of flame and dirt. The cannon fired another two rapid shots.

"RPG! RPG! They've got fucking RPGs!" The gunner shouted seconds before his turret ruptured amidst a concussive cloud of flame and super-heated metal.

#

"Shit." Ried jerked upright, his hands gripped the table's edge, his knuckles white. His ears pounded from increased blood pressure. His breath came in hyperventilating wheezes, and his heart thumped against his chest.

Looking around, he blinked his eyes until they refocused on his surroundings. A wave of embarrassment washed over him while bringing his ragged breathing under control.

Ried forced a reset on his composure and released his grip from the table and smeared away the sweat from his face.

Cleaning the diner's floor, a waitress turned and glanced his way.

Ried lowered his eyes, slid from the booth and stepped into the restroom. He braced himself on the washbasin and contemplated his reflection in the mirror holding a familiar shadow of torment. *Survivor's guilt, the shrink called it.*

He squeezed his eyes closed and flexed his neck muscles. "Fucking oath it's guilt." Turning on the tap, he splashed water on his face.

When the last drops of tepid water fell from his chin, he gave his reflection a contemptuous gaze. *Come on, Ried. Maybe it's time to stop running and settle down and sort your shit out.*

He massaged the front of his right shoulder, sighed, and left the washroom.

The waitress abandoned her monotonous sweeping and sauntered over to stand near his booth after he sat down. She gazed at the younger man and combed her mousey-blond hair around her right ear with her fingers.

Ried tried his best to ignore the hovering woman by concentrating on the mud-coloured liquid in the mug cradled between his palms. He caught her arching shoulders above an overemphasised straight back. Her actions gave off less subtlety than a rifle butt on his forehead.

"Are you, all right?"

"Fine, just a bad dream," he murmured.

The waitress bent down and retrieved an envelope lying near his foot. "I think you dropped this."

"Oh, thanks." He put the letter beside his empty plates.

She walked off through the swinging door into the kitchen. Her cloying citrus and vanilla-scented perfume lingered in her wake.

When she returned with a tray and cleaning cloth, Ried couldn't decide which smelled worse: the woman's cheap scent laced with the odour of stale cigarette smoke or the lingering aroma of the cattle truck.

The waitress tossed Ried's dirty plate and the newspaper on the tray. She moved the letter, reading the name and address written on the envelope. "Lavarack Barracks, huh?" She pried. "You're a long way from home." She leaned closer, wiping the laminate surface of the table above his thighs. "You on leave?"

"Discharged," Ried picked up the envelope and slid it into his pocket. He then picked up the cup, but instead of drinking, he swirled the contents. *Disillusioned is more like it.*

"I once knew a bloke in the air force," she continued. "Are you headin' home or takin' a holiday?" She slid into the bench opposite him.

The corners of his mouth rose and fell in a quick "you can go now" smile. "New job out west," he replied.

"So, you alone, Benjamin?" The woman stroked her earlobe, oblivious to his subtle rejection.

He shrugged and almost told her he preferred Ben or Ried rather than Benjamin. However, as always, he struggled to converse with the opposite sex. Besides, he didn't want to indulge her or her flirtations.

Behind the waitress, the truck driver entered the diner, and slouched his full soft body against the counter and tapped the service bell watching Ried and the waitress.

After a few seconds of awkward silence, Ried checked his watch. "I should be back on the road." He excused himself with an apologetic smile and exited the diner.

As the door closed after him, Ried heard the other man's jibe at the waitress.

"Strewth Linda, a bloke could starve waitin' for you."

\#

The jarring bump and the gravel drumming under his car blasted away the fog shrouding his concentration.

"Shit."

Christ, Ried. Are you trying to kill yourself?

He jerked the wheel bringing the car back onto the bitumen. The tyres squealed in protest, and the rear end swung about in erratic arcs.

Twenty metres down the road, Ried pulled over as his cheeks and mouth puffed with an exaggerated release of breath.

The surviving remains of the semi-digested steak sandwich clawed its way up his throat on a bubble of gastric juice. Ried swallowed back the burning regurgitation and forced his heart into a regular constant beat.

He reached across for the bottle of water rolling around on the floor behind the passenger seat, unscrewed the cap, and washed away the unpleasant taste. When the last of the liquid flowed across his tongue, he rubbed his eyes. *If you had any brains, you'd pull over and sleep.*

Instead, he massaged his neck and peered through the dozens of dead insects glued to his windscreen. A fitting metaphor should he fall asleep at the wheel.

Ried accelerated his car under the moonless star-filled sky.

On a typical night, plumes of light would herald the passage of cars and trucks driving along the highway. However, except for the few vehicles detouring west of Warwick, the only other headlights lighting the road were from his car.

The dashboard's pale green light reflected off his tired and drawn face, giving him a haunted, hollow appearance. A look worsened by the frown creasing his forehead after he glanced at the digital clock.

"Ten-thirty," he grumbled. *Christ. It'll be hours before I get there. Bloody roadworks.*

In the distance, a flickering glow pulsed in a cloud bank on the horizon. *And I am not in the bloody mood for a fucking storm.*

Resetting the cruise control, Ried stretched his legs and rolled his shoulders, an activity which did little in easing his fatigued muscles.

A quick check of his mobile's GPS confirmed his next fuel stop, a roadhouse, on the outskirts of Gore was fifteen kilometres away. *Don't give in now. You can sleep at the truck stop. Until then, bloody well stay awake and drive.*

However, within minutes, his body betrayed him; not from his heavy eyelids, but from the urging of a full bladder. "Well, when you gotta go, you gotta go," he said, bringing the SUV to a stop.

A blast of chilled air slapped his face when he stepped from the comfort of his car.

"Strewth."

He recoiled from the oppressive, wet, sweet, and sour odour of some nearby roadkill in slow decay. "God, I miss the smell of the bush." Around him crickets went on chirping in the long grass, oblivious to his sarcasm.

The pungent, cool breeze snaked its way past his collar and tickled the hair on his back, rippling his skin with Goosebumps and also hastened his need for a piss.

Ried hurried through the beam of his headlights, away from the highway, and released the pressure from his bladder. The sensation produced a sigh of almost pure rapture. A tart, metallic odour wafted up from the warm stream of urine near his feet.

A childhood ditty popped into his head. "Who wrote the new book Rusty Bedsprings?" He asked aloud with only the chirp of field crickets as his response, Ried cried, "I pee nightly!" He re-zipped his jeans, grinning at his joke.

With his back to the road, Ried closed his eyes and again stretched his tired body. With his callisthenics completed, Ried opened his eyes and found the storm clouds closer and now filling the sky.

Their internal lightning breaking the gloom, and in a group of bright flashes, he spotted a signpost pointing the way to a crop-dusting service and airfield.

Another soft pop of light raised his eyes. *Damn it. I was hoping it would cross–*

He squinted into the dark. "Sounds like something's in a hurry…"

The noise sounded like a medicine ball bouncing through the paddock's grass and salt scrub. Overhead, a lightning bolt streaked between two clouds, lighting the surrounding fields.

"Jesus.!" The blasphemy whip cracked in the night air.

Ried threw himself on the patch of urine-soaked ground when a large kangaroo leapt over a nearby bush. With a weighty thud, the marsupial's taloned paws landed, bracketing his head, before scraping the gravel back when the animal's powerful legs launched the kangaroo over both him and the car.

"Bugger me…"

He raised himself back on his haunches but slid on his rump instead when other Roo swooped out of the night and landing half a metre away from his right foot, before it too leapt away, its tail brushing the nape of his neck.

"Holy shit."

Ried scurried back against the front passenger wheel of his car. The air expelled from a short, nervous laugh condensed beneath his nose. Then, with comic slowness, he turned and peered over the bonnet watching the animals melt into the night.

He flinched when a long, blue-white ribbon of light skipped under the clouds.

"Holy shit!" His cry rolled over the paddocks.

A further series of brief flashes revealed hundreds of leaping marsupials pouring from the trees and shrubs in a tsunami of brown and grey fur.

The sound of their paws beating the ground, the snapping of branches and the whipped rustle of grass, drowned out the purr of the idling motor.

Overhead, lightning bolts continued pulsing, and in one of the flashbulb glares, Ried realised the animals were stampeding in one direction: his. *Oh, shit.*

He fell on all fours and scrambled around the opposite side of his small SUV. His scurry halted when the car shuddered from the impact of a stout wallaby. The stunned animal bounced back under the paws of the ensuing mob.

Ried watched on in shocked silence as the thronging mob jostled the wallaby backwards. A final kick from a giant red sent the battered corpse sliding from sight, down the road's slight embankment.

"Bloody hell." He held back the rise of panic and scuttled for the cover of the driver's side as the space around himself and the car filled with kangaroos and wallabies. *If I stay here, these bloody things will kick me to death.*

Ried dropped on his stomach and rolled under the car.

Another animal misjudged its leap, bounced off the bonnet, and skidded along the gravel, before it twisted upright and leapt across the road, avoiding the wallaby's fate.

After several minutes, the mob's numbers thinned, until only the sound of their continued flight echoed from the scrubland across the highway.

Ried's quick breaths puffed the dirt under his nose. He didn't move. Instead, he watched, listened, and waited. He stared wide-eyed through the letter-box view beyond the car's wheels. When no more kangaroos or wallabies came bounding out of the darkness, he crawled from under the car. *What the hell brought that on?*

Overhead, the dense cloud bank continued strobing with lightning. Then out of the clouds, a forked blue-white rope of energy lanced downwards before twisting skyward. *What the hell was that…*

Something about the kangaroos' stampede and the look of the storm didn't seem right.

Ignoring the damage done to the car, Ried jumped behind the wheel, started the engine, and sped up back along the highway.

Confusion replaced Ried's awe from the stampeding kangaroos when the night fell into abrupt darkness. *What the hell… What happened to the lightning?*

With a jolt, the car lurched from sudden wind squalls as the air became a frenzy of swirling twigs, leaves, and dry grass. All other signs showed the storm had vanished, leaving the wind in its wake.

Strewth… Ried scanned the night. *I've never seen a storm move that bloody fast.*

After several minutes, a reflection in the mirrors grabbed his attention. He frowned at the storm approaching from behind. *Can't be the same storm?*

His rear-view mirrors filled with reflected lightning. However, no claps of thunder or rumbling followed the flash. *I've never heard of a dry storm, in the middle of August?*

Ried watched the approaching squall on the side mirrors. *Two storms within minutes and right after a mob of Roos came charging at me out of the scrub?*

"And I thought the Ghan was full of weird shit."

The only sounds Ried heard came from the static screeching from the radio speakers which drowned out the rhythmic hum of the tyres on the bitumen.

Distracted by the ear-destroying shriek and hiss, he diverted his eyes from the road and silenced the radio. When he glanced up, Ried's arms locked straight, and he slammed both feet on the brakes.

"Jesus Christ!"

He heaved hard on the wheel. The vehicle's anti-lock braking system strained in protest sending shuddering jolts up his legs.

In place of the swirling flora and litter, the beams of the headlights filled with an assortment of cattle, horses, and wild deer. *What the–*

Every animal crossing the road seemed confused and careened off each other in twisted circles performing an abstract animal dance of absurd chaos.

Ried then noticed something far more disturbing than the whirlpooling behaviour of the beasts. Somewhere in the stampede's earlier path, many of the animals had become ensnared in barbed wire and fence posts. Foam and sweat, stained pink with blood, covered the terrified animals' chests, flanks, and legs.

In their dusty wake, the all too familiar aroma of fear, adrenaline, and blood filtered through the SUV vents.

Ried scanned the paddocks from where the manic herd came. "What the hell is out there?"

With the visions of terrified animals still haunting his eyes, he considered pulling over to investigate, but another burst of wind buffeted the car. "On second thought, I'll let the cops at Gore figure it out."

He slipped the gears into first and eased down on the accelerator. Above the speeding car, the clouds churned into a swirling eddy, illuminated from within by more flashbulb bursts of white-blue.

"Jesus. Is that a tornado?"

The car's movements became more erratic as Ried avoided the larger pieces of debris tossed about in the maelstrom winds around him. The storm then unleashed a solid wall of torrential rain and hail, which stopped within minutes, as if he passed beyond the curtain of a waterfall.

"Okay… That was quick

Another succession of gusting winds threatened to push him off the highway. "Pity the bloody wind didn't stop too."

He scanned each of the rear-view mirrors, the road ahead, and then glancing upward, his eyes caught the tumultuous clouds twisting into an electrified, reversed vortex. *What the fuck?*

He divided his attention between driving and looking up into the swirling inverted funnel laced with strings of crisscrossing energy.

"No way…" he whispered in reverent awe. *Must be a trick of the lightning.*

"I reckon it's time I was somewhere else."

When Ried increased his pressure on the accelerator every light in his car flared in intensity before the fuse box under the dashboard exploded in a crackling series of fizzling sparks.

His car sputtered and died.

Shit.

He tore off his jacket and smothered the spitting flames, and then threw his ruined jacket across the car. The sharp, pungent odour of burned wire and plastic smoke clawed at his throat and lungs, and with no power, the fresh air stayed locked on the other side of the glass.

"Damn it. Fucking electric windows."

More lightning burst from the cloud's funnel. The flashes rent apart the slate grey of the night.

Alone in the lifeless vehicle, Ried found himself hypnotised by the electrical tempest outside.

None of the arcing bolts touched the ground. Instead, the ribbons of energy curved back into the funnel without a single clap of thunder. Instead, everything going on outside suggested the sky was suffering a massive short circuit.

The car rocked and bucked from the increasing wind and battering from small airborne bushes and trees. He cringed when a shrub screeched and scraped across the bonnet.

When each returning bolt of light struck the funnel wall, an explosion followed by a gunshot blast creating dozens of micro-supernovae. Every one of those eruptions spawned hundreds of smaller bolts, glowing with the vibrant hues of the rainbow.

"Jesus. The whole fucking sky's gone mad!"

An unremitting dread crawled up from Ried's subconscious. He pictured the spiralling maw evolving into a ravenous monster, feeding on his fears and himself.

Instead, the world outside disappeared, hidden behind a mass of swirling fog pulsing with iridescent lightning. The mist swirled and churned with increasing speed.

At the sight of the glowing tempest reversing dynamics stretched his beliefs. Then debris and fog gyrating around his car disappeared within an inverted cyclone. The walls of the approaching vortex pulsed in indigo, purples, and brilliant greens.

Within minutes, the water droplets on the windshield, and the shallow puddles decorating the bitumen provided the only evidence of the storm's brief deluge.

"What the fuck is this?"

He followed several drops climbing up the glass. In disbelief, he looked on, intrigued by the upward flow of the water while the area around the car grew lighter with each passing second.

"This is bullshit." He tried opening the door, but when the fuses blew the surge locked the doors. "Fuck and FUCK."

With the darkness waning, he jammed himself hard against the windscreen for a better look at the funnel above his car. In the distance apex, an alabaster glow shone with the fierceness of a miniature sun.

Ried threw his arms and hands over his face. The cloud's inner wall flared into the blue-green fire, encircling the catapulted ball of white fire.

Bolts of energy spat out from the turquoise flames and assaulted the car and road. His body tingled and itched. Discharges of static electricity latticed his skin with every move he made.

Ried couldn't think. He couldn't speak. He could only scream.

With a sudden jolt, the front of the car angled upward. He ignored the pinprick stabs of pain and clutched the steering wheel. The rear end of the SUV seesawed as the field of electrostatic energy faded. Ried braced himself, expecting the tornado to lift and hurl his vehicle into the surrounding bush.

Then the car launched upward, the sudden g-forces slamming him back into his seat. The nerve-splitting sensation of a muscle tearing from the radial joint in his shoulder convulsed down his arm.

Pinned by the seatbelt, his head, arms, and legs, swung about as the car flipped and spun, swept farther into the vortex on ribbons of white and purple ionised flame.

Winded, stunned, and whiplashed, Ried, lurched forward with the unexpected head-spinning sensation of weightlessness and threw up.

All around him bolts of energy whiplashed the hapless vehicle. He snapped his head around to stare at the rear-view mirror.

"No fucking way…"

The scene reflected slapped his reasoning. He stared wide-eyed at the passing glimpse of the Western Queensland highway shrinking behind a closing iris of emerald fire.

The misshapen globules of his vomit merged into one larger spheroid. Ried pushed his open palm against the foul-smelling orb. His stomach heaved a dry retch when his fingers slipped past the thin, slick film, into the bile and gastric juice decorated with his semi-digested meal.

The rising temperature seared his throat and lungs. Ried felt like a piece of meat in a microwave. His nose burned from the rancid fumes of heated vomit. His mind threatened to shut down from the unyielding abuse hurled at his senses.

Then, the brutal force of gravity returned, multiplied tenfold. The car's unexpected drop crushed Ried against his seatbelt. He coughed out the air compressed from his lungs.

The belt latch snapped from his increased gravitational mass, and the gelatinous mass of vomit ruptured over him. Ried's head slammed into the front driver's side door pillar with an appalling smack.

His last recollection was the way the vortex turned inside out and spat the car out in a halo of tangerine fire. The expelled vehicle struck the ground amidst torrential wind and rain.

The impact jarred open the rear driver's side door and shattered the windows hurling glass through the rocking car as it settled in the mud, and water.

Tangled between the front seats and steering wheel, bleeding, and coated in his vomit, Ried passed out under the sound of the hammering rain.

#

The light washed away the blackness of his brief coma. He tried opening his eyes, but his right eye refused co-operation.

A shadow emerged, surrounded by a flaring corona. Ried blinked several times with his uninjured eye until the grey shape dissolved.

In its place appeared the face of an older man in his late fifties. His tanned face had deep laugh lines, with a moustache under a long equine nose protruding down between a pair of piercing blue-grey eyes.

Ried's dry lips parted, and his head followed the man who moved beside him. When Ried's hoarse rasp caught his attention, the stranger knelt beside him.

"Ah, you are awake." The old man rested his hand on Ried's shoulder and peered down with a tilted smile. "Easy, son. Just lay still, hey." With gentle, steady hands, the old man lifted Ried's head, allowing a small trickle of water to flow from a chipped enamelled mug and moisten Ried's lips and tongue.

"You're lucky we spotted you and your car this far off the road." The old man tipped the cup again. "I'm sorry, but until Doc Mitchum's had a look at you, I can't risk giving you any more." He lowered Ried's head and placed a wet cloth on the younger man's forehead.

As the old man lowered his head, Ried tried focusing on where he was, but all he caught were sparse shrubs and squat trees scattered across a mud pan of dry loam and dirt. Past the bushes stood tall eucalyptus against a bright, harsh pale blue sky.

Ried accepted the cool relief of the moistened rag. He lay there running a diagnostic on himself. His heart fluttered joy his toes moved in his boots. The fingers on his right hand reacted from his brain's commands. His left hand twitched with a partial response which released a stream of molten lead searing his nerves.

His right temple felt numb, and with each breath, his rib cage protested with starbursts of fire. All that agony meant he was damaged, but not broken. So, with a sense of morbid relief, he accepted the coal black veil of darkness shrouding his consciousness.

CHAPTER THREE

The old man wiped away a trickle of sweat running down his neck with his suntanned hand. Several hours had passed since they pulled the injured man from his wrecked car and the man chided himself for not shading Ried from the late morning's heat.

With a gentle hand, the old man placed his worn slouch hat over Ried's face and unfolded a tarp beside Ried. He then sorted several of the branches he collected earlier into size groups.

He brushed his hands against his grey denim pants, rolled up the sleeves of his khaki drill shirt, and set about building a shelter over Ried. When he fixed the last rope in place, the old man turned at the scrape of footsteps through the dirt.

A younger man in his late teens stepped into view from behind the wreck.

"What's the point, Father?"

The old man reached down, removed his hat from Ried's forehead, and turned toward the thin teenager, whose cheeks showed deep craters from acne scars.

He never understood why his son kept his shoulder-length black hair tied off in a ponytail

His son's face twisted into a frown above his mahogany-brown eyes. "With the shelter I mean. We should take what we can and leave him here. I mean, he's almost dead anyway."

The father's sigh carried the weight of exasperation. "And what if a Vigiles patrol found him?" He tested the last tie-down. "No, Nicholas, we are not leaving him here. Besides, do you know what Gallio would do to him?"

"Who cares?" Nicholas shrugged. "We don't know him, and if he's stupid enough to crash, then let Gallio find him."

A shrill whistle carried across the floodplain. The father and son turned toward the blurred figure of a man leading a horse and cart through the shimmering air.

"Jack, and about bloody time, too." When the father reached Jack, he snatched the reins. "I thought you were getting help."

Jack ignored the father's attitude and squatted in the lean-to's shade and wrinkled his nose. "Strewth, Dom. It smells like horse shit and old oil."

"Don't worry about the tarp. What about the help?"

"Sorry, mate." Jack shrugged. "Everybody's getting a tad more nervous with the increased patrols, and others just aren't keen on wasting their gas." He gave Dom a cheeky grin before finishing. "I got hold of old Doc Mitchum, though." He nodded toward the cart. "After that, I went back and got your horse and cart. I figure it's less conspicuous than your old flatbed."

"Fair enough." Dom looked disappointed. "Since Gallio and his pit bull arrived, the whole bloody region's too afraid to do much of anything."

49

Ignored by the two men, Nicholas strolled over and lay under the cart where he crossed his arms behind his head and closed his eyes.

Jack raised an eyebrow at Nicholas's dismissive behaviour but said nothing. Standing side by side, Jack outsized his friend in bulk and height, but unlike Dom, he sported a full beard and a thick mop of curly, dark red hair, streaked with grey from the temples.

"I don't wanna question you on this." Jack scratched under his chin.

"But you will," Dom sighed.

"Damn right, I will." Jack waved his hand toward the road. "With all the extra bloody patrols looking for those friggin' Nomads," he said, "are you sure taking him back with us is the best idea?" Jack studied the sleeping man. "Besides, would he even make the bloody trip back to town?"

"For the love of–" Dom threw his arms skyward. "I'll tell you what I bloody well told Nicholas." He jabbed a finger toward the unconscious Ried. "We are not leaving him here." He pushed his hat back on his head. "Besides, Julia would never forgive me."

"Okay, mate." Jack conceded. "I'm just letting you know my thoughts." He strolled around Ried's car, "I suppose you've considered the fact he could be one of 'em?" He stopped and inspected the SUV's rain-soaked insides. "I mean, this isn't your average bloody Junker."

"Yes, the car's different, and yes, he might be a damn Roman," Dom regarded his friend, "but the lad's hurt and needs help. Our help," Dom insisted. "Anything else we will sort out later."

Jack took in a breath and readied himself for more objections. However, Dom's expression, stance, and tone told Jack the discussion was over. "Fair enough." Jack shrugged as he placed a fresh cloth on Ried's head.

Dom smiled at his friend and whispered, "You're such a tosser." He moved across to the horse. "Come on you two," he said, grabbing the reins. "Nicholas, bring the machete and axe, will you?"

"Why?"

"I reckon your old man plans on hiding the wreck 'till later."

"And let's hope we haven't lost our knack at concealment," Dom quipped.

"Here's hoping." Jack flicked his thumb toward Ried. "What I wanna know is where you're gonna hide our injured friend."

"My place." Dom walked past Jack and patted his shoulder. "We'll take him there after Tom's had a look at him."

"Doc Mitchum won't be happy." Jack passed his eye over Ried. "He'll want to make sure the blokes not smashed up inside."

"When we get back to the farm, I'll send for Jennings and his portable X-ray unit–"

"Strewth, now you wanna involve the vet." Jack laughed at his friend. "I can't wait to hear old Mitchum's reply to that."

"Don't worry about Tom. I'll sort him out," Dom said.

"Anyway, just where at your place are you putting him?"

"We can put him in Julia's day cottage."

"Julia's cottage?"

Dom caught Jack's expression of slight disbelief. "I know what you're thinking, but Abbey's been cleaning the place up for a while now."

"And I suppose you're gonna get her to play nursemaid with our new friend." Jack's tone aired his concern. "And what if he is one of them and he wakes up to find himself stashed away by you?" When Dom slowed his step, Jack realised he might have overstepped his bounds.

"I'm sure Abbey will agree to it," Dom replied. "And if he is a Roman…" Dom let the sentence hang for a few seconds. "I'll sort it out."

"Well, I don't fucking agree with it," Nicholas spat.

"No one asked you and mind your tongue." Don shook his head and ventured out through the shimmering heat to harvest to gather his makeshift camouflage screen.

"I don't care what my father says," Nicholas complained. "I agree with you." He studied Jack. "We should take what we can and leave him for the crows."

"Do you now?"

"I don't get why my father's always helping everybody," Nicholas grumbled in a petulant tone, "or sticking his nose in other people's business."

"Sticking his nose in…" Jack drove his finger into the younger man's shoulder. "You're such a stupid little twat. You bloody well know how much everyone respects your old man around here."

"Oh, yes, the great hero of The Wars," Nicholas sneered. "You know he only helps everyone else is because father feels guilty about losing to the Romans."

"Guilty…" Jack's with narrowed eyes at Nicholas. "The only thing he should feel guilty about is bloody well having you."

Nicholas dropped the tools and tried to take a step away from the big man, but Jack's arm whipped out and grabbed his collar.

"And as for helping others out," Jack wrenched Nicholas closer, "it's who Dom is, and why I'm still alive." Jack shook his head in pity. "What you don't see is people asking him for help." He shoved Nicholas aside and retrieved the tools. "Come on. We've got work to do."

Back at the crash site with a cart full of harvested trees and shrubs, Dom told his son to strip the car of any luggage, papers and loose items to load in the small wagon and take back to the farm, while he and Jack waited for Dr Mitchum.

"I still reckon we leave him for the crows and sell off his stuff," Nicholas grumbled aloud.

"And just head straight back home," Dom said, "I don't want you going anywhere near town with that lot."

While Dom and Jack built a blind from the cut trees and shrubs, Nicholas did what his father instructed before climbing into the cart and riding across the floodplain.

Out on the road, Nicholas cast a spiteful glance at Jack and his father. "I don't care what he said. Any dick head who crashes his car that far from the road deserves to die and he will. So, why not sell his stuff and make a bit of coin?"

The horse's responded with a swish his tail to swat the flies tickling his rump.

Nicholas clicked his tongue and calculated what he would get for the stranger's belongings. Not a vast sum, but enough for a week's supply of 'E,' and while he was in town, he could spend more time with Gemma.

Proud of his disobedience and selfish decision, Nicholas relaxed on the cart's bench and flicked the reins to bring the animal to a trot.

#

A cohort of Roman motorbikes drove over a small rise in the road above the floodplain. The largest motorcycle, leading the squad, supported an open-framed sidecar whose passenger waved and bounced around.

"Stop, Praefectus. Stop! This is the area," he bubbled with excitement. "Yes, yes. This is the spot." With extended arms, he lifted an encyclopaedia-sized scanner and waved it back and forth in a series of long and short arcs. With each pass, the excitable Roman scrutinised the twitching needles and readouts on a small screen.

Near the centre of the screen, a bright green blip of light blinked so fast it almost became a solid dot. With a squeak, the little Roman launched himself out of his seat before the bike stopped.

Unlike his excited passenger, the rider dismounted his war bike which reflected the morning sun from its deep blue gloss paint. Various effigies and symbols decorated the forward cowlings, the most dominant, an embossed golden Aquila on each side above the protruding barrels of twin-mounted semi-automatic machine guns.

With arrogant, self-righteous ease and precise, controlled movements, the rider removed the ornate plumed full faced helmet. He scanned the area and each of the remaining dull-red Vigiles bikes when they pulled over in a protective cordon.

His light-brown eyes sparkled with a sense of pride, sat within his neoclassical face, crowned with trimmed dark black-brown hair.

The praefectus derived immense pleasure from reinstating what he called "lapsed discipline" over the last five years since his appointment by Marcus, his predecessor.

The cohort of Vigiles riders wore lightweight composite body armour over ink blue fatigues. Segmented manicas covered their shoulders. The high gloss sculptured chest and stomach section reflected the sun, as did the polished alloy grieves protecting their shins above thick soled, lace-up boots.

The praefectus wore a similar uniform to his men, except his body armour reflected a dark bronze rather than black. He wiped the dust from his boots and grieves before casting an eye over the surrounding scrubland.

"I see nothing unusual," he said, folding the cloth into the pocket of his burgundy tunic.

He rolled his shoulders and stretched his stocky, muscular body. The sculpted body armour and traditional leather manicas squeaked with his actions.

The smaller fidgeting and excited passenger leaked annoyance. "Yes, well, what we seek may be more than 'unusual.'"

The praefectus adjusted the cingulum militare around his waist. "You forget yourself, Decius. I'm not one of your lab rats."

Decius shuffled backwards and tipped his head in mute subjugation. His enthusiastic confidence waning.

Unlike the Praefectus, Decius did not wear the standard blue and reds of the military or Vigiles. He wore the uniform of the science auxiliaries: a dark green one-piece and a bright green sash draped across his left shoulder.

"Forgive me, Praefectus Gallio." Decius kowtowed.

Even though Gallio, who held the role of regional governor, wore no weapons, Decius still feared him. He stepped away and offered a comical but nervous salute before adjusting his black box until the screen produced a different image.

Excited by the result, Decius took out a metal rod from his pouch and connected it to the scanning unit using a coiled cable and proceeded in scuttling about the area with repeated adjustment of his oversized, wire-rimmed glasses.

The sound of two approaching bikes took the praefectus's attention away from the fidgeting little scientist. Gallio returned to his motorcycle, placed his helmet on the handlebars, and waited for the latecomers.

"You two fell behind. Why?"

"Praefectus, my bike developed a malfunction in the motor," the oldest rider snapped to attention with a brisk salute, "and while repairing it, we spotted a horse and cart in a gully, sir."

With cold regard, Gallio perused the two men standing at attention before him. Since MacMahon's recruitment, the human has proven himself a competent and useful lieutenant. He also held a valuable talent for extracting payments from many of the weaker businesses and farm owners.

The younger Vigiles, Donaldson, also proved a good choice. He held a certain naivety for upholding the law, and the legitimate duties of the Roman police force. Which made him an ideal addition to Gallios' display troops.

"It seemed abandoned," MacMahon finished.

"Abandoned?"

"I believe it belonged to a farmer or gypsy who'd stopped for a pi– To relieve himself in the bush."

"Did you see this farmer or a gypsy?" Gallio's scrutiny homed in on MacMahon

"Um, no, sir." MacMahon tried to hide his embarrassment. "They must've been deeper in the bush, poaching."

"I want you to continue down the road," Gallio commanded, "and investigate the gypsy camp near Yarraman. After which, you can go back to where you saw the cart and search for the missing owner."

"And if it's gone, sir?"

"Then search for both," Gallio continued, "and submit a full report to Mettius when you return to the barracks."

MacMahon glanced toward the Roman Centurion marching their way. He stiffened with an imperceptible shudder when the praefectus castrorum stopped a metre behind Gallio and adjusted the braided, blood-red insignia sash under his sword belt.

Gallio raised the corner of his mouth at the change in body language displayed by the two humans regarding his second in command.

Mettius's tall, muscular frame moved with the lithe, grace of a silent predator who watched the world through black on black eyes. There were times even Gallio found the total lack of white in Mettius's eyes unnerving.

Gallio also learned through time, Mettius cared little for people and their opinions about him. They either respected him, feared him, or died by his hand.

Unlike Gallio, Mettius always carried his small arsenal of weapons attached to his hip which included a Gladius and a Pugio – the traditional Roman sword and dagger – along with a semi-automatic carbine pistol holstered under his left armpit.

The weapons reinforced the notion of Mettius being the epitome of a humanoid predator. In fact, few matched Mettius's skill with a sword, shield, a dagger and a gun.

Gallio often indulged in the wish of having twenty Romans like Mettius. Then the Senate and Proconsul would understand the essence of true power.

A shadow crossed the ground near his feet. Gallio shifted his gaze upward to admire a circling eagle. *Ah, what better creature to signal good fortune.*

Without taking his eyes from the bird, he dismissed MacMahon and Donaldson.

When the two humans hurried to their bikes, Mettius issued instructions for setting up the portable command tent.

Gallio strode onto the sun-baked floodplain followed by Mettius.

"Praefectus." Mettius pointed toward a small, odd-looking collection of shrubs.

"Well spotted, my friend," Gallio replied.

When they arrived at the concealed wreck, they inspected the camouflage screen. "This screen shows a skill I've not seen in decades."

"Nomads?"

"No, I don't believe this handiwork is nomad or gypsy."

Mettius focused on the ground at their feet and crouched on his haunches. "Whoever they were, there were at least three men and a vehicle."

Gallio looked from his second in command to Decius, who trotted his way across the dusty plain.

"Have you found something–" The little scientist stopped with a squeal, his feet skidding in the loose dirt. The scanner jostled in his frightened hands.

A cruel smile creased Gallio's face. He felt sure the annoying little man came close to emptying his bowels and bladder.

Seconds before Decius's squeal, Mettius sprang from his crouch and with whiplash speed, drew his pistol to fix the muzzle on the point between Decius's eyebrows.

"Decius, if you come running in without announcing yourself again," Gallio approached the quivering man, "I will let Mettius shoot you."

A smile filled with ice and desire crossed Mettius's lips. He held his pistol pointed at Decius for another ten seconds before holstering the weapon in an effortless and precise movement.

"Oh, my… Please forgive me, Praefectus." Decius dipped his head and gave a feeble, shaky salute before he helped dismantle the camouflage screen.

At the sight of Ried's car, Decius bobbed up and down in glee. The earlier signs of his fear and shock gone.

"A gift from the gods… Yes, indeed. A gift of the gods." Decius walked around the smashed SUV. "Indeed, a blessed gift from the gods… Yes. Yes, a blessed gift." The little scientist fidgeted with his scanner. "I am detecting minute traces of plasma-based emissions… However, there are no residual radioactive artefacts, or other harmful emissions, or bacteria." He placed the scanner on the ground as Mettius and Gallio joined him to rock the car until it stood upright on its four wheels.

Gallio and Mettius stepped back to avoid the resulting small dust cloud. Decius opened every door to inspect the car's interior before he raised its unlatched hood, propping it open with a nearby stick.

The science auxiliary drooled in salacious delight when he explored, touched, sniffed, and scanned the engine bay. "This is a combustion motor, but nothing I have seen before."

Engrossed in the mysteries of their find, Decius ignored his two superiors and described the car's engine and electronics into the voice recorder on his scanner.

On finishing his diagnosis, Decius abandoned the engine bay and wandered around the car, finding, and cataloguing the differences between Ried's SUV and the older vehicles in current use.

Mettius, who had little time for the small ferret of a scientist, walked away and to study the ground around the car.

"Sir."

Gallio looked to where Mettius stood, studying the ground between the road and the car. "You've found something else?"

Mettius pointed to the faint tracks imprinted in the dirt. "Someone tried concealing the tracks of a van's, or a small truck, and over here…—" He drew Gallio's attention toward the right, "there are hoof prints and thin tracks."

"A cart." Gallio looked at Mettius. "MacMahon told me they came across one hidden from the road on the way here." He pointed toward the open gazebo.

Back under the shade of the tent, he asked for the map bag from his bike. "Something else is odd," he thought out loud. "Why is there no evidence showing the car being driven off the road?"

"The storm may have washed the tracks away."

"If the storm had brought more rain, then that would be true."

"Then how did it crash so far off the road?" Mettius asked. "It didn't fall from the sky."

"Excuse me, sir." With exaggerated caution, Decius approached them from behind. "It shouldn't be ruled out." He hesitated. "Of course, what I have is only a theory."

"Enlighten us," said Gallio.

Not often in such a bright spotlight, Decius's fidgeting mannerisms went into overdrive. The Roman scientist bobbed and fidgeted as he explained his theories. He reiterated how different the vehicle is, and where it sat on the broad floodplain, so far from the road.

"Decius, I assume you will offer something other than what we already know?"

"Yes, sir. I do Sir," Decius said, "I believe the car had travelled through a rupture in space and time itself."

Mettius and Gallio shook their heads as Gallio raised a dismissive hand.

However, Decius darted to the sidecar and returned with a canvas carry bag which he emptied onto the table. Shuffling the documents, he showed them readouts and reports printed from the weather instruments.

"The most interesting anomalies recorded all came from the sonar, pyranometer and kilometre systems during the storm," Decius said. "The accumulated data showed unique electromagnetic fluctuations, along with a range of abnormal gravity and atmospheric anomalies."

"What anomalies could come from just a storm?" Mettius's face twisted with scorn. "Ruptures in space and time – these are dreams of playwrights and fools… For thousands of years, the Empire has sailed among the stars, conquering countless worlds. Yet, no one ever recorded a hole in the galaxy." The Centurion dismissed Decius with a contemptuous glare, "Why? Because they don't exist."

"You know this how?" Decius's tone surprised himself. Mettius slid from the chair.

"I meant no offence, Praefectus Castrorum." The chubby little scientist cowered away from the returning glare of Mettius. "I am merely trying to explain a theory." Decius produced several of the fused lumps he collected from around the car.

"So, now you collect rocks?" Mettius scoffed and walked around the table.

"These are not rocks." Decius sighed. "You remember I noted residual plasm readings. Well, these resulted from plasma energy striking the ground." He sighed again. "My report will explain it all, including my findings on the vehicle."

"Decius, I've known you a long time," Gallio offered a humourless smile, "but this is the most fanciful theory you have ever had."

"Do you remember the records and scrolls from Novicus Patria?" Decius bravado continued.

"What about them?" Mettius sat on a folding chair, leaning against the armrest, and resting his head against his open hand.

"They told the legend of the ninth legion who fell from the heavens amidst a tunnel of fire and lightning." Decius settled into a lecturer's tone. "Those who wrote the scrolls assumed the heathen Brittany gods of the wood summoned a daemon to create the tunnel," Decius's face flushed. "But what if the portal which cast the Ninth across the heavens to create the Domino-Astartes was a natural phenomenon?" Decius knew he paraphrased the ancient scriptures and added his theory, but he wanted the military-minded brute beside Gallio to accept the possibility.

Gallio gave an impatient sigh. "Your point, Decius?"

"I believe the car, and whoever its occupants were, came through a similar dimensional portal which bore our ancestors."

Decius took a reflexive step back when he saw the disapproving look on Gallio's face. He considered offering further explanations, but instead, the scientist fidgeted and shuffled his feet.

"Decius, I will feed you to Cerberus if you don't keep still."

"Yes, Praefectus. I'm sorry, Praefectus. But, um, well…"

"By all the gods, man. Just say it."

"The vehicle, sir."

"What about it?"

"Surely, we aren't going to, well… leave it out here?"

"For a clever little man," Gallio replied, "you can be remarkably stupid."

Decius's face blossomed into a livid red flush at the insult. He tried out-staring Gallio, but his miserable attempt at defiance waned under the strength of Gallio's returning gaze.

"Of course, I'll have it brought back so you can play with it." Gallio pushed out his chair and considered the map. He left the cluttered table and made his way toward the edge of the gazebo's shade. With his arms behind his back, he contemplated the strange car on the dry mud plain. "Do you know how many occupants there were?"

"No, not until I run more tests."

"Well, somebody does." Gallio returned to the table and focused on the maps with Mettius at his side.

Decius stood and waited, ignored by the two men who stayed bent over the map chart, continuing their discussion. Hurt by his superior's rudeness, Decius exited the gazebo to continue with his on-site studies of the car.

Gallio peered over his shoulder toward the exiting scientist. "I have sent MacMahon and Donaldson to the Yarraman gypsy camp, but I fear they will find nothing. Send our spies there and see what they can uncover," he commanded, before returning his attention to the map.

"I'm assuming you want the farms searched?"

"Start with the closest – those three there – and then move on to the abandoned properties."

"Two full cohorts split into four groups should be enough."

"Agreed," Gallio said. "This will be an ideal opportunity for purging the region of any Nomads. It will also send a clear message to any others who would follow."

Mettius nodded with a cold, dead smile. "Burn the whole body rather than cut off the head."

"As for the farmers, there is a need for more discretion. The town council grows more suspicious with each passing week about our other activities. Instruct the others to hold off on our collections and filter down the sale of Enlightenment for a few weeks until we find who or what we are looking for. Then, flood the market with 'E' and increase the price by fifty per cent to cover what we'll lose."

"Won't the loss of revenue, raise issues with our supplier?"

"I'll use some of our reserve funds to cover any shortfall. The last thing we need is our benefactor, or his committee in Toowoomba, poking their noses around." Gallio rested his finger on the map. "I will call and talk to this one myself."

He moved around the table and stared across the floodplain again. "Have the trackers brought back here," he instructed over his shoulder. "I want the surrounding terrain searched for at least five kilometres."

"By your command." Mettius saluted.

"And ensure they give all reports to no one else but you."

"Sir." Mettius saluted again and left the gazebo.

CHAPTER FOUR

An ambulance dressed in faded paintwork and patches of rust pulled up between the back of Dom's house and the barn, scattering a brood of chickens.

Doctor Thomas Mitchum stepped out for his second house call since leaving Ried in Dom's cottage. He collected his bag from the passenger seat, closed the door, and headed toward the house when his friend's voice called out from near the barn. Mitchum waved his hand and waited for Dom and Nicholas as they rode to greet him.

"Dominic?" Mitchum reached up and shook his friend's hand.

"Before you ask, we've just been riding." Dom dismounted his horse and ignored the doctor's expression.

The doctor shook his head in weariness, something the slight drop of his shoulders emphasised. Thomas Mitchum was the town's senior physician and a combat veteran like Dominic and Jack. However, his battles weren't those of a Frontline soldier; they were those fought in the mobile triage hospitals.

His constant dour expression, shoulder-length grey hair and trimmed goatee, gave him the appearance of a nineteenth-century European aristocrat. Within the doctor's matured and lined face glinted a pair of bright emerald eyes, which defied his age and the facade of constant fatigue. They also hinted at a sharp, keen intellect beyond his sixty-plus years.

Many people considered the doctor brusque and on occasion a little recalcitrant, and not much of a conversationalist – an opinion he never denied or discredited.

"How are you today?" Mitchum asked Nicholas.

"I'm okay," Nicholas whispered after he dismounted.

"Good to hear it." Mitchum patted the teenager's shoulder. He turned to Dom. "I had a house call near Maidenwell, so I thought I'd drop in to check on how things are going."

"You've been down to the cottage then?"

"Not yet," the doctor waved a fly away, "but I spoke with Abbey earlier on the phone. She told me our friend is healing remarkably well. A little too well by her description." He followed Dom inside and waited for Nicholas to return after taking the horses into the barn.

Inside the dining room, Mitchum lifted Dom's shirt and dressings over the cuts inflicted by Nicholas on the night they brought Ried to the farm. "Well, they all seem to be healing nicely," Mitchum announced. "How are you feeling otherwise?"

"I'm okay."

"Are you?" Mitchum noted his friend's tone, but he had no intention of allowing Dom the last word. "Regardless, I still insist you refrain from any heavy or excessive activity."

"For how long?"

"Until I damn well say otherwise, and those damn stitches come out." He then turned to Nicholas. "How are the cramps and nausea going?"

"The cramps are mostly gone, and I only feel like throwing up when I first get up." Nicholas stared down at the floor, unable to face the doctor. "But this morning wasn't so bad."

Dr Mitchum examined Nicholas. The physical signs from the drug-induced psychotic episode two nights ago were healing well enough, but Mitchum wondered about the boy's psychological traumas from the other night.

#

Mitchum arrived after midnight, after a distressed Abbey called, on the same night Dom brought the young stranger to the cottage. The doctor walked straight into a scene of mayhem.

Nicholas and Dom were wrestling over the lounge room furniture, but this was not any father and son tussle. Armed with a bread knife, Nicholas screamed incoherent abuse and accusations at Dom, Abbey, and Molly.

It became clear to Mitchum even Dom's past hand to hand combat skills waned against the frenzied fever and the strength of a drug-fuelled Nicholas.

Mitchum dropped his bag on the floor and rifled the contents for a hypodermic and sedative. His nerves and manner kept in check from decades of emergency triage. His deft hands unsheathed the needle and clasp the vial filled with a milky liquid – the most potent opioid in his collection.

Without hesitation, he charged in to aid Dom who by then bled from several gashes and cuts. The free-flowing blood slicked Dom's hands, mixing with blood from Nicholas's own self-inflicted wounds.

Both Dom and Mitchum managed in hauling Nicholas to his feet as Molly's husband came in from behind, pinning Nicholas's arms and lifting the teenager off his feet.

The action fed Nicholas's rage, and he lashed out with his legs catching his father in the groin. Dom doubled over and fell back as the doctor thrust the hypodermic needle into the pulsing artery in Nicholas's neck.

The rapid beat of the teenager's heart aided the sedatives journey in his bloodstream. Within seconds Nicholas's screams became cries which became whimpers and ended with him slumped in the grip of Molly's husband.

#

Mitchum blinked and focused back on Nicholas. Most of the bruises from Molly's husband had lost their colour. However, when the doctor probed his abdomen, Nicholas flinched. "Still a little tender, hey?" He rested a gentle hand on the teenager's shoulder. "Well, just keep up your fluid intake. I promise the bouts of nausea will pass."

After completing his examination on Nicholas, Mitchum reached into his bag and pulled out a bottle of pale-blue liquid with the consistency of olive oil. "If the pain and nausea get too much, take three drops in some warm water."

"No, thanks." Nicholas slid the bottle back to Mitchum. "I'm done with taking anything from small bottles." He nodded toward the kitchen. "Anyway, Molly's been giving me some of her broth to help with the cramps."

"Molly's broth, hey?" Mitchum grunted and reclaimed the medicine to drop back into his bag. "Bloody native witch doctor's mumbo-jumbo."

Nicholas slid his chair back, muttered his thanks and left the two older men.

"I was surprised to see you two riding together."

"He showed up in the barn, saddled a horse and followed me out." Dom massaged his eyes and then wiped his damp fingers on his trousers. "The boy didn't say a word. He just rode beside me, never lifting his head."

Neither man uttered a word for a long minute until Mitchum broke the silence. "We need to find who is pedalling this poison," Mitchum repacked his bag. "I've been called out to three similar cases over the last month. God, when will people realise the stupidity of taking drugs." Mitchum rose and excused himself, "I suppose I should check in on your guest."

After inviting himself for lunch Mitchum and Dom sat on the front veranda, Mitchum patted his stomach. "Bloody hell, Dom. I'd gladly pay her double if she fed me like that every day." Mitchum lit a thin cigar he rescued from his breast pocket. He took a deep draw, feeling full and satisfied from Molly's repast of cold roast pork, assorted steamed vegetables, chased down with a double helping of scones with cream and jam.

"Don't kid yourself, mate," Dom said. "Yesterday, she fed me cheese sandwiches and fruit."

The two men drank coffee and talked for a while until the whine of Vigiles motorcycles coming down the drive broke the air of contentment.

"What do they want?" Dom's body language shifted as did the tenor of his voice.

"Do you think they have gotten wind of your guest?" He stood and watched the three riders stop several metres in front of the house.

"No," Dom said. "This is something else."

"I keep wondering why Marcus thought Gallio would make a better replacement," Mitchum mused, recognising the lead rider.

"I reckon, being nominated and then elected as proconsul clouded his judgement." Dom studied the Roman dismounting the bike, and as with every encounter, Dom found Gallios toned and muscular upper body a parody because of the Romans long spider thin legs.

"Well," Mitchum moved beside Dom. "Marcus, on the whole, was a good governor, but this one–"

"–Is an idiot." Dom finished the doctor's well-spoken sentiments.

"Mr Harris," Gallio said, after removing his helmet, and snapping down the bike stands. He rested his helmet on the seat of the bike and approached Dom.

"Gallio."

Gallio straightened his shoulders and twitched a stiff smile with the familiar manner Dom used to address him in front of his men. He returned his best, humourless and polite smile before addressing Mitchum. "Doctor, what brings you out here?"

"Just checking on my patients."

Gallio spotted the dressing on Dom's forearm. "What happened? A farming accident?"

For privacy's sake, Dom considered agreeing with Gallio's theory. Except Gallio was governor, and his excuse for a police force didn't seem to care about the growing drug problem.

"They're from my son. He had an overdose on that Enlightenment crap which turned bad," Dom glared at all three Vigiles, "but you lot don't give a shit about people taking drugs or even trying to catch the bastards peddling the garbage."

"Dominic, I came by to discuss other matters," Gallio rebuked, "not to discuss your son's drug habits or your opinions on our policing." He took a hasty step back when Dom marched forward in a flash of restrained temper. "However, the sale and possession of drugs is taken very–"

With the lightning fast responses born from combat and command, Gallio recovered his composure. He reminded himself who the two humans were, and how they, along with the former governor and other weak, liberal-minded Romans, worked to rebuild a sustainable society after the truce.

In truth, Gallio didn't believe Dom's acquiescence and neutral public stance toward the Romans, any more than he believed Decius's theory about holes in space.

"Dominic, I sympathise with what has happened to you and your family," Gallio said, raising an open hand to Dom. "So, please, understand I meant no disrespect."

Dr Mitchum studied the exchange between the two men, watching them ease back into their well-versed game of guarded diplomacy.

"It's been a trying time of late," Dom apologised, "between poor crops, a summer of little rain, and hotter days."

"Yes, I am sure life on the land can be difficult." Gallio pointed to the house. "Speaking of hot days, perhaps we can continue this inside?"

"All right."

Gallio tipped his head, smiling with the sincerity of a striking cobra. He followed Dom inside the house and sat down on the couch.

"Please, make yourself at home." Dom didn't hide his sarcasm. "What can I do for you?"

Mitchum followed Gallio and moved to sit on the opposite settee.

"No, Doctor," Gallio rose and pointed to the door. "I wish to speak with Mr Harris. Alone."

For several seconds, Mitchum held Gallio's gaze and his ground.

"It's all right, Tom." Dom walked Mitchum out through the kitchen. "If you still need to check on Nicholas, he's with his sister in Julia's old cottage."

Mitchum grunted, "Yes, well, I came here to check on him too." The doctor collected his bag from the floor, shook Dom's hand and left.

Sitting back in his chair, Dominic waited for Gallio to begin the conversation. Gallio, however, stayed silent, wandering about the room.

"I can assume from your comments outside," Gallio lifted the top page of an open notebook on Dom's desk. "The Cooperative will struggle with their quota this year."

"Don't fret. You'll get your tributes on time," Dom replied.

Gallio gave a feigned look of mild shock. "I never doubted it."

Dom walked over and closed the notebook.

Gallio offered his smile again and returned to the couch.

He settled back and set about discussing changes to the region's legislative requests by the Senate, along with several more items revolving around the town council and their common issues.

Dom sat in a casual pose and listened while Gallio waffled on. *All right, you son of a bitch. What do you really want?* "Gallio, I'm sure you didn't come here to discuss local politics, and the burdens placed on us by Toowoomba's legislative changes."

"Ah, direct as always." Gallio moved across the room toward Dom. "What do you know about the unusual storm the other night?" He sat back down and gauged Dom's reaction.

"Not much. Except it was a bloody inconvenience."

"How so?"

"For starters, it held us up overnight in Yarraman." Dom saw no point in lying.

"Yes, I know. I received a report from the outpost there which detailed those held over by the storm." Gallio crossed his legs and adjusted his tunic.

Of course, you did. Dom resisted the urge to step over and punch the Roman senseless.

Instead, he stood and went over to the drinks cabinet, returning with two glasses of local brandy. "And did those reports tell you it flattened about twelve hectares of my maze?" Dom handed the glass over to the Roman. "I also believe other crops in the storm's path were also ruined."

"Yes, I believe Mr Bennett and the Patterson's lost a sizable area of their corn crop." Dom took a sip and nodded. *He's fishing. All right, Dom... let's run out the line a bit.*

"Did it come close to the solar station at Tarong?"

"It did cross the reflector field," Gallio replied.

"Much damage?"

"A few reflectors and some localised damage." Gallio took a tentative sip of the brandy. "I'm more interested in what it left behind."

"I don't follow."

"On your trip back from Yarraman, did you see anything out of the ordinary?" Gallio studied Dom.

"Just some uprooted trees," Dom replied. "One of them made the bridge over Barker's Creek useless." Almost enjoying the game, he poured himself another brandy. "Which meant detouring over Cuthbert's Weir."

"Why not the main road through Nanango?"

"The weir crossing is the shortest route to Jack's place," Dom replied. *But you already know that.*

"Can I ask what you mean by 'out of the ordinary'?" Dom eased himself back in his chair.

"The storm may not have been an ordinary storm." Gallio held out his glass for a refill.

"You've lost me."

"I'm told it could have been a tear in space and time."

"Come again?" S*teady, Dom, just ease out a little more line.*

"My scientists tried explaining it, but alas, I am just a soldier." The Roman shrugged. "They described it much like a hidden and unstable tunnel through an impassable mountain range. Only, when something passed through the tunnel, it collapsed, trapping whatever passed through on this side."

"And you're saying something went through this one-way tunnel?" Dom leaned forward. "Something dangerous?"

"Not unless you consider an automobile as dangerous."

"I'm sorry?" *And the bait's taken.*

"It left a car behind?" Dom's behaviour and expressions would have done the travelling theatre group proud. *Time to start playing the line.*

"Yes, and the driver and or passengers are missing, lost, or even taken." Gallio leaned forward, resting the flat of his elbows on his thighs.

"How do you know it was occupied?"

"The assumption is, we believe, accurate because we found several tracks around the vehicle."

"And you believe whoever left the tracks took whoever was in the car?" *Almost ready for the net.*

"Is there anything I can help with?" Dom asked

Before Gallio could respond, they heard a vehicle coming down the drive.

Gallio went to the front door and raised a curious eyebrow at the weather-beaten blue Range Rover coming to an abrupt dust-raising stop near his men.

"Your friend, Mr Bennet, walks a thin line."

"He wouldn't be Jack if he didn't" Do goaded with a grin and a slight tilt of his head.

Jack eyed Gallio standing in the shadow of Dom's door before stepping down. He winked at the two men who brushed the dust from their clothes.

"G'day boys," he quipped with a broad smile and pleased with his efforts.

"Praefectus." Jack gave Gallio an exaggerated tilt of his head along with a half bow.

"Thank you for your offer, Mr Harris," Gallio called out after passing and ignoring Jack. "But we have the matter in hand." He approached the two Roman police, whispering to the taller of the two men.

Gallio hinted at a sneer toward Jack before he donned his helmet and mounted his bike and gunned the motor sending a wave of gravel and dust over Jack as he sped up the drive.

"Alien prick." Jack brushed himself down and gave Dom a silent 'does the bastard know' look.

Dom responded with a minute shake of his head.

"What did his lordship want?"

"Fishing and local politics, mostly," Dom responded, eyeing the taller of the two young Vigiles approaching.

"I am Fir–"

"I know who you are MacMahon." Dom snapped. "G'day, Michael." Dom walked past MacMahon, shaking hands with the other younger and plumper uniformed man. "I see service in the Vigiles auxiliaries is treating you well."

"Thanks, Mr Harris." Michael flushed.

Dom gave Michael a pat on the shoulder. He then stepped away and sized up MacMahon. Dom also caught Jack's casual sidestep toward him and took a deep breath, forcing himself to relax. Men like MacMahon used others with careless disregard for the sake of their own advancement, but Dom would enjoy watching such ambition break MacMahon

"Mr Harris," MacMahon stepped closer, "do you own a small, pale-blue or grey-painted, two-wheel cart or buggy with white-spoked wheels?"

"I do," Dom answered truthfully. "Why? Have you found it?"

"Excuse me?"

"Have you found it?" Dom repeated. "Some bugger stole it just over a week ago, along with one of my better stallions," he crossed his arms. "I reckon it was nicked by Nomads." He rubbed his chin in contemplation, "or do you reckon some gypsy kids took it as a prank?"

"Um… No, we haven't found it." MacMahon found himself on the back foot with Dom's rapid response and unexpected questions. "And you say gypsy kids took it?"

"No, I said Nomads, but if you know who pinched it then good." Dom pointed his thumb over his shoulder, "Don't bother looking for my horse, though. She came home a couple of nights ago."

"Sorry," MacMahon stumbled on, having lost all initiative from the questioning. "The horse came back?"

"Yes, but what about the cart?" Dom continued his own interrogation.

"If you're asking for it," Jack slid in with effortless ease. "Then it'd be a fair bet you haven't bloody well found it."

"We saw it a few days ago near the old Nanango road, this side of Barker's Creek," Michael answered in his usual polite and respectful tone. "We believe your cart may have been involved in an incident."

"Yes. Thank you, Donaldson," MacMahon snapped.

"Anyone hurt?"

"Hurt? No, why?" MacMahon frowned.

"Just a wrecked, weird-looking car," Michael added.

"Donaldson," MacMahon barked. "Hold your damn tongue."

"Well, what about my cart?" Dom pressed. "Where the hell is it now?"

"We are trying to find your cart, Mr Harris," MacMahon stammered, "that's why we—"

"Here's a thought," Dom moved toward MacMahon. "Stop frigging asking me about my stolen bloody cart, and just find it." He shoved a finger at the two Vigiles. "Better yet," he planted his feet and leaned within centimetres of MacMahon's face, "piss off and find the low-life mongrels selling the shit that almost killed my boy." Dom edged closer to MacMahon. "Now, get off my bloody land."

Jack rushed up and guided Dom two paces back from the two Vigiles. "Easy, Dom. Let it go," Jack whispered and then continued in a louder tone. "Okay, you two, I reckon you've got your answers. So, get back on those battery powered toys and bugger off."

MacMahon stood there with his hand clenched around his nightstick grip. "Good afternoon, Mr Harris, Mr Bennett." He strutted back toward the bikes with Michael by his side. "Who does that old fool think he is?" He whispered. "I would've taken the old bastard if that ape Bennett didn't step in."

"Not likely," young Michael replied, donning his helmet, and climbing onto his bike.

"No one fucking well asked you," MacMahon snapped.

Dom watched the two Vigiles officers steer their bikes onto the road before he marched back inside with Jack in tow.

"And?" Jack collected the two dirty glasses.

"Not much to tell," Dom called from the kitchen.

"Bullshit," Jack yelled back. "The bastard's checking you out?"

"He knows we stayed overnight at Yarraman."

"Yeah, well, those pricks have got spies everywhere." Jack walked toward the liquor cabinet. "At least Marcus had been easier to deal with."

"Gallio's a soldier, not a politician."

"Doesn't matter. The bastard and his lapdogs are all bent." Jack saw his friend's expression when he returned from the kitchen. "I know, I know, we can't prove it."

"Just remember, his best lap dog bites."

"Nothin a bloody bullet won't fix," Jack said, under his breath. "So, what else did you and his lordship chat about?"

"He told me they found the car."

"Shit." Jack almost spilt the drink he was pouring.

Dom helped himself to another glass and briefed Jack in on the conversation.

"I'm just glad a tree fell across the bridge," Dom added when he finished relaying the afternoon's events.

"Well, they obviously saw your boy and the cart." Jack scratched his chin under his beard.

"No doubt they saw the cart, but if they saw Nicholas with the cart, Gallio wouldn't have wasted time with just talking."

"I guess so."

"But I got the feeling our esteemed governor knows a lot more than he's letting on." Dom pondered his glass. "Let's hope when our guest wakes up, he can fill in the gaps."

CHAPTER FIVE

The next morning, a chill breeze flowed from the west to pass through the open window and caress Ried's face. His brow furrowed above pinched eyes. The morning glare lanced through his eyeballs stabbing the back of his skull.

With a soft groan, Ried rolled his head away from the stream of light. *Something isn't right? The ground. I remember lying on the ground.* He tried focusing on the memory, but it came out jumbled, like a jigsaw scattered on the floor. *There were stampeding Roos... A storm... Wait, I was in my LAV... but it was hot?*

His eyes flashed open, an action he at once regretted and slammed them shut. Letting his tight squint relax, he opened one eye and then the other. With each painful blink, his mind swept away the remnants of sleep, and found himself on a bed, in a room, instead of on the ground in the hot sun.

Ried rolled his head and squinted through the window into a hazy, and cloudless blue sky. Beyond the window, cast in silhouette against the morning sun waved the tops of several large gum trees, and on the breeze, came the melodic warbling song of magpies.

He went to massage his stiff neck. *Jesus.* He frowned at the IV needle in his hand. *What the...*

Reaching for the IV needle, Ried stopped at the sight of a folding camp bed with the sleeping figure of a woman under a sheet.

Ried called out, but no sound passed his parched mouth and throat. After several attempts, he raised enough saliva to ease the dryness in his throat. "Hey. Wake up."

The woman stirred at Ried's croaky command. "Oh, you're awake." She rolled over and pushed herself up. Sitting on the edge of her bed, she plucked a cotton dressing gown from the floor. She stood and covered her pale-green, cotton boxers and a T-shirt. "Sorry, I must have slept in." She stretched with a yawn.

The young woman walked around Ried's bed and closed the curtains against the morning glare. She flashed a smile before heading over to relight an old combustion stove.

Happy with her efforts, Ried's mystery roommate returned with a jug of chilled water and two glasses from a fridge which looked older than the stove.

His eyes followed the woman around the room. *Who the hell is she, and why is she sleeping beside my bed?*

He guessed the young woman was around his height, maybe his age less a year or two. Her wavy, mahogany-brown hair flowed down and caressed her shoulders, and the way she tied off her gown did nothing about hiding her subtle, full hourglass figure.

Feeling a little embarrassed from his close study of the woman, Ried gave the floor and the room more scrutiny than it deserved. *This place doesn't look like any typical hospital.*

The walls and ceiling comprised tongue-and-groove boards painted in a soft, buttery-yellow, and the ceiling painted white with dated light fittings hanging from the boards and flaking paint.

He paused his study of the room when he realised his roommate stood smiling down at him. She poured the water into a glass and passed it to him. He took the drink and tested the water with a sip before emptying the glass in quick successive gulps.

"Steady," she warned him. "You'll make yourself sick."

Ried felt the taut dryness recede from his mouth and throat. He held out the glass for more.

"Now, sip it this time," she scolded him.

"What happened?" He ignored her instructions and gulped down more water while searching through the fog in his mind.

"You crashed a few nights back, out on the flats during the storm," the young woman responded. "When they found you, Dad brought you here."

"Where's here?"

"My dad's farm."

"And your father is who?"

"Dominic Harris."

He handed her the glass for another refill. "I remember two blokes talking…"

"The other one was Uncle Jack." She refilled his glass. "He's not our real uncle, but we've called him that since we were kids."

Well, she's friendly enough…

"Are they the ones who took me out of the car?"

"Uh-huh. Along with my brother, Nicholas," she replied. "Let me tell you, Dr Mitchum was not happy they took you out before he arrived."

"And this is your farm?" Ried raised an eyebrow and again looked around the room.

"That's right." She caught his expression. "This was my mom's old day cottage," she said.

"Was?"

"She passed away." The woman's cheerfulness faded. *Shit...*

"I'm sorry."

"It was almost three years back." She gave Ried a weak smile

"So, your dad's farm. Where is it again?" He held out the glass. "Which is where?"

The brunette's company and her relaxed manner soon overrode his concerns.

"About ten kilometres south of town."

Ried continued drinking and raised a questioning eyebrow.

"Oh, sorry. Kingaroy."

"Kingaroy?" He shook his head. "No... It can't be..."

"Well, it is." She humoured him with a 'don't be silly' smile.

"But I was headed toward St. George when the storm hit me."

"St George?" She shook her head. "You must've hit your head pretty hard. Maybe your memories are mixed up."

"Not that hard." He ran his hand over the dressing on his forehead. "What the hell am I doing near Kingaroy?" He studied the young woman and the cottage, his ease swept aside by caution. "Why did they bring me to this farm and not the local hospital?"

"He didn't say. Just that it was better if you stayed here."

"On his farm near Kingaroy?" Ried didn't hide his scepticism.

"Yes," she took his glass, not quite snatching it. "Why, do you think I'm lying?"

"I don't know…" Ried hesitated. "I just find it weird he didn't take me to the hospital. It's like he doesn't want any questions asked by the cops or local authorities."

"Trust me. You don't want the local authorities involved," the brunette told Ried. "I suppose Dad's got his own reasons for not telling the Romans…" The last words came out in a whisper as her brow creased in a frown as she leaned closer.

"What?" Ried pulled back from the scrutiny of her emerald eyes flecked with gingerbread. His scepticism now replaced with suspicion at her sudden and close inspection. He scanned the room for a weapon and saw nothing he could use. Although, the way she wore the robe came close to qualifying as a weapon.

"Your face." She ignored his study of the room.

"What about it?"

Her eyebrows pinched a little, which highlighted her pointed nose. "Your black eye and bruises… They look almost healed."

Ried lifted his hands to his face, wincing when the needle pinched him again.

"You were pretty banged up when the doctor and I..." she trailed off when she lifted the bandage from his head. "Strewth," she whispered.

"Strewth what?" He shuffled pulled away in concern.

"The gash above your eye..." She knelt and reached under the bed. *Oh, shit!* Ried stiffened.

She dropped a first aid kit on the bed. "It's almost healed over the stitches." She sat beside him and leaned against him.

Ried's caution merged with a wave of embarrassment with her chests pushing against his shoulder, and her pleasant, musky odour sent his emotions into overdrive. He dragged more of the sheet across his lap and his; reaction.

"Hold still," she chided. "Benjamin, please keep still," she chastised him while she pulled out the last stitch and covered the partial scar with a Band-Aid.

Still cupping his chin, the woman rested the back of her other hand against his forehead and cheeks.

"You've still got a fever."

With no warning, she pulled back the sheet to inspect the bruise on his ribs.

A little intimidated by her behaviour, Ried dragged back the sheet, but she pushed his hand and the sheet away to check the other dressings on his ribs, arms, and stomach.

"Okay, just stop." He shunted her from his bed with his knees.

"Sorry." She sat back down on her bed. "I told the doctor how fast your cuts and scrapes were healing, but he didn't say anything yesterday when he saw you–"

"Hang on," Ried frowned and backed away. "How the hell do you know my name?"

"I looked in your wallet." She shrugged with a small, embarrassed smile.

"Really? And did you 'look' at anything else while I slept?" Ried quipped, lifting the sheet with his knee to conceal his body shape.

"Don't flatter yourself." Collecting the empty glasses and jug she gave Ried a hard glare. "All I've bloody been doing the last couple of days is playing friggin' nurse to you, my dad, and my brother." she stormed to the kitchen. One glass still filled with water tipped splashing the liquid across the table.

Before Ried could utter another word, she marched back in, waving her finger at him. He raised his open palms against her temper.

"And let me tell you, mate," she continued, "there are better things I could have been bloody well doing." The brunette thumped the chair beside his bed and sat down, grabbing his hand. "Now, I'll take this out. Then, you can clean up." She placed a thick Band-Aid over the exit wound left by the IV needle and pinched it down hard with her thumb.

"Christ." He winced from her firm grip and shoved her hand away.

"The bathroom's through there." She stood and pointed to the only door inside the cottage before returning to the kitchenette. "Oh, and I washed your clothes while you were asleep," she called out over her shoulder, "or is that also invading your privacy?"

Ried held his tongue and threw his legs over the edge of the bed. Two things happened: he pushed himself upright and then crashed to the floor in a wave of giddiness.

"Shit." With closed eyes, he swallowed away his nausea, and rose to his hands and knees before easing himself onto his heels, and falling back, tangled in the sheet, against the bed on the floorboards.

She rushed back to help him stand. "Sorry, Benjamin. The doctor told me you might be dizzy, but I forgot."

"No problem. I just got up too quick."

"I'll get a chair."

"It's okay," he assured her and then walked into the bathroom, supporting himself on the walls and door.

"Well, I'll wait out here then. Just in case."

With the water running from the shower nozzle, Ried took off the splint from his left wrist and inspected the yellow-blue stain of the healing bruise. Standing under the flow of hot water, he flexed his wrist for a few seconds, before a small bout of vertigo almost sent him falling against the wall.

"Are you okay in there?"

"Yep. All good." *Bullshit, Ried. You feel like crap.*

A few minutes later, he sat at the table and devoured a breakfast of oats, toast and coffee.

"So," he said after washing down his fourth piece of toast with a fresh coffee. "How about you have another crack at explaining why your father brought me here?"

"I told you, he didn't tell me."

Ried frowned at her response, crossed his arms, and leaned back in the chair.

"Don't give me that bloody look," she snapped. "You could have at least bloody well thanked me for nursing you."

"Okay–"

"If I'd known you'd be so bloody ungrateful, I would have told Dad to bugger off, and dump you in town." *Jesus, this one's got a temper. Come on Ried don't push your luck. Just figure out if she's a friend or a captor…*

"Look, this is all a bit of a shock and…" Ried mollified his tone the way he did in high school staring down a pissed-off teacher. "I'm sorry."

The young woman stared across the table with her arms folded.

"No, seriously. I'm sorry and thank you, Miss…"

"Abbey, Abbey Harris."

"Nice to meet you, Abbey Harris." Ried gave his best apologetic smile.

"Nice to meet you too, Benjamin."

"Ben or if you like, just Ried. Only my granddad called me Benjamin." He watched Abbey unfold her arms and then noticed how her eyes glinted with her smile.

"Do you remember what happened to you?" She asked while clearing the table.

"Not much. I remember driving on the highway toward Gore." He waited for a reaction. When none came, he continued. "Then, there was a storm which I reckon drove me off the road."

Ried puckered his brow, trying to recall more of his accident. Instead, he put down his cup feeling feverish again.

"You're sweating like a pig." Abbey handed him a tea-towel. "Are you okay?"

"I'm not sure." He wiped away the perspiration with the towel and hugged himself.

Abbey moved around the table. "Come on. Let's get you back to bed." She helped him back into the wrought-iron bed, and fluffed his pillows, brushing herself against him. *Christ. Is she doing that on purpose?*

"How long was I out for?"

"Since your accident, maybe four or five days all up."

"What!" He gawked at her in disbelief, his chills forgotten. "Shit. I need to make a few calls." His eyes explored the room. *No phone.*

"Have you seen my mobile?"

"You're what?"

"My mobile. My phone." Ried paused at the questioning look on Abbey's eyes.

"Sorry, you've lost me."

It was not the answer he'd hoped for. Ried climbed off the bed and went to his belongs stacked against a wall. He rummaged through the bags until he found his phone. When he turned the mobile over, he sighed at the shattered screen, "Shit." Ried tossed aside.

His suspicions came back hotter than his fever. He looked around the room again. *This place reminds me of a bad 80s movie. And what's with the bullshit about being near Kingaroy?*

He rubbed the front of his right shoulder for several seconds before charging out of the cabin.

"Where are you going?" Abbey called out.

Ried ignored Abbey and raised his hand to shade his eyes. He studied the cleared area around the little house.

To his back right, on the eastern side of the small ridge, ran a line of dense scrub. To his left, cut into the hill, was a campfire pit with three old, weathered, grey logs for seats.

The only path he saw branched off a vehicle track and disappeared up over a small rise to the right. Without hesitation, he stormed over to the path. *All right, Ried. It's time to find out what the bloody hell's going on.*

"Benjamin, please wait," Abbey called out, running after him. *Strewth, he's quick.*

When she caught up to him, she pleaded between breaths, "Benja… Ben, you still need to rest." She tried to grab his arm.

He twisted his arm from her grasp and held up an open hand. "Five days? I reckon I've rested enough," he barked, before heading toward a single gate set in a waist-high timber and chain wire fence, extending around the back of the main house. Ried swung the gate aside and headed toward the back steps of the house.

Standing in the open door at the top of the stairs, watching on with a look of concern, was an Aboriginal woman in her forties, her short, curly hair highlighted with grey streaks. Her hands rested in the large pocket of her jacquard cotton apron, which she wore over a floral, full-length, sleeveless dress.

"It's okay, Molly," Abbey said, making another grab for Ried's arm. "Is Dad inside?"

"He's in the dining room." Molly examined the young man through, hooded eyes. "Is he okay, Miss Abbey?"

Hearing raised voices outside, Dom stepped past Molly onto the top step.

"Mr Harris is it?" Ried freed himself from Abbey. "You need to tell me what the hell is going on."

Dominic stood dressed in denim trousers, elastic-sided boots, and a khaki, cotton, drill shirt. But, the man's commanding blue-grey eyes caught Ried's attention above his other features. Their colour gave them a hard look, but behind the tough exterior, Ried sensed a hint of compassion.

"Do I…?" Dom crossed his hands behind his back and looked at his daughter, who shrugged her shoulders.

"Sorry, I'm Benjamin Ried."

Ried climbed the steps with an outstretched hand, which Dom accepted on reflex. "Almost everybody calls me Ben or Ried."

"Benjamin Ried," Dom repeated in a hushed voice and went inside.

Ried took Dom's exit as an invitation to follow him through the kitchen and into the lounge room. When he entered the room, Ried paused at how the furniture seemed a little off.

Nothing was off in a bad context; it was just odd, looking neither new nor modern. The furniture appeared well cared for. Nothing seemed antique. Instead, the pieces looked dated and tired.

Standing against two of the walls were three solid, timber, vintage-style cabinets and shelf units full of well-worn books and a scattering of ornaments. In the corner behind the couches, Ried saw an old-style analogue phone – the kind with a rotary dial on its face – sitting on a timeworn roll-top desk.

"Are you feeling all right, son?"

A slow trickle of sweat ran down the back of Ried's neck and from under the hairline near his temple.

"Honestly, I feel like I'm burning up." Ried flopped into the wooden swivel chair in front of the desk to reach for the phone.

"Let's go into the dining room," suggested Dom. "Abbey, get the boy something cold." Dom moved beside Ried and helped him up. "Are you sure you're up to having a chat?"

"Yes," Ried insisted. "Abbey said you're the one who found me?"

"That's right. We saw your crashed car last Sunday–"

"Sunday? But I crashed on Thursday night." Ried shook his head and plonked down on a dining chair with a weary thump. "That'd mean I was out there for almost three days."

"I think you're a little confused, son. The storm came through Saturday afternoon and held us up overnight at Yarraman." Dom leaned forward to rest his elbows on the table. "That's how we discovered your car on Sunday. Because it wasn't there when we drove through on Saturday."

Ried didn't comment. Instead, he sat back with his arms folded, watching Dominic. *Why won't the man look me in the eye and why steer me away from the phone?*

"Can I ask where you were headed before you crashed?" Dom dismissed his guest's silent and arrogant pose.

"Out west, toward St. George. Then, this storm came and started to…" Ried paused when a flash of memory came back. He felt unsure whether to reveal what he remembered.

"Started to do what?"

"This might sound nuts, but I reckon it chased me."

"Storms don't chase people, son."

"Yeah, well, you weren't there, were you?"

"Benjamin… Is that your dad's name?"

"Excuse me?"

"Sorry, I just assumed."

"Look, what do you want with me?" Ried leaned against the table. "Don't get me wrong. I'm glad you helped and everything, but I want to know what's going on."

"Do you remember anything else about your accident?"

"Like I told your daughter, I drove off the road, and crashed from the storm." Ried leaned back.

Okay, this is getting tedious and a little more than odd.

"You don't remember how badly you were hurt?"

"No. Why?"

"You had a fractured forearm, two cracked ribs, dozens of cuts and scrapes, a black eye and the doctor said you had severe bruising and swelling around your ribs, spine and hips." Dom pointed to the Band-Aid on Ried's head. "Not to mention the nasty gash on your forehead."

"Give me a break. Your daughter told me it's only been five days since I crashed." Ried raised his eyebrows in disbelief. "So, by your account, I shouldn't have been able to crawl up here, let alone walk?" He pushed the chair back. "You lot must think I'm crazy."

"Sit down, son," Dom pleaded. "I don't think you are crazy. But understand in rescuing you, we took a hell of a flaming risk," he shrugged. "Or maybe I should just hand you over to the bloody Romans and let them deal with you."

"Romans." Ried leaned back and furrowed his brow. "Romans? Who the hell are– What the hell are you talking about?" He glared at Dom. "Just where the hell am I, and who the bloody hell are you people?"

"I'm trying to ask the same of you." Dom stood and went out to his desk and returned to his chair. "I went through this last night." He flicked Ried's wallet across the table. "Tell me where you came from, son. Because what I saw in there," he gestured to the wallet, "didn't make any sense."

"I guess looking through people's stuff runs in the family." Ried scooped up his wallet from the table.

"Where are your proper papers?"

"My papers?" Flabbergasted and disbelieving, Ried opened his wallet and removed its contents, spreading them across the polished table.

By then, Abbey had returned, dressed in her regular jeans and a checked blouse, carrying a tray with a glass jug of iced tea and three glasses.

"Look," Ried said. "I don't know what you mean by papers."

Ried's face dripped with perspiration. Mopping up his sweat as best as he could, he held up the plastic cards one by one. "This is my driver's licence, these are my gun permits, and those are my debit and credit cards."

"Credit cards?" Dom tapped two of plastic cards scattered on the table. "Credit cards haven't been around for decades." He then placed a finger on each licence. "And why bother to carry cards that show they are endorsed by the Queensland Government?" He slid them back toward Ried.

"Because they were." Ried held his stance.

"Here's the thing, son," Dom continued. "The Queensland Government hasn't existed for over thirty years—"

"Piss off." Ried jumped out of his chair. "What kind of bullshit is this?" The hair in his armpits matted with sweat as he wiped more sweat from his neck and face. "How about you tell me why you didn't take me to a hospital, and why you brought me over two hundred klicks from where I bloody well crashed?"

"I can assure you it isn't two hundred klicks to Barker's Creek," Dom replied. "And taking you to the hospital didn't seem prudent." He softened his tone. "Please, sit back down."

Ried stayed standing, almost preferring to fall against the wall in defiance.

Dom paused, and his brow gave a brief twitch when he recalled what Gallio said about a tear in space and time. Things about their guest came across as familiar and haunting. Dom's tone came out flat and direct. "If I took you to the hospital, then the authorities would have locked you up until the bastards figured out where you came from."

"Here's a heads up for you," Ried shot back. "I came from Brisbane and was driving to a new job in Western Queensland."

"All right, son, you—"

"I'm not your son."

Dom shrugged. "Okay, but you might want to sit down for this…" And then Dom explained, to the best of his ability, Gallio's theory of how Ried ended up in their world.

"Bullshit." Ried almost laughed when the explanation concluded. "You're telling me I fell through a hole in space?" *I don't know what weird, bloody game they're playing at. But, I've no intention of playing.*

"It's what their scientists reckon." Dom sat back.

"And just who the hell is this mob you keep calling the Romans?" Ried pinched the bridge of his nose before massaging his forehead. Despite himself, he snatched up a glass and gulped down the cold tea.

"It's complicated."

Ried palmed away the constant film of perspiration on his forehead. The action alone added to the pinched look of frustration he wore.

"Are you okay?" Abbey reached across for Ried's hand.

But Ried pulled his arm back, and swept up the cards from his wallet, glaring at them both. "You lot are fucking nuts," he spat and rushed from the house.

CHAPTER SIX

Ried ran through the gate back to the cottage and then slowed. He knew the cottage would be the first place anyone would go looking for him. In a split second, he ran at a crouch toward the barn diving headlong into the damp grass and dirt behind a water trough.

Hugging the moist concrete wall of the trough, he crawled on his stomach to peer around the end closest to the barn. From his vantage point, he saw Abbey and Dom standing at the back door, having a heated discussion until Abbey pushed past her father.

Dom trotted down the small set of stairs after his daughter, pausing at the gate, he surveyed the barn and sheds for a few seconds, before going back inside.

When Dom disappeared inside, Ried was about to run across to the open barn door and caught the movement of a vague silhouette in the shadows beyond the door.

"Clever bastard," Ried said and waited.

Once it was all clear, he darted inside the barn. The streams of light lancing the dust-filled air revealed bales of hay stacked below a small loft. Stacked in a corner lay disused or broken parts of a plough. Along the left wall, next to several horse stalls, ran an oil-stained workbench.

Nowhere in the barn did he see a car or motorbike.

"That'd be right…" He faced the line of stables and puffed his cheeks. "Okay, on horseback it is."

Behind his back, something metallic moved with a clink and tap.

"Shit." Ried's gut clenched and his diaphragm lurched. He crouched, turned and moved against the stalls. Ried baulked for several seconds at sound's source. Despite his fever, his blood chilled from the vision.

On the opposite wall hung the stuff of murder; scythes, long shears, double-bladed axes, and different-size cane knives.

"Bloody hell. Who else lives here? Stephen King?"

Farther along the wall, he spotted a rope and tackle system trailing from a winch motor in the rafters. An L-shaped rail jutted out from the wall left of the tools and farm blades. Slung along the rail sat six saddles and blankets.

Inside the nearest stall, a chestnut mare lifted her head, pointing her ears forward, stepped back and snorting at the intruder.

Ried kept his movements slow and controlled as he approached the stall. "Aren't you a beauty? You must be, what, fifteen hands high?" He admired the animal's long neck, draped in a well-groomed blonde mane and toned body and legs.

Three of which ended in white socks and a black one on her front left forelock, which the mare pawed through the hay covering the floor.

He ignored the casual pawing hoof and followed her snout past her full white blaze, punctuated by a reddish-brown star, and into her deep brown eyes.

"All right, you. Let's both stay calm, eh?" He eased himself back against the rail where he lifted off a saddle and blanket.

The mare watched Ried step toward her, snorted and rolled her head forward, and lifted her snout.

Without breaking eye contact, and with unhurried actions, Ried stepped inside the stall and placed the saddle and blanket on the ground.

"Good girl," cooed Ried as he stepped in front of the animal.

In reply, the animal bobbed her head and curled back her top lip taking a deep breath.

Ried kept still while the mare and himself measure each other.

"Easy girl… I'm not going to hurt you…" *Steady now Ried, a pissed off horse in a small stall won't end well for both of us.*

His face and hands became layered in slime from his sweat congealing the in the air, making him itch, but he knew breaking his moves now would spook the mare. So, he ignored the prickling sensation.

Ried stroked her neck with the palm of his hand in slow, tender passes while resting his other hand on her nose. His mother's words rang through his mind: *"Horses are no different from people. A soft, gentle caress is far more soothing and more respectful than a series of slaps, gentle or not."*

The horse's muscles shivered from his touch. "Shh. Easy, girl." He kept his movements slow and rhythmic. "How about you take me for a ride, hey?" Conscious of how her pawing front leg could lash out and cripple him, he continued caressing her under the chin.

After a moment, the mare calmed down and pushed herself against Ried.

"That's it. See? I'm not so bad." He reached for the blanket and froze when he heard voices outside. He slipped out of the stall and went up beside the door.

Through the open door, he watched Dom, Abbey and a young bloke with a ponytail standing at the fence. They debated while pointing in different directions. Approaching the barn came a man with well-tanned skin.

"Shit." Ried ducked back into the stall, taking care not to spook the mare or raise any dust. He held his breath when the man stopped at the door and counted the horses.

Two other horses whinnied, and the mare beside Ried lifted her head, snorted, and stomped her black-socked hoof on the ground.

Ried gritted his teeth and balled his fists in a muted curse from the animal's behaviour.

In the barn, the man approached the stalls, "Quiet, Devil."

But the closer the man came, the more agitated the animal grew. The muscles in Ried's arms tensed as he flexed his fists. Hurting anybody was not his first choice, but he had no intention of staying here as a prisoner or anything else.

The closer the man came; the more agitated Devil grew from his intrusion. She flicked and snaked her head with wide eyes and ears flat against her head and her breath puffing through her nostrils in rapid snorts.

Ried crept past behind Devil and peered through a split in the stall's timber wall.

The man raised his hands, cursed the horse, and walked out of the barn.

The moment the intruder left, Ried stood up beside Devil's head and looked over the stall. When the farmhand stepped from the barn, Devil's aggressive manner stopped, and she nudged her cheek against Ried's shoulder.

Ried reached up and stroked the mare's neck, "Hello Devil. I'm Ben."

With another quick glance at the open barn door, Ried eased his way out of the stall. He followed the outside voices as he approached the wall near the barn door and peeked through a hole in the timber boards.

Dom sent the man from the barn back along the cottage path as Abbey entered a shed about twenty metres away. Dom shifted and then sent the younger man with the ponytail after the tanned man before going back into the house. After several minutes he and the woman called Molly came out. The two had a quiet conversation after which she took off her apron and headed toward the barn as Dom ran after Abbey.

Ried scampered back into Devils stall and hugged the wall behind the horse. His breath stalled in his tight throat, knowing his luck was spent. However, the woman walked past him into the last stall and spent the next five minutes saddling a horse and then riding out through the back door.

His head flicked around when a cough and the roar of a motor came from the other shed. Squinting through a crack in the barn's wall, watched Dom and Abbey driving out in an open-backed Ute toward the front of the house. A sense of relief washed over his tension as he stepped back and finished saddling the horse.

He dragged his hand across his sweat-drenched face and wiped the gritty moisture down his pants and led Devil from the barn. By his reckoning, it must be near midday.

In the brighter light, he inspected her hooves and rechecked the saddle, bridle and girth buckles. Satisfied, he adjusted the stirrups and then lifted himself on the horse.

When Ried's weight settled in the saddle, Devil's ears rolled flat against her head, and she walked hind legs dipped. He leaned forward, and grabbed the horn of the saddle, and continued whispering near her ear until she relaxed. When he felt sure Devil accepted him in the saddle, he twitched the reins and rode past the house.

Once passed the main gate, he stopped, unsure of which way the old man went, or even which direction he should go in search of help. He looked both ways along the road and shrugged his shoulders. "Okay, do I go right or left?"

Without hesitation, Devil turned and walked down the road.

"All right, left it is."

#

The following day, Ried reached a T-intersection in the road. He paused and rested his elbow on the saddle horn. "No doubt about it. I'm lost." His stomach gurgled from hunger. He straightened back up, flexed his shoulders, and massaged his stiff neck. He nudged Devil into the shade of a stubby gum tree and stared into the surrounding hills and scrub.

Frustrated, lost, and confused, Ried wiped sweat from his face. His night in the country only worsened his fever and chills. The intersection across the road looked no different from the others he had passed.

On his left, the patchwork ribbon of dark-grey bitumen disappeared around a bend shrouded by trees. On the right, the road followed the gradual rise of a small hill.

Sweat trickled between his shoulder blades, and down his back. He walked Devil across the road toward a pair of rusty steel posts jutting out of a thick, woody patch of weeds and creeper vines.

Ried dismounted and tore away at the mass of thin wooded, vegetation until he revealed a faded road sign. He wiped away the dirt and grime built up over almost illegible letters against the signs oxidised and weather-worn colour.

He hawked back and spat on the sign and scrubbed away more of the accumulated decay and grunge until the bleached lettering revealed a name: *Kingaroy*.

"Bloody hell."

From where it lay in the grass and weeds, the sign's faded arrow pointed ahead of him. With little else to guide him, Ried mounted Devil, "Okay girl. The sign points that way. So, that's where we go."

After several minutes of riding, Ried's chills returned, and he shivered under his fever induced perspiration. With no other means of treating the symptoms, he kept riding in the warm, mid-morning sun.

Yet, as he rode, something niggled his senses and thoughts. Ried stopped Devil, shifted and twisted around, glancing at the sun shining down from above his right shoulder.

"The sun's on my right. This time yesterday, it was on my left… Which means I've turned myself around." He glanced back along the road and frowned at the shadows. *It's the middle of the day, but…*

Ried scanned the horizon and then squinted back toward the glowing white orb in the pale-blue sky. "It's way too hot for August, and the sun's in the wrong spot."

The warm breeze blowing in from the south-west soon evolved into a light wind, cooling his perspiration – an unpleasant sensation which enhanced his fevered chills.

His fever and the surrounding silence scrapped his nerves. "Where the hell is everyone?" He asked the Devil. "Christ, you would've thought I'd have seen somebody since yesterday?"

A short time later, he came across a bridge with the scarred remains of bitumen hanging on to the structures exposed broken and rotten timbers. The decaying bridge stood beyond reach in the middle of a swamp-filled gully.

Everything about the old bridge and intervening ditch spoke of something more than neglect. "Bloody hell," a feeling of defeat ebbed at him. "It's the same bloody bridge we saw yesterday." Shaking his head, Ried tugged on the reins and turned the horse around. "Christ. It's like I've stumbled onto the set of an Australian Walking Dead?"

On his left was the side road they took yesterday, a little farther along another side road ran off to the right into a wooded valley. "What do you reckon Devil, if we're gonna stay lost we might as well do it in some shade?"

After riding for four hundred metres down the road, the valley widened into dry paddocks of waist-high grass. Along the roadside stretched the remnants of barbed-wire fences and old, termite-ridden fence posts.

Along the way, his excitement grew when he spotted a track leading through the grass. Ried steered Devil along the path and reined her in by a broken gate made from rusted steel pipe.

Beyond the gate, stood the remains of an old farmhouse, surrounded by a field of swaying grass and weeds. Much of the house and the roof had fallen in on itself. The front stairs were gone; having long collapsed.

The derelict property enticed Ried with morbid curiosity. Halfway between the gate and the house lay the decaying hulk of a Land Cruiser flatbed.

Tree saplings forced their way through the rotten floorboards of its tray. Both doors were missing, exposing the interior of the cab. The remains of charred molten plastic draped from the rusted frames of the seats, dashboard and steering wheel.

Some areas of oxidised paint, stained brown, held fast on the hulk's body. The driver side front fender showed dozens of small black holes – old bullet scars from somebody's past target practice?

Ried continued along the track disturbing a small herd of grazing wild cattle who skittered at his approach. His first thought was the house had collapsed with age and decay, but on closer inspection, the scene told a different story.

He dismounted, dropped the reins over his shoulder, and walked toward the nearest wall with Devil in tow. The old farmhouse was nothing more than a weather-beaten facade hiding the shattered roof, walls and floor.

"Huh. Must have been one hell of a storm."

After tying the reins around a broken floor joist, he edged closer to the jagged back walls, avoiding the fresh patties of cow dung. Ried inspected several pieces of the shattered weatherboards. The way the timber had broken along with the signs of old charcoal hinted at something other than storm damage.

Ried's mind ticked off several scenarios to settle on something crashing into the house. "Whatever hit the building," Ried traced an imaginary line with his finger. "I reckon came in from this way and crashed somewhere over there."

Ried zigzagged through the waist-high rye-grass filled with cobbler pegs, and blackberry weeds toward a nearby tree line. Twenty-odd metres past the house and to the right, he spotted a weather-stained metal frame amidst the grass. "I guess it crashed closer than I thought."

When he parted the grass, he found the remains of an inline cockpit with the left and underneath side of the triangular frame crushed and twisted. Any padding on the seats decayed years ago to expose the frames and springs, the instrument panels were nothing more than broken metal with cracked or missing gauges.

What Ried found fascinating was the pieces of fuselage sheeting left attached to the framework. At first, he thought the metal was rusty, but when he rubbed away the grime, the light reflected from thin metal with a deep-bronze patina.

A few metres away, he kicked at a cylinder covered in the same ultra-thin sheeting. He knelt and wrapped his arms around the tube, and then rocked and tipped the short, fat barrel until it broke free from the soil and weeds.

He tugged the matted grassroots entangling a multi-bladed fan. "What the fuck..." He flipped the tube over. On the cylinder's outer casing, he found two opposing brackets, mounts and the segmented Venturi thrust controls. "What kind of jet nozzle is this?"

Ried dropped the cylinder and walked back past the skeletal cockpit, prodding the grass and weeds with his boot. Excitement and curiosity continued overriding his hunger and chills as he unveiled part of a broad delta-shaped object. He bent down to lift the metal and found it lighter than expected. *A wing?*

A brown and grey mass with legs moved when Ried lifted the wing. The lump was a lizard with a broad, flat head, which hissed at him before scuttling away on four squat legs.

"Shit. You'd be about the ugliest blue-tongue I've ever seen."

He waited until the grey and brown reptile waddled into the grass, and continued lifting the object, so it rested on one edge. The movement shifted something inside which let the daylight stream through a dozen holes punched through its thin sheeting. "Bullet holes?"

He let the wing fall back into the weeds and spotted some engraved and embossed symbols on the metal: a bull below a few letters in either Latin or Greek. Ried frowned at the images.

He dropped and then walked across the wing like object. The metal sheeting creased and dented under his weight before popping back out after each step. With the only evidence of his crossing being his footprints smudged in the dirt and grime.

Ried turned and bent back over the unusual wing and rubbed his hand along the metallic skin. "What sort of alloy doesn't dent?" Frowning, he turned and continue separating the surrounding grass with his boots.

A metre away, he lifted a rotting piece of plasticised material. "What the hell?" Ried studied the pattern of the pressed material. "Who wears body armour like this?" He went back to the review the etched symbols and then looked back at the body armour.

When he turned it over, several dried rib bones and vertebrae fell out with some composted soil. He dropped the armour in disgust and wandered back to the house. Along the way, Ried tripped and stumbled from a piece of metal half buried in the grass.

"Gimme a break." Ried kicked away at what tripped him. *What the hell?* He lifted the piece of metal and rolled his hand around. "A sword?"

He stood there, contemplating everything he found. The strange metal sheeting on the fuselage, the wing with bullet holes and the etched effigies, the back end of some weird jet engine, and a piece of armour and sword for a gladiator – It didn't add up.

He dropped the rusted sword. "It's official. I'm lost in a bizarre 'coma' dream, or I'm still asleep in the diner," he concluded, though neither gave rise as a convincing theory.

On his way back to the road, Ried stopped near the gate and gave the house one last look. The scene and old building resembled a derelict vessel on an undulating sea of beige and greys, a decaying guard hiding a bizarre secret.

"C'mon, girl. Let's get out of here and find some help." He tugged on the reins with a nagging, growing sense of unease and melancholy.

The rhythmic, hollow click-clack of Devil's metal shoes on the bitumen echoed back at him, a haunting sound in the still air.

Ried manoeuvred the mare into the grass and creeper vine beside the road. However, the swish and padded thud of the animal's hooves through the grass did little in easing his sense of loneliness and melancholy.

Strewth, there must be somebody working out here.

When he and Devil crested a small hill, Ried spotted a line of high-voltage towers with their cables falling to the ground. Smaller towers trailed off into the distance beside the broken towers. Unlike their taller companions, the wires on the smaller ones appeared in good condition and draped in an unbroken line from tower to tower.

The combination of mismatched towers running parallel to each other struck him as a little odd. Then again, the last couple of days were nothing but odd.

Ried stroked Devil's neck. "How about you tell me what's going on around here?"

The mare shook her head and flicked her tail.

"Well, something or someone is getting power, so let's see where they lead." Ried sat back and spurred Devil into a trot.

The motion of the trotting horse, the fluctuating fever, sweats, and growing stomach cramps, soon made him feel more than a little unwell. He eased Devil back to a steady walk, and patted his face dry with his sleeve, swallowing back the bitter bile burning his throat.

The images of the last two days played on his mind.

The ruined farms and bridges, the abandoned machinery and that weird ultralight plane. Then, there's the out of time look of the cottage and the furniture in their house.

"Hell, even their bloody phone looked like something my grandparents would've owned."

The horse gave a small snort.

111

"And what about all the weird bullshit the old man spun me?"

Devil swung her head around to look at him.

"What, no reply? I figured you'd be on his side." He rubbed the animal's neck. "And what happened to my car, eh?"

Ried tugged on the reins and almost fell from the sudden cramp in his stomach. The sharp, intense pain folded him over the saddle and left him resting on the mare's neck.

He took several deep breaths until the contractions eased enough to let him sit back upright. The seesawing fevers and sweats, along with the onset of cramps, ground down his strength. *Maybe I was a bit rash running off before I got all my strength back...*

The lack of water made his head throb from growing headaches, and his vision wavered in and out of focus.

"Come on, Ried. You're a member of the second R.A.R." He rubbed the front of his right shoulder. "You've been through worse. So, get your fucking shit together." Yet, he couldn't remember ever feeling this sick. Every muscle and organ screamed, trapped within a burning lava pit surrounded by a blizzard.

Unaware of her rider's torment, Devil continued down the road, feeling the weight of Ried shift before he passed out, slumped across her neck. She walked at a steady pace rolling her neck, shoulders and hips, keeping the non-responsive rider from falling out of the saddle.

CHAPTER SEVEN

Several hundred metres down the road, Devil meandered over into a patch of lush, wild couch grass, seconds before Ried rolled from the saddle. After a few minutes, the mare bowed her head and with soft taps, she nuzzled him until he stirred.

"Shit." He looked around. "I guess it's not a dream." He sighed and clutched the reins as Devil walked back helping him up.

Marvelling at the animal's intuitiveness, but still feeling a little weak, he hooked his arm under Devil's chin and slipped his hand through her bridle for support. He slid his foot across the thick carpet of grass while stroking the animal's cheek. "Did you know I would fall?"

The mare replied by lowering her head and cropping the top of the turf.

"You're not much of a talker, are you?" The sight of Devil cropping the grass and chewing sent his gastric juices in flux. "Well, at least one of us can eat."

In the distance, a flock of large, black birds flew around in circles, cawing, and squawking at each other. While watching the distant birds, a small swarm of little bush flies homed in on Ried's sweat moistened head, along with an annoying march fly.

Ried waved and slapped at the insects attracted by the salt from his perspiration. Then, he heard running water from within the nearby scrub, which stopped his windmilling waves and slaps.

"I suppose if I can't eat, then I can at least have a drink." He tied the reins around a small shrub and left Devil with her banquet of couch and ploughed his way through the dense foliage in search of the running water.

After several minutes of shoving and pushing, he stumbled out of the trees onto the edge of a small clearing split in the middle by a thin running creek.

Without the slightest hesitation, Ried jogged over to fall on the bank of the stream and pushed his head under the fresh water.

The flowing water hit him like a jolt of electricity recharging his tired, sweaty, and aching body. *Christ, that feels so good.*

Ried enjoyed the weightless feel of his arms and head floating in the cool creek. When he couldn't hold his breath any longer, he sat back on his knees and let the fresh water drip down his body, before leaning forward and scooping up handfuls of the thirst-quenching liquid.

"Look at what we've gone 'n' found, Muddgy."

"I reckon we've got us a townie who's lost and thirsty," another voice laughed.

"Bloody hell." Startled by the sudden intrusion, Ried turned, lost his footing and fell into the creek.

"And he's a cute one too," The second voice added.

Ried sat on the stream's gravel bottom with the water halfway up his chest, staring in mild disbelief at a man and woman. *Jesus Christ. Where the hell did Grizzly Adams come from?*

Ried pushed himself upright and waded to the bank, but paused mid-step when a slow, menacing growl came from behind the man's legs.

A muscular Rottweiler moved in front of the newcomer and rolled its lips back. The dog fixed its gaze on Ried and issued another threating rumble from deep in its throat.

"Easy now, dog." The woman patted the animal's head.

"Strewth. Give a bloke some warning before you sneak up on him." With protracted, cautious steps, Ried climbed out of the knee-deep water, shivering under his sodden clothes, *Easy now. Just stay calm. You've got nothing they could want...*

He paused as his caution and concern warnings rocketed skyward. Cradled in the man's arms, sat a clean, oiled, L1A1 self-loading rifle.

"We didn't sneak up. You shoulda listened to what's goin' on around ya." The woman grinned with a mouth full of yellow and brown stained teeth. "I like his clothes, Gazza." She took a few steps toward Ried, who took another step in the opposite direction, almost falling again into the water.

"Get away, Muddgy. They're not gonna be yours to have." The large man also approached Ried. "Now, don't you move, pretty boy," Gazza said. He looked Ried over. Trying to figure out why old man Harris wanted the stranger. *This bloke don't seem like anything special.*

"What is this?" Ried asked. "Have I walked onto the set of some new reality TV show?" He eased himself farther away from the creek. "You must have the crew and cameras well hidden." He moved a couple more steps. The dog noticed, and lowered its head, offering another ominous growl.

115

"I told ya not to fuckin' move, boy." Gazza continued staring at Ried.

Ried returned Gazza's observation. *Forget Grizzly Adams. I'm in some weird Queensland Deliverance.*

Without shifting his gaze, Gazza slid two fingers between his lips and blew a warbled, shrill whistle.

Oh fuck... Ried's blood turned to liquid nitrogen when the sound of the whistle brought the scrub around the creek to life.

More than a dozen men, women, and boys of mixed nationalities materialised from the surrounding bush. There were Caucasians, Aboriginal, and Asian – an eclectic bunch dressed in either skins and loincloths, or different combinations of repaired, faded, and torn clothes. Platts, braids, and dreadlocks decorated their hair and beards, and many sported crude tattoos.

Every one of them carried one or more weapons: spears, lethal-looking clubs, and large knives. Many of them also wore hodgepodge body armour, yet not one, apart from the man who spoke, carried any firearms.

"Oh, Shit." In an instant, Ried discounted the notion he'd stumbled onto the set of a TV show and went more with his deliverance theory.

"'Shit' just about sums it up," Gazza said with a smirk.

Reality show or not, it didn't take a script for Ried to understand who led them. The one called Gazza singled out two of his men from the encircling mob, who moved in Ried's direction.

Ried's foot slid back into the water when he took a defensive step back. Put off balance, Ried fell on his knees and fumbled on the bank's wet edge. Groping in his effort to stand, he concealed a tennis ball-sized rock in his fist. "What do you want?"

Gazza smirked. "We want you to come with us."

Okay, this is bullshit. "What if I don't want to?" Ried stepped into the more open ground. The dog rumbled another warning and stepped toward Ried, with every muscle coiled.

"No, dog. Stay." Gazza knelt beside the dog and rested his arm on the animal's shoulder.

"You don't hear so good, boy." The larger of the two new men waved a broad lethal blade at Ried. "The guv'na told ya, don't move."

"I'll tell you what." Ried matched the stare of the knife-wielding man. "I'll keep still if you do too." He then directed his attention at Gazza without taking his eyes off the knifeman and his friend. "Maybe we can work something out."

Gazza spat out a laugh. "Hear that? He reckons we can make a deal." Gazza turned off his smile. "Just fuckin' bag him," he said.

The two men grinned with savage delight as they charged toward Ried. The quiet one took a couple of swift steps and dove at Ried's legs.

But the man telegraphed his move, which allowed Ried to skip out of his grasp, only to stumble on the uneven ground, dropping his rock. Before Ried realised, the first man sheathed his knife and charged catching Ried off guard, with a brutal backhanded slap.

The man's fist carried the weight and power of an anvil which sent Ried cartwheeling and tripping over his own feet.

Unprepared, Ried fell hard. The landing driving the air from his lungs. In a quick twist, Ried rolled onto all fours sucking back his expelled breath and spitting out a mouthful of blood.

Dazed, Ried blinked and flexed his jaw with the sound of the cheering group muffled from the low ringing in his ear.

Spurred on by the group's encouragement, the brute picked up Ried by the shirt and pulled him closer. The larger man swore at Ried.

Ried shied away from the thug's foetid breath while wrapping his legs around his attacker's waist and dug his hands into the man's greasy hair.

With a grunt, the man reached for the hands locked in his hair.

Ried took advantage of the man's brief distraction, and in a whiplash move, rocked his head back, and then drove his forehead into his opponent's nose.

The impact sent a white flare behind Ried's forehead and shattered his attacker's eye socket and nose, sending out a stream of warm slick blood.

Ried's wounded and dazed attacker bellowed in pain and shock as he collapsed still holding Ried.

Stunned from the headbutt and fall, Ried didn't spot the second attacker who came in from behind. Caught by surprise, Ried grunted from the iron-clad grip of the smaller man.

Although smaller, the second thug was all muscle. The man tightened his bear hug, arched his back, and lifted Ried up to drop him back down.

The impact jarred Ried's legs and forced the air out of his lungs and without pause Ried's attacker retightened his grip and repeated the raise and drop move.

Ried's diaphragm strained under the relentless vice-like grip. His head and ears throbbed from the increase in blood pressure. His lungs wheezed, and heart beat a furious staccato in his chest.

In pure desperation, Ried raised his hands behind him groping and clenched his fingers into his opponent's thick, greasy hair.

With the man's head locked in his grip, Ried took a deep breath, clenched his teeth, and then drove his thumbs hard into the man's ear cavities, carving away the soft skin with his nails.

Ried ignored the man's cries, and twisted his thumbs deeper, burrowing for his eardrums. Once he felt the vice-like grip slacken from under his chest, Ried withdrew his thumbs, turned himself and his hands around and pried his thumbs into the man's eye sockets.

He then pushed the man back while shoving his index fingers into his bleeding ear canals.

The man screamed and thrashed, but this increased Ried's resolve. Lost in anger and the red fire of rage, Ried yelled, trying to squeeze the man's eyeballs from his head.

Terrified and blinded, the injured assailant thrashed about in a frenzy of panic which toppled both himself and Ried.

When they fell, Ried clamped his hands harder around the man's head, rolled across his body and twisted with a sudden jerk.

Ried rolled back around and recoiled at the site of his victims' blood smeared face oozing mulberry and honey-coloured fluid from his torn eye sockets and ears.

The first man, recovering from the headbutt and made a clumsy lunge toward Ried only he misjudged his move through blood and tear-swollen eyes.

Catching his breath, Ried spotted the man's move and rolled around, pushed down on his hands, and threw a desperate kick at the man.

His boot landed between the bigger man's ear and shoulder. The force of Ried's kick, combined with the other's momentum, broke the attacker's neck, sending him sprawling into the grass where his head landed with a bone-crushing thump on a large rock.

The man spluttered with a garbled cough, then rolled his eyes back and died after his next breath. A seeping pool of blood and cranial fluid matting his hair and staining the grass and soil.

Ried crawled over and relieved the corpse of its large knife. The side of Ried's face burned with pain, and several teeth moved when he pressed his tongue against them.

The red instinct and fire which fuelled his defences ebbed away. He stared in slow horror at the two men lying dead by his hand. Bile rose in his throat, which he swallowed back and stood favouring his twisted ankle.

The sight of Ried holding the knife, and standing over their dead comrades, turned the group's cheers into threatening murmurs and hard scowls.

Ried stumbled back returning their looks through his weariness, confusion, and anger.

Then, came the snarl and bark and his world shifted into slow motion.

Ried faced the attacking dog mesmerised at how the animal's paws spread out when they landed on the ground and the way his bloodstained hands gripped the knife's wooden handle.

The pent-up emotions from the last two days surged through his muscles, still boosted with added adrenaline.

His incoherent scream of rage, along with the dog's guttural bark registered as grumbling, phantasmal growls.

Chunks of dirt and grass floated in the air behind the dog's paws after it launched itself from the ground.

Everything around Ried moved with a nightmare's slowness.

The dog's face became an animated gargoyle with lips rolled back from teeth and fangs stained yellow and brown. The saliva flicked away in slow arcing globules.

Ried's own movements also became drawn and slow as he slid under the leaping animal and slashed the knife upward.

The unhurried blade entered the dog's fur puckering the skin inward along the knife's edge before the flesh split into a strawberry-coloured smile.

With a jolt, Ried stumbled back, hurled into real time.

The dingo crossbreed gave a short, high-pitched yelp, when the blade sliced past its ribs, and into its lung and heart. Still clutching the handle, the dead animals' weight and momentum twisted Ried around and carried them both into the creek.

When he stood and shook the water from his eyes, the crowd of feral people closed in on him.

The woman wailed at the sight of the dog floating in a spreading pool of crimson.

"You murderin' bastard."

His clothes soaked through and eyes wide, Ried stood, his nostrils flared with each deep inhalation.

Apart from the gurgling stream, and the increased drone of flies converging on the dead bodies the people and surrounding bush lay shrouded in silence.

Gazza moved forward, his gaze burning into Ried. *Fuck me. Fuck the colonel and fuck this bloke.* The sound of Ried's voice broke into Gazza's thoughts. "What'd you say?"

121

"I... I just want to go home," Ried pleaded, and then slapped at the sudden sting of an insect biting his neck. *Damn horseflies.* When he pulled his hand away, the flattened object in his palm was no insect.

Within two heartbeats all ability to stand or move deserted Ried and he collapsed onto his knees, glaring up at Gazza through blurring vision. "You fuckin–"

Gazza's shoulders slumped, and he stared at the blowgun wielding man behind Ried. "Damn it, Squat. If I wanted you to dart him, I would've fuckin told ya to." Gazza walked over to his two fallen men and stood over Ried. "There ain't no tellin what that shit'll do to a person." He pondered the young man laying at his feet. *This is gonna cost the Colonel double.*

When the darts sedative wore off, Ried found himself imprisoned alongside Devil in either a dark shed or cell lined with dank, mouldy hay. "Shit. Could this day get any worse or weirder?" He wanted to believe he lay in a hospital bed in a coma, experiencing one of those bleak, subconscious dreams.

But, if this is a dream, then how come it's all so friggin real? Sitting beside Devil, Ried recalled the fight with vivid, gut-wrenching clarity behind his closed eyes. "Jesus." He collapsed back against the wall.

The familiar voice of his platoon sergeant echoed from the back of his thoughts:

#

"Killing a man with your bare hands is not a job done lightly. It is primal. It is brutal. It is the most personal fucking form of combat you'll ever experience. But remember this. If afterwards, you feel squeamish or want to cry like a fucking baby, then you're alive, and you've done your job."

#

Ried pushed the sergeant's voice back into the shadows. He might well be alive, but his dream had transformed itself into a nightmare. "Christ, please let me wake up."

Beside him, Devil gave a small snort and shuffled her feet. "Hey, girl." He pushed himself out of the hay and checked out his surroundings. With measured steps, he walked around and reached out to feel the rough surface of a corrugated tin wall and wooden frame.

He groped his way around the confines of their prison. With his arm raised above his head, he jumped up and down in several places. "Well, I won't be riding out on horseback." By his reckoning, the whole building or shed seemed no bigger than a horse float. *Dream or not. At least the old man and his daughter didn't lock me in a fucking cupboard.*

Stepping over to the faint stream of light in front of him, Ried traced the outline of a door. He eased his shoulder against the metal lining, leaned into it, and felt the sticky mass of old spider webs brush his face. "Shit!" He slapped his face and stumbled back, colliding with Devil.

Ried continued beating at the dust-covered, gossamer threads. "Bloody spiders." When a piece of hay fell from his hair to land on his arm, he jumped back, slapping, and waving his arm about. "Oh, shit. Fucking spiders!" In a fit of embarrassed frustration, he lashed out with his foot at the door.

Ried spat out another curse when dislodged dust and grit showered down from the overhead timbers bringing about a series of bellowing sneezes.

Infuriated, he hammered the door with repeated assaults. "Hey. What's going on here? Let me out," he shouted between kicks.

He stepped back and in between deep breaths, the sound of voices; singing and shouting amidst children's laughter. With renewed vigour, Ried kicked at the door. All thoughts and discomfort from his twisted ankle gone.

This time, with each kick, the tin bent and pulled away from the door frame, but the timber frame itself stayed firm. "One or two good kicks more..."

Halfway through the motions of his next kick, something heavy banged against the side of the shed, and he heard a deep voice.

"Oi. Be still in there."

The loud bang against the corrugated wall and voice startled him. "Piss off," Ried shouted back, as he renewed his attack on the buckling door.

Then, without warning, the door opened, and the momentum of his unobstructed kick sent Ried sprawling out into the night.

Rolling himself over in the wash of lantern light, Gazza's voice came from behind the glare of an oil lamp. "I'd be keeping still, mate."

When Gazza lifted back the lantern, Ried found five sharp spears pointed at his neck and chest.

"Cause' this lot'll be good 'n' happy to stick you."

"What do you want with me?"

"Nothin'." Gazza lied, he scratched his ear and stood up, "but, you killed their mates…" Gazza let the sentence hang.

"You should've just let me walk," Ried murmured. "Then, they'd still be alive."

"Yep, and you'd most likely run off and dob us into the bloody Romans quick smart."

Ried frowned and tilted his head. *Who the hell are these Romans everyone's talking about?*

Misunderstanding Ried's expression, Gazza continued. "Those two clowns were only s'posed to grab you." Behind the lantern light, Gazza's eyes seemed filled with regret. "Now they're dead 'n' cold, and you're here."

With slow, steady moves, Ried stood and raised his arms.

Gazza broke into a bout of laughter.

Ried eyed each of the armed men and women around him and found nothing humorous.

"Put your bloody arms down, boy." He tapped one man on the shoulder and pointed over to the shed. "Get the horse."

Everyone shifted their attention to the shed when a wet, dull crack, followed by a shrill cry and a solid thud echoed into the night. Not long after a shadowed figure stumbled from the black rectangle of the shed's door to fall at Gazza's feet.

The man rolled around with his hands clutching his groin and uttering pitiful moans, curled into the foetal position and emptied his stomach.

"Fuckin' hell." Gazza issued a heavy sigh and rubbed his forehead before looking at Ried. "Get your fuckin' horse." He planted a solid grip on Ried's shoulder, "and don't be stupid about it."

Ried stepped over the crippled man and whispered, "Karma's a bitch."

He stopped a little shy of the door. "Easy, girl," he whispered. Stepping inside, he untied the reins and led Devil out. "It's all right, girl," he cooed, caressing Devil's cheek and neck. Still holding the reins, he took a step back and felt the pointy tip of a spear pressing into his ribs, just above the small of his back.

"Don't even think of being clever," the woman's tenor and spear tip implied anything but a casual threat.

Ried faced her and the rock-steady spear tip millimetres away from his liver.

"Back off, Molls," Gazza ordered. "Bring 'em to the big house."

Molls stepped up to Ried with a rope, and Devil lowered her head, rolling her ears, and shifting her stance.

Gazza held up the lantern. "For fuck's sake, woman. You want to end up rollin' in the dirt like him?" He nodded his head at the other man still curled up at his feet. "Just walk the boy back."

"I'm not a boy." Ried spat back.

Gazza shoved his face and lantern in front of Ried, looked him up and down grunted and walked off.

"What about Ned?" Molls asked, keeping Ried within reach of her spear and making sure she kept a safe distance from the horse.

Gazza contemplated the scene before him, scratched his ear and glanced over at the two other men. "You two take him down to Tilly's tent." When the men carried away, the comatose Ned, Gazza called over his shoulder as he marched off. "Come on, you lot."

Walking behind Gazza, the night's breeze carried an odour of cooked meat on wood smoke. The smells increased the pangs of Ried's hunger and made his dry mouth moist from saliva.

The scene of the approaching nomad leader in front of Ried, Devil, Molls, and her remaining companion caught the attention of a group of curious children dancing and playing near a crackling bonfire.

They came running up for a better look – along with a few of the adults – many of whom Ried could tell were drunk.

Seeing the growing crowd, Ried's anxiety level rose several degrees. He expected to have rocks, mud, rotten food, and even animal dung hurled at him.

Instead, the adults pointed and whispered, and the children did what children do – they giggled and emitted oohs and ahhs."

Unsure of how he should respond to the attention, Ried smiled at them, but not one person from the crowd smiled back or offered even a simple nod his way.

At least the villagers in Afghanistan smiled back. Discouraged by their lukewarm response, Ried ignored the onlookers and kept his eyes on the ground behind Gazza's feet.

"Christ. I really hope this is just one long, bad dream," Ried mumbled.

Gazza burst into another fit of laughter.

"What's so funny?" Ried glared at the laughing man's back.

"Bloody hell. You need a better dream," he said over his shoulder. "Now me, I'd be on a beach with a bunch of naked birds doin' me every pleasure." Gazza's face split into a huge grin at the thought. "Now, there's a fuckin' dream."

Ried held back his opinion and looked at the old high set Queenslander they approached. The fires reflections sparkled in the houses, single unbroken window.

In the farm's past, the original owners enclosed under the verandas to make extra living space accessed by French doors. From the bonfire's dancing light, Ried thought the old farmhouse seemed in a far better state of repair than anything else he'd seen since leaving the old man's farm.

"Tie the horse over there." Gazza pointed to the stump of an old mulberry tree.

"Can I at least take off her saddle?" Ried asked.

Gazza hesitated for a moment before he nodded his consent. He doubted their guest would do anything rash, but he waved Molls over to keep an eye on him.

When done, Ried put the saddle and blanket on the backrest of the bench under the veranda and flopped down from the weight of his confusion, weariness, and incredible hunger. "Any chance of getting something to eat?" He asked.

"Dunno," Gazza replied. "I'm not sure I wanna waste any of our food on you."

Gazza chuckled at the defeated expression of Ried. "Just pullin' ya leg," he said as he walked away.

Ried watched him go and went over the events of the last couple of days. *How does crashing in a storm lead to being kidnapped by a bunch of Doomsday Preppers?* Ried scratched at the stubble on his chin and tried to remember how many days the young woman at the farm said had passed since his crash.

Ried watched the one called Molls. Danger exuded from her pores. He decided not to let her or them intimidate him, so he adopted his own aggressive stance. After a few minutes, Ried grew bored with the silent game between his captors and himself, and he slumped back.

Closing his eyes, he massaged his temples trying to ease an encroaching headache. When he opened his eyes, he rested his chin in his hands and gazed at the strip of night sky between the overhanging veranda and distant tree-line.

What's with the stars? This far away from the town, the sky should be filled with them.

The sound of heavy footsteps distracted Ried's musings.

Putting a tray of food and drink down, Gazza handed him a small bowl of stew, and a mug full of some dark, reddish liquid.

Ried raised a cautious eyebrow after accepting the glutinous broth and dark coloured drink.

"Don't fret, boy. It ain't full of poison," Gazza assured him. "They'd bloody well hang me by my short and curlies if it was."

His hunger outweighed any trepidation, and Ried devoured the stew, ignoring the odd texture of the meat, and the earthy flavour of the gravy.

"I'm guessin' you ain't eaten in a while?"

Ried continued eating and shrugged his shoulders in response. After spooning the last chunks of the stew into his mouth, he replaced the empty bowl with the clay mug and sniffed the dark liquids odour.

He swallowed a mouthful and gagged on its pungent, sweet and sour taste. "What the hell…"

"It's good stuff, huh?" Gazza laughed. "We brew it ourselves from prickly pear and berries." He laughed again at Ried's reaction to the drink. "Try sippin' it, and then rest it on ya tongue before swallowin'."

With nothing else to lose, Ried followed the advice and found it did little in the way of making the drink more palatable.

Gazza nodded toward the big, chestnut mare. "You work for old man Harris?"

"Nope." Ried relaxed back into the bench and shook his head. "Why, do you know the old man?"

Gazza pointed at Devils rump, "That's his brand."

Ried took another more adventurous mouthful of the bush wine which sent waves of relaxing warmth radiating from his stomach.

"If you don't work for old man Harris?" Gazza asked. "Then how'd you end up with one of his nags?"

"Mmm. Oh, I crashed in a big bloody storm–" Ried lost the feeling in his cheeks. "What's with the stars?" The purple-red liquor made Ried more than a little relaxed.

"They's hidden by the clouds of dust. Now, what about the horse?" Gazza asked.

Ried gave Gazza a big, cheesy smile. "You mean Devil... I nicked her from the old man." His tone darkened. "The old bloke and his daughter held me prisoner for days and days," he puffed up his chest, "but I escaped after he gave me some bullshit yarn 'bout space tunnels... I told him to fuck off, and then I pinched the horse." He nodded in drunken pride, blinked, scratched behind his ear, and then pointed to the sky.

"What'd ya mean by them being hidden with dust?" Ried rubbed his nose again. "Oh, shit. Wuz the old bloke tellin' the truth?"

With a sudden pang of guilt, Ried glanced toward Devil, gulped down more grog and swivelled around wagging an inebriated finger at Gazza. "I wuz tryin' to head back to town when you lot showed up... Ried expression dropped along with his voice. "Fuck... are they really dead?"

"My blokes?"' Gazza shrugged, "Pretty much."

"Yeah, well... It was their fault anyway." Ried scanned the area. "So where is here?" Ried flopped back against the saddle feeling tired and then sat up pushing the mug against Gazza's arm. "She's a beaut, though," he blurted out.

"Who?"

"Devil," Ried said, "and the old man's daughter, too." He attempted to wink and gave up and instead, nudged his elbow into Gazza's ribs, almost falling over from the effort. He gave a comical yawn and then slumped against Gazza dropping the mug from unresponsive hands.

"Shit. He's a one-pot screamer." Gazza pushed Ried away and stood to stare down at his sleeping guest. "You're a strange one all right." He tried to make sense of the mixed messages the younger man gave him. "You pair take turns to watch him 'till the mornin'," Gazza instructed Molls and her companion as he walked away.

He paused a few metres away, giving Ried a frowning expression. In all his past dealings with Dominic Harris, Gazza couldn't recall seeing the stranger about. *So, where'd he come from? Mind you, it'd make sense that the old man and his daughter would help an injured stranger.*

He headed out to a nearby bonfire. "But, why was old man Harris so bloody insistent about findin' him?" Gazza stopped by the fire. *I reckon it's time we packed up and nicked off to the west… after I figure out a way to return him and the horse without pissing everyone off.* "I need another fuckin' drink."

CHAPTER EIGHT

Ried stretched and rubbed his cheeks and eyes while drawing in a long draught of the next morning's chill damp air. His stomach heaved, his breath tasted sour from his dry throat and mouth. "God. What did they feed me?"

In the distance, a chorus of crows greeted the day. On a closer front, his sleeping guards and their inharmonious snoring and grunting assaulted his ears. Ried hawked and spat in their direction and padded across the wet grass and tapped the empty pitcher.

"Fucking amateurs." Ried closed his eyes and listened for any other sounds of people moving about. A child cried while two more called out in a game, followed by a woman's voice berating the children. A subtle breeze carried the tang of hot ash and smoke. Nearby, Devil snorted and shifted her feet.

Still, Ried waited, but when there were no other signs of movement or people talking, he decided this was his best chance at escaping. He lifted the saddle and blanket and padded past the sleeping guards toward Devil.

Ried lowered the saddle on the damp grass and lifted the horse-blanket with a smug smile at his stealth when a gunshot shattered the morning quiet. In the same instant, a patch of ground erupted in front of the saddle.

Devil jumped and jerked her head, stretching her reins tied around the stump as Ried dropped using the saddle as cover.

Molls and the other man gave a squawk of surprise and pushed themselves up on unstable legs. Unsure where they should point their spears.

Ried peeked over the saddle as Gazza marched his way, pointing a long-barrelled, semi-automatic handgun.

To Ried's and everyone nearby surprise, he pushed himself up and stepped over the saddle.

"Not another fuckin' step." Gazza glowered at Ried. "I knew I should've fuckin' tied you up." The last comment aimed at Molls.

Ried hooded his eyes studying the man and the downward angle of his gun arm. *He won't shoot me.* Ried calculated his choices. He stopped, bent his knees and sprang to his left. His forearm struck the side of the male guard's head. Taken by surprise the man collapsed in a silent heap.

Before the man hit the ground, Ried dived, rolled and kicked Moll's legs out from under her. Continuing his rolling move, Ried snatched the end of Moll's spear and struck Gazza's gun hand with a vicious snap.

The spear's tip left a ragged gash along the back of his wrist and thumb and knocked the pistol from Gazza's grip.

Molls grunted and made a lunge for Ried's legs.

A move he sidestepped with ease as he scooped up the pistol in his hand, a heartbeat before Gazza's desperate grab clutched a handful of wet grass.

"Not another fucking step," hissed Ried with the automatics barrel aimed at the centre of Gazza's chest.

A crowd of onlookers, awoken by the gunshot, drifted in growing numbers from the other side of the old house.

The assembled mob created a human wall between the house and the broken fence near the horse.

The closest people pointed at the scene with their murmurs and catcalling growing louder while in the back a child cried. Others made wagers amongst themselves on the outcome between the young stranger, Gazza and Molls.

Who the hell are these people?

Out of the corner of his eye, Ried caught Molls shifting her stance. With a quick step, he moved closer and rested the tip of the spear against her throat. "Don't even think of being clever." His arm stiffened. "Isn't that what you said." Ried shifted his stance pressing the spear tip harder against her skin. "it's good advice."

For a brief second, Molls considered defying Ried's suggestion. However, the warmth of blood pooling around the tip of the spear curbed her defiant thoughts.

With the handgun trained on Gazza's chest, and the spear keeping Molls at bay, Ried glimpsed a man moving toward them under the veranda. *Fuck me...*

Another shot rang out, and a child screamed as the lantern hanging above the man's head exploded. The near brave man stood fixed on the spot with lamp fuel running down his contorted face.

The bullet may have struck the lamp more by accident than design, but for Ried, it produced the desired result.

"All you lot hold off," Gazza instructed. "Molls get behind me and don't be stupid either." He locked eyes with Ried. "You're pretty handy with that," he said, "but I'd be guessin' you ain't never shot a man."

"Not with a pistol..." He eased himself away from Gazza, "yet." Ried's expression and tone gave showed calm control, but his inner emotions ran amuck.

Gazza smiled at the comment, but his smile faded when he recognised something behind Ried's eyes. A look he'd seen on dozens of men over many years. Regardless, he tried his own version of verbal bravado. "Anyway, there ain't enough rounds in there for us all."

"True. But what difference does it make?" Ried told him. "I killed their mates, so, I'm as good as dead anyway."

"How's about you drop the gun so we can make a deal?"

Ried dropped the spear and cupped the gun in both hands. He adjusted his stance, squared his shoulders, and stood firm with his feet at shoulder width. He shuffled his left foot just in front of his right and leaned forward at the hip.

"You're joking. After you lot attack me, drug me, kidnap me, and then fucking well shoot at me?" Ried's voice never rose an octave. "You figure now's a good time for a deal?"

During and after the wars, luck and intuition kept Gazza alive. Now, as then, he went with his intuition. *Strewth… Old Harris can go fuck himself. I ain't losing anybody else.*

"All right, you lot. Drop your kit and back off." Hearing the odd murmur behind him, Gazza shot a quick glance over his shoulder. "Fuck me. Are you all fuckin' deaf?" His voice growled. "Drop your kits and get the fuck back."

Behind Gazza came the sound of grunts and curses as people followed his directive, dropping their knives, spears and other assorted weapons.

Ried held his stance and watched the crowd shuffle back.

Gazza rolled his head forward. "Done. Now, get on your horse and piss off."

"Just like that?" Ried asked without lowering the pistol.

"Yep, just like that."

Ried bent his gun arm at the hip, keeping the pistol trained on Gazza. He stepped back and untied Devil's reins with his free hand and manoeuvred the mare around so he could saddle her. At no time did the pistol waver from Gazza's direction, even when he mounted the horse. "Which way to the old man's farm?"

"You're shittin' me..."

"Which way?"

"North-west, about thirty klicks," Gazza answered. "Head left past the creek. Take the third road on the right and keep goin' 'till you reach a wide T intersection with an old service station. Then go right until your first left. The rest you can work out your fuckin' self."

Ried walked Devil beside Gazza, leaned in and whispered through a smile while keeping the pistol aimed at his kidnapper's chest. "I'd look to your own house before you bother chasing after me."

Conscious of how and where Ried pointed the gun, Gazza twisted at the hip. In the back left of the crowd, three men stood apart locked in a heated, yet quiet discussion and staring at Gazza.

"Fuck me," Gazza rumbled in an unhappy tone. He looked back at Ried. "Don't s'pose I can have the gun back?"

Ried smiled and reined Devil toward the creek while keeping a distance from the crowd's edge. Without looking back, he tossed the weapon into a nearby Lantana bush and smiled at the rising voices in the background. *Yep, karma's a bitch all right.*

After crossing the creek, Ried rode on for about fifteen minutes and then dismounted so he could readjust the saddle and girth belt. Satisfied, he and the saddle wouldn't roll off the mare's back, he remounted and started at the sound of an approaching truck.

He scanned the road and the surrounding bush for a hiding place. Except the scrub and grass taunted him with a definitive lack of options. "Christ. Well, after the last twenty-four hours, things couldn't get any worse." So, he reigned Devil over to the side of the road and kept walking in the hopes the driver would pass on by.

When the truck crested the rise, Ried raised his eyebrows at the old Bedford pulling over beside him. "Isn't there anything around here from the twenty-first century?"

When the stout, older driver stepped down from the cab, he lifted a small towel from his trouser pocket and mopped his brow before redressing his long, blond comb-over.

Ried could feel the morning heat through his cotton drill shirt, yet the man wore a tweed sports coat over a white, collared shirt tucked into corduroy jeans.

"Hello, young man."

Ried relaxed a little with the man's jovial features and casual nature.

The driver returned Ried's smile as he walked up and fed the animal three lumps of sugar with an air of familiarity.

"Care to explain why you are on Julia Harris's horse?"

"I stole her." Ried couldn't see how a lie would change his situation. He also noticed the man took a firm hold of the reins just past the bridle.

Oh yeah, karma is definitely a bitch. Ried squirmed under the balding man's long scrutinising stare.

"You're the young chap I X-rayed?" The man squinted voicing mild curiosity. "You seem to have healed rather well."

"You took X-rays of me?"

"Yes."

"So, you're a radiographer?"

"Good heavens, not. I am the district's vet."

"Bloody hell, the hospital must be bad if they took me to a vet."

The vet's ruddy cheeks wobble from his head shaking rejection. "No, my dear boy, I visited you at Dom's farm."

"A vet with a portable X-ray machine?"

"That's correct. It might be a tad old and cumbersome, but my unit has proven itself useful on many occasions." The vet puffed in a proud statement and then he shifted closer dropping his voice. "It was all quite clandestine. Neither Mr Harris nor Mr Bennett would explain what happened to you." He walked around the mare. "I will admit I was rather curious why they tended your injuries in Julia's old cottage, instead of the hospital. Considering the extent of your... injuries."

"Can you help me get back to the Harris place?" Ried dismounted and held the reins out toward the stranger. "I think I owe him an apology. Mister -"

"Yes, of course." The vet held out his hand. "Lester Jennings."

"Benjamin Ried. But please, just call me Ben or Ried," he said, accepting Jennings outstretched hand.

"Glad to meet you, Ben," Jennings said with a broad smile. "Now, let's load up Devil and get her back home, eh?" He tied the reins through a large hinged ring mounted

139

on the truck's side, opened the rear door, and slid out a ramp from under the floor's frame. He locked the ramp in place and walked Devil inside the enclosed truck followed by Ried.

Jennings leaned against the open door while Ried tethered Devil and then unsaddled her. After which, he set about clearing a spot for himself beside her.

"Good heavens, son. You can't ride back here."

"Why not? Besides, you don't even know me."

"Which won't change if you're locked back here." Jennings watched the gentle way Ried stroke the horse. "Excellent choice." He beamed stepping down the ramp.

"I don't suppose you have anything to eat?" Ried asked.

Jennings climbed into the truck's cab and came back with a basket covered with a clean, white piece of calico. "This should do the trick." He lifted the cloth to reveal goat cheese, grapes, dried pork, a cob of bread, and a bottle of white wine. "It was gifted to me this morning." Without prompting, Jennings recounted his overnight visit and consultations within the small community at the old hamlet of Maidenwell, tending their various pets and animals.

Ried avoided the goat's cheese and instead helped himself to the bread, fruit and meat. Jennings, however, sampled everything in the basket.

"You don't eat cheese?"

Ried shrugged and continued chewing on the pork. On his deployment in Afghanistan, he had eaten his share of goat cheese, but he never gained a taste for it.

Jennings continued to devour the cheese with a handful of grapes. Without prompting, he uncorked a bottle of wine which he passed over to a reluctant Ried, who took a sip of the homemade wine. He would have preferred water, but the light, sweetness of the drink seemed palatable enough, especially after the taste of the nomad's potent home brew.

"So, you say you stole Devil?"

"I know I shouldn't have, but-"

"Yes, that is true," Jennings said, "however, I'm most curious why she let you."

"She does have spirit, but Devil's like any other horse."

"Ah, that part is not quite true." The vet explained how Dom's wife, Julia, found the newborn mare beside the remains of her mother, who someone shot and butchered for meat. "Julia Harris always had a way with injured or lost people and animals, so she adopted Devil and hand reared her.

"From then on the animal became very protective of Julia and refused to let anyone else ride her." He broke out into a jovial chuckle. "In fact, it took about two years of constant visits, before Devil would let me treat her without Julia."

"I think Devil tolerates me because I give her sugar." He smiled at his own joke. "The animal always lets Dom groom her, but nothing else. And since Julia's passing, Devil pined for her surrogate mother." Jennings raised an eyebrow and glanced sideways between more mouthfuls of food and wine. "Yet, you saddled and ride her from Dom's barn."

"My mum is the best horse person I know. She made sure me and my sisters all grew up around them. I suppose I picked up her genes." Ried shrugged and then broke into a broad grin. "Devil did give one of those feral blokes a good thump."

"Feral?"

Jennings's expression morphed into one of horror when Ried talked about the people who had attacked and kidnapped him.

"Dear lord. Those were Nomads, and you escaped them?"

Ried saw the colour drain from Jennings's face, while he scanned the surrounding bush. After several minutes of exaggerated convincing him the Nomads weren't coming after them, Jennings calmed down and continued eating and drinking.

In between mouthfuls, he patted Ried's shoulder and reassured him Dominic's relief at finding them safe would outway any anger.

After consuming most of the food in the basket, Ried could feel his strength and alertness improving. The warm sun and a full stomach mellowed Ried's tension and mood.

He stretched himself to ease the stiffness from his awkward night's sleep on the bench and two days of riding. Even the fight and escape from the Nomads seemed a distant memory.

Ried stood beside the truck in the sun and listened as the breeze rustled the leaves, serenaded by the chirping of cicadas. He closed his eyes and absorbed the calm and beauty of the morning.

Off in the distance, a faint and unusual whining sound weaved into his moment of bliss. Ried walked out to the middle of the road. "What's that noise?"

Jennings put down the empty basket and joined Ried. "Oh, dear me."

"Relax I don't think it's the Nomads."

"No, but what is coming could be much worse." Jennings's jovial mood turned to mist evaporating in the air. "Hurry. Get in the back. There's a storage shelf above the cab where you can hide." He nudged Ried toward the rear of the truck.

"Hey, stop pushing."

"Hush, boy. Please, just do what I ask." With persistent pushing, Jennings's manoeuvred Ried toward the back of the truck. He ushered the protesting Ried into the vehicle and pointed at the shelf. "Quickly now. Get yourself up there and keep quiet."

Jennings's abrupt change in manner, along with his hyper nervous insistence, resembled similar reactions to some Afghan villagers portrayed when suspected Taliban troops were nearby. Before he could ask what spooked him, Jennings slid the ramp inside the truck and closed the door, leaving Ried and Devil standing in the gloom.

Unsure of what just happened, Ried followed Jennings request and climbed onto the storage shelf above the truck's cab. He wriggled closer to the side and peered through the truck's timber slat wall.

Jennings cast a furtive glance at his truck and sponged his face before wringing his hands at the sight of a sizeable group of dominating dark red motorbikes coming stopping nearby.

Ried shifted his head to get a better look at the plum-coloured machines and wondered which bike gang the riders belonged to, but the glare blotted out any view of the gang's symbols or colours.

The look of the riders mounted on the bikes spooked Ried. This gang looked almost militant, with their ink-blue uniforms, heavy black boots, and moulded body armour. He shifted around for a better look and remembered the old farm.

Bloody hell... It looks like what I found yesterday.

The helmets on the riders' heads were also a polished black, with plating covering their ears, and a dark, polarised, drop-down visor, which covered the riders' eyes. *These blokes look like the hero of those comics Simmo always read? Some sort of policeman, judge and executioner.*

The movement of Jennings toward the lead rider who dismounted broke Ried's abstract train of thought. Ried squirmed around for a better look at the bike rider who Ried assumed was the gang's sergeant-at-arms.

A blood-red sash wrapped around the man's waist under a broad, dark, leather belt, decorated with a dozen leather straps situated over his groin. On each hip, Ried could see pouches and the handle of a knife, but then Jennings stepped in front of the rider blocking Ried's view. *Who the hell are these blokes?*

"Dr Jennings."

"Centurion Mettius."

Ried frowned and mouthed the word Centurion.

"Why are you here?" The man looked around and studied the truck.

When Ried saw the man's black-on-black eyes, he almost swore aloud. *Jesus, that's just creepy. Who the hell would cover their whole eyes with black contacts?*

"My truck overheated," Jennings lied, "and while it cooled down, I thought I'd have breakfast." As a way of showing he spoke the truth, Jennings collected the empty food basket. His manner not unlike a timid child producing the evidence of his completed homework.

"Next time, for your own safety, I suggest you find a better place to stop." Mettius ignored the basket. "This is scavenger territory." Before Jennings could respond, he looked past Jennings, when he heard a noise from inside the truck.

Ried looked over his shoulder toward the horse. *Jesus Christ, Devil.*

"I'm taking a horse back for treatment," Jennings said.

Ried watched as Mettius scrutinised Jennings and then signalled the first three riders who join him beside the truck. Ried tensed, his ears pounding with the blood pumped by his adrenaline-fuelled heart.

He heard them move around the truck, watching their shadows and silhouettes through the slatted side walls. With exaggerated slowness, Ried slid toward the front of the shelf area and waited.

Ried couldn't understand why, but the big bikes, the armoured riders, and their ominous, blacked-eyed sergeant-at-arms Jennings called Centurion Mettius all raised Ried's internal alarms. His gut told him something was wrong. Very wrong.

Behind him, Mettius had opened the truck's rear door.

Ried froze from the increased light exposing the back of the truck.

"You see? Just a horse. There's no need for your pistol," Jennings said.

Holy shit. Ried's gut knotted from Jennings warning.

"What's under the blanket?"

"More wine and cheese. In gratis for my service."

A long silence followed Jennings continued lies. When the door of the truck closed, Ried closed his eyes and willed his heart to slow down its juddering beat.

"Are you looking for somebody?"

Ried swore at the vet's question, and then every muscle tensed when Mettius spun on his heel.

"Why would you ask that?" Mettius demanded through squinting eyes.

Jennings pulled out his little towel and mopped his head.

Ried felt sure the Jennings was about to shit himself.

"Well…" He avoided the cold, black-on-black eyes staring back at him. "Um, I've seen your patrols over the last couple of days, and, well, they don't typically comprise so many men."

"We are seeking the scavengers, and one or more escaped prisoners." Mettius moved his face within centimetres of Jennings. "Or those in league with any of them."

"I'll be sure and report anything I see," Jennings said as he dabbed at his perspiring face

"You look unwell." Mettius held Jennings in his black stare.

"Too much wine and cheese, I fear." Jennings did not try to fake his nausea. His fear of Mettius did that for him. Jennings tried to smile as he continued mopping away the dripping perspiration.

"Just be on your way," Mettius barked after marching off and mounting his bike.

Ried watched the twenty-plus bikes ride past.

"All right, my boy. You can come out now."

"They were armed?"

"Obviously."

Ried paced in a circle while frowning at Jennings answer. *It's a bloody, bold move for any bike gang to display their weapons.* "Who are the scavengers they talked about?"

"I believe they were referring to the Nomads."

146

"Shit. The Nomads?" Ried grabbed Jennings's shoulders. "We have to follow them."

"I will do no such thing." Jennings back away, his eyes wide with terror. "Those are armed men."

"With a clear agenda against people armed with spears and knives."

"And it has nothing to do with us," said Jennings. "So, we should do what the Centurion instructed."

Bloody hell. Ried continued pacing.

Jennings's ashen face paled into chalk.

Whoever those riders were, they scared the shit out of him. Ried knew forcing the man's help was a pointless exercise. So, he gave Jennings a swift nod of understanding. Ried thanked Jennings for the food before running down the road after the bikes.

"Wait," Jennings called out after a moment. "I'll do it." He looked miserable. "I'm not sure who's madder; you for running after them, or me for driving you."

Ried patted the vet's shoulder and climbed into the cab after him.

After a stop-start, six-point turn, Jennings followed the bikes. A few minutes down the road, Jennings rounded a bend and pumped the brakes as the last motorcycle veered off the road.

"I don't suppose you have a rifle?" Ried asked, climbing out of the cabin.

Jennings shook his head.

That'd be right. "Can you take Devil back and tell them I'm sorry?" Ried flicked the door closed.

Jennings fumbled his way out and went around to stop Ried, who vanished in the tall grass and bushes.

"Oh dear, what will Dom say?" Jennings mopped a heavier film of perspiration from his brow. "Stupid

fellow… Going after Mettius and back to those Nomads."
He patted his flushed face and paced a figure eight while
frowning at the spot Ried disappeared. "Oh, dear…"

CHAPTER NINE

Breaking through the bushes, Ried winced from the trucks revving motor when the vet drove away. Ried stopped midway across the stream and hoped the bike riders didn't pick up its noise.

Once across the creek, Ried scrambled up the bank and into the field of long grass and weeds before he slowed and dropped into a crouch when he crested a broad rise.

On his left, the track cut through the grass toward the house and nearby sheds. The last dust cloud from the passing bikes drifted in the breeze across the fields dotted with clumps of lantana, wild bougainvillaea, and a few small stands of trees.

When he reached the top of another small rise twenty metres from the farmhouse, he lay down and parted the long grass. In the distance, the angry shouts of men, and the cries of scared women and children competed with a flock of cawing crows.

Without hesitation, he darted and wove his way through the long grass and bushes and using the farmhouse for cover as he drew closer.

He skirted a stand of Wattyl bushes and crouched beside an old collapsed, timber rail and paling fence and picked up a piece of the broken fence rail. Armed with his makeshift club, he rounded the stump of an old, fallen gum tree which led him to the far side of the house.

Once there, Ried dropped and crawled past the house and up behind a squat ironbark growing through another section of the fence. Keeping low he used the trunk of the tree and raised roots for cover as he shifted to look between the palings.

Sixty metres away, a group of the armed riders herded the Nomads together with heavy-handed pushes and shoves. Unable to see everything going on, Ried flattened himself and crawled with exaggerated stealth around the tree for a better vantage point.

Twenty-something to one. Ried wondered whether his decision might well have been a little hasty. *Why come back to help the people, who twenty-four hours ago, kidnapped me? Maybe Jennings was right, and I am mad.*

Ried lay there in the dirt, desperate to ignoring the mixed feelings of helpless frustration and growing indecision.

He peered back around the tree. His tactical logic argued with emotion on his next course of action while a voice told him to leave. Those people were not his problem, and besides… how could he help?

The scene dissolved to the bus stop at his old high school.

#

"Ben, Don't," his sister pleaded.

Across the road, four boys from the Senior football team harassed another student and his girlfriend. When the boy resisted the leader of the bullies slapped the boy down and kicked him while his mates laughed and mocked the screaming, crying girlfriend.

Becca step in front of her brother. "No, you can't help them, and if you try, they'll beat up on you."

150

"Move Becca," Ried warned. "I'm gonna teach Gilmore, and his dickhead mates enough is enough."

"And end up like the kid on the ground?"

"Better than just walking away…"

His sister was right. He ended up on the ground, but so did Gilmore and one of his sidekicks.

The memory, along with the sounds of a scuffle coming from inside a nearby henhouse resolved his internal debate.

Without a sound, he shifted around keeping his profile low. Then with careful movements, Ried hugged the ground on his approach.

Inside the henhouse, one biker dragged a small girl by her hair – who sobbed in shock, too terrified to even scream. Aside from the rider and the girl, an old couple who tried, with little success, to tug the child free from the rider's grip.

When the old woman slapped the rider's helmeted face with a branch, the man tossed the young girl aside, grabbed the old lady's arm and twisted her to the ground, and then slammed the heel of his boot against her chest.

The woman uttered a brief cry and slumped back in the dirt.

Ried winced, there could be no mistaking the sound of her ribs and sternum breaking under the blow.

The old man and child scrambled over to the woman who lay twitching in the dust.

The rider flicked his rifle around and with both hands around the barrel, he clubbed the old man between his shoulder blades. Not content with the damage caused by the gun, the rider dropped the weapon and pulled out a mat black metallic nightstick.

In a fluid, well-practised move, he raised his arm holding the baton and with his other hand, the helmeted thug grabbed the man's shirt, ready to club him when a shadow fell across the old man and girl.

The rider dropped his victim and whirled around drawing his pistol, a move he never completed. Because of a length of timber striking his helmet with such force, it shattered his visor, nose and cheekbones.

He never uttered a sound or felt the bone fragments lacerate his brain's frontal lobe because his neck snapped; killing him in an instant.

The rider's head rolled forward, his face a wet mass of blood and torn flesh. He took a drunken step sideways in death before falling in the dirt like a discarded rag doll.

The child ran into the arms of the old man, their faces both streaked from the rivers of tears. His hands lifted the woman's head to rest on his knees where he stroked her hair and face while whispering for her to answer, but her unseeing eyes stared at the roof of the henhouse.

Ried put a gentle and consoling hand on the man's heaving shoulder. Ried reached down and closed the old woman's unseeing eyes before he dragged the rider's dead body aside.

With fast hands, he stripped the dead rider of his equipment. A compact rifle, a semi-automatic pistol, and pouches of ammunition. Ried then slid a sheathed sword and dagger from the weapons belt.

He put the carbine rifle aside for himself and placed the pistol beside the old man's feet.

Instead of taking the weapon, the old nomad reached around for the small sword and broad, flat dagger and then squeezed Ried's forearm in gratitude.

Unsure what to say Ried replied with a curt nod and stripped the rider of his body armour. Without a word, the old man and girl slipped past the rusted and torn wire of the henhouse.

Ried ran his eye over the lightweight tactical vest. On closer inspection, he decided the moulded leather and plastic armour would work well in close quarter hand-to-hand but gave little or no ballistic protection.

He lifted the pistol wiped away the dust realising it looked like the one he had taken from Gazza. The rifle had a similar grip to the semi-automatic handgun, and a compact, Bullpup-style stock.

A quick inspection confirmed the same magazine fitted both the pistol and carbine. Ried thumbed out one round from a loaded magazine.

The bullet and casings resembled a nine-millimetre round and tapered to a hold a snub-nosed lead bullet six millimetres in diameter. There was nothing extraordinary about the brass casing with four opposing grooves running two-thirds down the length of the projectile.

Thumbing the round back in a magazine, Ried recognised the ammunition projectile for what it was – a lethal short-distance, high powered, anti-personal round.

Satisfied with the two guns, Ried inspected the black alloy nightstick with its vertical rubber grip a third of the way along its shaft, which held a kind of compression lever.

At the back, the shaft ended in a dial of sorts. Pinching the knob, Ried gave the dial a twist. With a soft clack, two small, silver pins poked out of the opposite end. When he squeezed the grip, an electric bolt arced between the two protruding tips.

"Cool."

Impressed with his collection, Ried fastened the belt around his waist, sliding the nightstick back into its ring. He then discarded the empty sheaths for the sword and dagger, before adjusting where the holster, magazine pouches and nightstick all sat on the belt.

He pressed the butt of the rifle tight against his shoulder to get a feel for how it sat in his arms and sighted down the triangular barrel through its rear peep and blade site.

The carbine rested against his shoulder the same way his army-issued Austeyr F88 C did. But, unlike the Australian combat rifle, the thug's carbine didn't have a forward vertical hand grip.

Instead, the forward section of the stock ran two-thirds of the barrel length to merge into a guard sweeping back and connecting with the base of its pistol grip. Several centimetres below the barrel were four knuckle duster-style rings.

He slid his fingers through the finger holes and wrapped his right hand around the pistol grip, surprised with how the weapons configuration kept the carbine rock-solid for either firing from the shoulder or the hip.

Also, the rifle's compact body, breach, stock and curved frame with the knuckle duster rings made it a formidable close-combat tool.

By the time Ried completed inspecting his new weapons cache, only one voice now echoed around the old farm. Easing himself around for a better view, he saw the tall, lean man who had spoken to the vet.

Ried took his time in studying the sergeant-at-arms and the armed riders near the Nomads. He shifted his attention to the line of armed men who encircled the kneeling and terrified group of unarmed people.

The body language and stance of the armed men told Ried one thing. Questions or no questions this was a prelude for execution.

He bundled his cache of weapons and crawled back behind the fence. Regardless of his small arsenal, a tsunami of helplessness again swamped his resolve. Mathematics doesn't lie. *You're facing an unknown foe who outnumber and outgun you twenty-plus to one. Shit. The proverbial snowflake in hell had better odds.*

Ried watched on through the fence, a physical metaphor for his cage of indecision. He wiped a sweaty palm down his trouser leg and remembered what his grandfather said:

"The world loves a brave hero, but only the family mourns a dead one."

Out in the open, standing in front of his captives and unaware of the incident in the henhouse, Mettius continued his pacing in front of his prisoners. He again asked the Nomads if they harboured any strangers.

The response, "fuck off," echoed around the old farm. Other similar and cruder cries followed the first. With their bravery bolstered, several men threw catcalls and laughter toward Mettius.

Mettius signalled his men to bring out the chief offender.

A woman, with a newborn child wrapped against her chest, stepped up to slap, kick, and punch the thugs who wrestled someone from the group.

With a nod from Mettius, the armed men also shoved out the woman and baby until she stood beside the man Ried recognised as the one who he coated in lamp oil.

A rider swung his nightstick against the back of their legs causing the couple to collapse on their knees.

155

Mettius waved his men back and circled the couple – a leopard stalking its prey.

"Do you wish to say something?"

The male nomad focused on a distant point. "Piss off."

This raised several bursts of nervous, defiant laughter from others in the crowd.

In response, Mettius backhanded the man.

The rebellious nomad took the brutal slap, tipped his bruised face, and spat a mouthful of blood over Mettius's boots.

Mettius raised an eyebrow at the stained phlegm sliding from his boot and then with a face devoid of expression, he lashed forward and grabbed the nomad's hair, and hauled him to his feet, before throwing him onto the ground.

When the man stopped rolling in the dirt, he raised himself into a crouch and then leapt at Mettius.

Unsurprised by the nomad's action, Mettius, in one swift move, drew his sword and swung it in a graceful arc at his oncoming assailant. He then stepped aside as the headless torso, spouting blood from the severed flesh, landed with a hard thud on the stunned woman's feet.

The headless body twitched and discoloured the ground with a slow spreading beetroot stain. A metre from the Nomads front ranks the decapitated head stared back, a surprised grimace frozen on his face.

Wailing in shock, the woman threw herself and the baby over the body. Behind her, Mettius stood over them. He drew his pistol, and fired three shots, silencing both mother and child.

FUCK. SHIT... Holy shit.

Ried stumbled back and slumped down with his back against the tree. His heart pounded against his ribs in horrified grief. His vision blurred, his breathing came in gasps. Pulling his knees against his chest, Ried could feel himself slipping into shock.

Who the fuck are these people?

The sudden shouts and wailing cries from the Nomads routed Ried from his emotional shutdown. A voice of righteous anger screamed within him.

Ried flicked around and shouldered the rifle. Instinct and training took over from the raw emotions when he lined the sights on the murderer who wiped the blood from his tunic as he rubbed his boot against the dead woman's dress.

He contemplated the cleanliness of his boot and issued further instructions to drag out another six men and women and have them kneel to face the other Nomads.

Ried focused on his own breathing and the rise and fall of his chest as he held the carbine in a firm hold. The front blade hiccupped in time with his heartbeat. Ried calmed himself and then focused on the voice of a cold killer.

"Defiance will only lead to a long, dark sleep, in your own blood," Mettius said. "Now, I will ask again…" He prowled behind the closest kneeling man who sneered and spat on the ground, a second before a rose-coloured cloud filled with pieces of his skull and pulverised brains, exploded from his forehead.

"Enough!" Gazza bellowed and barged from the crowd to stand between Mettius and Ried's rifle.

"Move, your dumb bastard," whispered Ried.

"Ah. The noble chieftain shows himself," Mettius mocked in a loud voice, raising his sword to Gazza's throat.

"We came across some bloke yesterday," Gazza told him. "He killed two of my boys and then bolted."

The two men faced off and pivoted around Mettius's sword.

"Which direction?" Mettius asked, pointing the pistol at the head of a kneeling woman, while still holding the sword under Gazza's chin as they continued walking in a circle.

"Shit," Ried cursed and rolled around the tree. Then, Mettius and Gazza stopped their macabre waltz which gave Ried a clear shot at Mettius who now rested the barrel of the pistol against the woman's head. "No more," Ried uttered between breaths.

If Mettius was protected by a patron god, then their intervention came when Ried squeezed the trigger.

The same second the sharp crack of the rifle's report echoed around the old farm, one of the other riders moved between Mettius and the incoming round.

Mettius flinched, taking a small step back when the spent bullet slammed into his body armour, followed by a dark-red arterial spray and pieces of the rider's heart muscle and sternum.

The interceding rider gawked in shocked wonder at the fist-sized hole in his chest. He tried speaking, but instead, he coughed on blood-filled foam dribbled from his mouth as he fell sideways.

The ground around Ried erupted in dozens of dry dust and dirt geysers. Concussive cracks tore splinters from the tree and fence. Ried rolled back behind the stump, and when the shooting stopped, he rocked back to see several riders approach him in a brisk walk, casting nervous glances between themselves.

Without hesitation, Ried rose and kneeled on one knee and fired four quick rounds. Even before the last bullet left the barrel, Ried ran past the henhouse. The rapid shots from his carbine found their mark on two of the men.

One collapsed, face down, with a small hole below his eye, and the other dropped to the ground, curling himself into the foetal position, and holding his stomach. He soon passed out; his life flowing into the dirt from his lacerated liver. The third and fourth faltered and ran back.

Before the second Roman hit the ground, Mettius saw Ried run and disappear amongst the landscape. Something about the stranger's movements and shooting abilities ignited Mettius's internal alarms; the shooter was no nomad.

Ried used the small rise the old farmhouse sat on for cover as he ran in behind the car-sized woodpile. He spared a look over the timber wall searching for Mettius.

With the riders distracted and confused, Gazza and the Nomads needed no instruction to charge the armed men around them.

Outnumbered, the armed riders fired a few shots at the fast-moving Nomads, who overwhelmed them in a vengeful and brutal melee of hand-to-hand fighting.

Despite Gazza standing over Mettius by a full head, the Centurion weathered the fury of blows and punches delivered by Gazza. In fact, Mettius countered and struck back with equal determination and stoic efficiency until the fight devolved into a simple brawl.

Everything around Ried slowed down. Once again, he felt detached. Like a person watching an ultra-slow-motion film. His tactical training urged him to use the phenomenon to his advantage, but he found himself gapping in awe at the slow comical movements around him.

The riders and Nomads continued to wrestle in a hanging cloud of dust. Amidst the melee, blossomed the flowering plumes of discharged rifles and pistols. Sunlight reflected off arcing swords and knives. Arterial blood rained dark crimson drops, mist, and streams against the bright, dust-fringed sky to splatter across anyone nearby.

In the open, Mettius floated through the air behind his roundhouse kick to Gazza.

The figures of six more men move forward, past their two dead comrades, toward the mound of chopped wood he hid behind. Without hesitation, Ried turned to run behind the nearby barn. His breaths sounding like blacksmith bellows.

Back at the woodpile, lazy clouds of dust and woodchips surrounded the six riders who slid to a protracted stop, their faces contort in confusion when they found nothing but the odd, cut pieces of wood which had fallen from the pile.

Ried's thoughts came across clear and concise under the veil of slowness, he gauged the risks and charged at the men from behind the barn's protection.

Irrespective of how clear his mind worked, Ried's body moved as though trapped in treacle. In front of Ried, an elongated bubble of expanding gas flared from his carbine barrel.

Before his foot fell for a second step, he fired two more rounds. On his third shot, the world and time whiplashed back to normal.

His bullets found their targets before the men knew what had happened. The three of them fell to the ground, one in a pool of his own vomit mewing pitiful sobs for his mother. Another saw the hole near his groin spitting blood half a metre high, in time with his rapid pulse and passed out. The third man wept from the pain in his torn shoulder.

With the speed of a running gazelle, Ried came up behind them with his rifle raised and his finger tensed on the trigger.

A survivor heard Ried's approach. His head swivelled toward Ried and stared cross-eyed at the black muzzle of a carbine, centimetres from his face.

"Your call," Ried hissed from a dry throat.

The younger man refocused on Ried's grim face and then back at the large, looming black hole and wet himself.

One of his companions, seduced by a moment of heroism, drew his pistol on Ried, who, with a quick twist from the hip, turned and shot the man in the throat.

The bullet tore through the man's larynx and windpipe, shattering vertebrae, and severing his spine. The almost heroic rider's body jerked and fell back against the stack of wood. His fingers convulsed on the pistol's trigger, sending a bullet cutting across Ried's thigh.

Waves of fire flowed through Ried's leg which buckled, bringing Ried down on one knee. Despite the pain in his thigh, Ried kept the rifle pointed at the two uninjured men. With a grunt from behind clenched teeth, Ried pushed himself upright and stepped back.

"They're dead, but your other two mates should live," he said. "Plug the holes and wrap them with firm pressure, but first, kick away your weapons." Ried's calf muscle twitched from the touch of his warm blood tracking down past his knee.

Shifting the weight from his wounded leg, Ried caught the swift movement of a shadow and the glint of sunlight off metal.

He raised his rifle deflecting a sword arcing down at him with such force the blow sent him staggering backwards.

On instinct, Ried grabbed the barrel of his rifle to counter the thrusts and lunges from the sword-wielding attacker.

The new assailant pirouetted from one of Ried's swings to face him with both sword and knife. A combination he used to thrust and counter against the batting action of the rifle.

When his attacker moved in, Ried recognised the man's blood-smeared face; Mettius.

The Roman moved with calm, measured thrusts and cuts – the actions of someone who knew how to wield a sword and knife – while Ried's moves smacked of desperation, and a desire to stay alive.

He batted and lunged out with the carbine until his manic parries, twists and swings gave him the upper hand.

Mettius faltered against Ried's undisciplined and desperate assaults. The Roman's brief loss of footing gave Ried the time he needed to flick the rifle around, hold its grip, and pull the trigger.

His mind froze in horror at the hollow clack of the firing pin striking an empty chamber.

Mettius gave Ried a cold, "you're dead" smile, made even more chilling by those obsidian orbs he had for eyes.

Ried tossed the empty rifle at Mettius, fell on his side, and swept his legs toward the Roman's knees. His frantic action connected.

With a surprised cry, Mettius crumpled when his left knee folded causing him to twist, so his face bounced against the wood pile.

Those few brief seconds Mettius lay stunned gave Ried enough time to reach for the nightstick in his waist, twist the dial and shove the weapon at Mettius while squeezing the lever. The electric arc caught Mettius on the right arm below the shoulder.

Mettius cried out, dropped his sword from his limp hand, and lunged forward to backhand Ried with a fist. The blow caught Ried just below his ear and sent him skidding across the dirt.

A storm of bullets shredded the top of the pile into a cloud of splinters, bark and dust. Mettius allowed his anger and frustration to take control which resulted in exposing himself from behind the wall of chopped firewood.

Whoever was firing at Mettius gave Ried the opportunity to reach across and snatch a carbine left by the other riders.

Taking fire from his left and from behind, Mettius sprinted across to the barn, the ground exploding around his feet from Ried's wild shots.

During the fight between Mettius and Ried, the two other riders grabbed their wounded companions and fled the scene.

Ried pushed himself up, tossed the empty carbine aside, drew his pistol, and followed Mettius – but a gabble of loud yells and victorious cries soaked through the ringing in his ears.

With the pistol still raised, Ried walked between the woodpile and the barn, pausing when he faced the now armed Nomads.

For the second time that morning, Gazza told his people to stand down, and he brought his full attention to Ried. "Easy, lad," Gazza crooned. "Put down the gun, hey?"

Ried blinked, and his breathing steadied as the adrenaline-fuelled red fog melted away. He stood there drained and noticed the young, liver-shot, rider now dead and lying face down on the blood-soaked ground.

Christ. He's just a kid. Ried let the pistol hang in his hand for a few seconds, before he slid the gun into the holster, and raised his arms.

"Put down your bloody arms." Gazza pointed at Ried's bleeding thigh. "You, all right?"

"Hurts like a bitch, but I'll live. What about you?"

"I reckon Tilly's got a job ahead of her." Gazza flinched when he touched the wounds on his bruised and battered face, with a hand seeping blood from torn skin and knuckles.

Ried watched in disbelief as two Nomads with spears who wandered amongst the dead and wounded.

"What the fuck?" Ried's hand moved to grip his holstered pistol after seeing the Nomads plunge their spears into at least three wounded men.

"Don't." Gazza grabbed Ried's arm.

Ried snapped his arm away from Gazza's reach when the two spearmen approached.

"Sorry, guv'na. They were passed even Tilly's help."

The depth of sadness in the man's voice slapped at Ried's assumption.

"Jimmy had a busted neck and was suffocating. The poor bastard couldn't feel nuthin' from the chin down."

What stung Ried was the flat, factual way the Nomad told them as he wiped the tip of his spear with a rag.

"The other bloke had his guts split wide and was spillin' his insides into his armour."

"What about the third one?" Ried asked.

"Old mate was hurtin' like hell from bein' shot in the chest and gut. I stuck him to ease his pain before he fuckin' well bled out."

Regardless of what the nomad said, Ried struggled with the brutal, antiquated way of dealing with dying men. Unsure of what else he could say, he went over to inspect the growing pile of dead.

Ried stood and watched the Nomads hurl more bodies on a growing pile.

"The bastard's not there," Gazza said when he walked up behind Ried. "He did a runner with the others."

"Who are they?"

"Them?" Gazza said, "They're the fuckin' Vigiles."

"Are they some sort of bikie gang?"

"Bikie gang? Did you hit your fuckin' head?" Gazza laughed. "Bikie gang… That lot's the Romans' idea of police. Only, the bastard who governs this region is a…" Gazza paused. Something in Ried's expression merged with Dom's request. "Where the fuck are you from?"

"Not from around here," Ried murmured.

Before Gazza could comment, they heard a yell from the other side of the farmhouse.

When Gazza and Ried walked past the house, a few of the Nomads joined them with Lester Jennings being hustled and looking terrified.

"What the hell are you doing here?" Ried asked the petrified vet. "You can trust me when I say he's no spy," he told Gazza, stepping past, and pulling the frightened Jennings aside. "You were supposed to take Devil back."

When the nomad who caught him walked away, Jennings mewed a pathetic whimper, and Ried thought he would faint when Gazza approached them.

"Don't worry, old man." Gazza patted Jennings's shoulder. "We ain't gonna kill you."

Unconvinced, Jennings turned to Ried. "When you ran off after the Vigiles, something told me I should wait around." Nervous sweat saturated Jennings's face and neck. "I did drive the truck down the road after you disappeared into the bushes. But, instead of continuing, I turned into a side track, and out of sight."

Jennings explained how he had left the truck and went back toward the creek which he crossed, hoping to persuade Ried to go back with him. "But when the shooting started, I panicked and hid in the bushes."

Upon finishing his tale, he saw Muddgy approach with a pitcher of their cactus brew and old tin mugs on a tray.

Ried started to warn Jennings about the drink, but the vet swallowed the contents of the mug in two gulps. His face flushed, and he coughed and spluttered, much to the amusement of his onlookers.

When Jennings finished his bout of coughing, Ried watched the man take another drink.

Turning away from the blustering Jennings, Gazza told Ried about his plan to head west, past the reach of the Romans. But first, the farm needed cleaning up.

"Cleaning up?"

Gazza's expression matched his matter-of-fact tone. "The pricks will be back in force and lookin' for blood. Only, when they get here, they'll find nothin' but ash n bones."

The two improbable allies clasped forearms in a silent parting after which Ried handed him the pistol belt and told him to look in the old henhouse.

Gazza turned to go, but then asked, "What's your name?"

"Ben Ried."

The nomad contemplated the young man before him. "So, Ried, you wanna tell me why you came back?"

Ried shrugged. "It seemed like the right thing to do."

"Fuck me. You're a strange one all right." He slapped Ried's back, almost choking on his laughter before walking away.

Jennings mopped his brow using his sleeve. "Savages. He didn't even thank you." When Ried limped away, stopping at an open water barrel to wash his face, and the bullet graze.

Jennings came up alongside Ried and cast a concerned look at the wound on Ried's thigh. "I'll dress that back at my truck. Unless you plan on running off again."
Ried patted his face dry with his forearms. "And go where?" He whispered.

CHAPTER TEN

Gallio entered the governors' house as glinting stainless steel flashed across the hallway, clattering, and spinning along the polished floorboards.

"Leave!" Mettius's command sent a distraught medical auxiliary rushing past the door.

"Medici?" Gallio approached the man collecting dishes, instruments and dressings from the floor.

"Praefectus." Startled by Gallio, the young medic, dressed in a powder blue jumpsuit, snapped to attention.

Gallio tilted the young man's face to inspect the cut near his right eye and a matching wound in the corner of his mouth. "Continue collecting your equipment. And remain in the hall."

Mettius paced Gallios' office, and each time he passed an ornate and delicate resin framed mirror, he scowled at the reflection. On the third circuit of the room, Mettius unsheathed his pugio and swung his hand to drive the pommel into the looking glass.

"Stay your hand," Gallio commanded.

Mettius sheathed his dagger, fixing his eyes on Gallio's reflection as he entered the room. "I want him crucified and his entrails cut from his living body."

"Who? The Medici you just expelled from my office or our mysterious stranger, or perhaps the nomad leader?"

"You choose now to mock me?"

168

Gallio sat behind his desk and poured two glasses of wine. One thing he had learned about his second-in-command – from when he was a boy and through his service in the Empire – was knowing when to stay at arm's length of his wrath. However, Gallio was still Mettius's commander.

"Perhaps just a little. Now, sit down so the Medici can tend your wounds."

Mettius sat opposite Gallio and allowed the nervous young medical auxiliary to bathe his bruises and suture the gash along the right side of his jawline.

After the medic treated the last wound on Mettius, he stood back, saluted, and scampered from Gallio's office. Left alone with Mettius, Gallio leaned forward, rested his elbows on the desk, and steepled his fingers.

"What is the debt?"

"Seven dead, nine wounded, of which three won't live beyond the week." Mettius massaged a livid bruise on his right bicep.

"That looks painful," Gallio said. "Now, have you calmed yourself enough to provide a report?"

"You'll have it by sunrise tomorrow," Mettius responded. He reached across for the wine Gallio poured for him and winced.

"I look forward to reading it."

Mettius ignored the caustic tone of his commander. "Why keep it?"

"Keep what?"

"The mirror."

Gallio sighed. "It was a gift from your mother to my wife."

"Yes, but they are both dead."

"Which is why I keep it…" Gallio often found Mettius's lack of emotional attachment useful. Yet, as a friend, he also found Mettius's emotional disability a sad enigma.

Gallio gave a slight frown above a contemplative pout. He poured himself another wine and picked at the platter of fruit and cheese.

"Now that the Nomads have weapons." Gallio paused on the implied threat. "So as of now, no patrol leaves the compound with fewer than six cohorts."

"Sixty troops per patrol?"

"You disapprove?"

Mettius's shoulders arched back a mere fraction at the jibe. "No, Sir, six cohorts as you command."

Gallio unrolled a lithograph of the region, "and have the perimeter expanded by twenty kilometres. The bikes you left behind will give them the added capability to travel farther."

At the second implied failing, Mettius faltered when he placed the glass on the table. He stood, adjusted his tunic, saluted and headed toward the door.

"Don't forget, Centurion, I want the report on my desk by sunrise."

Mettius stopped without turning and gave Gallio a curt nod before marching from the office.

Gallio pushed his chair across the floor and walked over to a cabinet. He lifted a key from his pocket and opened the doors. Inside sitting on a marble base rested a metal framed, octagonal glass plate. On either side of the marble base stood a vase of flowers and pewter statuettes. One being Juno, the goddess of Marriage. The other being Diana, the goddess of hunting.

He glanced over his shoulder at Mettius's heavy footsteps resonating along the hall. With the faintest sigh, Gallio pressed a sensor button on the plates frame. The crystal glowed until the smiling and waving holographic images of his wife and two sons coalesced.

"Zosima, your nephew still can't grasp the concept of defeat. Petilius, be sure to watch over your younger brother and mother in Elysium until we are united. Not yet, though. First, I must build a new Empire from the ashes of this benighted planet."

Inside the cottage, Ried sat cross-legged against the overturned wrought-iron bed surrounded by his clothes, empty bags, and the rest of the upturned furniture.

Outside on the veranda, Jack's shadow crossed the oblique patch of light cutting through the dust motes. Another shadow passed through the beam of sunlight, followed by several thumps on the door.

Ried ignored the shadows as he massaged his bruised, bleeding knuckles.

Another series of blows threatened to knock the door off its hinges.

Just leave me the fuck alone.

When more heavy knocks resounded, Ried got up and opened the door and returned to sit by the bed.

Dom took two steps through the door. "Shit." He wiped his hand across the back of his neck and exchanged a quick glance with Jack before both men turned and walked back onto the veranda

Through the open doorway, Ried saw a man older than Dom walk up to the veranda wearing a sports coat and an old fedora. In one hand, he carried a leather bag, and in the other, a cracked, worn, and over-filled briefcase. Something about the man was familiar, but right then, Ried didn't care if he knew him or not.

The newcomer spoke from the doorway, "Ben, do you mind if we clean up?"

"Suit yourself."

Dom, Jack and the stranger tidied inside the cottage, being careful not to touch Ried's belongings. Once they finished, the older man ushered Jack and Dom outside.

Ried sighed listening to their soft conversation.

"Strewth. He's made a right bloody mess," Jack said.

"Did you notice his knuckles and the smeared blood on the wall?" Dom said.

"I dare say he's angry and confused," the stranger replied.

"Well, given what Jennings relayed about our friend's morning and his adventures," Dom poked his head around the door frame, "I reckon this may only be the start of it."

"Yep. It's a fair bet he's got the gist of his predicament," said Jack.

Ried listened to the three men's discussion, while he righted the bed and gathered his scattered possessions.

"What's going on?"

All three men turned in unison when Abbey skipped up onto the veranda.

"Hello, Dr Mitchum."

"Hello, Abbey."

"Why are you all standing out here?" She asked, pushing past the men.

"Abbey, wait– bloody hell," Dom whispered.

Jack followed Abbey and planted himself against the inside door frame.

Dom and Mitchum edged closer.

"The lad's repacking his stuff,"

Abbey stopped a little farther in than Jack, where she watched Ried repack in silence.

"You can come in," Ried said with his back facing her. When he finished packing his last bag, he sat on the bed, holding a folded piece of paper, postcard and envelope. Beside him lay a photo of two women standing before an enormous black gate, with a royal emblem bolted to the vertical bars.

Abbey sat down with the photograph between them.

Ried answered Abbey's silent question in a mournful whisper, "My mother and sister on holiday in London." He picked up the photo, running a dirty finger around the image of his younger sister.

"What's she holding?"

"A teddy bear dressed in a soldier's uniform." He tried smiling. "Becca bought it for me as a good luck charm for Afghanistan." He wiped his nose and smeared away a streak of sorrow rolling down his cheek. He tipped his head back and gave a short, painful laugh. "Christ, did I cop some flak from my mates in the barracks when they saw it."

Ried dropped his head and gathered the snapshot, postcard and letter. He slid them back into the envelope, before guiding the envelope into a pocket on his backpack.

He muttered a curse, dropped the bag on the floor, got up and walked around the bed to stare out of the cottage's rear window.

Abbey watched his back in silence as he rested his head against the glass and his arms crossed.

For several minutes Ried stood there with his shoulders rising and falling. His breaths came in constricted gasps. After half a minute he mashed his palms against his eyes.

Unsure whether to console him or leave him alone, Abbey fidgeted on the bed. Her growing sense of sympathy urging her to reach out, but instead, embarrassment flushed her cheeks. *Time to go. I reckon I've intruded enough.*

"This is all wrong," he said resting his forehead on the glass.

"What is?"

"Everything," his response was brusque, edged in disbelief. "Wild Nomads, modern-day Romans with guns, swords and motorbikes." He gestured outside. "Deserted farms left to rot, roads, and bridges in ruin, and I can't even guess what that weird, crashed plane I found is or was."

He turned and slumped against the window frame. "It's just wrong. The whole bloody lot of it." He pointed his finger at Abbey. "Your old man telling me there's been no Queensland Government for decades." Ried paced the room. "And when I asked for my mobile phone…" he tossed her a frown. "You reckon you didn't know what I was talking about." He finished his rant and slid down the wall.

Abbey shifted on the bed. She wanted to sit beside him offer her sympathies and comfort him. Instead, she replied in a meek little voice, "well, I don't."

With a grunt, Ried stood and marched out to join the three men.

"How are you feeling, son?" Mitchum asked when Ried walked over to them.

Dom and Jack did a double-take in the doctor's gentle manner and voice.

"Bloody hell, Jack," whispered Dom. "That's twice this week, old Mitchum's used the same tone."

"Uh, don't tell me the old bastard's getting soft," Jack said.

Ried ignored Mitchum and walked over to Dom. "I'm sorry I took your horse."

Dom looked awkward before responding. "Well, she's back now. So, no harm done eh."

"Can you tell me more about how I got here?"

"I think Dr Mitchum can explain it better." Dom gave Mitchum a quick, apologetic shrug.

"All right." Mitchum threw Dom a veiled look. "Let's go inside then."

Ried followed the doctor as Dom and Jack brought in the two chairs from the veranda. Once the four men settled themselves around the table. The doctor did his best to appear casual. Jack and Dom did the same, while Ried focused on a knothole in the table top.

Abbey stared at the four silent men, excused herself, and left them all sitting in silence.

After a few minutes, Jack shifted in his chair and looked at Ried. "We hear you've been busy."

Ried shrugged. He watched the doctor take out a wad of notes from his briefcase, along with some journals.

"You won't need that," Ried said when he saw Mitchum drop a syringe full of clear liquid into his coat pocket.

Jack frowned at Ried, and then the doctor. "Won't need what?"

"The Needle," Ried said, "I'm assuming it's a sedative."

Dom raised an eyebrow at the doctor.

"Yes, well, a precautionary measure," Mitchum said without removing the pocketed syringe, "Dominic told me you don't recall much about how you ended up here?"

"I didn't," Ried said, "until this afternoon after I came back." He paused and raised his eyes when none of them spoke. Taking a deep breath, he told them everything he could remember, from when he saw the stampeding kangaroos, to the inverted, lightning-filled tornado, and the ball of electricity.

The three older men listened to Ried's tale, after which Dom told him everything that happened after they found him, including Nicholas's drug-induced rage, and the Romans' visits.

"So, who's this Gallio?"

"He's our regional governor, magistrate and the Vigiles' praefectus." Dom glanced at Ried. "The blokes you had a run-in with are called the Vigiles – the Romans' version of a police force."

"They have an unusual way of policing," Ried said. "This governorship, how long has it been going on?"

"Only the last couple of years for Gallio," Dom replied. "Before him, the last governor had been Marcus, who now rules the Senate in Toowoomba. It was Marcus who recommended Gallio for the role."

Jack chimed in, "Marcus was a decent bloke, for a Roman. He knew how to treat people. But Gallio? He's a true prick through 'n' through."

Dom raised his eyebrow at Jack who shrugged in response. Dom brought his attention back to Ried. "The one, you and Lester, ran into this morning is Mettius – Gallio's head lap dog. Not someone you'd want to get on the wrong side of."

"Bit late for that," Ried mumbled leaning back and inspecting the wound on his thigh which already scabbed over under the dressing. He pressed the tape down and asked Mitchum about why he was healing faster.

The doctor turned into an enthusiastic school teacher. "I believe the unique or unusual energies occurring which you endured may have set off a mutagenic reaction."

"Mutation?"

The doctor nodded with a sheepish shrug and expanded on his hypothesis about the strange fevers and chills. Using his notes and charts, he explained how Ried's haemoglobin factors were different when compared to everybody else's.

"You took my blood?"

"Only after Abbey informed me of how fast you were healing—"

Ried stopped him and read through the relevant paperwork, graphs and charts.

"These ones with the high readings are yours?"

"That's right because of what happened our blood has higher concentrates of carbon dioxide, sulphates, hydrochloric and hydrofluoric derivatives – along with various traces of radioactive particles."

Mitchum flicked through the papers to place one on top of the others. "While your tests showed many similar elements with significantly lower levels. The same results came back for any fluorides, chlorine and hydrocarbons.

"Would I be right in saying these trace elements and differences between our blood has something to do with these Romans?"

"In a roundabout way," Mitchum responded.

"Okay." Ried looked at Dominic. "Can you explain more about these Romans, and what happened?"

"Well, I'm not much of a historian, and I'm definitely not a scientist."

"Fair enough. Then tell me in the words of a soldier."

Dom paused, leaned back in his chair, and crossed his arms. "What makes you think I'm in the military?"

"Maybe not anymore," Ried nodded toward Jack, "but at some point, you both were."

"You reckon?" Jack quipped.

"Christ, it stands out like a pair of dog's balls," Ried shot back.

"You see it because you're one yourself," Mitchum pointed out.

"Not anymore."

"Ah. That explains the scar on your shoulder," Mitchum remarked.

"I got it on my last stint." Ried focused on Dom again. "So, what about these Romans? Because the Roman Empire I knew stopped being great about five or six hundred years ago."

Dom paused and went over a conversation he and Jack had with Mitchum about alternate worlds. "There were ancient Romans here, but they fell afoul of the Greeks, who ended up ruling much of Europe, North Africa and western Asia. But, growing religions and the spread of the Turkish Empire–"

Ried raised his eyebrows.

"Sorry, our Romans; they came from outer space, claiming to have conquered over half the galaxy."

"Space Romans?" Ried muttered. *Why not?*

"At first, we figured they stole the name from our history," Dom said, "but it turned out this Roman Galactic Empire is similar in culture and name."

"So, what they just landed and then invaded you?"
Asked Ried

Dom laughed despite himself. "They didn't 'land' or attack us in the way you think. Yes, they invaded us," Dom's mood became sombre, "but they did so by infiltrating our society over several decades changing the social, fiscal and political shape of the world. I guess they'd been studying us for a while because they played on our fears and weaknesses – like terrorism, economic downturns, etcetera.

"We believe they started messing about with the world economy back in the 1950s. Except, for every type of economic downturn or collapse they engineered, the world recovered with stronger markets and policies. Their next gambit came in the form of terrorism. Now, that galvanised the world… Fear, kidnappings, suicide attacks and mass genocide, became a far better tool at destabilising the globe.

"Over time, the superpowers banded together and fought against the growing terrorist groups. Even the UN peacekeepers became more aggressive in their response. But it was like stopping a sandstorm with a wire basket. It seemed for every terror leader taken down, a new, more charismatic, influential and Roman one took their place.

"Over time, Roman agents infiltrated the Security Council and once entrenched they dissolved the current, ineffectual peacekeeper force by replacing them with a newer, more lethal force called the Praetorians."

Dom's historical account paused when Abbey returned with sandwiches made from leftovers and a thermos of coffee.

While they all ate, Dom continued, "They were swift, brutal, and did their job with absolute impunity. The larger, more powerful nations committed unprecedented amounts of men, material, and money to the Praetorian force. This left most countries – including Australia – vulnerable, with weak and depleted armed forces." Dom poured himself a coffee.

"So, the bastards attacked our economies again and ramped up a more aggressive terror campaign against every countries stock markets, banks and heads of state. The planet quickly collapsed into a shit heap.

"When civil unrest grew rampant, and out of control, the Romans made their next move and marched the Praetorians into every nation's capital city declaring martial law.

"Then, their main invasion forces arrived from giant spaceships in battle barges and drop ships by the thousands."

Dom explained how The Wars dragged on for over a decade, and then, in desperation, the surviving military and political leaders on Earth used nuclear weapons against the Roman planetary strongholds and their orbital ships.

Despite himself, Ried listened with a growing curiosity while Dom explained how the massive spacecraft hit by the nuclear missiles exploded in space or crashed into the planet, setting off a series of volcanic eruptions along with devastating earthquakes and tidal waves.

The atmosphere filled with volcanic ash and radioactive dust clouds which created the long winters, followed by several years of hot summers.

Dom's tone grew in bitterness. "None of that influenced the continuing, bitter skirmishes between the survivors of both sides. Until, for the sake of everyone's survival, they had agreed to cease all hostilities."

"A truce?" Despite all he heard, Ried's voice leached criticism and disappointment. "More like a surrender declaration, since they're the ones in charge."

"You might well be right," Dom said. "But back then, there wasn't any organised military to continue our defence, and even though both races suffered from the winters, the Romans still had a greater military and occupational force. So, selling it as a truce was our only chance at any peace and survival."

Ried shrugged. "I guess we'll have to agree to disagree," he said. "But if they're 'aliens,' why do they look like ordinary people?"

"Now there's a wonderful piece of irony. Over the year's mankind fantasised about weird looking aliens. Yet, when they arrive, they look like us."

"So, if all the countries bolstered this Praetorian force with your own military, Ried said. "Why wasn't there any sort of rebellion or mutinies?"

"Remember what I said about militant terrorism. Well, it was the human troops sent in to fight the terrorists while the Romans stayed back and watched our armies wither.

"Then, with the military units depleted, the clever bastards rebuilt the Praetorians by recruiting teenagers and those who could be manipulated and trained–"

"Bloody well brainwashed you mean," Jack said.

"And it's still hard to fathom why many of our young people wanted to be one of them." Mused Mitchum.

Dom continued. "Following the truce after the post-war skirmishes, older teenagers and out-of-work blokes signed up to the Vigiles because it was a job."

Ried let everything Dom said register, as best it could. He picked at the knothole before facing Mitchum. "Would these changes I've gone through change how I perceive time?"

"In what way?"

"Before I got taken by the Nomads and during the fighting against these Vigiles, it felt like everything slowed down."

"I think you're referring to combat time," Dom suggested.

"No, I know what combat time is. This was different. It wasn't my brain drawing things out from shock. It was like I could see and react faster than normal."

"We know that whatever you experienced during your crossing has made you heal faster," Mitchum said, "So, it is possible it may have heightened your senses."

Mitchum leaned back in his chair with his arms crossed in contemplative thought. "What you experienced might also be a response to certain neurological chemicals combined with adrenaline. But without more tests," Mitchum shrugged, "all I can do is speculate."

Ried had no intention of being the doctor's lab rat, so he turned to face Dom. "One other thing. What time of year is it?"

"Why?" Asked Abbey.

"The sun's in a different spot," Ried said and continued picking at the table.

"That could just be an alternate world effect," Mitchum replied.

Without looking up, Ried decided the next question needed asking. "All right, What date is it?"

"The 12th of January 2021," Dom answered.

The blood drained from Ried's cheeks, and the synapses in his brain ceased firing for a few seconds. "But… I crashed in August 2014…" His mind spiralled out of control. He pushed the chair away from the table and went outside, where he paced the veranda, squinting at the dark sky littered with faint lacklustre stars.

Ried tilted his head back and ran his hands down over his face, before marching back to the group.

"Let me see if I've got this right." Ried paced out a figure eight. "I'm seven years in the future, in some other dimension, on another Earth invaded by an alien race of futuristic Romans," he strode back to the table and leaned on the back of his chair, "which you lot tried to fight off, almost destroying the planet in the attempt." In an outburst of frustrated anger, he shoved his seat against the table disturbing the plates and cups. "OH, and let's not forget, a planet I'm now stuck on. And getting mutated in the process…"

Ried's anger created a shroud of sadness over the table. His voice dropped to a whisper, and he sought the doctor's eyes with a pleading expression. "I can't go home, can I?"

The doctor gave Ried a small shake of his head. "I'm sorry, son."

In response, Ried gripped the chairs back.

Dom and the others feared he would smash it, but instead Ried stormed off into the night.

He sat on the closest silver-grey log by the fire pit with a thick film of moisture covering his eyes.

183

From inside the cottage came a brief argument, the closing of a door and soft footfalls through the dew-soaked ground.

"The doctor said this might help." Abbey sat beside him holding a bottle of brandy and two cups.

Ried contemplated telling her to go away. Instead, he took the offered bottle and a mug which he raised skyward. "Here's to me and a new fucked up world."

Abbey watched Ried skull the contents and the next refill. When he filled the third cupful, Abbey put down her cup and rose from the log.

"Ben?"

"Just go Abbey…" He wiped his cheek across his shoulder.

Abbey turned and walked over to the path. Behind her, Ried swore followed by the echoing thump of the slamming cottage door.

***

PART TWO

CHAPTER ONE

Shards of shattered crystal rebounded from the wall amidst droplets of wine.

"How can one human being vaporise?" Gallio screamed at the four provincial Vigiles commanders.

"Sir, my scouts and spies report no unusual comings or goings from the Yarraman province or with the gypsies…" The grey-bearded man trailed off from the withering glare of Gallio.

"Tesserarius Denver, I do not want verbal rhetoric mimicking your transcripts." Gallio leaned in on Denver. "I want him found!" Gallio emphasised his request by backhanding Denver.

"Praefectus. This obsession is causing a breakdown in our day to day policing–" Denver froze with an increasing, hot, sensation within his chest.

Gallio rested his cheek against Denver's "I do not care about policing and nor does Toowoomba." Gallio whispered. He stepped back and jerked the Pugio from Denver's ribs.

While holding Denver's hair in his fist, Gallio vented his frustration in a flurry of rapid stabs in the dead Tesserarius chest and abdomen. With his anger abated Gallio faced the remaining three Vigiles commanders.

"I will give you each another six weeks to find the off-worlder and those Nomads." Gallio let Denver's body crumple at his feet.

The three officers issued faltering salutes and fled Gallios office.

Mettius gave his commander a fresh glass of wine. "Sir, perhaps we should scale back our efforts to falsify our desire to find the off-worlder."

Gallio rested his blood-slicked dagger on the desk and accepted the glass. "I will not lure them out with the actions of a sheep." Gallio pressed the intercom on his desk. When his secretary entered Gallio pointed to Denver's leaching corpse. "Have this removed." He marched from his office with Mettius in tow. "I want patrol intervals reduced by half, and I want you to visit each Vigiles outpost from the eastern border to the western plains and ensure you enforce my instructions."

"By your command."

#

Jack's beat up land cruiser pulled up in front of the Harris house. He stepped from the vehicle, closed the door and leaned against the front guard.

"You want me to get you a blue-n-white striped apron?"

"What for?" Asked Abbey. She turned back to pruning a hedge of camellias with more gusto than needed.

"I figure the way you're carving those bushes you might as dress like a butcher."

Abbey swore and tossed the secateurs in the dirt as she sat on her haunches. "Uncle Jack, what's going on with Dad?"

"I dunno. Dom seems okay."

187

"He's not, and you bloody well know it," Abbey remarked. "I've seen him go out of his way and more to help people, but he avoids Ben, and he won't say why."

"Dom will be all right. The lad's arrival just stirred up some old war memories."

Abbey responded with a slight smile, but she could tell Jack also worried about Dom. "It's not just that," Abbey said, When Molly and I came back from town the other day, Gallio called by for the third time in as many weeks."

"Ah."

"I can tell Dad's worried Gallio knows about Ben," Abbey said. "So, he and Gallio keep playing those stupid political games where neither says what's really on their bloody minds."

Jack scratched his chin under his beard. "How's your brother?"

"Nicky's gone back to drinking and spending his days and most nights at that pub." Abbey stood up and washed her hands from the garden tap. "When he does come home, Dad has a go at him, and then the two of them end up having huge bloody rows."

Jack put a consoling arm around his goddaughter.

"If you want Dad, he's out riding the south-west fences after some calves went missing."

"Okay, but I just came here to see how Ben is doing."

Abbey crossed her arms and pouted. "He can bloody well rot in that cottage."

"I'm guessing the last four weeks haven't got any better since Will found him curled up on the floor."

188

"No. Ben won't answer the door, and when he does, he screams abuse at us." Abbey sunk against Jacks' chest. "Molly leaves him food by the door which he eventually takes inside and then tosses the basket outside." Abbey looked in her lap and wrung her hands together. "Don't tell Dad, but I've been hiding in the bushes with his old binoculars and watching the cottage…"

"And?"

"Ben's a mess. He hasn't shaved or bathed in weeks, and from what I saw through the window he hasn't lifted a finger to wash a plate or tidy up…" She pushed herself away from Jack. "He even told Dr Mitchum to bugger off."

"Just remember what the lad's been through," cautioned Jack. "But he seems like a strong bloke, so I reckon he'll come around."

"But when?"

"Time will tell lass, time will tell."

On the forty-third day, Abbey strolled down the path leading to the cottage, wondering what mood their guest was in. She steeled herself for another awkward food drop.

However, when she got closer, she noticed the door was open with Ried sitting on the small veranda, clean, shaved and dressed in fresh clothes. She stopped two metres in front of him, with one arm hooked through the cane basket's handle, and the other resting on her hip.

"Good morning," she said.

"Morning."

"Are you going out?"

"Not really," he replied. "Well, yes, maybe."

"Okay, so long as you're sure."

"Do you mind if we turn lunch into a picnic?"

"A picnic?" Abbey put the basket down and crossed her arms.

"What, you're just going to stand there?"

"A picnic would be fun," she conceded, "but not if you aren't going to talk." She kept her arms crossed, raised her eyebrows, and waited for his answer.

"Fair enough."

"Do you have somewhere in mind?"

"I was hoping you could suggest something."

"Well, I do know of a spot."

In response, Ried spun and darted into the cottage, appearing a minute later with a bottle of water, two tin mugs, and the blanket from his bed folded under his arm. He walked toward her to pick up the basket.

Abbey gave a small smile and headed around the back of the cottage with Ried following behind her. At different intervals during their walk, Abbey attempted to start a conversation, but Ried's responses were vague and stilted.

"Where are we going?" Ried asked when the small talk waned.

"It's my secret place," Abbey twisted around with a hint of mischief behind her smile. "I usually ride there, so it might be a bit of a hike on foot."

"No worries." After a few metres, Ried increased his stride to walk beside her. "By the way, thanks for all the food and stuff."

While his tone and smile held a reserve, Abbey blushed, bowed her head, and quickened her pace to conceal her flushed cheeks, hoping he didn't notice.

They walked in silence for a while. Ried fell behind and studied the scenery on either side of the path and in front of him. Including Abbey and how she walked in her firm, fitted jeans.

After almost tripping on a rock from watching Abbey, Ried averted his eyes back to the surrounding bush, which differed little from his excursion on Devil.

The most common shrub was small wattle trees, she-oaks scattered amongst dogwood, open clumps of lantana, blackberry bush, tall and dry grasses, and some of the largest prickly pear cactus he'd ever seen.

"Why do a lot of the older trees look so crook?"

"They're the ones left standing after the long winter and bad rains."

"Bad rains?" Ried remembered what Dom told him about the nuclear and volcanic winters. "You mean acid rain?"

"I suppose so."

"I guess the snow must have been rank too."

"Dad reckoned all the water needed distilling." She gave a small shrug. "I don't remember the snow and cold. But I do remember the summers."

"Why? Were they hot?"

"Hot and wet," she replied, "filled with massive storms and floods." Abbey waited for a response, but Ried kept walking in silence.

After a while, they stopped at the top of a small hill which overlooked a deep, forest-lined gully dotted with moss and lichen-covered boulders.

"Come on, this way." Abbey pointed to a little path on the right. The track wound through the rocks under the eucalyptus trees and ended at a small glade. A rock-strewn creek divided the gully floor. From the trees, the screech of birds echoed through the trees. The cause of the noise came from a flock of white, sulphur-crested cockatoos perched amongst the branches across the ravine. Their white feathers contrasting against a canvas of the green, brown and greys.

The splash and flow of a waterfall feeding the creek serenaded the raucous call of the birds. Behind the noise came the high-pitched burp of frogs, chirping cicadas, and the subtle swish of the higher leaves dancing in the breeze.

Along the creek bank, several well-fed water lizards sunned themselves in the gold-tinted rays of sunlight lancing through the trees.

Ried inhaled the air and sounds of the small valley's microsystem. An overdue welcome contrast from the broken weed-filled world Ried found since his arrival.

When they reached the bottom, Ried continued to follow Abbey through dense, blue-green couch and clover fighting against dark-green, leafy vines creeping over rocks, shrub, logs and tree trunks with thin hard thorns along every runner.

Abbey led him along the bank of the stream toward a broad, flat rock standing free of the barbed creeper and radiated a subtle warmth from the sun.

The stone slab was the perfect place to throw the blanket over for their picnic, but not before Ried made sure they were clear of any 'widow makers' from the trees above.

"What's a widow maker?"

"See those large, dead, overhanging branches?" He pointed across the creek to a tall gum tree on the other bank. "That's what the cattle drovers back home called them," he explained, holding her hand to help her settle on the blanket. "Cause if one of them broke loose and fell on you…" he slapped a hand on his thigh to emphasise his point, "…you aren't going home." With his last comment, Ried's face darkened.

Abbey feared he had withdrawn into himself again.

Instead, Ried inhaled, forced a tight smile, and helped her empty the basket of food to make lunch.

During their meal, he leaned back on his elbow with his gaze fixed on the opposite side of the creek.

Curious about what Ried fixated on, Abbey followed his silent stare and spied the object of his attention: a healthy-looking brown wallaby, standing amongst the rocks and boulders.

"There's a group of them living between here and the foothills," she said.

"Mob."

"What?"

"Where I come from," Ried said, "we call a group of them a mob," He dropped his gaze from the wallaby with the realisation he spoke of his home for a second time with no anxiety threatening to shut him down. "He looks in good nick."

"And the birds, too." Abbey nodded toward the cockatoos. "Each year, there are more of them about. Dad reckons nature is healing itself."

The conversation dwindled, so Abbey left Ried with his own thoughts. She rolled on her side studying him and twirling a lock of hair around her finger, admiring his profile.

The afternoon light highlighted his coco hair with a tinge of red. A hint of sympathy crossed Abbey's face. She recalled the healed scars on Ried's shoulder, arms, and back when he arrived and wondered what happened to him when he was a soldier.

Oblivious of her scrutiny Ried refilled his cup and brushed away an ant crawling along his leg.

What sort of person are you Ben Ried? Regardless of the past weeks, I can tell you must be a good person, or you wouldn't have gone back and helped the Nomads who kidnapped you.

The corner of her lip creased in a smile. *I would have liked to meet your mom and sister… Oh, God. What if somewhere out there he's got a girlfriend?*

The thought of Ried having someone waiting for him to run back into their arms gave Abbey a tight sensation in her chest and stomach. She sat up and wiped away a drop pooling in the corner of her eye, feeling angry and ashamed.

A glance in Ried's direction showed him looking at the gurgling creek. Relieved he didn't see her brief rise of jealousy, Abbey brushed some hair away from her face while regaining her composure.

With an unexpected start, Ried cried out, leapt up, staggered two steps back and fell off the rock. Tangled in the barbed vine, he tripped over a small log. "Christ all bloody mighty," he pushed himself up. "That's… the biggest friggin' spider I've ever seen." His face ashen, Ried darted the perceived safety of the blanket.

"Are you okay?" Abbey now on her feet, grabbed his hand in concern only to step back at the sight of the giant tarantula scurrying into the dry leaves and searching for safety with its two front legs raised in defence.

194

Ried scanned the surrounding undergrowth and tree litter for more giant arachnids, before, with dramatic hesitation, he allowed himself to sit back down.

"I get the feeling you don't like spiders?"

"Yes– Um, no– Yes…" He surveyed the ground around them. "Well, actually, no," Ried admitted. "Especially when they're that friggin' big." He ran his hand through his hair. With each breath, the colour returned to his face. "Please, tell me there aren't more mutant creatures roaming about. I'm not sure I could deal with any giant scorpions or zombies."

"No giant scorpions and everybody knows zombies aren't real." She pushed his shoulder, knocking him off balance. Except, Ried still held Abbey's hand when he fell, dragging her from the rock and landing on top of him.

Lying there, they locked eyes. Right then, Abbey only wanted Ried to close those beautiful hazel-green eyes and kiss her. Instead, she pushed herself away and cleaned up the lunch scraps. With a faint, nervous flutter in her voice, she said, "We'd better head off before it gets too late."

"Abbey." Ried stood, "Abbey."

She continued putting things into the basket, kneeling with her back facing him to hide her embarrassment.

"Hey," he whispered, kneeling in front of her and lifting her chin, "are you okay?"

Her cheeks still flushed, she stopped packing the basket, keeping her breaths steady as she wiped her hands across her thighs.

"Yep, I'm fine." She lied, pushing his hand away.

Abbey looked everywhere but into his eyes as he helped her up. Her mind whirled, wishing she could change the subject, but also not wanting to break the intimate moment.

"Look, these last few weeks have been like some sort of bad dream." For a few seconds, Ried looked at his feet and then lifted his gaze back to her face. "But you've added some light to it, and well... even if it's not a dream, I'm glad you came instead of watching me from behind a bush."

"Oh..." Abbey's heart imploded. "You saw me?" She averted her face, her voice softened. "I was worried about you. That's all–"

He lowered his head and kissed her lips with a brushing soft caress.

Abbey's pulse increased by the power of ten, and the nerves in her face tingled on the verge of exploding. For a split second, she panicked, until her heart stilled her fear letting her return the kiss.

Ried pulled back when she returned the kiss. "You're right... I think we should... you know, start heading back."

She grabbed the basket and stood while brushing her fingers across her lips, before moving past Ried, and giving him a gentle "about time" smile.

A short time later, they walked along the gully's ridgeline. Ried headed back along their original path but stopped when he didn't hear Abbey's footfall behind him.

"What's wrong with the way we came?"

"This way's shorter," she said with a coy smile, pointing to a path running parallel to the gully.

"Shorter? Then why come the long way?"

"If you must know, your behaviour over the last few weeks had really pissed me off."

"You don't think that's a bit childish?"

"Maybe."

"Maybe?" Ried raised his eyebrows, "I reckon I've had a bloody good reason for acting the way I did."

"True enough," Abbey replied, heading along the new path. "Anyway, why'd you clean yourself up and wait on the steps for me?" She asked over her shoulder.

"I realised I smelled like a septic tank."

"And if Molly or Will came down to drop off the food?"

"Then…" an invisible hand wrapped around his throat. "I would have said sorry and thanked them…" The last part spoke in a mumbled whisper."

"Good thing I came along then."

"I suppose." Ried faltered.

"And would you have kissed Molly?"

"What? No." *Oh for fuck sake Ried.*

Abbey continued walking with her back to him and speaking over her shoulder. "So down on the rock, why'd you kiss me?"

Oh, crap. "Just to say thanks… I guess." *Strewth you sound pathetic.*

Abbey stopped and turned around. She opened her mouth to speak, but instead, she sighed, frowned, and rotated on her heel to continue along the path.

"What?"

"Nothing," Abbey hissed. "It doesn't matter," she murmured to herself, quickening her pace.

#

Two weeks later Ried and Abbey were riding through the eastern paddocks of Dom's farm.

"I don't get your father," He said after a long silent ten minutes.

"What's to get?" Abbey replied in a cautious tone.

"Come on. The man pulls me from my wrecked car, have you nursemaid me," Ried said with a smile. "And then lets me use your mum's cottage, but he won't visit or let me leave the property."

"You know that's just to protect you."

"Yeah, well I don't need his protection," Ried replied in a dour tone. "To be honest, I feel like a prisoner."

"Don't be ungrateful," Abbey chirped at him. "At least Dad is letting you help out. Because if you were his prisoner, then you wouldn't step a foot out of the cottage."

"Look, I'm not ungrateful…" He caught the expression she returned. "And I kind of get why he's keeping me away from Gallio and Mettius, and I do enjoy working with William and the other farm hands…"

"There's a 'but' coming isn't there?"

Ried reined Devil to a stop. "To bloody right there is. I'm stuck on a planet, I don't know where, which reminds me of my own Earth, but is very different on so many levels and… Well, I just want to see more of it."

Abbey noticed a familiar expression in his eyes which softened her resolve. "Meet me in the main house for breakfast tomorrow morning." She reined her horse closer to Devil and then squeezed the hand resting on his thigh. She tugged the reins of her horse and gave the animal a gentle heel. "Last one back to the barn makes lunch." Then with a flick of the reins, she galloped up the ridge.

Inside Dom's house, Ried stood beside the doorway leading from the lounge to the kitchen. His back straight and shoulders square above his crossed arms.

"I don't think it's a good idea," Dom said, "not yet anyway." He avoided Ried's steadfast gaze.

"Really Dad?" Abbey asked. "Keeping him prisoner on the farm isn't right."

Ried raised his eyebrows. *Did she just say, prisoner?*

"Besides," Nicholas chimed in, "with all the time gone by, I reckon they've given up looking for Ried."

On Nicholas's comment, Ried frowned. *Okay... Since when does Nicky step up for me.*

"I suppose your useless mates in the pub told you that."

"No–"

"That's what I thought?" Dom walked over to the desk and poured himself a Brandy.

"At least when I get drunk, I wait till after lunch and do it with my friends." Nicholas stormed from the room after delivering his barb.

Ried shifted his weight and stepped up to the sofa separating him and Dom. "Am I your prisoner?"

"What? Don't be absurd." Dom gave a flick of his hand holding the empty glass

"Then let me off this bloody farm." Ried rested his palms on the couch as he leaned closer to Dom.

"God, you sound as ungrateful as my son," Dom said after draining his second shot of Brandy.

"Just the opposite," Ried's expression shifted, and his voice took on a more severe tone. "But keeping me your special guest who can't leave will destroy that gratitude." Ried marched around in front of Dom. "On second thought you tell me why I should be grateful?" Ried didn't wait for an answer. "Was it because you rescued me, then gave me food and shelter. Well in my books, the last two don't differ from what the governor of a prison does."

"Dad?"

199

Dom didn't look at Ried or his daughter. Instead, he skulled a third helping of liquor.

Ried continued his line of questions. "Or is there more to it than just hiding me."

"Enough," Dom said when he slammed down the glass on the coffee table. "I've got an appointment with Tom after lunch. So please, do join us." Dom sat at his desk, shuffled around papers and letter before issuing a quiet command, "I have work to do. So, get out."

"Dad." Abbey's face paled at her father's tone and dark manner.

"Both of you."

#

Never in his wildest dreams did Ried imagine the highlight of his day would be sitting in the back of a Ute on a simple drive into town. He felt relaxed from a growing sense of freedom and smiling at the absurdity of how he felt.

The closer to Kingaroy they drove, the more signs of civilisation came into view. There were more power lines, and unlike the overgrown and neglected paddocks he saw after stealing Devil, the hills and fields they now drove through showed healthy signs of cultivation.

One property boasted a significant citrus orchard, while another grew what appeared looked like olive trees.

Ried pointed to a converted service station. If there's not much petrol, what are they selling for fuel?"

"Liquid methane mostly," replied Nicholas.

"Methane?"

"From a plant to the northeast."

An abandoned church they drove by stood out in stark contrast to the maintained farms. The weatherboard walls, after decades of sun and weather, had become a patchwork of bleached timber and decayed paintwork.

The bell tower, once the centrepiece of the church's architecture, lay scattered and broken in long grass and bramble weed near three dozen tilted or broken headstones.

On the outskirts of town, Nicholas pointed out a ramshackle cottage industry built on the remains of a light industrial estate. Most of the buildings consisted of rusted, corrugated iron sheeting, recycled brick, and timber slabs.

"What's in there?" Asked Ried.

"Tanneries, two or three blacksmiths, and one good old mechanic's shop next to a junkyard."

Ried followed where Nicholas pointed and saw rows of car bodies stacked five or more high. Trundling among the towers of vehicle corpses was a crane carrying the gutted remains of a truck.

"What are all the little buildings?"

"Those are shrines.

"Shrines?"

"For the Roman gods," Nicholas said. "See the most decorated ones. They belong to Plutus, the god of wealth." Nicholas pointed out another common one. "That's one for Vulcan, the smith god."

"Do you believe in their gods?"

"I grew up with them. So yeah, I suppose I do." He nudged Ried, "and don't ask Abbey or Dad if they do."

"Okay."

Half a kilometre down the town's main road, Dom pulled over opposite a grocery store. Farther along the street stood an impressive building with an ornate frieze on its gable. The buildings cared for appearance contrasting the surrounding, neglected, storefronts with boarded over windows and doors.

The heady scent of wood smoke and fresh bread wafted from a bakery on the corner of a laneway. Not every building hid behind timber boards. Ried spied a bric-a-brac shop and a weathered two-story pub. A group of uniformed men entered through the pub's wide double doors.

A distinct sound built in resonance. Ried tilted his head and frowned trying to place why he knew the sound. They stepped from the footpath to cross the road when the source of the low whine rounded the corner; sixty Vigiles patrol bikes sped by, followed by an equal number of armed men on horseback.

"It seems they haven't given up searching for you," Abbey said to Ried.

"Or for his nomad friends," her brother added.

Dom gave Nicholas a 'told you so' look before reaching behind the passenger seat of the Ute. When Dom found his prize, he pushed a faded, sweat-stained, broad-brimmed hat into Ried's hand. "Here. Put this on, just in case one of those blokes you let go is around and recognises you."

"You're kidding," Ried said. "That was over two months ago."

"This isn't a debate."

Ried shrugged and dropped the oversized and moth-eaten apparel on his head. "How do I look?" He gave a theatrical pose.

They all replied with shrugs and nods.

"Strewth. Talk about a tough audience," Ried quipped.

Dom took Abbey aside. "We shouldn't take more than half an hour at the clinic." He flicked a thumb over his shoulder. "You two wait in Maud's 'til I get you."

"I'd rather we wait at the café." Abbey stuffed her hands into her jeans and watched them walk toward the doctor's surgery, before following her brother and scrutinising the building with a 'must I' scowl.

The pub's rusty, corrugated, bull-nosed awning covered a full-length veranda, which also spanned the footpath. The front entrance doors were a three-metre-high, double-hung affair suffering from a haphazard and hurried repaint.

Intricate lead lights depicting flagons of beer, a slaughtered cow, and naked women decorated the top third of each door.

"Ugh. Talk about gross."

"Don't be a snob," Nicholas said. "Father's got a point. This'll be the best place to catch any rumours floating about." He opened the pub's door. "At least I'll get another chance to see Gemma." He beamed with joy.

"Who's Gemma?"

"Um… She's my… friend."

"A friend, huh?" She smiled at her brother's expression flushed with embarrassment.

"Just leave it."

"I've noticed you and Ben have been getting on these last few weeks."

"Except for calling me Nicky, Ben's not a bad bloke," Nicholas said. "Also, he doesn't patronise me like Father. But he's a bit of a contradiction."

"I hadn't noticed."

"Well, he is. He's got an odd sense of humour. He likes a drink but hates smoking, and he's easy to talk to. Even when he's sober. He can ride Devil better than Mom could, but when I ask what it was like to be a soldier, or what happened at the nomad camp, he shuts up and goes all reclusive. Like Father." Nicholas picked his earlobe. "I mean, what could be so bad about being a soldier?"

"Let's hope we never find out," Abbey said.

"Anyway, what's with you and Ben?" Nicholas asked, giving his sister's shoulder a light punch.

"I don't think there is a 'me and him,'" Abbey said with a little more regret in her voice than she intended.

#

Heading back down the street after seeing Dr Mitchum, Dom, and Ried found Abbey sitting outside the local café with a young man in a Vigiles uniform, who appeared three-too-many drinks past inebriation.

"I told you both to wait in the pub."

Ried walked up to Dom. "I don't think Abbey would be out here unless she had her reasons."

Dom flicked Ried a humourless, 'this is family' look.

"What's with him?" Dom pointed at Michael and looked around. "Where is your brother?"

"Dad, stop," Abbey snapped back. "We were inside, but we had some trouble. So, I thought bringing Michael out here would help sober him up," she explained. "Nicky is still inside with some girl called Gemma."

"I'm sorry, Mr Harris," Michael slurred. "Who are you?" He asked, spotting Ried.

"I'm a friend just helping out for a bit," Ried replied.

Michael's curious frown slipped beneath an idiotic grin, his head bouncing like a ball on an elastic string.

"Don't mind him, son," Dom said to Michael. "Can you make your way home?"

"My sister lives at the end of High Street," he stood grabbing the table. "Shit… Who's moving the ground… Thanks for the coffee, Abbey." He pulled an exaggerated face when he turned to face Dom. "Mr Harris, you mind your step with MacMahon and the others. The pricks had it in for Nick for ages," Michael gave a sloppy nod, adjusted his uniform, and then headed down the road taking a step back or sideways every few metres.

"Abbey," Dom eyed the old pub. "Is MacMahon the reason you two are out here?"

"Yes, but I'll explain later."

Ried leaned closer to Abbey. "Your drunk friends got a crush on you," he said with a wink and lopsided grin.

"Mike's not my type," she said, turning to hold Ried's eyes for a few seconds.

Oblivious to her gaze, Ried turned to Dom. "Who's this MacMahon bloke anyway?"

"An arrogant piece of shit," Dom said. "A few of us reckon he's pushing drugs, and on the take with–"

A sonic boom rang out from the pub doors followed by Nicholas who stop started as he crossed the street.

When Nicholas realised his family stood together and watched him, he paused and assert himself, but by the time he joined them, his eyes overflowed with tears.

"Nicky." Abbey met her brother first and put her arms around his shoulders.

"What's wrong, son?" Dominic walked in between them steering his son into the chair vacated by Michael.

"It's Gemma," he sobbed. "Maud's gone and sold her…" Nicholas dragged his sleeve across his cheeks and nose, "…to that fucking goon, MacMahon."

"Who's Gemma?" Dom shifted his eyes to his daughter.

"Nicky's girlfriend. I think." Abbey puckered her brow. "Hang on, Maud was holding a razor at MacMahon's groin before we came outside."

"It seems old Maud and MacMahon are playing some bullshit game." Dom's voice carried an edge of cold steel.

"Sorry. Did Nicky just say she sold her?" Ried asked.

"Yes. It's a part of the great Roman culture. Unfortunately, the idea made its way back to ours," Dom answered. "The Romans believe they had crafted slavery into a socially acceptable and civilised way of life." If rancour and disgust took human shape, then Dom became their vessel. "But the bastard, money-grubbing pricks amongst us seized the opportunity and ran with it."

Ried's stomach churned stinging his throat with bile. *I suppose some concepts manage to transcend galaxies and dimensions.* Well, universal behaviour or not, selling people was wrong. Plain and simple.

"For all their hypocrisy, the Romans tried banning and condemning any humans running a slave den," Dom fixed his glare on the pub's entrance, "except, it's all piss and wind. The only thing they did was create an underground black-market business." He walked off the footpath as a motorbike pulled up beside him.

Ried studied the bike. It looked like an old Harley frame with an LPG gas cylinder in place of the original tank. *Yet another thing to give this world a Mad Max feel.*

The rider cut the motor. "Dumb question. But is everything okay?" Jack asked.

Around his friends and family, Jack was a gentle giant with a mischievous sense of humour, but Ried sensed someone you should not take lightly.

"If you call selling young girls okay," Dom hissed, "then yes, everything is bloody fantastic." He started toward the pub.

"You three stay here," Jack instructed the younger adults as he hopped off his bike to follow Dom.

"Not a bloody chance," Ried said.

"No, son," Jack said. "You better keep a low profile."

Ried ignored Jack's instructions and kept pace with the big man. "Give me a break. For months, everyone has been asking me why I went back to help Gazza and his people." He looked at both men. "Correct me if I'm wrong, but I reckon it's the same bloody reason you two are going in there."

Dom expression gave Ried a voiceless, "wait here" command.

Ried lifted off the hat and waved it at Dom. "I'll keep this pulled down and stay behind you, but I am still going with you."

Dom nodded with a resigned sigh. Jack patted Ried's shoulder, and together, the three men walked across the road.

"Be careful, Father," Nicholas called out. "MacMahon's not alone."

Dom twitched his head in understanding, before continuing his march toward the pub.

"You know, I reckon your boyfriend might be okay," Nicholas said, cuffing away more tears.

"I told you, Ben's not my boyfriend." Abbey retorted watching Ried disappear through the door of the hotel.

Nicholas rocked his head back a fraction at his sister's terse reply. "Fair enough."

CHAPTER TWO

The three men paused in the foyers gloom. Once their eyes adjusted, they made their way to the bar. Resting against the bar beside Jack, Ried tipped his hat back to give the room a quick survey.

Jesus. Talk about the wild west.

A light blue and grey fog of tobacco smoke shrouded the expansive room. Wandering through the haze and between dirt and sweat-stained male and female farmers, mechanics and labourer's, the establishments working girls went about plying their trade. Drinking around other tables sat men and women whose trousers, skirts, blouses, shirts, and footwear showed themselves as anything but manual labourer's.

Near the opposite wall a few groups of men in the dark blue fatigues of the Vigiles drank, laughed, played cards, or hustled each other over a pool table made from red stained mahogany. All the pockets on the side facing the bar used calico in place of the tattered remnants of netting. Dogeared lengths of tape covered several long tears along the table's outer edge of the felt.

Why do cops always play pool? Ried pulled the brim of the hat down a little when one of the closest Vigiles glanced his way.

From the far corner a piano, an out-of-tune vocalist, and two guitars impersonated music in the background.

Their efforts ignored by most of the pub's patrons.

Screeching through the music came a voice calling out from across the room. Ried shifted his attention to the human shriek and did a quick double-take when he spotted the owner, a woman who he doubted would not be much over one and a half metres in height.

The woman's mouse-coloured, unwashed hair hung from her head and surrounded her pug-nosed features in a matted, pageboy-style cut.

She wiped her hands on a beer and food-stained apron tied over her grey cotton blouse; the linen stretched taut over her bulbous stomach below a pair of voluminous, semi-exposed breasts streaked in pale stretch marks.

"As I live and breathe…" The approaching woman's waddling gait went past comical as she approached on drumstick-shaped legs beneath a high cut a denim skirt. "Dominic Harris, what brings you and your friends here?" She asked, coming up behind Jack slapping his rump.

"Bloody cheek," Jack said.

"Maud," Dom leaned against the saloon's long, curved serving counter. "Do you still carry that old cut-throat?"

"What, not even a hello?" Her arms shot outward in theatrical shock revealing white crusted sweat-stained armpits.

"The razor?"

"Don't know what you mean," she rested her hands on her gelatinous hips and bat her eyelids.

"Come on, Maud. How long have we known each other?" Dom's surveillance of the room stopped on MacMahon, who held a young, red-headed woman with alabaster skin. After a long pause, he addressed Maud. "I know you sleep with the bloody thing."

When Ried caught sight of the group of uniformed men

capturing Dom's attention, the memory of the teenage boy wearing the same uniform laying dead flashed behind his eyes. He pushed the vision aside and studied the scene at the table.

Ried nudged Jack's arm and nodded where Dom's fixed his stare but noticed Jack's gaze had already homed in on the group with the young woman.

Ried frowned at the others in the room and shook his head. *What the hell is wrong with this lot? Any fool here can see she's there against her will.*

Balling his fists, Ried took a step forward, as Jack's hand on his shoulder – a simple reminder of their earlier agreement. Ried exhaled a hushed grunt from under the gentle restraint and moved back behind his friend.

"Now, cut the bullshit and toss the blade." Dom's consistent tone and steel-grey eyes emphasised the request.

Maud's own deep-set eyes swivelled in her round, face before producing her best "we're all friends here" smile.

Dom's expression and stance remained stoic.

In head tipping defeat, Maud lifted her skirt with one hand and slipped the razor from her garter.

"Shit. That image is not gonna go away," whispered Ried. *Talk about losing a dollar to find five cents.* The array of emotions crossing Maud's face, when she let go of the blade almost, made Ried laugh aloud.

"Charlie, you still have that old .38 and knife?" Dom asked, facing the crowded room. "How 'bout you come on out and then drop them both by the door."

"It's okay, luv. Do what Mr Harris says, hey."

Charlie shifted his bulk behind the bar. His head moved from Maud to Jack, then the stranger in the hat, and then resting his defiance at Dom's back.

In a blur of movement, Jack swept over, slapped his

hand on the back of Charlie's neck, and catapulted the surprised man's head onto the stained bar top. The force of the blow shattered Charlie's nose and drove his broken teeth through his upper lip.

Before Charlie's limp body could slide off the bar top, Jack clamped his hand around Charlies holding the .38 revolver. With minimum effort, Jack dragged the unconscious man over the counter, and let him drop with an unceremonious thud on the floor.

Kneeling beside the prone barman, Jack tossed Ried a wink as he slid a hunting knife from inside Charlie's boot. He gave the leather and bone handle an appreciative nod before throwing the knife into the rubbish bin near the door.

Jack held up the revolver. "Tch, tch. Don't you know guns are dangerous?" He patted the barrel of the pistol on the moaning man's bald head.

With deft hands, Jack flicked open the cylinder ejecting the bullets into his palm as he rose. He sidestepped back by Ried where he dropped the pistol in the bin.

"Keep 'em safe." He grabbed Ried's hand and passed him the ammunition.

Ried slipped the rounds into his pocket and bent down to collect Maud's cut-throat and followed Jacks lead by tossing it beside Charlie's weapons.

Impressed with Jack's speed and ability, Ried appreciated the company he now shared.

The quick altercation between Jack and Charlie silenced the singer, piano and guitar players.

The scraping of chairs and shuffle of feet across the discoloured, uneven floorboards drew Ried's attention from the prone Charlie.

At the back of the saloon, making their way toward the

door leading to the saloon's beer garden, Ried saw four men who displayed a fervent desire to leave.

The first man, dressed in overalls smeared in dry red mud, stumbled back into the room. The other three also hopped back in retreat when Nicholas and Abbey blocked their path.

With a snap of his wrist, Nicholas flicked the solid door closed and threw the top and bottom pad bolts home. The loud hollow thud of the door and the click-clack of the lock raised the tension within the pub from mute to palpable.

Without instruction, Abbey, and her brother ushered Maud's girls upstairs.

Ried smiled and wandered across to the diminutive publican and local madam. "Maud," he said, "I've not long bought myself a property, and I'm looking for some… company and they tell me you can help."

"Don't know what you mean." She put a hand on each hip and replied in horror. "It ain't legal."

"True," Ried's mind ticked in successive thoughts. "But if I wanted legal, I'd get married." Ried bent closer to Maud, his voice a conspiratorial whisper. "Well, how much for one of the young girls?"

Maud puffed out her ample chest. "What you playin' at." She flicked her thumb at Dom. "you ain't-a friend of theirs, or you wouldn't be askin' for paid help.

Ried draped his arm across her shoulder holding his breath at her sweet and sour body odour. "You're right, I'm not with them. I just happened to follow them in."

"Yeah, how come he gave you the bullets?"

Ried glanced back at Jack. "Shit, would you say no to somebody that big?" Ried continued in soft tones as he dropped the bullets into her apron pocket.

With everybody in the smoke-filled room focused on

Ried and Maud, Dom noticed one of MacMahon's associates slide off his chair, and retreat from the table.

"Don't leave on our account, son," Dom suggested in quiet.

The man paused mid-move before flopping back in his seat. MacMahon himself fidgeted under the older man's hard gaze.

Dom looked over his shoulder with a less than happy expression at the play between Maud and Ried.

Maud flicked a look at Dom and then the young stranger. "I reckon you got something crossed," she said, "cause you're barking up the wrong tree."

"Come on, Maud," Ried said, "I've done some research, and I know you've got good clean merchandise and I've got a saddlebag full of coin."

The compliment and mention of money caused Maud to weigh the stranger in a new light. "They ain't cheap."

"Fair enough." Ried made a great show of deep thought as he edged closer to MacMahon's table to look over the young redhead

Dom moved in near Ried and studied the five men seated alongside MacMahon. He offered them all a benign smile. Behind his back, Dom made his left hand into the shape of a pistol, before he showed two fingers on his right hand.

Jack hawked up some non-existent phlegm and nodded his head twice.

Ried saw the exchange and squinted a little closer at the table and its occupants. He counted three nightsticks and two pistols. Armed or not, those blokes are definitely outgunned.

"How much for this one?" Ried asked in a booming, clear voice.

MacMahon shifted and drew the girl closer. His intent and actions telegraphed she was his possession.

All the nearby customers exchanged various looks and glances. Their heads nodding in unspoken agreement: Move away and do it now. Chairs scraped across the timber floor; others toppled over. People bumped into tables, spilt drinks, and knocked over glasses in their exodus.

"No one leaves." The tenor and pitch of Dom's raised voice carried across the room. People shuffled, but no one left.

Wow, now that is what I call a parade ground voice. When Ried returned his attention to MacMahon's table, he spotted Jack walking with a casual air of indifference to one of the fallen chairs.

Ried held back a grin when Jack rested the chair on his shoulder. *Hell, there's no threat in that move at all.*

During the prolonged silence, Ried moved a step sideways making his position the final piece in corralling those at the table.

Maud sensed a storm coming and rushed up to stand near Dom. "Come on Mr Harris, let's go back to the bar. My shout eh…"

"Not all that thirsty," Dom said staring hard at MacMahon. "Besides you haven't answered him." He said tipping his head at Ried.

Maud shrugged and shuffled back to Charlie. "I've already told him he's barkin' up the wrong tree."

Ried tracked her movement in the looking glass hanging behind MacMahon. "Come on, Maud," Ried called out. "We're talking about you making an excellent profit," Ried said.

Maud fidgeted while skipping her eyes between Dom,

Jack, Ried and MacMahon. "I done told you before. She ain't for sale cause it ain't legal." She cast her eye over the patrons in the hope her lie convinced everyone her word rang true. The white stain under her armpits softened with added perspiration. It figured old man Harris was in town with that snivellin' little bastard of his. Her twitching gaze caught MacMahon's eye. And fuck you too…

Ried cast a look at Dom and then to MacMahon and then in the mirror at Maud. "I'll pay you, let's say triple what he paid."

Dom shot Ried an expression sheathed in fire.

"Hah, you got it wrong," Maud focused on Dom and called out with shaky bravado. "She ain't even the girl."

"Which girl?" Ried seemed confused by her statement.

"Whoever it is you're lookin' for."

"Funny." Dom turned to face Maud. "I don't remember anyone saying they were looking for a girl except him." Dom could not hold back his "got you" smile when he saw Maud's false bravado turn into spoilt beer.

"Piss off, you lot. The deal's been struck," MacMahon spat, standing up and pushing Gemma aside.

Maud's screech shattered the plate glass silence. "Hold your filthy tongue, MacMahon."

"She's mine bought and paid for." He emphasised his point by shaking her wrist, with his other hand resting on the butt of his pistol.

"Shit," Maud blurted out and went to the bin and faltered when a farm hand pulled it away from her. She glared at the younger man. "No more free booze or girls for you, Eddy Danaher."

"Shut your bloody mouth, boy," Jack's growl rolled across the tables.

Maud closed her eyes and pouted before flicking her

attention between Jack and MacMahon. "Shit and double shit…"

"Grownups are talking." Jack finished.

MacMahon's arrogant defiance wavered in an instant against Jack's tall, bearded hulk, and he sunk back into his chair, pulling Gemma onto his lap.

"Well, Maud, how about it?" Insisted Ried

Maud lifted a thin, dark-olive cigar from her apron, and lit it with an old lighter in her shaking hands. "Triple, hey?" She pulled back on the cigar. "All right, done deal," she said, exhaling the blue-grey smoke from between her teeth. "But I want your coin now."

Ried gave Dom a defeated look.

"Bullshit," MacMahon cursed. "I paid for her. So, she's mi–"

Jesus Christ, enough of this bullshit… "No." The word exploded from Ried with the concussion of an exploding hand grenade. He moved forward, but Dom held his hand out and shook his head. Ried inhaled, and then released the breath in a sigh of acceptance.

MacMahon glared back at Ried and rose from his chair. "What's the matter sport. Won't old man Harris let you off the leash? His taunt drew nervous laughs from his man around him but backed down when Ried barrelled past Dom.

Ried parked his face a nose-length from MacMahon's sweat sodden features. The rancid alcohol and tobacco smell on the man's breath polluted Ried's nose.

"You think you can?" MacMahon sneered.

"It'll be the easiest part of my day." Ried's poker-face stare matched his unemotional tone.

"Maud, give this officer back his money," Dom's command dripped with contempt as he came up behind

Ried to rest his hand on his shoulder. "Not today, son."

"Yeah, the old man's right. Not today."

Ried wanted to take the smile from MacMahon's face and shove it up his arse.

"Leave it be." Dom pulled Ried back by the arm as Dom brought his full attention back to MacMahon. "Papers?"

MacMahon sat back and crossed his arms. "Fuck off, old man."

"Papers." Dom snapped his fingers. "And your pen."

"Come on shit for brains," Jack said to MacMahon. "You do not want him to ask a third time."

Meanwhile, Ried stepped across placing a gentle arm around Gemma's shoulders and spotted MacMahon's fingers dig into Gemma's thigh.

Gemma's body scrunched from the pain.

Ried narrowed his eyes and slipped his hand around MacMahon's wrist and pinched his fingers into the soft flesh.

MacMahon's smug smile evolved into a painful sneer with the pressure of Ried's fingers crushing a nerve cluster.

Ried kept on his stone mask and increased his pressure watching MacMahon's fingers blossom open. With his other hand, Ried guided Gemma away from the MacMahon's lap.

When Ried released his wrist, MacMahon pulled his numb hand back and massaged the bruised flesh.

The young woman stiffened at Ried's touch.

"It's all good," Ried smiled. "No one's buying anyone. We just came to help you."

She shot Nicholas a desperate plea, and when he nodded with a smile, she faced Ried, Dom and Jack, ignoring MacMahon's hate-filled stare.

"What's your name, love?" Dom asked.

"It's Gemma, sir. Gemma Harris," she muttered with her eyes turned on the floor.

Ried's eyebrows almost launched from his face. Okay, I did not see that coming.

Gemma's announcement went off like a stun grenade amongst the patrons within earshot.

"You and Nicholas?" Dom asked her, glancing around to give his son a small nod and a hint of a smile.

Jack lowered the chair from his shoulder and scratched under his chin while Ried gave Nicholas a thumbs-up behind his back. From the stairs, Abbey moved beside her brother and gave him a hug.

"Yes, sir. A little over six months," Gemma said. "Maud knew about us." Her lashes pooled with released emotions. Her voice quivered with held back sobs. "But the old cow didn't care. To her I was just property," Gemma finished, wiping at the rivulets of anger trickling down her cheeks. "Maud even made Nicky pay when he…" Gemma cast her eyes down. "You know, visited me," she said between sobbing breaths.

Ried searched out Maud's reflection and held it in his hard stare.

"Shh, it's all right," Dom soothed the heaving girl. "You head over to your husband." He rested his arm on her shoulder and kissed the girl's shaking head.

Gemma ran over to Nicholas as Dom shifted his attention back on MacMahon. "Papers, on the table or I will reach down into that black throat of yours and tear out your spine.

"Come on Quince," the bald man beside MacMahon said. "Strewth the little sluts not worth it."

Jack lunged over and backhanded the man's mouth.

218

MacMahon unfolded a document from his breast pocket and threw it at Dom.

"You get nothing," Dom glanced at Maud's reflection. "Give the money to Gemma."

MacMahon leapt from his chair. "Like fuck, she will–"

Dom lashed out with the speed of a striking cobra and drove his fist into MacMahon's stomach.

MacMahon folded over from the force of the blow. With a swift follow-through, Dom grabbed the hair above MacMahon's neck and rammed his face against the worn, greasy floorboards.

With Dom's entire weight on him, MacMahon wheezed, gulping for air, and vomiting up his belly of beer and food.

Dom ignored the odorous puddle and leaned closer, whispering into his ear.

Seeing his friend beaten and held down, the bald Vigiles took a step from behind the table.

In response, Jack lifted the chair beside him and slammed it on the table showering the shattered chair across MacMahon's table and associates.

Many of the patrons swore, and a woman yelped in fright. The small, bald accomplice flinched and glowered, but held his ground.

Using the distraction, Ried raced in to snatch MacMahon's nightstick out of his belt and rammed the rounded business end into the man's throat. "What would happen if I turned the dial all the way around and squeezed my hand?"

The bald man sneered through his bruised bleeding lips. "You're all fucking dead men."

Dom stood up to put his hand on Ried's arm, easing it back. "All of it, on the table now," he instructed, and then relieved Ried of the nightstick.

When the others hesitated, Jack kicked the table. The remaining three men took the cue and tossed their belts and sticks on the table faster than a cracking whip.

Jack looked over at the young Vigiles who sat beside the bald man. "What's your name, son?"

"It's Oliver Edwards, sir."

"Okay, Oliver Edwards, take all this stuff, and throw it in the rubbish bin by the bar." Jack stopped the young man when he passed. "You look like a bright lad. I reckon you should find better friends, hey."

MacMahon clawed himself upright and moved closer to clutch a fistful of Ried's shirt. "Gallio and Mettius will kill you for this. Fuck, I will kill you for this."

Ried slapped MacMahon's hand away and retrieved the document which he then held above his head and wove his way around the saloon. "All of you lot, listen very carefully."

He turned to face MacMahon and his men. "Tell everybody, from this day forward, the trade in human beings has stopped. Forever!" He walked back to Maud threw the paper in her face. "It's wrong." He whirled back to the room. "Is this what you rebuilt your world for? The buying and selling of other people like cattle or worse? Like they were nothing?' Ried's tone went from commanding to one of pleading. "Christ, you've got to be better than that," he pointed at MacMahon's table, "or them."

Many returned his disdainful gaze with guilty nods and murmurs of affirmation. A few of the more intoxicated patrons motioned or told Ried to piss off. Others, out of their own embarrassment, focused on their drinks, hands, the floor, or their footwear – anything and anywhere to avoid Ried's accusing glare.

With Ried dominating the saloon, Dom detoured over to Maud, who fell back against the unconscious Charlie. "As for you," Dom's eyes reflected the hardness of diamonds, and his voice spat icicles, "The girl gets the money, and you'll hand back double for every cent my son paid you for seeing his wife."

"Yes, Mr Harris. Absolutely, sir... Consider the deal brokered." She trotted around the bar and into her office to return after several minutes to hand Dom a cash box.

Dom took the box, opened it. He looked at the money, not caring if Maud cheated him because he'd made a point. When he closed the lid, he noticed MacMahon and his men vacated the pub via the beer garden door.

Abbey, Nicholas, and Gemma came down beside Dom, who dropped the nightstick into the bin with the other assorted weapons. Nicholas hugged Gemma and then his father in a short, awkward embrace before he approached Jack and Ried.

"Thank you, Mr Bennett." Nicholas offered his hand to Jack who accepted it with a wink. He then turned to Ried with his hand outstretched.

"Anytime, mate." Ried accepted Nicholas's hand.

Abbey also walked up to Ried and gave him a kiss on the cheek with a whispered: "Thank you."

Jack patted Ried's shoulder and picked up the garbage bin of weapons. He followed Dom's now-larger family outside, leaving behind a deafening silence within the saloon.

Dom fell behind to ponder his son and newly found daughter-in-law walking with their arms entwined. He then noticed Jack still carrying the rubbish bin.

"You plan on keeping that?"

"Tempting." Jack considered the wastebasket with its cache of weapons and then walked into the café. He spoke with the waiter, palming him some money before returning to the others on the footpath. "They'll hold it for an hour or so, and then return it," he said, picking up his helmet with a lopsided grin. "Who'd have guessed your boy went and got himself married?"

"All these months and he never told me." The disappointment flowed with Dom's words. He studied his son and new daughter-in-law. "You were right, Jack."

"About what?"

"Time. It always tells you," Dom said, and then held out his hand to Jack. "Thanks for your support in there."

"Just like the old days." Jack beamed through his bushy beard when he clasped his friend's hand.

"And weren't you supposed to hang back," Dom frowned at Ried. "Not go in and announce yourself. Or ask about buying a girl."

"I don't reckon that was ever going to happen." Ried matched Dom's expression and tone. "Besides you charging straight to MacMahon told her you wanted blood. So, I added some confusion."

Dom grunted.

"The shit's gonna hit the fan over this," Jack said, getting on his bike.

"And we'll duck if it does," Abbey chimed in.

Jack let out a short burst of hearty laughter. "You lot are all bloody mad. You know that don't ya?" He yelled over the bikes loud exhaust.

Dom's eyes followed Jack down the street before his gaze landed on the Temple of Venus, built by the Romans in place of the old church they had demolished. "Do you think they got married in there?" He asked.

"Probably, but to be honest, Dad," Abbey said, "I don't care, just so long as they're happy."

"A real romantic. Just like your mother." Dom hugged his daughter. "Let's hope it's not a dying concept."

"What's not a dying concept?" Asked Ried.

"Romance," Dom answered.

Abbey flushed and rushed over to Nicholas and Gemma.

CHAPTER THREE

The next morning, Ried joined the Harris's around the dining table, discussing a small intimate barbeque for a post-wedding celebration. But by mid-morning, the plans for a quiet gathering escalated to include the entire town gathering.

It didn't take long for the entertainment ideas to grow into an intense debate about what Nicholas and Gemma should wear. With brother and sister lost in a warm discussion, Ried took the opportunity and asked Dom outside for a quiet word.

"What's on your mind?"

Ried scratched and tugged his ear in hesitation. "Now, this might sound weird, but something got me thinking about Dr Mitchum suggestion our two worlds were alternate, rather than parallel."

"Go on."

"Well, there was this kid in my class who had the same name as you. So, maybe the Dominic Harris I knew, is my world's version of you."

"Makes sense," Dom's voice softened, "because I reckon, I went to school with this world's version of you. In fact, we were pretty good mates."

"That'd explain a few things." Ried sat on the patio floor against a post. "Like why you've kept me at a distance and when you did look at me, I could see something in you would change."

"I'll be honest. Seeing what or who you looked like knocked me for a six." Dom fiddled with his wedding ring. "After Tom had cleaned your face, the first thought I had was you being Ben's son, and the more I saw of you... Well, let's say it stirred up long-forgotten memories."

"Because I reminded you of him?"

Dom shook his head. "Just the opposite."

"Okay, now you've lost me."

"Ben had a temper, and he knew how to push people around. But being young and his best mate, I accepted his flaws." Dom sat on a chair near the door. "When everything in our world started going to shit, it grew clear our opinions were very different." Dom's shoulders sagged.

"Just before our final year, the class broke out into a heated, political discussion. Not before long, it had turned into a full-on row, and soon, we both faced off shouting at each other. That's about the time I realised Ben's views had turned very militant.

"For whatever reason, I turned away and was struck hard from behind. I ended up in a coma for several months." Dom pushed himself from the chair. "I later found out Ben hit me with a stool. Of course, he got suspended and never came back."

"Do you know what happened to him?" Ried brushed a fly from his cheek.

"He joined the Praetorian guard," Dom said. "Then through the Wars, he'd gained the rank of tribune – a rare feat for a non-Roman. He even took on a Roman name. From what our intel reported, Ben had earned a reputation as a brutal, sadistic commander, whose belief in the Romans was absolute. When we met again, I was a lieutenant-colonel commanding what had become nothing more than a guerrilla army.

"One of our last jobs put us in the Coolum foothills on a search-and-destroy mission. After several days of hide 'n' seek, we'd were giving the bastards a run for their money. But the Romans called in more reinforcements. An entire legion of Praetorians, with Ben in command.

"Jack and I moved our boys around to support the local militia who'd copped a flogging. Our advance turned into a bloody melee of close-quarter and hand-to-hand combat." Dom's eyes and his voice drifted back into his past.

"Call it fate, or just dumbass luck, but Ben and I collided back to back. God, I flew into a rage after seeing the way he butchered my men. I went berserk. I suppose I vented eight years of fighting against him.

"I don't know how long we fought, but I remember him getting the better of me. I got desperate and called out the childhood nickname we used. When he heard the name, he stopped and stared down at me… For just a split second, the old Ben returned. But then the bastard in him came back."

Dom closed his eyes as the memory engulfed him. A full minute elapsed before he opened them to gaze into the horizon.

He continued with a tone of sadness and pity. "I took advantage of his weak moment and drove my sword hard up and under his ribs. My blood boiled with revenge and I kept pushing 'til I saw its tip come through his shoulder. We both fell, and I landed on top of him." Dom's voice changed tenor, "and I watched his life drain from his eyes."

The last comment from Dom resonated with Ried. He knew how Dom felt. His own time doing the right thing for his country and its allies had left its own marks. The kind that didn't wash away in the shower.

Dom's eyes refocused, returning from his past. He took a long, deep breath, which he released in a prolonged exhalation. "Thank you for not saying sorry," Dom said. "As someone who'd seen combat, at least you understand where I'm coming from. Besides, if anyone should apologise, it should bloody well be me saying sorry to you."

Before Ried could respond, they lifted their heads at the sound of a vehicle coming down the drive. When the armoured truck drew closer, Ried recognised the occupant in the passenger seat as the same Roman officer from the nomad raid.

Before the vehicle's wheels stopped, six armed Vigiles jumped out of the back with their rifles raised and aimed at Dom and Ried.

The Roman officer sat in the van for a full minute, with his black eyes fixed on Ried, before he climbed out to march up to Dom.

"Mettius," Dom called out. "Let me guess. You're here about yesterday?"

"This is an arrest warrant for you, your family, servants, and house guests."

Dom's composure slipped for half a second before he stiffened, stepped off the porch, and marched up to the Roman. By this time, the commotion had drawn Nicholas and the two girls outside.

"Anything my family has done is because of me–"

"Spare me your rhetoric of honour and bravado," Mettius spat back. "You committed treason by striking an officer of the Empire." His emotionless gaze considered Nicholas and Abbey and decided neither of the humans posed any credible threat. Then, he fixed his black-eyed stare on Ried.

"I see we can add harbouring a fugitive and murderer to your charges." Mettius studied Ried the way a doctor examines a new virus – deciding how best to eradicate it for the good of everyone.

Ried weighed Mettius in return. The shadowed image of a dead mother and baby replaced the Romans face. Ried straightened his back drawing a sharp breath to quell his anger.

Mettius eyed the two men and offered his best imitation at a smile.

The sight of Mettius's black on black eyes and his smile sent waves of tremors along Ried's spine. Ried doubted he would ever see a colder or more dead expression from anything or anyone. Except what Ried experienced went beyond fear. Because the alien standing before them epitomised everything imaginable about being a cold, and efficient killer.

"I should arrest you all," Mettius swung those obsidian orbs between Dom and Ried, "but my orders are clear." He produced a sealed scroll. "I have a pardon for your family and servants, on the proviso you and the off-worlder surrender, with no resistance."

"What's this off-worlder shit?" Ried ignored his internal warnings and put a foot forward and into the barrel of a carbine pressing against his chest.

Mettius strode up to Ried. "Do not test me," he palmed away the rifle, "or I will finish what I began... Regardless of my orders."

"Can I speak to my children first?" Dom interrupted.

"No." Mettius turned on his heel. "Put them in the back."

Four of the guards approached Dom and Ried, who, with no other choice, walked toward the van. One man, Ried recognised, was the young Vigiles from behind the woodpile. At the back of the truck, Ried turned to look back at everyone on the veranda.

When Ried paused, one of the other guards raised his carbine butt first and angled it between Ried's shoulder blades. However, the young Vigiles stepped in and grabbed the other's arm, before he could swing the rifle down.

Stepping up into the van, a familiar voice spoke from the shadows.

"Jack." Ried and Dom shuffled over to his friend sitting on the floor with both arms manacled above his head.

"I see the gang's all here," Jack said.

"Rose and the girls?" Asked Dom.

"They're good 'n' safe," replied Jack.

"You?" Dom eyed the split below Jacks eyebrow circled in dry blood above a mound of swollen flesh encasing his eye.

"I'll live."

When the van turned past the gate, an engine howled, and gravel ricocheted from the sides of the armoured car which lurched sideways.

Mettius barked at the Vigiles behind the wheel.

"Sorry, sir. It was the Harris woman."

#

Dom remained silent since the guards dropped the heavy iron grate over their cell. All he did was pace. Not even the evening's rainstorm deterred Dom from tracking back and forth, creating a shallow trench of red mud.

The same thunderstorm left Ried wet, cold, and shrouded in bleak emotions. *Now would be a good time for this to actually 'be' a real nightmare.* Ried curled into the foetal position under the wet blanket shivering so hard his back hurt while Jack leaned against the dirt wall sleeping.

Their captors traversed the galaxy and conquered worlds, but Ried thought their methods were more barbaric than modern, and a hole in the ground for a cell did nothing to dispel his theory.

Christ. Is there any bloody thing about this world that isn't a contradiction? Ried rolled over at an odd noise approaching their pit.

Several pebbles plopped on the mud floor and Gallio, humming to himself, stopped to shine a bright torch down on the three men.

Ried shielded his eyes against the yellow glare while Dominic glanced back at Gallio through the beam's harsh glare.

"I'd apologise for the storm." Gallio lifted his face and empty palm toward the sky. "Unfortunately, we have yet to control what Jupiter does with the weather."

"What do you want?" Dom asked.

Gallio's smile gave the impression of sympathy and friendship, unlike his eyes now bright with arrogant triumph. "You struck an officer of the Empire." He waved a finger at the three men the way a parent does with a naughty child.

"If he's what you consider an officer," Dom said, "maybe you should rethink your recruiting process." He moved across to the crude toilet, unzipped his fly and urinated.

Jack stirred awake. "What's with the bloody li–" Jack said. "Oh, it's just you." He slid from his wet cot and replaced Dom at the toilet.

Gallio's expression iced over. He straightened his back, all traces of levity gone. "Perhaps, if you offered a public apology to the men you insulted and attacked–"

"Piss off," Dom said.

Jack hawked and spat a wad of phlegm down the earthen toilet. "You're the one who should bloody well apologise."

"I should apologise–" Gallio frowned. "Why in the name of Mars should I apologise?"

Dom sloshed through the mud-slicked floor and lay down on the wet bed covers and rolled over, showing his back to the Roman. "If you honestly don't know, then it'll take too long to explain."

Gallio faltered, switched off the torch and marched into the dark.

#

The prison van pulled up beside Kingaroy's old town hall steps. The door opened and flooded the dark interior with bright mid-morning light.

Bundled from the van, Ried blinked to ease the stinging light stabbing his eyes. When his bruised retinas returned to normal, he raised an eyebrow at the friezes adorning the halls portico.

Supporting the panels of relief work, stood four Corinthian-style columns, and beyond those, the architecture of the building appeared unchanged from its original design – smooth, chamfer board walls, with an expansive overhanging soffit above several oversized hopper windows.

Gallio strode out to the steps from behind the pillars. His chest and shoulders set firm, and he oozed self-righteous pride as the sun reflected from his shining armour and full battle dress. Under his right arm, he carried a helmet adorned in a horsehair brush, dyed blood red, to match the cape folded back over one shoulder.

"I'd like to kick that smug alien prick's face," Jack said through swollen, bruised lips.

"Take a number," Ried quipped.

"Take a what?"

"It means get in line."

"Quiet, you two," Dom said watching the first of five cars pull over in front of the prison van.

"Who are all the people in the cars?" Asked Ried.

"The town council," Jack said.

"town council?"

"Each region has a six-member council as part of the truce accord."

Ried counted five people, two women and three men, climb the stairs. He shuffled around in his shackles. "It looks like the last one is running late."

Dom held up his cuffed hands and pointed up the stairs. "Actually, he was the first one to arrive."

"Ah," Ried said watching how Gallio gave a benevolent nod toward each member of the town council as they entered the hall. Once all the council members entered the building, two armed Vigiles pushed the giant double doors closed.

"I'm sorry, you two. It seems I've made a right bloody balls-up of things."

"Bullshit," Jack said. "You were protecting your family. Besides, the little prick had it coming."

Dom didn't get the chance to respond because Mettius walked around the corner to approach Gallio.

Several people who gathered across the street heckled the two Romans. However, a hard look from Mettius reduced the catcalls to sullen murmurs

Ried stepped around to check out a crowd of onlookers and then raised his eyes to the Centurion with the black on black eyes.

"It looks like our esteemed governor sent out the word about our arrest," Dom mused.

The guards on the steps ignored the prisoners, and watched the growing crowd with keen eyes, searching for any hint of trouble.

Gallio donned his helmet and strode before Dom. "For too long, the people of this region have shown little or no respect toward the Empire." He considered the crowd from beneath his dress helmet. "Well, today's hearing and sentencing will give them cause to think otherwise."

He glanced up at the fluttering assortment of flags. *Yes, today their appreciation of the Empire will change.* Gallio spared his prisoners one last glance before pivoting on his heel and marching with Mettius to the side entrance.

"Here, Sam Tobin. You should be ashamed of yourself." A woman's voice called out to one of the Vigiles guards from across the street after Gallio disappeared into the courthouse.

"Yeah, this whole thing is all bullshit!" shouted another voice, before a series of small bags exploded across the steps.

"Looks like someone's getting restless," Ried said when another paint bomb splashed on the steps nearby. He wiped the drop of the emulsion from his cheek. "Their aim could improve, though."

When the last liquid bomb ruptured on the stairs, the incensed guards who retreated, raised their carbines toward the crowd.

Ried stiffened. "Oh, shit." He flicked his head between the armed Vigiles and the vocal people, who ignored the implied threat of the raised weapons.

Jack eased himself between Ried and the steps. "Don't. You'd be dead in a heartbeat."

Ried grunted and crouched down in the shadow of the armoured car.

Ten minutes later, an official cavalcade of vehicles came down the road to part the crowd and pull up in front of the hall.

Four single rider motorbikes lead the cavalcade, behind those came four motor trikes, in front of two dark blue limousines. To the rear of the cars came four more trikes with four motorbikes in the back.

The large trikes piqued Ried curiosity and concerns. "Jesus. They have armoured trikes?" Ried said in awe.

"They call 'em chariots," Jack said.

"Figures."

The moment the cavalcade stopped, the eight chariots positioned their heavy weapons toward the gathering townspeople while the remaining riders lined the footpath between the vehicles and the town hall.

"Oh, shit," Ried and Jack repeated in a concerned tense whisper.

One rider read something other than fear in the three prisoner's eyes and body language. He shifted his gaze from the people gathered across the street, to the heavy weapons, and then marched over to the chariots, and spoke to the gunmen. They all gave a curt nod and pointed their muzzles toward the road.

"Am I right in saying those blokes aren't the local police?" Asked Ried

From inside the limousine, six men stepped out. Two of them wore bright, ornate togas – the first with dark blue and red piping, while the second man wore a bright, pale lime, with three broad bands of red piping laced with gold filigree.

"Strewth, Dom. What the hell is Marcus doing here?" Jack asked.

"What, that bloke in the dress is your former governor?"

"Yep."

"His name is Marcus Civilis Emeritus," Dom said. "The others are his entourage, and the blokes in the dress uniforms are his personal Praetorian Guards."

Ried studied the armoured Praetorians dressed in ink-blue trousers and tunics covered by bright, polished brass and black-gold armour, helmets resembling those worn by German soldiers in World War Two.

Attached to the wide leather belt around each soldiers' waist hung a sword, a pistol, a broad dagger, and an elongated oval plate with eight short rods protruding over the rim. Also hanging from their belts draped a curtain of gold studded strips across their groin.

"Those dish things with the rods," Ried asked Dom, "are they radios?"

"It's the boss and frame for their collapsible energy shields."

"Energy shields. Cool." Except, the expression on Dom and Jack's faces told Ried the shields were anything but 'cool.'

The leading Praetorian from the car approached Gallio's guards, who, after a second's hesitation, lowered their weapons. Each of their faces clouded over from uncertainty and shadowed guilt when confronted by a Praefecti Praetorio, an officer of the Senate's elite Praetorian guard.

Behind them across the street, the crowd shifted in a wave of murmurs.

"Oi, Marcus. You in on this too?" Shouted one man from the crowd.

The man in the lime toga faced the crowd, offering them a beaming, beneficent smile. "My good citizens and friends," Marcus's voice boomed. "I am here to ensure justice is dealt in a fair manner, and see those accused are served with its wrath or its blessing." Marcus knew he would get no verbal thanks for his political rhetoric, but when the protesters fell back of their own volition, he bowed his head in gratitude.

Marcus signalled one of his guards over and issued instructions for the men to stand at ease. When the guard's eyes darted to the crowd, Marcus placed a hand on the man's shoulder. "Centurion. Let us not give them further cause to stain these streets in blood."

With a salute, the Centurion marched away as Marcus approached the three men. The pallor of his face grew lighter, and his shoulders drooped at the sight of their clothes stained with mud, unwashed hair, and faces streaked with grime. *Gallio, what a reckless fool you have become.*

"Who authorised the use of chains on these men?" Marcus demanded.

"Primus Pilus Mettius, sir." The young driver of the van produced a nervous salute.

Marcus ignored the driver's salute. "Remove them." He clasped Dominic's hand. "I am truly sorry, my old friend." He reached out to shake Jack's hand. "You certainly looked better when last I saw you." With his greeting to Dom and Jack concluded, Marcus faced Ried. "Benjamin, please, also accept my apologies."

"Have we met?" Ried said rather than accepting the apology. "Or have you been looking through my wallet too?"

The proconsul raised his eyebrow at Ried's questioning rebuttal. He moved away to confer with one of his senior officers, who saluted and marched into the hall.

"Now," Marcus said on his return, "shall we go back and get you cleaned and fed?"

Marcus walked behind the three men with his arms spread out, guiding them back to the small truck. "For the sake of appearances, you will need to go in the van which one of my men will drive."

Ried let Dom and Jack climb in first as the crowd dispersed. When he stepped up, he watched Marcus and his guards enter the hall and then looked up at the series of friezes on the hall's facade.

Until then, Ried paid no attention to the designs adorning the gable. In the centre, at its apex, a raised effigy of a Roman eagle with wings spread wide and holding a laurel wreath above an embossed *IX*. Carved beneath the Roman numerals were the letters *S.P.Q.R*, and the figure of an ancient Spanish bull below the letters.

No way... It's just a coincidence.

CHAPTER FOUR

The prison vehicle carrying Dom, Jack and Ried, followed by Marcus's cavalcade drove through the gate of the Vigiles barracks. After stopping, the three prisoners stepped out of the van. The men from the first pair of bikes marched past Ried and inspected a small house near the west side of the parade ground.

"What the hell are we doing back here?" Ried asked.

The Praetorians emerged from the house and signalled the guards behind Ried and the others.

Marcus walked up with the escort. "Gentlemen, you will remain a guest of the garrison," Marcus pointed to the door leading into the small house. "Until the conclusion of our investigation."

Ried walked through the door followed by the rest. He counted four doors leading from a hallway starting from an open plan living, dining and kitchen area. He went over to the sink and tested the tap and searched the cupboards until he found a plastic glass which he filled, drank and refilled. Behind him, Jack growled

"So, we're still under friggin' arrest?"

"In a manner of speaking," Marcus replied, "yes, you are still under arrest." He pointed to a tall cupboard next to Ried. "In there you will find coffee, tea canned food and bread.

"What about Gallio and his butcher?" Asked Ried when he opened a cutlery draw to see only plastic utensils.

"Butcher? A rather apt description for Mettius. One would almost believe you have had prior dealings with the Centurion."

Ried pursed his lips while shaking his head. "Nope. I just heard stories."

Marcus offered Ried the hint of a smile. "Have no concerns regarding Gallio, he may be the Vigiles' Praefectus, the region's governor, and a Tribune in his own right," Marcus said. "However, I am the Legatus Augusti Pro Praetore."

"Which means what?" Ried asked.

"I outrank him."

"Fair enough," Ried said. "But if you outrank him, why bring us all back here and not let us go?"

"It's simple, son," Jack answered as he sat at the table, looking across at Marcus. "We're all bloody well guilty 'til they friggin' prove otherwise."

"Indeed," Marcus agreed. "However, you forget the vast legal advice, both civilian, and military, at my disposal." He focused on Dom. "It is unfortunate, but as I said, you must remain here in the compound."

"But not in the comfort of the guest quarters," Dom said.

"Yes and no, during each day of the inquest, you will be incarcerated in the pits," Marcus said, "and then at dusk, you will be escorted back here for the night. At no time will any of you be in chains." Marcus levelled his gaze at them. "Understand this – if you try to leave these quarters without a guard or permission, you will spend the remainder of your time in the box."

240

"I know I will regret asking this, but what is the box?" Ried wandered over to a window and scanned the open ground behind them.

"It is a steel container, 1.2 square metres in size, and is bolted to a small sledge to ensure it is always in the sun," Marcus joined Ried. He pointed toward the pits on the far left. "This time of year, those last three are in the shade for most of the day. We will provide clean blankets and fresh food for the day." He guided them back outside and led them toward their daytime holding pits.

"It was Abbey who told you what happened?" Dom asked.

"Yes, and I must tell you that your daughter voiced her concerns," Marcus considered how he should continue, "shall we say, rather passionately, regarding the whole affair."

"Abbey's her mother's daughter all right."

"Indeed. Your daughter presented some of the most colourful oratory expressions the floor of the Senate house has heard in quite some time."

Jack shook his head. "Strewth, Marcus. Just say the girl swore."

On the way to their respective daytime cells, Ried caught a pitiful moan echoing from the nearest pit. In the next cell, another voice sobbed between bouts of anger. Walking behind the others, Ried considered their Roman escort and again wondered about the disparity of this civilisation.

When they crossed the path, Ried recognised MacMahon lying on a bed in the second pit.

MacMahon looked up when they passed, fixing his eyes on Dom before directing his glower on Ried.

Ried paused. "So, your boss locked you up too." He gave MacMahon a wink. "Karma sure is a bitch."

MacMahon raised his hand and made a pistol with his fist to point at Ried and pretend to shoot.

"You missed," said Ried behind the raised middle finger of his hand.

After Dom climbed into his designated pit, Jack scratched under his beard. "Well, old Marcus is certainly keeping it real."

"So, how long will he maintain this bullshit charade?" Ried asked.

"Time will tell, son. Time will tell."

For the next few hours, Ried alternated between circling his cell, looking toward the sky, and playing tic-tac-toe on the dirt floor, the latter of which he soon tired of. So, he did push-ups, crunches and squats, until he reached the point of exhaustion. He then lay back on the bed contemplating the recent changes to his life.

Later in the afternoon, he grunted from his boredom and distracted himself by counting the giant blowflies, which buzzed and hovered in languid circles around the hole in the timber box over an abyss of putrefied, composting human waste. After a time, the thrill of counting flies soon became tedious. Besides, he kept losing count.

Ried flopped back down on the bunk. "See, Ried, this is what happens when you refuse to sleep on long drives. You end up on another Earth, in another dimension, dealing with Romans from space, and then getting chucked in a fucking dirt hole. Twice." He glanced at the toilet and sighed. "I'd give my left nut for a TV and a decent burger with fries."

Gallio entered his office in a controlled rage, further fuelled by the sight of Marcus sitting at his desk. He negated the obliged salute and approached his polished teak and rosewood desk and leaned across on his balled fists.

"What gives you the right to cancel the hearing and take my prisoners?"

"You forget yourself, Praefectus." Marcus pushed a scroll across the desk. "This will explain why." He adjusted his lime-green ceremonial toga before he refilled a wine glass.

Gallio snatched up the scroll, his knuckles white from his grip. He held the document and pictured himself beating in Marcus's skull with it. However, the two Praetorian guards behind Marcus dissuaded Gallios murderous desires.

"Forgive me, Proconsul." He looked down at Marcus, producing a false and yet convincing sycophantic smile. "I offer my sincerest apologies."

"You do?" Marcus raised an eyebrow at Gallio's impertinence. "Please, sit down."

Gallio sat opposite Marcus. He kept his back straight and inflexible, letting the scroll slip from his hand to roll across the table.

For the next several minutes, the two men sat in quiet reserve with Gallio refusing to let the proconsul's attitude diminish or penetrate his composure.

"You have been busy, and, I might add, somewhat secretive."

"Proconsul?"

"Dispense with the pretence of innocence, Gallio," Marcus said. "I assume you received the coded instruction to report anything beyond the norm after the unusual storm cell?"

"Yes, I received the instruction."

"Yet you chose not to respond. In fact, you instructed your science auxiliaries not to report what they found?"

"I didn't see the point of wasting the Senate's resources on a crashed motor car," Gallio replied.

Marcus shook his head and breathed a sigh of disappointment. "Ah, but not just any motor car." He unlatched a case and take out a portfolio file full of papers.

Gallio glanced at the file with a raised eyebrow. He then poured himself some wine with one recurring thought: *Betrayal*. "Decius," he whispered.

"You said something?"

"Yes. The name of your spy," Gallio said. "The senior officer of my scientific auxiliaries, Decius."

"Decius?" Marcus laughed at the suggestion. "Cast your suspicions elsewhere. Decius is too much the scientist to dabble in the dark art of secret diplomacy. In fact, his only vice is inadequate security and improper storage of his work."

"His security measures reflect the standards I expect of this compound."

"Yet I obtained copies of his work, his notes and various pieces of the off-worlder's vehicle." Marcus opened a folder bound with a blue, satin ribbon and read part of a page.

"The similarities between certain metallurgical attributes showed evidence of the base mineral elements, and the atomic structure of the alloys matching those of the ancient relics housed in the Senate emporium."

"If you are about to tell me that the off-worlder came from the same place our ancestors did, I should inform you, Decius, with our limited resources, had already presented a similar theory," Gallio studied Marcus. "You and the Senate. You don't really hold with that theory?"

Marcus paused in reflection. *How much should I tell him and how would he react if he knew the truth?* "It is indeed our strongest and best theory," Marcus poured himself another drink and looked back at Gallio. "Which would make us his descendants. In an obscure way."

"The whole concept is pure fantasy." The thought of his ancestors and the off-worlder coming from the same place, but at different time intervals in another dimension, insulted Gallio. "In truth, I don't care where he comes from. He killed several of my men, and publicly spoke out against our ways." When he finished, Gallio sat back with his arms crossed showing Marcus he considered the subject closed, and the off-worlder's fate sealed.

Marcus slid out his chair and walked in front of a window clasping his hands behind his back Marcus contemplated his next words and the early night for a full minute before he turned to look back at Gallio. "We found nothing to substantiate any of those allegations."

"WHAT?" Gallio launched himself from the chair. *More lies and betrayal.*

The two Praetorians moved between Marcus and Gallio, each with one hand on their gladius's sheath, and the other on the hilt of the sword.

Marcus waved his guards away. He seemed neither concerned nor threatened by Gallio's tantrum. Instead, he strolled back to the desk and produced another file, which he placed in front of Gallio. "Apart from the accounts by your Vigiles and those of Maud, no one else came forward to corroborate your men and their report."

"What of the off-worlder and his actions at the nomad encampment?"

"It is all there in the file," Marcus said, "There is no doubt somebody shot your men, but the descriptions of the unknown attacker were general and vague." He sat down, "and with the nomad camp now nothing but ash and burnt bodies along with no collaboration from a surviving member of the nomad clan. The Senate closed the incident due to insufficient evidence."

Before Gallio could respond, Mettius entered the office and gave a stiff salute.

Marcus left Mettius standing at attention with his arm outstretched for a full two minutes. "You wish to make a report, Centurion?"

"The prisoners. They are being escorted from the cells."

"Correct. Until completion of the investigation, the three humans will spend each night in the guest barracks and returned to the cells at dawn."

Mettius gave an imperceptible glance toward Gallio, who gave an even more subtle nod in response.

"You wish to add something else, Centurion?" Marcus regarded Mettius.

"No, Proconsul." Mettius snapped to attention with his eyes fixed on the far wall.

"Then, you may go." Marcus dismissed the Centurion with a casual flick of his hand. While Mettius made a point of saluting Gallio rather than the proconsul before marching from the room.

"I see your half-breed still tries to be a proper soldier of the Empire." Marcus knew the half-breed reference would gall Gallio, and he enjoyed seeing his governor struggle with his rancour at the term.

"He's a better soldier than most," Gallio looked sideways at the guards in the room, "including your precious Praetorian guard."

"He is no more an actual Roman soldier than this desk is." Marcus pointed after the departed Mettius. "Your… creature is nothing more than a well-trained pet."

"At least Roman blood flows in his veins," Gallio said. "You know damn well Mettius had proven himself on countless occasions. He is a true son of the Empire," Gallio held Marcus's stare, "regardless of the fact his father was Alterian and his mother, a Roman."

Mettius's entry and service to the Empire came about because of Gallio's guile and persistence. However, for Mettius, it meant he could never marry or father children. If he did, then those offspring would spend the rest of their lives in nothing better than slavery: the males turned into eunuchs, and the females sold to work in brothels until they died, yet, Mettius accepted such a sacrifice for the honour of serving the Empire and its glory.

"What about Harris and Bennett?"

"They will serve two weeks in confinement for striking a sworn officer of the Empire." Marcus put his hand up, stopping Gallio from voicing his thoughts. "I will take no further action on them. But, let us not forget why they chose such a course of action." Marcus consulted the file in front of Gallio.

Gallio flinched and found controlling his anger and frustration a continuing challenge. He closed his eyes and inhaled several breaths, using the small, rhythmic action to compose himself.

Upon opening his eyes, he focused on the wall behind the proconsul where two power lances hung in an X behind a traditional scutum above his legion's decorated banner.

Again, Gallio's mind filled with murderous thoughts. He calculated his chances against Marcus's bodyguards if he leapt across the room for the shield and a lance. He knew to fight the two guards in the confines of his office, and a third from those in the hall, would end with his death before he could strike a blow against Marcus.

No. You have not lived and fought for over a century to die such a wasted death. Especially with what is at stake.

"Sorry, what did you say?"

"Your Senior Constable MacMahon," Marcus repeated, "who, according to the witness accounts, played a part in the illegal sale of a citizen." Marcus held up his hand. "I say illegal because a Roman slave merchant had not brokered the sale." Disappointment reflected in his voice and eyes, as he tossed the file across the desk at Gallio.

"Not only did this Maud detain the girl unlawfully, but I found out this Gemma married Dominic's son over six months ago – in the house of Venus, no less." Marcus studied Gallio, waiting for a reaction before he continued. "The next part I found truly offensive," He continued. "Apart from keeping Gemma in servitude, this Maud also forced her husband to pay for conjugal time with his bride."

"Your friendship with Harris has clouded your judgement." Gallio dismissed the file with a swipe of his hand.

"And the growing paranoia you harbour for the man has clouded yours."

"The little slut never sought permission to marry," Gallio said in deference to Marcus's earlier statement. "I can assure you, you will find no evidence of illegal activity for the sale of the girl." In truth, Gallio didn't care one way or the other for the proconsul's moral debate or the legalities of slavery. He only cared about losing an asset. "The publican bought and paid for her via a Roman broker."

Marcus opened another file. "I assume you are referring to this." He produced Gemma's original bill of sale, taken from Maud's records. "It is a fraudulent document. An excellent one, but a forgery, nonetheless." He handed Gallio the paper.

Gallio studied the bill of sale. His outward countenance remained composed and aloof, but inside, his self-control faltered. *Damn those gypsies and their slave merchants. Thieves, every last pagan one of them.*

He sat up a little straighter, ensuring his tone matched his composure. "Thank you for bringing this matter to my attention," Gallio said. "I will ensure a full investigation is started—"

"Gallio, do not misunderstand what is happening," Marcus interrupted. "A thorough investigation is required. In fact, one has been underway for some time." He reached for the formal scroll Gallio had discarded at the start of the evening.

Gallio again accepted the scroll, and this time, he broke the Senate's seal and read the document. He glanced at Marcus with a confused frown before his disbelief let the parchment slip from his fingers.

"By what right?"

"I will repeat, an investigation is underway." Marcus leaned back and steepled his fingers. "The preliminary findings supplied enough evidence to raise a unanimous vote of no confidence."

"Unanimous? But you—"

"Recommended and instated you to be my successor." Marcus poured himself another wine. "Your recent actions now make me regret ever having made such a decision."

Gallio pushed the chair back. "What of the off-worlder?"

"Released with Harris and Bennett at the end of their two-week confinement."

"That decision will be our undoing." Gallio felt far older than his 175 years. The campaign to conquer this blighted planet handed him its last curse.

First, my son during the Russian invasion. Then, the death of my wife when their ship crashed and sank in the waters of the Antarctic. And now, the Senate usurp me from this post. Gallio stood and headed to the door with no formal dismissal or salute. He stopped at the door with his back to Marcus. "I am disappointed in you, Proconsul."

Marcus neither commented nor reacted to Gallio's comment. Instead, he savoured his drink and watched Gallio disappear into the shadows of the hall.

#

Six days later, in the holding cells, Ried lay with his back on the dirt, and his legs bent over the bed frame. He had counted his thirtieth stomach crunch when Mettius blocked the sun.

"Huh. That time already?" Ried gyrated on his backside to lean against the timber bed, knowing he would get no reply from his stoic observer. He squinted through the grate covering the pit and tilted his head to the right and then the left.

"So, what do you want to talk about today?" Ried snapped his finger. "Oh, I forgot. You're one of those blokes who just like to watch." He stood, dusted himself down, and sat on the edge of the bed. "Here's the thing. I've had a gutful of you and your bloody voyeuristic shit. So, either say something, do something, or fuck off."

He rolled himself out on the straw mattress and ignored Mettius by tucking his hands behind his head, focusing on the clouds, reciting a few songs, and then closing his eyes.

With his eyes shut, he concentrated on the sounds around him – anything to take his mind off the Roman's perverse, ritualistic stares.

After a few minutes, Ried expected to hear Mettius's retreating feet crunch across the gravel. Instead, a handful of stones trickled into his cell, followed by a shadow sliding along the pit's earthen wall.

When Ried turned around, he found Mettius standing on the grill, pointing his sword in a relaxed grip above Ried's chest.

The sun glinted against the polished blade pointing at Ried as alien, and human contemplated the other in unwavering silence. Ried breathed in a steady breath and shifted his eyes from the sword to stop and shudder at Mettius's cold half-smile beneath his alien, black on black orbs. Then, without warning, Mettius raised his face skyward, sheathed the gladius, spun on his heel, and strode away from the pit.

Ried tilted his head to track the sound of Mettius's receding footsteps, unable to shake the disconcerting sensation of becoming an unwanted addition to someone's menu.

#

Two weeks later, from his vantage point under the shade of the governor's veranda, Marcus watched the activities outside the gates of the Vigiles compound. With orders to stand down, the captain of the guard watched the people gathering at the gate. Like the proconsul, the captain seemed intrigued by the people's reaction after the three men appeared.

During the emotional praise and cheers, Dom's family and friends closed ranks around the three men, as they crossed the street to drive off in their various cars and utes.

Marcus brushed a fly from his cheek watching the dust trail of the last vehicle disappear from existence across the nearby paddocks. The scene and the people's reactions convinced Marcus, his choice in Dominic had been the right one. So long as he could control the man from the shadows, and without his knowledge.

However, the people's response to the off-worlder gave Marcus cause for thought. *Perhaps, Gallio's prediction was not so infantile in its premise. Which means, Benjamin James Ried will need a subtler strategy.*

Marcus sighed and meditated on his next course of actions surrounding Dominic and Ried. Both, he feared, would tax all his clandestine tactics and abilities.

"Forgive my impertinence, Proconsul," his assistant interrupted. "What if Mr Harris chooses not to accept your offer?"

"Then, you will have the promotion of a lifetime," Marcus replied.

CHAPTER FIVE

Twenty-four hours after Dom, Jack and Ried's acquittal, the backyard of the Harris residence became a maze of tables, gifted with food and desserts. Under the eaves against the house, two, crude, four-metre benches of sawn timber lay hidden beneath kegs, crates of homemade beer, spirits and sweet drinks.

Hay bales lined the fence between upended empty wine barrels. A collection of pallets and logs draped in ribbons overlooked a dance floor of plywood. In the stage, the members of a bush band tuned their instruments.

Molly, Abbey, Nicholas and Gemma fussed about the growing number of partygoers. Ried wanted himself to relax and enjoy the moment. Instead, he prowled amongst the throng casting glances beyond the party.

"Whatever your looking for won't happen here," Dom said behind Ried.

"How can you know that?".

Dom shrugged, "I don't." He handed the younger man a beer, "but my gut does." Dom patted Ried's shoulder and joined a group near the bar.

Ried pulled back on a long draw of the beer and massaged the scar on his shoulder and then did a casual patrol amongst the wagons, cars and trucks. *Come on Ried stop being paranoid and enjoy the party.* Yet the vision of Mettius standing over his pit kept screening through his thoughts.

By seven o'clock, Dom stopped mingling and left the party to the young and energetic. Two weeks of imprisonment, well treated or not, was not something a man of his age recovered from in a matter of hours. So, he chose his time and made his way to the front patio with Dr Mitchum in tow.

"How do you feel?" Asked Mitchum who joined Dom on the front veranda.

"For the love of God," Dom complained. "If you ask me how I feel one more time—"

"I'm your doctor and your friend, so I'll damn well ask it when I bloody need to."

"I'm tired, but otherwise, I'm all right."

Mitchum gave a mollified grunt and sat down. "So then, are you going to do it?"

Dom pursed his lips, and his head dipped between his shoulders.

Mitchum dismissed the response with a curt wave and returned to the party.

From behind the house came the crash and clatter of plates, followed by raucous laughter.

"Sounds like they're enjoying themselves," came a comment from the dark.

"Bloody hell," Dom twisted toward the voice, "I'd forgotten how flaming quiet you are." He pointed to the chair beside him. "Where's your toga?"

"I did not think it was suitable attire." Marcus moved from the shadows dressed a long-sleeved, cream, cotton shirt and pale-blue chinos, with a matching black, leather belt and riding boots.

"And you'd be friggin' right," Jack voiced his agreement after he stepped out of the front door carrying two beers. One of which he gave to Dom and keeping the other for himself.

"It is good to see you at home again." Marcus held out his hand.

"You know damn well it's not my home," Jack responded, accepting the offered hand with a reserved shake.

"Still guarded, I see."

"Still the politician, I see," Jack shot back. "Tell me something. If you had always planned on dropping the charges, why'd you keep us, prisoners?"

"A necessary illusion," Marcus smiled back.

"And choosing Dom for governor. Is that also an illusion?"

"Politics, mate. Nothing but politics." Dom leaned toward Marcus. "You got the Senate to agree on me as governor, so the people would stay in line."

"Ah, nothing slips by you, does it, my old friend?" Marcus seceded with a head tilt. He studied both men. *It would seem Dominic and the hair-suit, Jack Bennett, understand more keenly than I recall.* "Dominic is right. Gallio and his own propensity to elevate his status along with his associate's behaviour left us little choice." Marcus locked his gaze on Dom.

"Assigning a Roman to replace Gallio meant we could not ignore the risk of this region falling into rebellion. However, promoting a non-Roman with Dominic's character and history would move us all to a… more unified end." Marcus batted away a hovering cabbage moth. "The sad truth is that our choice of Gallio proved somewhat damaging."

Dom held Marcus's gaze. "Speaking of damaging, what'd you do with him?"

Marcus lifted his chin in contemplation. "He has been… recalled."

"Bloody hell," Jack mumbled over his beer. "Why do politicians never give a straight bloody answer?"

"All right, I'll do it," Dom blurted out.

"What?" Jack spluttered on a mouthful of his grog.

"You will?" Marcus raised an eyebrow. "I sense a proviso is coming."

"You're damn right." Dom pushed himself out of his chair. "I'll do it on the proviso we get complete annexation."

"Full annexation will be a difficult sell," Marcus conceded.

"Well, Proconsul," Dom paused, "if you want a unified end to all this, you better start working on a good sales pitch. Gallio and his thug have put the whole region on a cliff's edge."

"And you just said the Senate's worried about rebellion," Jack finished.

"Which the Senate would ensure ended with a quick resolution," declared Marcus.

"You're right. It would be short," Dom still considered Marcus, "and they know what the actual cost would be." He rose and made his way inside.

"Oi, where you off to?" Jack chased after Dom.

"To join the party," Dom waved his empty glass. "And get pissed."

Planting himself on a hay bale beside Dom, Ried asked. "So, this Marcus bloke," Ried eyed Marcus sitting aside from the revellers with the two men. "What's his game?"

"His game would be anyone's guess," Remarked Dom. "Marcus is a decorated soldier, and one of a dozen Romans of notable rank who survived the wars," Dom said. "Between us, we turned a bunch of starving people and a dying town into a profitable and healthy community."

"It must've been challenging work." Ried tried to fathom the complexity of rebuilding a broken world and remembered what the core of engineers went through in Afghanistan.

"Too bloody right," Dom smiled with pride. "With Marcus's help, we built the solar and methane plants. Within two years, people wandering the bush came into town, and its population increased."

"Except for the Nomads?"

"Not everybody agreed to the truce."

"Is that why the Romans are hunting them down?"

"Others, Roman and human see the Nomads as a pervasive threat."

"I'm guessing you aren't one of the others?"

Dom saluted with his beer. "My only concern is if some person or persons got the different clans to unite."

"Are there many of these clans?"

"More than they know," Dom said watching Marcus. The Romans talk a good front about unity, but this is a very fractured country. Gypsies, Nomads, Romans and the southern regions free people. All of us moving around on a spinning top trying to maintain a balance."

"Is that why you and Marcus worked hard at rebuilding?"

"I did it to grow stability, commerce, and I wanted the truce to be a less one-sided affair. As for our esteemed proconsul, I think Marcus saw what we did as something else." Dom sipped his beer. "We gained so much from a growing agricultural, primary and blue-collar industry, but we had lost things too." Dom's pride faded into sadness. "In a way, what I did became a double-edged sword."

"How's that?" Ried found the homebrew easy to drink.

"Because the Roman generals and tribunes used what Marcus and I had accomplished to rebuild their own version of government."

"And your mate Marcus was one of those generals?"

"Yes." Dom admired how quick Ried understood things. "And the bastard played his political hand well." Dom put down his empty glass. He squeezed Ried's shoulder in a firm parental grip. "So, you mind Marcus. He might claim friendship, but I wouldn't trust the bastard as far as I could throw him." He patted Ried's shoulder and went inside.

Over the next hour, Ried tried mingling, but he felt like a zebra amongst the wilder beasts. After some smiling nods and the occasional pat on the back from people he didn't know, he made his way to the makeshift bar and helped himself to another drink.

"If you're drinking Nielsen's homebrew," Abbey said behind him, "you might want to go easy on it."

"Hey there." Ried turned and smiled at her. "It's not so bad. Especially after the nomad stuff."

Abbey leaned on the bar, her elbow and forearm brushing against his. "I'm sorry I haven't seen you much since the party started."

"That's okay," he replied. *Jesus, Ried. Is that your best line?*

"Well then, I'm glad you're 'okay' with it," Abbey responded with a touch of frustration.

"No... I'm not– Well, I... I am, because I know you've been playing hostess–"

"Playing hostess..." Her frustration shifted to annoyance.

"Don't look at me like that. I didn't mean anything by it."

"Ben?"

"Abbey?"

"Are you married?"

"Married." Ried laughed. "Ah, no. Why?"

Abbey squeezed his hand, and gave him one of her unreadable smiles, before she took her drink and headed toward Jack's wife, Rose, and their two daughters.

Bloody hell. What'd I say now? Ried watched her cross the yard, once again admiring the way her hips gave slight twerks with each step. He sculled the rest of his drink.

He switched his beer glass for a stronger drink and wandered over where a group of revellers gathered around the doctor and Jack.

For a few seconds, Ried locked eyes with Marcus, who raised a glass in a salute before continuing with the card game he and two impassive men played. *Strewth. Why not wear a sign saying we're his bodyguards?*

Out in the dance area, Ried saw Nicholas and Gemma hugging each other – oblivious to everything around them – their moves slow and out of sync with the gypsy bands.

Is that what love does? Makes you dance to a different tune?

Near the band, which belted out a rowdy tune, Abbey and Rose laughed and joked. Yet, during the entire conversation, Abbey stole glances at Ried over the rim of her glass, while playing with her hair and ear.

On at least two occasions, Ried smiled back, before a loud roar from the group around Jack grabbed his attention, and he joined the chorus of cheers and calls.

"G'day."

"G'day," Ried replied, shaking the offered hand. "What's going on?"

"These two buggers do this all the bloody time," the other man said and then wiped a tanned hand across his tobacco-stained moustache. He roared out a gravel-throated cheer when Jack downed another glass of liquor. "Ol' Doc Mitchum challenges Jack, and the next time, Jack will challenge the Doc."

"Who normally wins?"

"Ol' Mitchum. Every bloody time." He gave a shout when Mitchum flicked his head back to gulp down the liquor and waving the empty glass.

Jack burped a harrumph and raised his glass sloshing some of the amber liquor. The watching crowd went quiet. Ried shuffled closer, hypnotised by the slow, unsteady action of Jack lifting the glass to his lips.

Ried saw something shift in Jack's posture and took a swift step back.

The inebriated bear called Jack, pulled his chin back, swallowed and let slip a long-muffled burp with an odd expression in his glazed eyes.

Those closest to Jack followed Ried's lead and also took a step away. Someone from the group tossed a bucket at Jacks feet.

Jack flicked the bucket away with an unsteady gait and, in silence, while still holding the glass centimetres from his lips. He landed like a falling elephant amongst the cheering crowd.

Two drunk but brave souls tried to catch Jack, which resulted in all three men tumbling to the ground and scattering several others like falling bowling pins.

Mitchum jumped to his feet, belching a drunken exclamation of victory before he too passed out in the arms of the nearest onlookers.

Shaking his head in bewilderment, Ried helped carry the unconscious men into the house.

The end of the game also seemed to announce the end of the night. He laughed when he heard wives berating their drunken husbands, while they smiled and thanked the Harris household for the party.

The night air filled with an eclectic mix of noises from the clattering clip-clop of horse hooves, the assorted rumble and clatter of engines, and the raucous laughter of drunken men mixing with the debate about who would drive. When the last vehicle turned onto the road, the scrapping chirp of crickets and the occasional burp of frogs soon filled the silent void.

Lost in his own reflections, Ried collected the abandoned plates and glasses left scattered about the backyard and stacked them into piles on the tables.

"Domestic duties suit you."

"Shit." Ried dropped the plate he was scraping clean.

Behind Marcus stood the two men who played cards with him through the night. "I guessed they were yours."

Marcus leaned on the table beside Ried. "You do not trust me?"

"After what I've seen," Ried returned to cleaning the plates. "The answer is tipping in favour of no, I don't."

Abbey came over and slid her hand through Ried's arm.

The action raised a benign smirk on Marcus. "Well, I cannot blame you." Marcus dusted the sleeve of his coat and then asked his bodyguards for some chairs. Before Marcus sat, he gestured for Ried and Abbey to sit with him. "After all, your brief time in 'our' world has been less than inviting," Marcus said. "The incident at Maud's." Marcus lit himself a long, thin cheroot. "And your regrettable involvement at the nomad compound."

Ried shuffled in the chair as every muscle locked in tense readiness. "What do you want?" His internal warning chimed, and his mind replayed Dom's recent words.

"If you knew about Ben and the raid," Abbey squeezed Ried's hand, "then why did you let him go?"

"Power and politics." Ried held the Proconsul's gaze.

Marcus gave Ried a hurt look. "Benjamin, I wish to make things right between us, and I also desire to know you better. Which is why I would like you to stay in a small villa at my estate. The view from its front deck is marvellous."

"You're kidding." Ried sat back with his arms crossed.

Marcus sighed. "No, the offer is real, as is the view," The casual levity in his voice hardened. "And may I suggest, you do more than consider it." Marcus rose as did Ried. "It would be awkward for all parties involved should the Senate learn of who you are and your involvement in the raid." Marcus stepped back with a smile and squeezed Ried's shoulder. "I will be here for another week, ensuring Dominic is successful in his transition. I expect your acceptance by the time I leave."

#

The following morning, Abbey hammered on the cottage door until Ried unlatched the lock and let her in.

Ried's bloodshot eyes and grey complexion halted Abbeys entrance.

"God, I was wrong about no such thing as Zombies."

"Hilarious," replied Ried in a voice sounding anything but.

"Benjamin, you need to tell Dad,"

"Morning, Ben. How'd you sleep?" He quipped when she stormed past him. "Not good, Abbey, but thanks for asking."

"Well, will you?"

"I will, but not about the threat." Ried dragged himself to the kitchen area.

"Why not?"

"Because we both know, Dom wouldn't take the job if he knew." Ried set to lighting the stove. "I'll tell him that I want to leave so I can learn more about this world." He abandoned his efforts to set the kindling alight.

"I know you want to see more, but not this way." She backed away when he approached. "I won't bloody lie to Dad," Abbey said with crossed arms.

"C'mon, Abbey. You're being unrealistic and–"

"Don't you even think of saying overdramatic." She marched up to him, drilling her finger into his chest.

"Bloody hell," he barked, rubbing his chest. "It would only be 'til Dom got settled into his new role."

"Bullshit." She whirled and took three paces and then whiplashed around and retraced those three steps in two quick strides. "I don't trust him to let you go and… and… Well, I don't trust him." She sniffed back and palmed away an annoying tear.

"I don't trust him either…"

Abbey ran from the cottage.

He squeezed his hand around the kindling, but the little hardwood splinters pricking his palm did nothing to assuage the guilt stabbing his heart.

After lunch, Ried sat at the table in Dom's dining room, listening to the mood around him as everyone discussed Marcus's threat and its ramifications.

"All the debates and whining won't change anything. You all need to understand, Marcus will take Ried by force if he refuses to accept the offer," Dom said.

"I knew the bastard had something planned," growled Jack sitting in the creased clothes he wore at the party. "Alien pricks, the lot of 'em."

Ried pushed himself from the table. "It's settled then."

"No, it's bloody not." Abbey shot a "don't you dare let him go" look at her father, who glanced at Jack for support.

"I have to go." Ried's eye contact drifted from Abbey to everyone else around the table. "At least this way, Marcus will keep his word with Dom, and I'll be under his watch."

"I don't understand." Nicholas frowned.

"To Marcus and the other Romans, Ben is an added threat in an already unstable region," Dom explained. "But Marcus also knows he needs to keep Ben safe, so I will remain an ally and a loyal citizen."

"So," Nicholas said, "if Ben stays, Marcus is afraid it will trigger some sort of rebellion?"

"Like I said last night, it would be bloody and short," Jack said.

"It wouldn't matter," Mitchum interceded. "History has proven time, and again even a small rebellion has long-term repercussions."

"Jesus. We're going in circles." Ried rubbed his scarred shoulder. "I'll phone him tomorrow and tell him to expect a house guest by the end of the week." He pushed his chair under the table and walked from the room.

Tears welled up in Abbey's eyes. "I'm going with him."

"You can't, Abbey." Dom's voice drowned with sadness and sympathy.

"Why not?" Abbey pleaded in the tone of somebody who reached a wall too high to climb.

"Because others in the Senate will use you as leverage against Marcus and me."

A single tear rolled off Abbey's chin. With an angry swipe, she wiped her eyes and nose. "We can't let him go alone."

No one replied. In the kitchen Molly's lunch preparations copied the anxiety, Nicholas concentrated on the edge of the table. Gemma wrung her hands. Abbey fixed her gaze on her father's downturned face.

"He won't be alone." Jack broke the awkward silence. "I'll be with him."

Except for Abbey, everybody threw weak objections at Jack.

"How the bloody hell is that better?" Dom's question silenced the room.

"Because I'm not your daughter."

"What about Rose and the girls?" Asked Dom.

Jack's face contorted. "She'll be fine. Rose will understand…"

Nicholas pursed his lips and leaned his elbows on the table, his words flowing fast. "Father will be in town at the governor's house. Molly and William can look after Mr Bennett's farm, and Mrs Bennett can move up here." He stood and moved behind Gemma and locked eyes with his father. "Me, Gemma, and Abbey can take care of them and the farm." He looked at his father. "I reckon being governor will be enough for you to deal with."

"All right, it's settled." Jack gave his quick response. He slid his chair back and walked around the table. "I'll see you lot in a couple of days." He offered his hand to Nicholas and scratched under his beard. "I reckon keeping the boy safe from those mongrels will be easier than telling Rose."

#

In the Vigiles compound the following day, Marcus sat in Gallio's office signing scrolls, reviewing plans, and getting the final documents ready for Dominic's acceptance and signature.

At midday, a Praetorian officer marched across the carpeted floor, and stopped a half-metre from the desk, offering a crisp salute.

"Arillius," Marcus said, "have we word from our emissary?"

267

"No, and he is past overdue."

Marcus threw the stylus he held across the desk. "Gallio better not think he can play us for fools." He leaned back in the chair and pursed his lips to release a long, frustrated sigh. "This debacle needs to end. Quickly."

Tribune Arillius saluted, turned on his heel, and marched from the office with a smile.

Rocking in the chair, and lost in thought, Marcus ignored Arillius's departure. The disappearance of Gallio disturbed him. It was the former governor's lack of action that Marcus found most troubling because it contrasted with the soldier's normal behaviour. *And now, Dominic and his ridiculous notion for independence* – a request Marcus had not predicted, and therefore, had not prepared himself to deal with.

Alone in his office, Marcus worked through the afternoon to devise various means of ensuring Dominic performed his role of the governor under Marcus's veiled guidance and skirt the ridiculous notion of annexation. However, should Dominic pursue the desire for independence, it would need the creation of darker politics to destroy the dream. In his mind's eye, Marcus sketched the mechanics.

First, invite a small but measured amount of violence and rebellious acts upon the weaker senators. Then, implicate Dominic and those closest to him. Dominic's impeachment would, of course, end with a tragic outcome. The entire affair proving how humans are incapable of self-governing in peace. Thereby allowing the quorum continuation with their plan to gain absolute rule.

As for the off-worlder, I will hand him over to the Frumentarii, as initially intended.

Pleased with the foundations of his plans, Marcus poured himself more wine when Flavianus rushed into the office.

Flavianus bounced on the balls of his feet. His short, string bean body looked almost comical with his agitation.

"Calm yourself, Flavianus," Marcus said.

"Proconsul, the... Praefectus Castrorum you sent has... um... well, returned."

"About time–" Marcus looked over to the door at two of his Praetorians setting down a timber chest made from rough-sawn slabs.

Seeing the box, Marcus sighed. He controlled his rising anger at Gallio's melodramatic action – sending the Praefectus's head back in a box.

Marcus rose and walked over to study the chest, and how it settled into the plush carpet. With a cautious hand, he lifted the lid and then stiffened, his blood colouring his cheeks the way mercury rises from heat.

Removing the closest Praetorian's sword, Marcus probed the foul-smelling contents, the late Prefectus Castrorum, layered by the red-black ooze of congealed blood.

Marcus handed the sword, smeared with gore, back to the guard. "Remove this from my sight." Marcus adjusted his cloak and stared at the dark puddle on the carpet.

"Pointless and archaic barbarism!" He sidestepped where the grate rested and marched into the hall accosting Flavianous. "Who delivered it? I want them arrested and the flesh whipped from their bones." His tone dripped with ice and venom.

"According to the guards at the gate, it was the local veterinarian, Lester Jennings."

"The vet?"

"Yes, sir. It seems several Vigiles stopped the vet and instructed him to deliver it as a matter of urgency."

"Where is Jennings now?"

"In the hospital."

"The hospital?"

"Yes, sir. When the centurions opened the crate for inspection, the vet saw the contents. They both report the man had vomited, before falling back in shock, striking his head against the rear of his truck."

Stepping outside and into the fresh air, Marcus closed his eyes, taking several long breaths to wash the bitter metallic taste from his nose and throat, and counted backwards from one hundred.

After his meditation, the proconsul wondered what game Gallio was playing, when the Vigiles Tesserarius marched up to Marcus.

"Cassius. Whatever it is, can it not wait?"

"I don't think it can wait, sir."

Marcus studied the guard commander's agitated state and took the report to ease his suffering. He opened the folder and read the contents. "Thirty-six men deserting their post?"

"Yes, Proconsul. They also broke into the armoury and equipment stores and released MacMahon and the other prisoners from the cells."

Marcus prowled the lawn and dismissed Cassius with a wave. "Horses killed, and the patrol bikes sabotaged? These are acts of treason. Gallio and his pet must be insane." He flicked the file at his assistant. "Did the vet at least say where he took possession of the crate?"

"Yes, Proconsul." Flavianus trotted after Marcus, who entered the house and marched down the hall. "Near where the raid occurred against the local Nomads."

Marcus raged back into the office. "Flavianus, I want every map of the region on my desk within the hour and send for Cassius." He pointed to the port wine wet patch. "And have that filth cleaned."

Five minutes later Cassius marched into the office trailed by cleaners.

"Ah, Cassius, I want your best rider ready to leave in half an hour."

"I know just the man."

"Can he be trusted?"

"Yes sir, but wouldn't a coded message via a Sub-Ether unit be quicker?"

"Not when Gallio now possess two units." Marcus lifted a sealed scroll from the desk. "No commander we need to do this via an older method."

"Should we warn the Governor-elect?"

"No. For the time being this is a Roman matter and will be dealt with by Romans."

"As you command." Cassius turned to leave but paused on an afterthought.

"What is it, commander?"

"Sir, until we have established Gallios whereabouts or his intentions, you should not travel without your full escort."

Marcus sat at his desk and steepled his fingers. "I think that would send a message to the people that something is afoot." He noted Cassius's expression. "You do not agree?"

"With respect. No sir, I do not."

"Perhaps you are right to be cautious." Marcus tapped his fingers together, "would adding a chariot and two extra bikes ease your concern?"

Cassius tipped his head. "Yes, sir."

CHAPTER SIX

Two days later, and thirty kilometres away, Gallio gave the twilight's glowing beauty no appreciation. The burning, red-orange ball of plasma, sitting in a tangerine and lilac sky, paled against the fire of vengeance blazing in his mind's eye.

He would seek retribution against the demon off-worlder and the human. The first for being the spawn of Hades and Harris who kept the people's acceptance and respect of their rightful masters at bay.

Raising his head, Gallio stared through the shadowed gum trees with a pure sense of self-righteousness.

All will suffer when Mettius and I sweep across this blighted country with sword and gun. First Toowoomba, then Armidale followed by the other polluted southern Senate houses. Then I will dismember that pompous, weak and sycophantic Proconsul.

"Forgive me, sir," said Mettius, coming up beside Gallio. "You wanted to know the status of our vehicles."

"Your tone and face foreshadow something less positive."

Mettius ignored Gallio's jibe. "Apart from the low battery charge on the bikes, the rest of the equipment appears in good order,"

"What about the prison van?"

"The front suspension snapped along the track."

"So, the gods have decreed our temporary fate. We'll maintain camp here while the bike's batteries are charging," Gallio said, walking beside his friend.

"Is it wise to stay for so long?"

"With his forces depleted, the remaining bikes disabled, and the horses slaughtered, Marcus will not risk an expeditionary force until he has sufficient reinforcements, which should give us about three days."

Gallio patted Mettius's back. "When the bikes are ready, I want two scouts to search the western roads between Kingaroy and Toowoomba. Marcus will know we are listening to the sub-ether frequencies, so he'll send a rider for more reinforcements." He closed his eyes in thought. "Has there been any report from the men watching the Harris farm and the barracks?"

"None yet."

"Do any of the bikes have enough charge left to carry someone back to the barracks?"

"Only one chariot."

Gallio nodded. "My rank and bravado should secure the Aquilae Nidus, but it's what we do next that will require more men if we are to succeed…" Gallio walked in silent thought. "Tell MacMahon to join me. He is persuasive enough to rally more support."

"What if the human is recognised?"

"There is that chance," Gallio replied. "But in war, there must always be a risk."

In the evening light, parakeets filled the trees in a raucous chorus of chirping, whistles, and squawks. The branches shimmied from a moving, blurred collection of bright red and green birds feasting on the flower's nectar. *Perhaps this world does have some of the best, albeit vocal, flora, and fauna of those he helped conquer.*

During his campaigns, Gallio discounted the mystical fantasies of worlds with wondrous beasts, luminescent oceans and exotic plant life. Instead, he discovered worlds of coarse monochromatic landscapes dominated much of the galaxy's habitable planets.

Much like the Erodinian campaign. A world, filled with harsh deserts, hewn from bedrock by swirling sand and dust storms. If not for abundant quantities of fuel and minerals needed to maintain the four Classis Infinitum – the fleets of infinity – the empire would have shunned the world, and Mettius would not be at his side.

"Sir, you sent for us?" MacMahon saluted.

Gallio studied MacMahon and the three men standing nearby. He knew the human had his own secret agenda, and no doubt, the beating inflicted after the debacle in the pub, added fuel to those desires.

A lamb with a wolf's ambitions. Gallio dipped his head with the slightest hint of mirth crossing his lips.

"Do you believe there are many men at the barracks we could sway to the cause?"

"Between us, we know of at least two dozen."

Gallio held back his disappointment. "How many of those are equites?"

"Around six, maybe a few more."

The former governor concealed his disappointment at the numbers but conceded even twenty-four additional men were better than none. He drew the men around him and issued instructions for their mission.

After their briefing, Gallio watched them saunter away. *I would have preferred hells three-headed dog, Cerberus. Instead, I have a lamb leading two goats...*

The analogy sparked inspiration for a multi-pronged tactic. "Yes, three jaws breathing fire. The left and right as a diversion while the centre head bites down on our enemies."

Once they passed from Gallios earshot, MacMahon curled his lips into a smile. "All right, boys. We'll get the numbers his lordship wants and afterwards we'll have ourselves some fun."

"Would settling a score be part of the fun?"

"You bet your hairy arse it does, Hicks. And another thing," MacMahon said, "I want you clean for this job. So, no more 'E' 'til we're done."

MacMahon's lieutenant wiped a hand over the silver film of sweat coating his bald head, and grunted his less than enthusiastic response, while the third man snickered.

"What the fuck are you laughing at? You dumb lump of shit," Hicks snapped.

"I may be a lump of shit," Mouse slapped his smaller friend's back, "but I'm smart enough to know how that stuff fucks with your brain."

#

The same evening, Ried and Abbey sat on one of the weathered logs facing a small bonfire near the cottage. They drank the doctor's brandy in the wake of a campfire meal Ried served.

He poked the fire which crackled and spat with each jab. He concentrated on the areas between the burning timber, and the glowing white coal bathed in bright blue flames.

Ried stared into the flickering dark-orange glow, his legs tingling from the heat soaking through his jeans.

"No one's ever cooked a damper and billy tea for me before," Abbey said, breaking the silence between them. "In fact, until tonight, I'd never heard of a damper." She pulled her woollen coat tighter.

"One of the best bush tucker meals my grandfather ever taught me to make," Ried said, as he repositioned a slab on the coals launching dozens of bright cinders through a gossamer grey cloud of smoke.

The sound of the fire, the dancing shadows and the eucalyptus-scented wood smoke added to Ried's nostalgia.

Abbey let her gaze take in his shadowed silhouette as he stoked the coals. "I'm sorry you've lost your family and your world."

Ried rocked back on his heels and sat with his back against the log. "Now, here's where this whole dimensional crossover is fu– a bit weird," Ried said. "From my perspective, they're alive and well."

A geyser of sapphire flame hissed outward from a melting pocket of sap. Ried waited for the flare to finish its cycle of life before he continued.

"But my family will mourn my loss never knowing what happened or that I'm alive."

Ried's words came out brave and logical. Yet, Abbey's sympathy swelled. Since her mother's death, she learned to grow past her pain and loss. "It takes time for the hurt to go away." Her gut instinct told her Ried's grief must be like an open wound. "Maybe something will come along to help fill or replace the empty space in your heart." Her hands played with her maroon scarf as she edged closer to him.

Ried didn't pick up on her subtle actions, but he did pick up two of her words which raised a faint, dark smile. *Space and time. What a bloody joke.*

A piece of log, its foundations rendered to ash, rolled amongst the coals, launching another fountain of glowing sparks skyward. Their brief life extinguished after colliding with the cold air.

Ried followed their flight to oblivion and noticed the sky seemed much brighter than usual. He could count over two dozen stars, some brighter than others.

"You know... Apart from my family, I miss my sky." He shifted on his haunches and raised his face toward Abbey. "If I sat on a ridge like this back on my Earth, I'd see the whole Milky Way and th–" He waved his hand upward but stopped when a far-off sizzle and pulsing light caught his attention.

With Ried's unexpected pause, Abbey turned to see what captured his focus.

Above them, travelling across the dotted stars, flashed a cluster of blazing streaks.

"Another piece of falling space junk. Dad calls them a final eulogy for The Wars."

"I wonder what causes those colours?" Ried's finger followed the rippling bow wave of fluorescent greens, reds and blues.

"I think it has something to do with radioactive dust and ash."

The glow from the falling debris faded. "Everywhere I look," Ried said, "I see so much that is as different as it is the same." He ploughed a trench into the soil with the heel of his boot. "I know this is... Earth," Ried spread out his arms, "and much of it resembles mine. Only..." He dropped his arms.

Pushing aside the plates with her foot, and putting down the glass of liquor, Abbey slid from the log to kneel between the fire and Ried. The fire's heat blasting through her woollen coat added more colour to her already flushed cheeks. "Am I doing something wrong?"

"Sorry, you've lost me."

"Be serious."

"I am," Ried replied with a frown. "I don't know what you're referring to… oh…" His abrupt understanding of the expression Abbey wore, slapped his face with the force of a swinging anvil.

Ried's diaphragm seized, his stomach muscles clenched, and his ability to speak vanished. He swallowed several times and forced himself to draw in a breath. He sat there shy and mortified, suspecting he looked like an idiot.

"I knew it." Her tone and manner fell flat. "All these weeks, I thought you liked me."

"Like you… I do like you."

"Not like me." She pushed herself back up. "I mean, do you 'like' me?"

"Ah. Well, yes. I…" *Shit. Even in an alternate universe, they're the same.* Ried knew he liked her – a lot. Yet, he kept a part of himself back.

"So, what is it then? Am I so wrong in assuming you like my company? I mean, you keep giving me signals, and when I get close, you back off and put up some invisible damn wall." Her eyes tracked Ried's every move.

He stood, shuffling his feet.

Abbey rushed on. "I mean you kissed me on that picnic."

Ried tried to say something, but all he managed was a confused look and sigh.

"That's it," she fired back at him and turned away.

278

"Abbey… Please–"

"Please what?" She snapped. "It's pretty obvious I've made a right bloody twit of myself."

"No, you haven't," he said, reaching for her hand. "It's me."

"Oh, now you're patronising me." Abbey tried pulling her hand from his firm grip.

"Bloody hell," he said. "I had to get picked up and dumped from my home and world to find a woman who, from the moment I took a glass of water from her, stirred the oceans around my heart." *Jesus, did I say that?* "So, yes, I like you and–"

"And what?" She paused in her attempts to free her hand.

Ried dropped her hand, and sat back down, rubbing his thumbs in his palms and staring at his feet. "It scares the absolute shit out of me. Christ, I'm more comfortable field stripping a rifle than I am around you lot." He caught Abbey raise her eyebrows

"Not you or your family. I mean women… in general…" Ried restarted gouging out the dirt. "But then when you're around, I get the same sensations I used to get before we went out on patrol, only worse."

"Those same feelings?" She rested her hands on her hips.

"Yes. No. Well, yes. Only, different–" *Fucking hell, will someone just shoot me.* "–but in a good way," he added. "Then, when I'm not near you, it hurts 'til I see you again."

"Oh…"

"And what about your dad." He waved his arms up in the air. "Christ, I stole your mom's horse, and he bloody well forgave me. And, I mean, well, you're his daughter and…" He shrugged, regretting the fact he spoke at all. He leaned forward on his thighs. *Christ. I don't blame her if she thinks I'm a complete dropkick.*

"Dad's not here now." Abbey knelt closer to him, reaching for his face.

"No… No, he isn't," Ried replied. *At least she didn't call me a moron.*

#

Serenading kookaburras heralded the coming of dawn.

Ried lay in bed watching the ceilings features emerge with the mornings light. After last night, he told himself he should be rejoicing with the birds outside. Instead, his head floated and bobbed in waves of dark emotions.

Little by little, he disentangled himself from under Abbey and slipped out of bed. With exaggerated slowness, Ried scooped up a towel, wrapped the cloth around his waist, and padded his way over to the kitchen.

After relighting the coals and wood in the stove's firebox, he sat and listened to the cooker's metal casing creak with the growing heat.

His thoughts became a lizard crawling in a glass jar, desperate for escape. The soft caresses on his bare shoulders startled him, breaking the lizard's prison.

Abbey draped her arms over his chest, kissing the nape of his neck. "Morning," she whispered.

"Hello," Ried said, crossing his arms over hers, and letting his head fall back to rest between her neck and shoulder.

Abbey squeezed him against her naked body for a minute before walking around to kiss him while undoing his towel.

"Abbey?"

"Shh." She knelt in front of him.

Ried smiled at the splash of water and Abbeys soft singing from the bathroom. The last two hours spent in bed with Abbey were by far the best way to spend the post-dawn period.

A knock at the door broke his mood when Nicholas invited himself into the cottage.

"Ben– Oh, good. You're up," Nicholas studied the room. "Strewth. You're even tidier than Father is." He noticed Ried's belongings stacked in two neat, separate piles and dipped his head.

Ried wondered if his younger friend's reaction came from guilt. If so, Ried ignored Nicholas's discomfort.

The first group of luggage comprised a soft carry bag and a small suitcase. The other collection had an army issue backpack and a sizeable and cumbersome duffel bag fastened with double zips. Resting against the second pile lay a small case secured by a padlock.

"Nicky is there somewhere I can store some of my stuff?" He pointed to the duffle bag and padlocked case.

"What's in them?"

"Just stuff I want to keep safe."

"And stop calling me Nicky," Nicholas chided, "you know I hate it."

"I know," replied Ried with a smirk as he shoved his young friend's arm.

281

"Father's got a dry room under the barn in–" Nicholas stopped when Abbey emerged from the bathroom dressed in a pair of Ried's boxer shorts and a T-shirt. He held her gaze with raised eyebrows before pursing his lips and furrowing his brow. "Abbey?"

"Don't you dare give me that look, Mister 'I secretly married my girlfriend?'"

"Um…" Nicholas faced Ried "Do you still want to go into town this morning with Jack and me?" Nicholas followed Abbey who collected her clothes and went back into the bathroom but not before blowing a kiss at her brother.

He tossed a withering glare at his sister.

"Molly also asked if you were coming up for breakfast." Nicholas pouted at Ried. "So… You and my sister –"

Ried enjoyed Abbey's little brother trying to sound protective. "Spent the night together. In my bed." He slapped Nicholas's shoulder blade.

Nicholas's mouth and jaw moved as though he spoke. Except no words came out, so he dipped his head and walked out.

After Nicholas left, Abbey came out of the bathroom and helped Ried clear away the dirty breakfast dishes. An awkward silence filled the cottage.

Ried then moved his bags out to the veranda, while inside, Abbey made the bed. A wash of shame and guilt came over Ried when he watched her. A reaction further heightened when Abbey brushed her cheek with her palm.

Ried cursed fate and all its accompanying bullshit. He wanted to stay, but he had given Marcus his word – not to mention his promise to Dom. *How the hell did I get myself into such a fucking mess?* He fell against the door frame and rubbed the scar on his shoulder.

"I keep getting this odd feeling I'm not going to see you again," Abbey said nudging him aside and locking the door.

"I'm guessing you don't mean me going into town?"

"Don't do that."

"Do what?"

"Treat it all like it is some bloody game."

"I said I'd be coming back." He adjusted the backpack across both shoulders before stepping from the veranda. "I've no bloody intention of staying with Marcus any longer than I have to."

"Then why go at all?"

"We've been through this. The bastard's got me tied in with the raid."

"That's what I mean," Abbey said to the sky and then looked across at Ried. "Marcus will use that to make sure you don't come back."

Ried shifted the pack again hoping the expressions from the action hid his own concerns on the subject.

A few minutes later, he took the case Abbey carried and headed into the barn and groomed Devil while waiting for Dom. "Now, you behave yourself with Abbey and her old man," he told the horse.

"Oi, not so much of the old man," chided Dom from behind.

"Sorry."

Dom waved the apology away, patting the top of Ried's shoulder when he stepped around the young man's luggage. "Nicholas said you wanted to put something in the dry room?"

"Yep, this lot here."

"Well, give us a hand."

Together, they moved several bales of hay and some open crates filled with machinery parts and tools from a time-worn canvas tarpaulin.

Ried took Dom's lead by grabbing a loop of rope tied to two corners and rolled back the tarp filling the air with a cloud of old, dry hay and dust.

Set into the floor under the tarp lay a large, rectangular, metal door and frame.

"A safe door?"

"And a heavy one at that," Dom replied, "It came from an old munitions dump near Crows Nest."

Ried almost commented on the fact Crows Nest didn't have a military base but remembered that was on his Earth. So instead, he asked, "How old is the thing?"

"Apart from the lock and frame, I'd say the door's almost a hundred years old."

Recessed in the door's edge facing the barn's rear wall was a clunky-looking number pad, the kind which might have belonged on a calculator. On the opposite end ran a long piano-style hinge with a twelve-millimetre spine, fixed with over a dozen one-way screws.

Ried's mind ticked over with curiosity and with growing interest, he continued watching Dom, who grabbed a hook and rope from the nearby wall to slip through an iron ring near the keypad.

The thick twine passed over two wide metal pulley wheels before wrapping around a winch drum, and motor bolted to a reinforced collection of rafters.

An insulated cable ran from the winch to a mobile gantry controller, with a palm-size, green, yellow and red buttons on its face. Dom unhooked the control box from the wall which he swung across to Ried, before bending over the pin pad to enter the code.

"What happens if you lose power?"

"The whole setup runs on solar," Dom said. "connected to a converter, which feeds a Twenty-four-volt capacitor for the winch motor, and a deep-cycle, twelve-volt battery for the lock and inside lights.

"Huh."

"The capacitor holds enough charge to open the door twice a day."

"What if the door comes down when you're inside?"

"There's a basic intercom to the kitchen." Dom pointed to a series of thick ropes and chain hanging on the barn's wall. "The triple block 'n' tackle system is the manual backup." Dom stepped back. "Okay, bring it up."

Ried pressed the mushroom-shaped green button. The old winch gave an electric cough, and a screech as the drum took the strain and wound in the rope.

The motor groaned under the effort, and the rafters creaked as the line stretched until the fibres almost reached their snapping point.

Ried flinched when a sharp, metallic crack signalled the hinge shifting on the pin. Then followed a smaller series of creaks and pops until the door stopped at an angle of about sixty degrees.

After he secured the door, Dom carried Ried's cases down to the dry room.

Ried smiled and gave an imperceptible shake of his head at how the crafty old bugger manoeuvred him, so the door obscured his view of the space below the floor.

#

Back in the house, Dom poured Ried a Scotch. "Molly told me Abbey didn't come back to the house last night."

"Ah…" Ried shuffled his feet. "She spent the night with me in the cottage." *And here comes the "I'm her father" bit.*

"Don't worry, son. This isn't the betrayed father routine," Dom said. "I saw it coming weeks ago, even if you didn't. Although, your timing isn't what I'd call ideal."

Talk about an understatement. Ried swallowed the drink in one mouthful. "No, sir, it isn't." he croaked from the sting of the amber liquid.

"Now, aside from that, you and Jack watch each other's backs while you're with Marcus."

"Understood."

Dom walked outside at the familiar sound of Jacks four-wheel-drive as Ried went back into the kitchen to grab his coat.

"Are you leaving already?" Molly asked

"No, I'm going to town with Jack and Nicky."

"Miss Abbey needs you here to say goodbye."

"We said our goodbyes this morning."

Molly took Ried's hand. "You're a good person, Mr R, but you are as dumb as a rock."

"Excuse me?"

"There are never enough goodbyes for a woman in love." She patted his cheek. "So, off you go and spend what time you have with her."

"Um, okay, but we'll be back in plenty of time." When Ried walked into the lounge room, Abbey fell against Ried's chest and hugged him with her shoulders rising and falling with soft, drawn-out sobs.

Ried rested his head on hers and ran his fingers through her hair. *Bloody hell, she smells good.* Each time he moved, she squeezed him tighter.

"Hey," Ried reached for her elbows.

"What?"

"You squeeze me any harder, and I'll snap in two."

"Good, then you'll have to say here."

He pulled her arms from around him, and held her chin, before kissing her the same way he did on their picnic. "Remember, you're my light." He kissed her again and skipped through the door.

"What the hell are you doing?" Dom asked from his chair on the patio.

"I need to go into town for a bit."

"Like hell. Marcus will be here soon."

"Tough. If Marcus wants me that bad enough, he'll have to friggin' wait."

Before Dom could reply, Jack's family walked between them to greet Abbey.

Ried winked at Abbey and went over to Jack's rust stained Range Rover where Jack's wife, Rose, took him aside.

Rose wasn't a big woman. In fact, Ried guessed she stood a few centimetres shorter than Abbey, but Ried saw strength and passion far more significant than her petite stature. Grey streaks highlighted her black-brown hair tied back at her shoulders. Her olive complexion worked well at concealing her actual age, but her red-rimmed eyes couldn't hide her sorrow.

"Jackson told me your second name is James."

"Sorry, Mrs Bennett. I don't follow."

"Your names. Do you know what they mean?"

Ried shrugged his shoulders. "Not really."

Rose gave him one of the best maternal smiles in existence.

"Benjamin means 'the right hand, ' and James means 'usurper.'"

"Okay."

"I want you to be my right hand and bring my Jackson back."

"All right, I pr–"

"Don't promise. Just say yes."

"Yes."

CHAPTER SEVEN

Ried stood on the footpath diverting the flow of foot traffic. The occasional complaint and disapproval from around went unnoticed by him as he opened the small jewellery box covered in luxurious, purple velvet, and lined with cream satin.

Inside the palm-size case, glinting in the mid-morning sun, rested two chains coiled beside a heart-shaped gold pendant, inlaid with a single diamond and garnet.

With his arms full of bags and an assorted of gift-wrapped boxes, Jack strolled up beside Ried.

"Nice," Jack said, eyeing the piece of jewellery. "What's with the crooked line down the middle?"

"It's where they join to make one." With his finger, Ried separated the gold heart.

"Strewth, your giving Abbey a something which looks like a broken heart?"

Shit, I didn't think of that. Ried closed the box. "It's supposed to be a metaphor about how we feel when we are apart…" He slipped the box into his pocket. "Shit."

"You're not good at this relationship stuff, are you?"

"It's a work in progress." Ried shrugged, "at least I had the jeweller send the bill to Marcus."

Jack bellowed a short laugh. "Good on ya. Let's hope he adds–"

A high-pitched scream ripped the air. Jack and Ried swore when a man yelled.

"Nicholas?" the pair said in unison wondering which direction the cries came from. A second high-pitched shout rolled from building to building along the street.

Without hesitation, Jack ran across the road and hurled his gifts in the back of his Ute. Ried weaved and dodged through the people who slowed and gathered near the entrance of an alley.

A terrified child came running from an alley colliding against a wall of curious onlookers.

Without slowing, Ried scythed through the growing group of people and down the laneway.

Jack scooped up the frightened child.

A woman screamed again,

"Mummy," the young girl cried out.

"Bloody hell…" Jack passed her on to an older woman and charged after Ried, pausing when he glimpsed three Praetorian's jogging down the street in his direction.

#

The laneway led to an old memorial park behind Maud's beer garden. Dominating the park was a hexagonal stone pillar, on which stood a pair of sandstone legs from the knees down.

Running headlong down the path, Ried spotted Nicholas trying to shield a young woman from the assault of two men.

Hicks, the small, bald, bull-terrier of a man was the bloke Jack backhanded in the pub. The one MacMahon called Hicks, who went in on Nicholas wielding a Vigiles nightstick. His accomplice, nicknamed Mouse, sported a trimmed mohawk and goatee, and brandished a large hunting knife, with its hilt forming a set of knuckle dusters.

Hicks swung the baton, striking a hard, glancing blow knocking Nicholas off his feet.

Mouse, the larger of all the men now in the park, moved in on an opening and snatched for the woman's arm.

Nicholas recovered enough to charge forward and drive his shoulder into Mouse's chest, who laughed when Nicholas bounced off his broad muscular frame.

Still laughing, the thug clutched a handful of Nicholas's ponytail, and wrenched the younger man to his feet, twisting Nicholas's head around.

Nicholas clawed at the meaty arm and hand wrapped in his hair.

While finding amusement with Dom's son's actions, Mouse drove the knuckle-dusted hilt of his knife into the young man's exposed ribs in a quick succession of rabbit punches. When Nicholas hung limp and wheezing in his grip, Mouse tossed the subdued Nicholas aside.

Dom's son hit the statue's pillar with a bruising thump, his head bouncing off the sandstone block. Incoherent, Nicholas slumped to the ground beside the woman.

Hicks raised the Vigiles baton above Nicholas, ready to cave in his skull, while his accomplice moved on the cowering woman huddled next to him. Neither man, with their cruel focus on Nicholas and the woman, noticed Ried's charging entrance.

Hicks wolfish grin contorted when his larger friend fell on him with a surprised grunt. The blow from Ried's airborne feet forced the air from Mouse's lungs with an audible crack.

Prepared and braced for his landing, Ried followed through with his body's momentum. The second he hit the ground Ried rolled upright and rushed over to Nicholas and the woman.

Behind them, Hicks grunted, pushed, and squirmed himself out from under his incapacitated partner, who howled and swore in protesting pain. Free of Mouse's weight, Hicks scrambled for the fallen nightstick, clutched the weapon and moved in on his new enemy.

"Ben," Jack yelled.

Ried flicked his head around, sensed the danger and rolled on his back avoiding the arcing prongs of the nightstick. In one continuous flow of movement, Ried twisted his hip and kicked out at his assailant.

Tangled in Ried's legs, the man staggered and tripped over his own feet barking a curse when his hip and elbow thumped the ground. His street fighting experience gained the advantage over Ried. The man recovered with ease and continued swinging with the charged baton.

Ried spat his own hushed curse and reached out for the man's wrist and arm. He twisted his own body to avoid the end of the truncheon – crackling with raw blue energy between the prongs.

In desperation, Ried clamped his hands around his opponent's, which locked the thug's finger around the Taser's trigger lever. The move became a wrestling match in a game of will and brute force.

Determined he would gain the upper hand, Ried gritted his teeth, braced his feet, and dragged Mouse up and twisted his arms around.

The thug outsized Ried in mass and muscle. However, Ried resisted with every muscle and tendon in his body constricting with determination.

Both men see-sawed to gain the upper hand and control of the nightstick.

During the muscle tearing wrestling match, Ried gained the advantage over his opponent.

Ried's cheeks puffed filling his lungs. His arms coiled and brought the electrified prongs of the nightstick into the Hicks groin and gained a painful lesson from his mistake. The arcing current surged through both men. They convulsed as one, dropping the nightstick.

Ried staggered against the sandstone plinth, while the thug fell sideways, striking his head on the old concrete path edge with a concussive thud.

With twitching muscle spasms, Ried spat a wad of bile and phlegm at his feet. "Oh… Shit… That fuckin' hurt," moaned Ried, as Jack helped him stand.

They both went to help Nicholas and the young woman next to him while Ried kept massaging his twitching abdominal muscles.

Ried registered several comments and remarks. People filed from nowhere and gathered in front of the gate leading to the pub's beer garden.

At first, Ried thought his eyes having just received an electric shock, played a trick when the gathering parted.

"You're joking." Ried used Jack's shoulder to lever himself upright.

Jack twisted around when someone called out a name; MacMahon. "Son-of-a-bitch."

MacMahon, armed with his own nightstick and pistol, strode toward them, ignoring his downed comrades and his gun pointed at Ried.

The world shifted into sudden, slow sharpened clarity. A quadruple blossom of orange fire and smoke erupted from the muzzle of the pistol.

Ried shoved Jack aside and dived over the unconscious Nicholas and crying woman whose features became a stretched face of horror.

Jack landed on his backside two metres away surprised with Ried's lightning fast moves and flinching from four concussive cracks splitting the air.

The bullets ricocheted from the statue's base and showered Ried's back with stone shards and hot splashes of lead.

When Jack leapt back to his feet, he took two quick side steps before another two more rounds ruptured the ground where he stood. Once again, Jack showed – for a tall and solid man – that he could move with surprising agility and speed.

He released a throaty bellow of fury, and in two giant strides he grabbed MacMahon's collar and slapped the pistol from his hand.

With his finger still on the trigger, MacMahon fired off a round, missing the young woman's head by millimetres.

By the time his pistol hit the ground, MacMahon had twisted free of Jack's fingers and moved into a crouch. With deft skill, MacMahon held his nightstick, spun the charge dial and squeezed the lever all in one smooth action as he stabbed Jacks midriff with the crackling Taser.

Twice in the space of two minutes, Jack let a younger man's swift, agile action catch him off guard. Jack doubled over from the high-voltage tips scraped against his stomach.

A second too late, Ried straightened with his hand out as a warning. His own movements now slow and a little uncoordinated as he moved in on MacMahon from behind.

As Ried's arm locked around MacMahon's throat, Ried flinched when the world and time returned to normal.

Taken aback by Ried's lightning fast assault, MacMahon dropped the nightstick and reached behind his head. He clawed and scratched while trying to twist out of Ried's constrictive hold.

Ried's mindset shifted from a defensive mindset into a red fog of hate-fed raged. He tightened his grip and rolled his body until MacMahon's feet lifted from the grass and his lower back arched over Ried's bent and raised hip. Imperceptible sensations of grinding of bone and stretching of tendons vibrated through clothing and past skin sending Ried's nerve ending alive signalling a message to Ried's vengeance centres; crush MacMahon.

The rogue Vigiles eyes bulged, his cheeks sucked in with his efforts to draw breath past the muscular band crushing his windpipe. MacMahon's nails dug and tore at Ried's flesh.

The crowd cheered with MacMahon's actions resembling a desperate, wounded beast sensing death.

Ried braced his legs to keep his balance against MacMahon's wild thrashing and manic struggles. Then a frantic sweep of MacMahon's legs struck one of Ried's knees.

The unexpected blow put Ried off-balance, sending the two combatants crashing to the ground. MacMahon's weight and the impact stunned Ried breaking his stranglehold.

The temporary loss of hold shifted MacMahon's survival driven mind into action. He lowered his head and buried his teeth into Ried's forearm.

When Ried's arm jerked away from the bite, MacMahon wrenched himself around and buried an elbow under Ried's floating rib.

Ried flinched when the blow compressed his diaphragm. Despite having the wind belted from his chest, Ried's determination did not falter, and he increased his stranglehold to pull MacMahon closer.

MacMahon kept squirming until his teeth locked on Ried's forearm where he clamped his jaw closed. The surge and taste of warm blood filled MacMahon's mouth as he bit harder and shook his head.

Ried cried out when MacMahon tore a piece of his skin loose between his teeth. He rolled away clamping his hand on the jagged hole in his arm.

MacMahon spat away Ried's blood and flesh and scampered away with wild eyes.

Crouched on the path with blood flowing from under and through his fingers and palm. Ried dismissed the dull ache from his diaphragm and the white-hot sting in his arm.

His facial expressions and narrowed eyes gave clear instruction to MacMahon, the day, and himself was not done.

His boots pushed against the crumbling concrete path as he catapulted himself headlong toward MacMahon, who scrambled away like a wounded spider.

Ried's dive ended when his shoulder collided with MacMahon's solar plexus. MacMahon doubled over, allowing Ried to wrap his arms around MacMahon's waist.

Then, with a guttural roar, Ried lifted MacMahon off his feet and slammed him back to the ground. Stunning them both.

MacMahon rolled over, spitting a glutinous wad of bile mixed with phlegm, and blood. He held his ribs with one hand and clawed for his pistol with the other. When Ried's shadow fell across him, MacMahon mewed a pitiful whimper with tear-drenched eyes.

"Please… No more."

Ried ignored the request and with the speed of a striking snake, Ried clamped his fingers around the wrist of MacMahon's outstretched arm.

MacMahon kicked and tried to pull his arm free as Ried wrenched and lifted his arm. "No! Please–" A river of boiling oil ran through MacMahon, and his scream became a gargled cry when Ried pushed his foot under the Vigiles chin to rest across his throat.

A gargoyle's mask of fury and hatred shrouded Ried's face. He glared into MacMahon's eyes while rotating his arm.

MacMahon's neck and head pivoted backwards under Ried's boot. His body arched off the grass. His strangled pleas grew shrill and desperate, and he lashed out at Ried with his legs.

To avoid MacMahon's thrashing legs, Ried changed his stance and shifted his foot from MacMahon's neck, to step back, and smashed his other boot onto the prone man's ankle joint.

Recovering from the Taser's electrical shock, Jack pushed himself upright, transfixed by Ried's cold determination and the terror on MacMahon's face.

The added pain of a broken ankle was the final blow to MacMahon's battered body. He shuddered and blacked out.

Oblivious to MacMahon's incoherent state, Ried twisted back around to reposition his boot across his opponent's neck, and again pulled on his arm.

Gritting his teeth, Jack fought against the convulsing muscles in his stomach and moved up behind Ried.

"Fuck off, Jack."

Jack ignored Ried's cold tone. He knew all too well the dark demon's hand-to-hand combat brought out in a man. He cupped his hands around Ried's shoulder and squeezed, his thumbs burying them into the soft flesh of his young friend's armpit.

The compacted nerves in Ried's armpit shrieked. The strength in his arm faltered under the numbing, electric jolts. He drew in an angry breath, and his body tensed to renew his task.

"Benjamin, don't!" Jack increased the pressure of his contracting hold. "Come on, son. Let it go."

Ried swore through the pain, refusing to obey.

Jack shook his head and pinched deeper.

The crushed nerves sent a shock wave down Ried's arm and into his brain. He released MacMahon to collapse against Jack. Ried's body trembled, and his pinched nerves sent fire ants to gnaw and sting the flesh of his arm and ribs.

Footsteps hitting the ground in a drum beat rhythm, heralded the Roman soldier's arrival with their pistols drawn and their shields activated. The lead Praetorian signalled a halt and surveyed the scene before him.

He spied MacMahon at Ried's feet along with MacMahon's incapacitated cronies a few metres away. He holstered his pistol, thumbed off his shield and moved aside when two paramedics and DR Mitchum hurried past.

The people, the park, and the closest Praetorian standing before him, filtered their way into the receding blood tinged fog in Ried's awareness. He took a long, deep breath to regain his composure.

"Christ, Jack…" He remembered the death of the two Nomads at his hands, and how it tortured him. He turned to stare at the unconscious MacMahon.

"Take a breath, son," Jack counselled the younger man. "Let it go."

Ried shuddered, ashamed of his murderous desire, yet, he felt cheated for not fulfilling the goal. And then, he remembered why he ran into the park. "Nicholas."

Jack helped him over to their unconscious friend cradled in the woman's lap.

Ried shifted the hair above Nicholas's right eye revealing a deep gash and a nasty bruise discolouring the skin around his temple. The younger man's swollen, broken nose still seeped blood. Ried noticed Nicholas's arm hanging limp and twisted at the elbow.

The familiar, gruff voice of Dr Mitchum barked short instructions as another two paramedics came up the path carrying collapsible stretchers under each arm.

As a medic joined Mitchum who knelt over Nicholas, the first Praetorian signalled his men to move the growing crowd back, as a cohort of Vigiles appeared via the pub's beer garden.

Ignoring the Vigiles arrival, the second ambulance attendant checked Hicks pulse, shook his head and lower the man's arm. The paramedic scribbled on a notepad and moved across to Mouse.

Almost an hour had passed since Nicholas's admittance into the Kingaroy Base Hospital. During that time, Ried paced around the waiting room, his thoughts clouded.

Oblivious to the pale-green walls dotted with water-stained prints in faded timber frames, he navigated his way around the odd assortment of furniture scattered across the old linoleum floor tiles.

Ried looked over to Jack who was resting on a settee with his eyes shut. His head leaned against the wall, and his feet resting on a small table littered with well-thumbed magazines and books.

How the hell can he be so calm? Especially after what happened. Christ… What will Dom say when he gets here?

Ried rubbed the scar on his shoulder again. With a soft sigh, he wondered out into the hall. A passing nurse gave Ried a polite, bland, unemotional smile.

"Is there any word on Nicholas?"

"I'm sorry, Mr…?"

"Just Ben will do."

"Ben," she smiled again, "the doctor is still with your friend. He'll see you when he has finished."

Ried returned a half-hearted smile of gratitude. *Is it a cosmic rule that nurses must give the same bloody inane answers*?

Stirred awake by the voices, Jack rose from the settee. "Come on, son," he said, "Doc Mitchum might be a gruff old bastard, but Nicholas couldn't be in a better set of hands."

"What the hell was he doing in the bloody park, anyway?"

"He was there because of me."

The answer came from the woman at the park, whose face and neck wore the unnatural decorations of bruises. Holding her hand was the little girl who had run out of the alley. The slim woman called herself Lizzy and introduced her daughter, Susie, who hugged a rag doll.

The nurse helped Lizzy to a couch with her daughter, then left. Ried did his best not to react at the blotches of blues, purple and maroon on her throat and face.

"What happened?" Jack asked.

"Nicholas came by Maud's for Susie's birthday. Then, Maud saw MacMahon come into the pub. She panicked and pushed us out into the park. But there were two of MacMahon's men standing guard by the gate."

Lizzy gathered her composure. "The one with the Mohawk grabbed me by the throat." She rubbed the nape of her neck, and for a few seconds, her breath quickened. "Susie and Nicholas tried to stop him." She dabbed away some tears. "Nicholas punched at him, and Susie tried to pull me free… only…" She wiped another tear away with the back of her hand.

"The big man was hurting Mummy," Susie said from under her mother's arm.

She reached out with a shaking hand accepting the cup of coffee, Jack handed her. "I kicked the big one in the balls, hoping he'd let go, but he threw me hard against the old statue."

Ried stepped out into the hall and came back with a blanket which he spread over Lizzy and her daughter lap.

Dr Mitchum paused when he entered the room. His shoulders hung with a weighted droop, reflecting his disposition and energy.

Jack and Ried mistook Mitchum's tired gait and his sigh for something else.

Susie slid from the couch and tugged on Mitchum's trouser leg. "Is Uncle Nicky going to be okay?"

"He'll be fine," Mitchum said. "The other doctors and nurses will make him all better."

Jack led the doctor away from Susie and Lizzy.

Mitchum headed toward the side bench and poured a coffee. "He took a beating. But it's nothing he won't live through." Mitchum kneaded his own stiff neck. "You know, they also beat up old Maud and Charlie."

"Is Charlie okay?" Lizzy asked. "He always treated the girls, especially me and Susie, like his sisters."

"I'm sorry. We couldn't save Charlie. His injuries were just too severe."

"What about Nicholas? How bad is he?" Ried asked.

"He's got four cracked ribs, a bruised lung, a fractured jaw and nose, and a broken arm."

"Flamin' hell," Jack whispered massaging his chin under his beard. "Can we see him?"

"No. I've had to put the boy under sedation."

Ried paced the room again before collapsing with a tired thump against the door frame.

"Don't fret too much, son." Mitchum walked over and put a reassuring hand on Ried's shoulder. "His injuries are not life-threatening."

"What about MacMahon and the other two?" Jack asked.

"Our mohawk-haired friend has two broken ribs and a punctured lung. The bald one was dead at the scene." For several seconds, Mitchum focused on a spot of worn linoleum floor before facing Ried. "And MacMahon? Well, I reckon he'll wish you finished him off."

"So, the prick will live?" Ried asked.

"Yes, but he won't be enjoying it for a while." Mitchum massaged the bridge of his nose. "Between a ruptured spleen, torn diaphragm, sprained ligaments in his shoulder and wrist, along with a partially crushed larynx and a broken ankle… I'd say he'll be downright miserable."

"Perhaps you should have finished the bastard off."

They all turned around, curious to see who issued the statement. Ried recognised the Roman who sat with Marcus at Dom's party. Behind him, two more Praetorians stepped up to flank the waiting room's entrance.

"Is that your medical opinion?" Mitchum retorted.

"No, Doctor. My ethical one."

"Ethics. That's rich coming from a race who still buy and sell people," Ried replied in a voice loaded with sarcasm.

"I do not expect you to understand our ways, off-worlder."

Ried clenched his fists and straightened his back. "Too bloody right." He strode up to the Roman. "I bet Marcus has had you lot investigating Gallio, and our arrest just happened to give him an excuse to show up."

"The proconsul may well have his own investigation underway. However, Marcus knows nothing of ours." The Roman rested his hand on the hilt of his gladius. "And nor will he." He studied Ried, the same way a small boy examines a jar of tadpoles.

Undeterred by the Roman's implied threat, Ried prepared to quiz the Roman further, but all the lights flickered and went out. Standing in the darkened room, a dull, crumpled thump vibrated through the walls, followed by a slight tremor. Mitchum barged past the Praetorians and disappeared down the hall amidst confused staff.

Ried, Jack and the Praetorian sprinted down the opposite hallway and through the foyer doors. Once outside, they jogged along the hospital's wall toward the street leading to town. A call from Jack brought Ried sliding to a stop.

When Ried turned back, Jack disappeared down a back alley. With a quick double skip, Ried ran to the laneway and up an external fire escape after Jack two steps at a time.

Ried bounded from the metal stairs and across the hospital's roof. Beyond the town's rooftops, several billowing, greasy black clouds mushroomed skyward in the south-east.

The Roman soldier caught up and stood beside them. "Gallio."

"I reckon the bastard's taken out the power plant," Jack confirmed.

Before Ried could respond, another explosion erupted with a concussive rolling boom behind some hills a few kilometres from town. A blossom of orange, blue and red flame expanded into a rising mahogany brown and grey cloud.

Nearby, a bell tolled, followed by the growing whine of an air-raid siren, the shriek ricocheting along the roofs.

"The methane plant," the tall Roman spat before he jogged back to the fire escape.

Ried kept his eyes on the trail of smoke, his stomach drowning under the weight of burning coal. "Jack, where is Dom's farm from here?"

Jack pointed. "Over that way–" His finger locked on the horizon to the right of the smoke. "Shit!" Jack whirled after Ried.

CHAPTER EIGHT

A mob of two dozen kangaroos enjoyed the early afternoon sun while they grazed on the roadside. Several turned their heads with twitching ears at the approaching hi-revving growl.

The big muscular buck scratched himself and returned his attention back to the grass. Next, to him, a young female lay down in the shadow of her mate only to spring up when a reverberating squeal of tyres disturbed the air.

Six of the startled animals zig-zagged along the road in front of Dr Mitchum's van whose occupants – except for the driver – cried out. Each passenger clutched the first solid within reach when the vehicle skidded and drifted around the panicked marsupials.

Ried threw Jack an "are you trying to kill us" look.

Jack ignored the targeted swearing and kept his focus on the road.

Ahead, beyond the trees, several thin columns of dirty grey smoke rose in the still air. When the careening van crested the rise, Ried and Jack released a collective sigh when they realised the plumes of smoke came from the front of Dom's house, rather than the building itself.

The drive from town to the farm, on an average run, would take around twenty to twenty-five minutes. However, by Ried's watch, Jack had completed the trip in under seven – including the time to get the keys from Dr Mitchum.

Behind him, the three Praetorian guards from the hospital each wore pallid complexions, a result of sliding and bouncing all over the floor from Jack's urgent driving, and his phenomenal avoidance of the fleeing kangaroos.

When the van reached the gate of Dom's driveway, Jack spun the wheel to the right. The van's back end drifted toward the solid ironbark posts at the entrance's left. Ried's eyes stayed fixed on the timber post, waiting for the impact, when Jack flicked the steering wheel the opposite way.

Everyone recoiled at the screeching snap of the rear bumper clipping the post on the right. The quick, scraping impact sent the old ambulance fishtailing down the gravel drive. Jack gunned the motor, gaining control via the van's acceleration.

Dom's driveway ran a little over five hundred metres back from the road – a very short five hundred metres under the vans breakneck speed.

"Jack?" Ried gripped the seatbelt and dashboard.

"Hold on, boys."

Jack wrenched the handbrake and flicked the steering wheel. The van slewed across the gravel a full 180-degrees. A billowing blanket of dirt and stones spewed across the patio three metres from the rear of the vehicle.

The dust hung for several silent seconds before drifting over the house. Jack and Ried sprung from the vehicle and threw themselves behind the open doors.

"Where the hell did you learn to drive?" Ried asked.

"I reckon Doc Mitchum's gonna have something to say about his missing rear bumper," Jack remarked, ignoring Ried's sarcasm.

They crouched close to the front guards and peered through the van doors windows, each man listening and watchful. Crows cawed across the fields and from the gutters of Dom's roof, serenaded by the far-off bellows of cattle.

The three Romans stumbled from the back of the van. In a series of awkward moves, they drew their pistols in stiff, outstretched arms, taking up a triangular formation, and dropping to one knee.

Ried shook his head and glanced across the bonnet at Jack, who mouthed the word "wankers."

Swarms of hovering flies and gnats filled the air. A metallic, acrid, sweet, and sour stench mingled with the dust. Saliva pooled in Ried's mouth ahead of the rising bile from his stomach.

The gut-turning bouquet came from the bodies scattered about the front yard. Drying pools of blood, urine, and intestinal fluids soaked the ground around the corpses. Each one's ash-coloured face frozen in the last millisecond of mortality's abandonment.

Two of the bodies were from Marcus's bodyguards. The others wore a mix of Vigiles uniform and civilian clothing.

A few metres to the vans left lay the shattered, burning wreck of a war trike. Jack dashed to investigate the bike, and the eviscerated, smouldering remains of the rider.

He scanned the area before picking up one of the fallen machine guns, along with the weapons' tangled ammunition belt. He hefted the heavy weapon with ease and looped the belt of linked ammunition around his arm before he darted back to the cover of the van.

While Jack searched the shattered trike, Ried moved over to the closest body where he secured a pistol from the dead man's holster. However, rather than move the corpse, Ried unclipped the gore-soaked sling from a carbine under the bodies arm.

The writhing mass of black, iridescent blue, and silver insects ignored Ried. Their sole interest, the abundance of food in the blood, torn flesh, and grey matter oozing from the golf-ball-size hole in the back of the man's skull.

With his shirt pulled up to his nose to try to filter out the odour, Ried continued his inspection of two other bodies.

A garbled voice and groan brought Ried spinning around with the carbine raised. "You're fucking kidding me…" he lowered his gun with a mixed look of pity and disgust at the closest Praetorian from the van spewing a stream of vomit at his feet.

A light breeze blew in from the east which gave a two-folded relief: the first when it cooled the sweat on Ried's neck, and the second by clearing the malodorous air.

Back behind the cover of the van, Jack watched Ried's hands explore the weapons he garnered. The younger man emptied the four magazines and cycled the two pistols and carbine. With steady, assured hands, Ried reloaded three of the mags to full capacity and then slammed them home and released the open slides to put a round in the breach.

What Ried's next action raised an eyebrow of admiration from Jack. With each gun having a loaded round in the breach, Ried dropped each magazine and added another round in each one.

Satisfied, Ried then pushed both handguns into his waistband – one in the front and the other in the back –and then tapped Jacks shoulder pointing towards the splintered, and broken woodwork around the windows and adjoining walls.

"Whatever happened here went down quick," Ried said in hushed tones, testing the carbine against his shoulder.

Jack nodded his agreement watching several shadows crisscross the ground. Above them, the cloudless sky filled with a growing number of circling crows who glided down to land around the dead bodies.

"Would Dom have any guns in the house?" Ried asked, ignoring the birds' gurgling, clicking calls.

"An old, double-barrelled pheasant gun and a bolt-action 208." He flicked a thumb toward the Romans. "These bastards don't want us armed with anything that shoots faster than theirs."

Ried motioned Jack to follow him over to the Praetorian's body. "These blokes weren't killed by a shotgun." Ried pointed down to the wounds on the dead man before he stepped across to another corpse, pointing out the rough, three-centimetre opening below his sternum.

Jack squinted at the black and burgundy hole. "This is an exit wound."

With a grunt, Ried rolled the stiff body over to see a small bullet hole in the Roman's back. "Oi, you. How many men were here with your proconsul?"

"You shall address me as Centurion Arillius."

"Yeah, whatever." Ried stood and moved toward the roman. "And the question still stands."

"There were four bikes and two chariots."

Ried responded with a puzzled expression.

"Nine men including Marcus's driver," Arillius clarified.

Ried's went back to Jack, his thoughts racing, "You notice anything odd?"

Jack scanned the carnage across the front yard. "Bloody hell. There's only the one burnt out trike." He turned back to Ried. "Soldier boy either hasn't noticed or is too stupid to care."

"Not just that," Ried said pointing the carbine at the far end of the patio. "What's wrong with that bike?" Ried made a slow concentrated stare at each window and the open front door facing them.

"It looks in pretty good nick—" With a slap of understanding, Jack twisted to point his machine gun toward the house. "They've left a bloke behind just in case."

"It's what I'd do."

"I see nothing further to gain by staying here," Arillius said when he headed toward the van.

"Hold up mate." Ried stepped inside the Romans personal space.

Arillius stood to his full height glaring down at Ried. "It is obvious we have arrived too late, and I must report this."

Ried lowered his voice. "You three go through the house. Jack, you come with me around the back."

"I will not take orders from you," hissed Arillius

"And we have the keys to the van." Ried spat back.

Jack kowtowed. "Centurion, could you please check inside the house?" His manner and toned dripping with sarcasm. "Bloody hell son," Jack whispered behind Ried. "Now's not the time to start a fight with them."

"Tough shit," Ried murmured when he reached the corner of the house. He scanned the open ground on his left. With slow, cautious steps, he edged through the garden along the wall.

He paused at the rear corner beside a shrub and peeped into the back area behind the house. Shifting his weight onto his left leg, Ried leaned out with the carbine sitting in his left shoulder. He rotated at the hip to scan the area around the barn, and across to the machinery shed.

More bodies littered the yard behind the house. One hung face-first over the rear fence rail with a crow tearing at the man's back, pulling away shreds of blood-stained cloth and flesh.

Slumped nearby against the fence was the second body. The third and fourth lay by the open double gate, and the fifth, another Praetorian, lay crumpled at the foot of the back stairs.

Jack slid up to Ried, nodding toward the machinery shed. "Dom's old flatbed truck is gone."

Through the walls came the muffled sounds of the Romans searching the house room by room. Ried gave Jack a dour look from the thuds, bangs and the crash of falling crockery or glass.

"Arrogant pricks," muttered Jack

Ried padded along the fence.

Jack admired the way Ried moved. The younger man walked in a quick march, bent with a slight crouch and leaning into the carbine pulled tight in his shoulder, every action fluid. No wasted energy or time. Where Ried looked, the barrel pointed. Weapon and man merged into a single deadly and quiet entity.

Jack followed Ried through a pair of open, double gates leading into the backyard and froze when a horror-fuelled, blood-chilling scream came from the house.

Ried dropped on one knee, his left leg bent at an almost perfect right angle, the sights of his small, semi-automatic rifle locked on the dark rectangle of the open back door.

The wail turned Jack's warm blood into ice. Within seconds, a figure jumped down the back stairs, skidding to a stop when he saw two guns aimed at him. He dropped his blood-smeared sword, fumbling with the carbine slung across his chest.

Two rapid, sharp, concussive cracks reverberated off the back wall of Dom's house before the man's gladius touched the ground.

Jack swore.

The newcomer jerked in his step and collapsed to his knees with two expanding patches of dark red staining his pants. He grunted with pain and pushed himself upright. In a state of anger and disbelief, he pondered the bullet wound in the top of each thigh.

The gunshot man, dressed in a Vigiles uniform, lifted his face toward Jack and Ried. His cheek trembled before he let loose an agonised bellow of rage.

The wounded man's shaky hands raised his carbine and took two awkward, drunken steps forward, before collapsing on his side, the stump of his neck spurting crimson fountains across the ground.

"FUCK." Ried pointed his rifle at the second Praetorian from the van who sheathed his sword in a casual, self-righteous manner while grinning at the decapitated body in front of him.

Ried stood with his carbine trained on the smug Roman. His hand flexed and massaged the pistol grip in frustration. The urge to shoot the Roman soldier boiled high on his emotions. Like a vulture, Ried circled the decapitated body, while fixing the Praetorian with a cold, squinting glare.

The sword-wielding Praetorian said nothing to Ried's actions, all he did was raise an eyebrow, give Ried a shrug and then turn away.

"Don't you take another fucking step."

Ried dropped the carbine and stared down at the bodyless head in frustration, anger, and a fear of defeat. Without a word, he walked over, knelt, and clamped his hands around the head. Ried swore at the lifeless face and stormed over to the larger Roman.

Before the Roman could react, Ried released a bellow of pent-up despair and bludgeoned the gruesome cosh into the Praetorian's face.

Stunned by Ried's savage onslaught, the Roman tripped over his own feet as he backed away. The Praetorian wiped his torn lip and bloody nose glaring at Ried now standing over him, shaking the battered head.

"If I wanted him dead, I would have shot out his fucking heart!" In a final vent of anger, Ried hurled the head over the fence.

The Roman stood and spat out a broken tooth. He reached for his sword with his eyes fixed on Ried's as Jack stepped up beside his friend.

"Praetorian," Arillius called out from the back door while supporting the Roman, who Ried saw vomit by the front patio.

The Praetorian held up Arillius, said and did nothing except fix his glazed eyes on the blood saturated bundle of rags and towels where is wrists and hands should have been.

The third Roman in front of Ried held his ground.

"I require your assistance," Arillius said as Jack lifted the muzzle of the machine gun while Ried moved his hand gripped the pistol in the small of his back.

"Now," Arillius commanded.

Several minutes later, on the patio, Jack set about making two tourniquets and stopped when he noticed the wounded Roman's dull, vacant expression. Jack shook his head and let out a soft, sad sigh dropping the slings and closed the man's unseeing eyes.

With the remaining daylight, Jack, Ried, and the two remaining Praetorians collected all the bodies and placed them in a heap beside the machinery shed. After completing the gruesome task, Ried and Jack returned to the patio, lit several candles, and sat side by side in silence.

Between the two men stood the undamaged luggage belonging to Jack and his family, along with the two smaller bags of Ried's belongings.

Jack took out a flannel jacket from his suitcase. "No point freezing my butt off while his lordship decides what to do next."

Ried's own self-pity accepted the nibbling cold as part atonement for his failure to keep Abbey safe. With a grunt he made his way over to the war bike they spotted earlier and kicked the machine over before returning to sit by Jack.

"Feel better?" Asked Jack.

"Not much."

A short while later, the two Romans came out of the house, Arillius passed the remaining Praetorian a curtain to bundle all the weapons gathered from the dead bodies, including those held by Ried and Jack.

"You seem familiar with our carbines," Arillius said to Ried. "You also have a habit of striking Roman citizens."

"Be thankful the bastard's still breathing," Ried responded without looking up.

"For the record," Jack said to Arillius, "it was Dom, not Ben, who flattened MacMahon."

"We need to go back to town. Now," demanded Arillius.

"Look, Centurion now's not the time to start ordering us about." Jack stood and faced the Roman.

"Consider it a firm request." Arillius contemplated the broad-shouldered man before him. The candles sallow light and flickering shadows morphed Jack's bearded features into a monster disguised in the form of a man. A man out for revenge.

The soft purr of an electric bike foreshadowed the growing bright light which spotlighted Jack and Arillius standing toe to toe.

Arillius stepped back and raised his hand to shade his eyes against the harsh glare as the bike stopped beside the doctor's van.

The blurred shadow of the rider dismounted and crossed into the light's corona.

"Mr Bennett?"

"Who's asking?" Jack squinted at the talking shadow.

"It's me, Michael Donaldson."

Michael's arrival and the ensuing conversation brought Ried back from his brooding withdrawal. He shaded his eyes against the light and rose to stand beside Jack, where he studied the teenager, in his armoured Vigiles uniform, with suspicion. "What are you doing here?"

"They told me I could find Centurion Arillius out here."

Arillius marched toward Michael. "Did you get through?"

"Yes, Centurion." Michael saluted and took out a sealed scroll from his satchel. "My instructions were to hand this to you."

Arillius opened the sealed parchment to read in the motorbike's headlight.

Michael walked over to the patio. "What happened here?"

"Gallio–" Jack paused curling his fists into tight balls. "Rose, my daughters… The prick has taken everybody."

Ried cast his eyes down to the dirt and then at Jack. "Jesus, I'm sorry Jack I didn't even think about Rose and the girls…"

Jack gave Ried a weak smile. "Well, they're not in the house. So, I reckon he's got them all hostage to get at you and Marcus–" from the corner of his eye he saw Arillius drop the scroll and stomp their way, unsheathing his gladius. "Hello…"

Michael skipped aside, slack-jawed when Arillius approached with his sword arm tensed.

Jack moved in to protect Ried who pushed him aside.

Arillius ignored the three humans to accost the remaining soldier and push him hard against the wall. Arillius braced his forearm across the man's throat, his gladius held up, so the tip pressed into the Praetorian's stomach, angling upward under his chest armour.

"Bloody hell," Ried and Jack cried out in unison.

"I now understand why you killed the renegade." Arillius pushed the sword a little harder and kicked aside the machine gun dropped by the pinned Praetorian.

Ried frowned as the meaning in Arillius's statement registered through his confusion. "Oh, Christ. He's insurance to make sure no one talked."

"Did I miss something?" Jack asked.

"Gallio is one of several lieutenants in an organisation we have been investigating." Arillius leaned closer to the Praetorian's face. "We believed him to have gone rogue some time ago, and most likely acting beyond their sphere of influence."

"So much for the great Roman space empire," Ried sneered. "You lot can't even control your own soldiers." Ried directed his attention to the Praetorian under Arillius's hold. "So, just what plan is your arsehole boss running?"

"What if Gallio doesn't have a 'plan'? What if he's gone crazy, and this sod is here to clean up?" Jack added.

"The big one is almost right," the pinned Roman answered. "For some time Gallio showed signs of becoming unstable and a threat to all parties. So, we were sent to either re-educate or exterminate." He looked at Arillius. "I do not know of his plans or the whereabouts of their people."

"Then you are of little use," Arillius whispered and pushed the sword farther up behind the man's armour.

The sharp weapon sliced through his victim's lung and heart until the tip broke through the skin beside his collarbone.

The Praetorians mouth opened in shock releasing a river of foaming blood and spittle. His boots slid and skipped on the smooth, concrete floor. His traumatised eyes asked one silent question beneath a small, confused frown: Why?

Arillius kept the sword in place and watched the soldier die. Then when his victim gave a final, small spasm, Arillius withdrew his sword. The unsupported body slumped onto the veranda floor. In frigid silence, Arillius wiped his blade on the dead Roman soldier's sleeve, avoiding the spreading, viscose puddle leaching from the eviscerated Roman.

"What the fuck?" Ried stared at Arillius. "Shit… Why?" He stabbed his finger toward the dead soldier. "Christ. What the hell's wrong with you lot?" Ried lunged forward, grabbing the Centurion's shoulder manica to spin him around and slam him against one of the patio posts.

"He admitted to knowing nothing of Gallio's whereabouts," Arillius eased Ried away with the point of his sword, "which meant his usefulness expired."

"And you fucking believed him?" A faint copper odour wafted from the sword.

"Be careful, off-worlder."

"Or what?" Ried barked, ignoring the tip of the blade resting against his sternum. "You'll decide I'm of no further value?"

For a second, Ried thought Arillius might make that decision. Instead, the Roman lowered his sword and shoved Ried aside. He strode past Jack and across the drive, mounted the motorbike, and rode off into the night.

"Bloody hell, son."

"What?" Hissed Ried. "These bastards are hiding something from us."

"Maybe," Jack stabbed Ried's shoulder, "but making enemies of 'em all is likely to get you bloody well killed in the process."

"Yeah, I know." Ried's faced creased with a petulant frown, and he stormed into the house. Somehow, the death of the Praetorian at Arillius's hands slammed a steel door shut, barring them from finding Abbey and the others.

Jack left Ried alone inside with his thoughts. "Come on Michael help me move this bloke."

Before Jack and Michael had carried the body from the veranda, Ried charged out of the dark, empty house. "Jack, bring the van around to the barn."

"What?"

"I don't think they got everybody."

"What the hell does that mean?"

"Just bring the van."

CHAPTER NINE

Down in the barn, Michael followed Ried who moved around under a candle's glow, as Jack parked the van at the barn's entrance. The harsh light from the van's only working headlamp cast Ried's and Michael's moving shadows against the back wall.

In the back corner, the rope Dom used for opening the safe door stretched between the floor and the winch. Ried handed Michael the candle and scrambled around a stack of disorderly hay bales and overturned crates.

His eyes traced the dark line of the power cable suspended between an old tarp hanging on the wall. Ried tore away the tarp and snatched the control box from its cradle. "Let's hope Dom was right about the capacitors charge." He slammed his palm down on the green button.

"What–" Michael jumped back at the sudden grinding noise from the winch.

Jack joined Ried and Michael with a confused look. "Why are you opening Dom's dry room?"

Jack and Michael both flinched when the hinge gave a final scraping crack as the door opened, casting a gold-tinted light into the barn. Ried hit the stop button, and they all walked toward the open door and waited. Jack gave Ried a questioning look.

Then Jack's ears pricked up at the mouse-like voice calling out from beneath their feet.

"Stephanie?" Asked Jack.

A young girl's voice responded. "Daddy?"

Jack dashed down into the hidden room.

Ried followed Jack down a set of metal stairs, stumbled on the last expanded metal tread when he saw the room which by the look of its depth, he guessed the space ran two-thirds the length of the barn, and almost as wide.

On the longest walls stood a series of steel lockers separated by two double bunks and lining the wall at the opposite end were shelves filled with crates and sealed boxes.

Under the bunk beds, Gemma sat on a mattress with Rose's head in her lap. At the site of his wife's pale complexion and her blood-stained dress, Jack paused and fell to his knees hugging his two daughters, staring down at his wife with moisture filled eyes.

Gemma patted away some perspiration from Rose's face between wiping away the tears staining her own cheeks. On the floor next to the mattress, lay used bandages and field dressings leaching congealed rivulets of blood on the concrete floor. The position of the wound, Rose's laboured breaths, and the amount of blood loss showed her hold on life was losing grip.

Jack lifted the dressing on her wound before he kissed her forehead. With gentle and slow moves, he lifted Rose's head to take Gemma's place. Ried knelt beside his friend, whose large hands caressed his wife's cheek with delicate touches.

Gemma, Michael and Ried moved aside when Jack's daughters shuffled over to sit on either side of their father.

Ried squeezed his friend's shoulder and ushered Gemma and Michael up into the barn.

When Ried stepped into the dark barn, doubt and guilt argued their cases. If he had stayed, then maybe Rose would not have been shot. But then, what would have happened to Nicholas if he and Jack didn't go to town? Anger and a sense of uselessness replaced his numb grief.

Gemma paced in circles wiping her eyes and wringing her hands trying to clean away the blood staining her skin.

Ried knew Gemma could slip into shock, but he needed to know what happened and where Abbey and her father were.

Gemma sniffed, inhaled a long breath and spoke down at their feet. "The proconsul arrived about a half-hour after you left. He and Dom went into the dining room, and I went outside with Abbey and the girls to go for a walk around the farm. Rose said goodbye to Molly and Bill who left in Mr Harris's Ute. After lunch, we played card games, and that's when we heard the explosion at the power plant.

"Two of Marcus's guards came inside and said somebody was coming down the driveway. We all thought it was you returning from town. Then, the second bigger explosion happened, and someone started shooting at the house. Dom rolled the couches over and told us to keep down." Gemma fixated on the back of her hand where she rubbed a patch of dried blood.

"God, it was all so loud. I was so frightened." She flicked a smile at Ried. "But Abbey was a rock… she had been so calm when she pushed the twins and me into the kitchen. Then, another explosion went off near the house, I saw Mr Harris rush down the hall, and come back with a gun.

"He started shooting through the front door. The proconsul went to take the gun, but Mr Harris pushed him aside. He fired more shots through a window. Two of the proconsul's guards ran past us. So, Mr Harris told us all to follow them.

"We ran down the stairs and headed for the barn, but some men appeared from behind the barn, and started shooting at the house. Mr Harris and the guards started shooting back. I heard another explosion out the front, and the shooting stopped." Gemma looked at her feet. "Mr Harris spotted some men near the truck in his shed..."

Ried wanted to ask her how many men but decided to let her keep talking. He knew by her manner, flickering eyes and the way she spoke, Gemma was close to hysteria.

She looked at Ried, her cheeks shiny from the tears flooding from her red-rimmed, bloodshot eyes. "The proconsul and one of his men went back inside. Mr Harris made me, Rose, and the girls, hide under the back stairs and then ran back inside. Then one of the Roman soldiers fell on the stairs after he got shot, so Abbey picked up his gun and started shooting at the ones near the truck.

"Except, the gun jammed or something... Mr Harris ran back outside. Both he and the proconsul started shooting at the men moving up from the truck shed. Abbey ran inside saying something about a shotgun. Then, the shooting stopped, so... so Mr Harris called out to Abbey and then made us run to the barn." Gemma's voice dropped to a whisper. "Then, he came out from behind the machinery shed, shooting at us."

"Who came out?"

Gemma looked up at Ried, her face a canvas of white-washed skin.

"It was Mettius. The one with those horrible black eyes." Gemma's head fell against Ried's shoulder. "It all happened so quick…" She palmed away more tears and wiped her nose against her sleeve. "Rose jumped in front of the twins when we ran into the barn. I think Mr Harris hit Mettius because he cried out and rushed back toward the front of the house.

"When we got into the barn, Mr Harris opened the dry room just enough for us to get in." She wiped away some more tears. "He knew Rose had been shot, so he told me where I could find the first aid stuff, and which cupboard had food and water. I don't think he knew how bad Rose was. He just said he had to get back to Abbey.

"When we climbed down, he switched on the lights, and then closed the door behind us. He told us to be quiet because of the speakers." Gemma tried to describe the sounds coming from the speakers before everything in the house went quiet.

She broke down again when she told Ried she didn't know how to help Rose. "All I could do was keep replacing the dressing to soak up the blood. Oh, God. There was so much blood."

When Gemma finished her recount of the day, she asked why Nicholas wasn't with them. Ried fidgeted, unable to look at Gemma as he told her what happened in town.

He expected her to go ballistic and blame him. But instead, she wrapped her arms around him – before she collapsed, her chest pitching in convulsive grief.

"This is all my fault…"

"No… No, it's not." Ried told her. He held Gemma knowing there was one person to blame. Himself.

Michael shrugged out of his jacket and slipped it around Gemma's shoulders.

Ried passed Gemma to Michael when Jack's daughters came up from the dry room, their wet faces wet and ashen. The way they carried themselves crushed Ried's heart under more bricks of guilt.

Gemma raised her head and covered her mouth when she saw the two girls. She inhaled a quick breath and pushed her own grief aside as she moved to console Jack's daughters in their moment of despair.

"Mummy's dead," Stephanie said. The young teenager's chest convulsed in long, drawn-out sobs.

"No, she hasn't," her sister cried. "She is just sleeping until she gets better." She looked at the surrounding adults with pleading eyes. "Gemma?"

Rebecca held her sister. "Emily, Mummy's never going to wake up because she's with the angels." Stephanie looked at Ried. "Isn't she?"

"That's right, no one can hurt her again." Ried glanced at Gemma and gave a small pathetic shrug.

Gemma mouthed it's okay as she led the girls toward Mitchum's van.

A moment later, Jack came out carrying his wife.

Ried eased himself up to approach Jack. "You okay, mate?"

Jack lifted his eyes from his wife's pale face. His expression was one of surreal disbelief. "I'm okay, but Rose is tired. I'm going to take her home to rest."

Ried nodded and walked over to Michael. He whispered instructions for him to gather some blankets and a mattress for the back of the van.

Ried turned back to Jack. "You can't walk home, mate." He tried keeping his tone soft and level. "How about I drive you?"

At the sight of Jack and Rose, Ried's own fear for Abbey and Dom escalated. Inside his head, the voices argued.

His heart burned with the unknown. He wanted to offer his sympathies and tell his friend everything would be okay, but with Rose looking so peaceful in her husband's arms, the words "sorry" and "okay" seemed pitiful and inadequate. Instead, Ried walked past him to help Michael with the mattresses.

#

Ried's watch twitched past midnight when he returned to the cottage from the hospital. Stepping through the door a glint of moonlight reflected from the bottle of Dr Mitchum's brandy. Ried ignored the bottles subtle temptation and instead fell on the bed.

Fatigue weighed him down, yet sleep eluded him. With a desperate sigh, he rolled from the bed to retrieve the brandy. He eyed the bottle and reckoned the remaining amber liquid was more than enough to bring on sleep.

With the last of the brandy consumed, Ried slumped into a troubled slumber. Guilt fuelled dreams taunted him with visions of Dom and Abbey lying dead at his feet or chained to a wall and tortured. Other flashing images held the distorted, bulbous faces of Gallio and Mettius, laughing and stabbing him with their swords and daggers.

When the morning sky opened in pale purple and greys, Ried decided to saddle Devil and head off in search of Abbey and Dom. But first, he needed a few of his things from Dom's dry room.

His determined march along the path faltered, and instead of going to the barn, Ried headed toward the main house to let Gemma know his decision. He stopped at the gate and massaged his tired eyes.

"Good morning, Ben," Molly said from behind. "Did you sleep all right?"

"Molly." Ried turned with a start. "What? Oh, yes. Fine, thanks," he lied. "Um, aren't you supposed to be down at Jack's place?"

"Yes, but my place is here at home with you and Gemma. There are others who can help with the Bennett farm and family."

Ried's weariness played tricks on him. For a few seconds, he believed he was dreaming. What else would explain Molly speaking in precise, well-enunciated English?

She smiled at Ried's confusion. "Dom and Julia had found, no, rescued the last of my family from a Roman slave party a year before Abbey was born." Molly rested a reassuring arm around Ried's shoulders. "If you're wondering where the simple housekeeper is, you shouldn't. I am still here."

"Back in the early days of The Wars, I was a school teacher and community leader." A shadow clouded her eyes and face. "You know first-hand, that the Romans – for a race capable of interstellar travel – are barbaric and ignorant. Even more so when it came to people with a skin colour different from their own.

"For millennia, my people had lived on this great continent." Molly's eyes sparkled with a cheeky smile. "Then for two centuries, we survived the white men from Europe." Her expression darkened, and the grin faded. "But, the invaders from the stars couldn't tolerate any coloured person was equal to them. So, they took it upon themselves to eradicate or enslave any human not born with Caucasian skin tones.

"And it failed. Many of my people banded together and fled inland. Now no Roman ventures into the heart of our country, and those who tried never returned. Over time, they left us in relative peace. We were tolerated or ignored."

Ried shrugged, unsure of what to say.

"So, Julia Harris suggested I act in a simpler, down-to-earth manner, so as not to attract the attention of the Romans."

"And you didn't mind?"

"No. In fact, I agreed with Julia, because I understood what was at stake. I'm sorry for the deception, but I've played Molly the maid for so long I often forget to drop the persona. Now, there is breakfast in the kitchen along, with a full pot of coffee, to help after your bad night." Molly pointed to the barn. "In the meantime, you've got a friend waiting for you."

"Friend? In the barn?" Ried made his way to the barns darker interior, his curiosity waning under a wave of frustration. *I reckon I've had enough surprises.*

By Molly's relaxed manner, Ried doubted it would be anybody unwanted. But since he arrived in this world, his caution bar sat on a higher scale. Even more so after the last twenty-four hours.

Over to his left, past the horse stalls, a shadowy silhouette of a man loitered near the hay bales.

"What the hell?" Ried froze and scanned the large shed. "Shit… Are you crazy?" He approached his 'friend.' "What happened to heading out west?"

"We only went as far as the old Barakula State Forest," Gazza replied. "The Romans think the place is cursed by the Aborigines, so they don't go there. Anyway, some gypsies told us what's been going on."

Ried straightened his shoulders when he sensed the presence of others before six of Gazza's people stepped out of the dark. "Of all the places to go, why the hell would you come here? I guess you know Molly, but what if somebody else sees you lot?"

"You're right. Molly 'n' her hubby knows all about the Colonel and us," Gazza said.

"You and Dom?" Ried sat on a nearby hay bale, now even more tired from confusion.

"My older brother and I fought beside the Colonel and Major Bennett at the end of The Wars, and a few years later during the long freeze, I started workin' with the Colonel against the Romans. Nothin' big." Gazza shrugged. "Just some stealin' and raidin'."

"How many of your clan know about your arrangement with Dom?"

"Just this lot," Gazza said. "The rest, including Muddgy, would've fuckin' strung us up if they knew."

"So, why are you here–" Ried turned at the sound of somebody entering the barn. "Shit."

"Molly said you were in the –" Jack froze when he saw the small group of Nomads. "Bloody hell." He turned on Ried. "What the hell's going on here?"

"Jack, ah… these are friends of Dom's. They heard what hap–"

"Bullshit." Jack measured the nomad leader.

Ried's world spun. Without thinking, he shouldered his way between Jack and Gazza.

"Don't blame Ried, Major."

Jack's meaty hand pushed Ried aside. He squinted in a frown at the nomad. "Bugger me… Phil Andrews?"

Gazza and Jack matched each other in height, size and strength. At Gazza's camp, there had been no doubt who commanded, but his whole demeanour changed before Jack.

"No, sir. Phil died at Coolum. I'm his brother, Garry," Gazza replied.

Jack stepped back and marshalled Ried toward the stalls. "Is that the same Gazza from your little outing?"

"Yep." Ried didn't know what Jack would do next. The last thing he wanted was to test loyalties. "Apparently, he's been working with Dom to harass and steal from the Romans since… wait… you're kidding…"

"Sorry?" Jack asked.

Ried kicked up dust and hay when he marched back to the Nomads. "Dom sent you out to look for me. That's how you found me near the creek?"

"The Colonel did ask me to find you," Gazza told him. "Truth be known, I didn't give a fuck whether we did or didn't. He said he wasn't sure if you were a Roman or not, but he still wanted you found." Gazza smiled. "It was just dumb fuckin' luck we stumbled on you having a bath."

"I wasn't having a– It doesn't matter." Ried noticed Devil getting agitated and walked over to soothe her. "You still haven't said why you are here."

"I told my mob enough was enough with all the Roman bullshit. So, we came to offer our help, and if it comes down to a scrap… then all the better." Gazza clenched his fists. "Besides, I didn't like being run out of my land." He then looked at Jack, lowered his voice and extended his hand. "Molly told me what happened yesterday with your wife…" He stepped up to Jack. "Sir, I wanna pass on our sympathies for your loss…"

The expression on Jack's face sent alarms through Ried.

Jack's entire body slumped. For a moment, his eyes filled with angry tears, and he looked decades older as he turned his back rubbing the back of his hand across his eyes. His chest expanded from a deep inhale. He straightened his shoulders and faced Gazza.

"Ah…" Jack's sigh carried away his brief emotions. He gave a smile curbed by sorrow when he accepted the nomad's hand and wishes. "Thank you."

"I'm gonna send the word out to other nomad chiefs to keep an ear out for the bastards who stole the Colonel and Abbey. He might be a townie, but most of the clans respect the Colonel. Mind you, they'd never say it."

"I suppose you trust these other clans?" Asked Jack.

"Most of 'em. It's true we don't like townies and sometimes each other, but we hate the fuckin' Romans more." With that said, Gazza and his troop filed out the back door.

Ried looked at Jack and shrugged before following them out. *What the fuck?*

For a full minute, Ried peered into the meadows and patches of scrub, but Gazza and his group had disappeared as if the ground and surrounding grass swallowed them whole. In the distance, a flicker of sunlight reflected off the creek flowing from Abbey's gully.

The reflection raised a bubble of salt water to etch his eyes. Ried dipped his head, swallowed, and pinched his nose between his thumb and finger and wiped his face across each shoulder.

All right, God. If you really are out there, then give me something, anything, to show me where Gallio and that cold bastard have taken Abbey and Dom.

Ried wasn't sure whether he should trust Gazza and the Nomads to find the information that could lead to Abbey and her father. *The question now is... Do I wait, or search for them myself?*

"Bugger me," Jack said behind Ried. "I'll tell you this. Old Dom couldn't have found a better bloke for the job. Back in the day, your mate Gazza and his brother were nick-named the Bush Wraiths..." He looked out across the paddocks. "It looks like his skills haven't faded with time."

"Yeah, well, the day they took me, I could have sworn they appeared from the leaves and grass." Ried kept his back to Jack.

After a few minutes, Ried sat on a bale of hay in front of Devil's stall. "I sort of get the scattered people gathering together after your 'wars'..." said Ried. "either as Nomads or the gypsies and then others gravitating to the growing towns." He gave Jack a confused look, "but it's the math I can't get. Stuff just doesn't add up."

"I don't follow."

"Dr Mitchum said this is an alternate Earth."

"I guess so."

"Well, unless things are radically different to the one, I came from, I'm guessing this world would have had around five or six billion people on it when the Romans invaded, and this version of Australia would have had… what… nineteen to twenty million."

"Sounds about right."

"So, even after casualties and losses, the numbers don't make sense."

"I wondered when you'd get around to stuff like that." Jack dragged over another bale of hay to sit on. "The Roman pricks resorted to their own version of population control. After conquering a town or city, they would kill off a third of the population outright – men, women, children, it didn't matter to them. From those left alive, the bastards took half up on their spaceships, and the rest of the people were left to establish a Roman-based culture."

"One-third of everybody? That leaves a lot of bodies to dispose of."

Jack plucked a fistful of hay and let it fall through his fingers. "There weren't many bodies… Because the Romans used what they called Immolators. Huge tanks armed with massive flamethrowers."

"They incinerated them?" Ried looked dubious.

"Worse." Jack shook his head. "The shit fired from those tanks was so hot it melted glass, concrete, steel and anything else it touched. All it left behind was a foul-smelling tar-like sludge. But the pricks didn't stop there. Anyone who protested, resisted, or batted an eyelid the wrong way, met the same fate." Jack's tone changed. "That's when a worldwide resistance movement started, and The Wars continued, and more people died through fighting, torture and worse."

"Are there any of those tanks left?"

"I bloody well hope not."

"What about the ethnic groups? Surely there would've been a diverse set of cultures."

"There was. Why?"

"Something Molly told me."

"Ah, what can I tell you. The Romans came here with a near-white policy, which they enforced. The longer The Wars went on, the more lethal their actions became." Jack sighed, "We picked up radio chatter about them using Navis Mortems."

"Navis Mortems?"

"Translated it means Death Ships," Jack's remark held the bitterness of hatred. "Giant flying bricks with hundreds of massive pulse cannons and immolators on them. They rained down on Asia, South America and most of Africa and the middle east... Cities, people and their history turned to dust and flames."

"But what about those people living here?"

"They were hunted down and either killed or enslaved." Jack scratched under his chin. "I reckon something snapped in what was left of our world leaders, and they launched the nukes... Some said it was the Commies who fired first, but it didn't matter. Because from that point our world changed." Jack's eyes filled with regret and sorrow. "It's a fair bet most of those orbital ships were full of our people when they got blown up or went down."

Ried slumped, unable to comprehend the enormity of what his friend and Molly told him. He swallowed to keep breathing. An act of genocide by an invading force, and an act of genocide involving your own people to save your own race. *Fuck me*... "I'm – I don't know what to say."

"It's history, son. Nothing you can say or do will change it." Jack rested his hand on Ried's shoulder. "Just pray for their souls and move on. And pray your Nomads can help us find Dom and Abbey."

"You never struck me as the religious type."

"You'd be bloody right, but my Rose was…" Jack headed toward the barn's entrance and thumbed away another tear.

***

PART THREE

CHAPTER ONE

A group of five men carrying toolboxes and ladders came around from the front of Dom's house. Ried recognised the man he spoke with from Jack and Mitchum's drinking game laying out a canvas drop cloth and paint pots.

"What's going on? Who are all these people?" quizzed Ried stopping with Jack at the backyard fence.

"These fellas are here to fix Mr H's home," Molly said from the clothesline, holding a basket of dry clothing and sheets.

Ried raised an eyebrow at how Molly spoke.

Nearby, a young, dark-haired woman threw blood-stained towels, curtains, and linen on an open fire.

"I'll leave you lot to it." Jack's mood sobered. "I'm off to make the arrangements for Rose's funeral."

"You had breakfast this morning, Mr B?" Molly lifted out one of the cotton napkins from the basket to hand to Jack, who used the cloth to mop away the swollen tears glistening on his beard. "I reckon not," Molly answered for him. "First, you eat. Then do what you need to."

Despite his reluctance to eat, Jack helped himself to coffee and pancakes. Ried sat across from him, feeling awkward and saying nothing, while in the background Dom's house evolved into a mini construction zone.

"How are the girls?"

"Time will tell," Jack replied between mouthfuls.

"So, why did you come here this morning?" Asked Ried pouring a coffee.

"I wanted to see if you were okay."

Ried held the coffee cup at his mouth for longer than necessary. *Jesus Christ. Rose died in his arms, they kidnapped Abbey and Dom, and he wants to make sure I'm ok…* Unable to voice a response, Ried gave a partial shrug.

"I also wanted to make sure you were still here and coming to Rose's funeral."

Ried's cheeks warmed from embarrassment, and he dropped his eyes to concentrate on his plate of untouched food. "To be honest, I wasn't sure you'd want me there after everything that's happened."

"Strewth, son," Jack said. "You're as much a pawn in all this as the rest of us."

Ried understood Jack's sentiment, but in his heart, he didn't agree with it. "Maybe."

Jack put a meaty, yet gentle hand on Ried's shoulder, "And I have a favour to ask."

"Name it."

"I'd like you to stand beside me as my second pallbearer."

Okay… That was not the answer I was expecting.

Apart from the construction repairs around the house. All he could hear in his head was the last conversation Rose had with him, or rather, one word rose from that talk; Usurper, and it announced itself in a white light of accusation.

"What about Dr Mitchum? I thought, apart from Dom, he was your oldest friend."

"It's okay, son," Jack assured Ried. "I've already spoken to the Doc. Besides, it was his idea."

Ried opened his mouth to decline the gracious and personal offer, but then he heard himself say, "I'd be honoured."

After Jack left, Ried abandoned his unfinished breakfast and wandered through the house to see more men sanding, filling, and painting. Without a word, Molly's husband came up behind Ried and steered him back to the kitchen, but instead of eating he went outside and threw up.

He gripped the step to stop from collapsing; Dom and Abbey's kidnapping, Rose, the Nomads in the barn, Jack's request, and all the people fixing Dom's house overwhelmed Ried. His knees folded and he all but fell on the lower step, his emotions spun in tightening circles.

Molly came down with a glass of water and led him away from the house.

Ried gripped the top rail of the fence, stretched his arms and squeezed his eyes shut. "Why are they even here?" He drew a deep breath and looked across at Molly. "It's only been a day. Bloody hell, Molly. Dom's gone, Abbey's gone... and all they can do is fix his bloody house."

"They may have been taken, Ben..." Molly leaned on the fence beside him her voice quiet. Her own heart wallowed with angst at the loss of Dom and Abbey, but the young man beside her tore at her maternal instincts. When she first saw Ried, his aura shone told her he came for a reason. Now his aura pulsed in dark reds haloed by a muddy dark blue blending to an almost black fog. "But I don't believe they are lost." She nodded toward the house. "Many people love Abbey and Dom but remember those same people are also hurting. Fixing the house is their way of saying and believing they'll be back."

340

When Molly reached for Ried's hand, he pushed himself away from the fence and stormed through the gate.

Molly stood, still holding the full glass of water and watched Ried's head bob out of sight as William, with tools in hand, leaned on the fence beside his wife. "Our young traveller seems broken and angry."

"We are all angry. "

William flinched from his wife's tone.

Molly gripped her husband's hand for his forgiveness. "Ben is troubled with bad spirits," she said and passed the glass of water to William. There was no point wasting it. "I also don't believe the Rainbow Serpent brought him to us, change its mind and break him." She chided her husband in a soft "what have I told you" voice.

William had learned many years ago not to argue with the Dreamtime magic his wife and her mother's line were strong in. Yet, that didn't keep his pragmatic side from nudging her belief. When the need arose.

"What about the boss and Abbey?"

"Their future's intertwined with Ben's path now."

William opened his mouth but caught the expression on his wife's face. So, he made a prudent decision and kept his opinion unspoken. With a smile and wink, William held her hand and kissed her cheek. "There are times I prefer Molly, the housemaid," he teased, whispering in her ear, and swinging his hammer up for a soft tap on her bum.

After another fretful night, Ried rode Devil past the front gate, deciding to hold off on his quest to find Dom and Abbey. He would give Gazza another day after the funeral for Rose, and then he would start his own search by visiting the Vigiles barracks and finding out what they knew, and he didn't care who he upset or who suffered.

Two hundred metres down the road, he came across a small roadblock guarded by townspeople and six Vigiles, including an officer and Michael Donaldson.

"Easy, girl," Ried soothed the animal. "You wanna explain?"

The Vigiles officer caught the subtle tone in Ried's voice. "There may not have been any local sightings or reports on Gallio's whereabouts, but as a precaution, we set these up on all the roads leading to Mr Harris's and Mr Bennett's properties."

"Sorry, who are you?" Ried studied the officer.

"I am Cassius Gellius Scapula. The Vigiles' Tesserarius."

"Sounds official, and very Roman," Ried scoffed. "So, are these your new recruits?" His voice seethed with sarcasm.

"No. I think you misunderstand." Cassius offered his hand to Ried. "The cordons are not official. They are purely for added safety."

The tone of the Tesserarius and his manner chastised Ried enough for him to lower his aggressive stance, but not his caution.

"I have also secured the road to the church and the cemetery for the funeral tomorrow," Cassius added, still holding out his hand.

Ried dismounted and took the offered hand.

"My family is eager to meet you."

342

"They'll be at the funeral?"

"And the service. You may not believe this," Cassius smiled, "but there are many Romans who have worshipped one god and disagree with our Senate's attitude to dominate rather than work and live in peace."

"One god?"

"Yes."

"Okay." Ried cast his eye over the blockade and the mix of Vigiles and townspeople. With a perplexed shake of his head, he mounted Devil and rode away.

#

The following afternoon after laying Rose to rest, many of those at the service went back to Jack's house for a wake organised by the local quilting association.

Ried studied the people and the event. Unlike the homecoming party held at Dom's, this gathering overflowed with quiet reverence and earnest conversations.

Throughout the day, a continuous stream of people treated Ried like a member of the household, thanking him for everything he'd done to help Jack and Dom's family. Ried's weak, false smiles and thank you's concealed an overpowering conviction he did not deserve their support or gratitude.

What contributed to that belief was Nicholas's petulant, latent anger. The baleful stares from Dom's son soon soured away the platitudes passed on by the others and further fuelled Ried's guilt. By seven in the evening, he made a quiet exit.

"Where are you off to?" Jack asked from the shadows.

"The cottage." Ried faced the gate leading into Jack's driveway. "Jesus, Jack. This is all because of me." His guilt fermented into anger as the gravel crunched under his spinning heel. He held Jack's gaze. "All those people… all bloody day long, they kept thanking me for what I had done to help, when Abbey, Dom, and Ro-Rose…" Ried let the sentence fall away before continuing. "Oh, and let's not forget, Nicholas, who hates me for what happened."

"I wouldn't pay too much heed where Dom's boy is concerned. Nicholas will always be a spoilt little twat."

"It is not just Nicholas." Ried sighed and ran his fingers through his hair. "Don't you get it?" His question hung heavy with regret. "This is my fault… all of it. Shit." Ried pointed back to Jack's house. "Maybe Nicholas is right. Maybe I should've fucking died after the crash," Ried whispered, turning back toward the road beyond the gate.

Jack's long legs carried him to block Ried's path. "And now you're just gonna walk out on us?"

Ried stepped around Jack, refusing to let his friend's size and manner intimidate him. "Yes."

Jack clamped his hand around Ried's arm. "This isn't just about what happened at Dom's place, is it?"

"Fuck off, Jack." With surprising power, Ried freed his arm and held the large farmer's eye.

"That's twice you've said that to me," growled Jack.

Ried caught the underlying tone in Jack's voice and straightened to his full height, squaring off his shoulders.

Jack moved in and stabbed a finger into the younger man's chest. "I saw the look on your face with MacMahon, and it's one I've seen before."

"Leave it, Jack." Ried had never seen a live Grizzly bear, but right then, Jackson Bennett gave a damned good impression of one. Still, Ried held his squared-off posture. He didn't doubt he could take down Jack, Ried also did not doubt, by the end, Jack will have broken him as well. "You don't know what you're talking about."

"Try me?" Jack waited for a response from Ried, and when none came, he continued. "That scar you keep rubbing. I bet it's got something to do with what's eating you up inside."

Ried's jaw clenched under a twitching cheek muscle.

"So, how many men did you lose?"

"My whole damn squad." Ried's defensive stance crumpled when his eyes lost focus from the black memory, and he massaged the scar on his shoulder. "My entire troop all died, and I got sent home with a medal and three stripes."

"Do you think they gave you a medal because it was your fault? It was war, son. Sometimes shit happens—"

"Don't you bloody dare patronise me? You weren't there."

"Back off, Ben. I know full well what war is about and what can bloody well happen." Jack pointed out into the night. "And if you reckon riding off alone to find them and getting yourself killed in the process is the best way to resolve your guilt and anger, then you're a bloody idiot."

"I can't stay here." Ried also pointed out into the night. "Not while those bastards have Abbey and Dom."

"Dom's a tough son of a bitch. He'll take care of her."

"For how long? A week? A month?" Ried spread his arms to emphasise his point.

"All right. Where are you gonna start looking?"

"I'll figure something out."

"No, Ben. Just give it a couple more days," Jack pleaded. "Gallio's ego will get the better of him, and then we'll have something to work with."

"What? You really believe that?"

"Time will tell, son. It always does."

"You know what," Ried responded, tapping Jack's chest with two fingers. "Time can kiss my arse!" Not waiting for a response, he turned and marched into the night.

Jack sighed, watching the darkness swallow Ried. With his arms folded, Jack stood listening to the younger man's footsteps fade into silence. Behind Jack, a familiar step came crunching through the gravel.

"Have you seen Ben?" Mitchum asked, stopping alongside Jack. "He wanted me to drop him back at the cottage."

"He decided to walk," Jack replied as he headed back along his drive.

Mitchum grew alarmed and trotted after Jack. "And you let him go? What if Gallio's thugs are still about?"

"Believe me, Doc. I'd be more worried about them," Jack said. "Look, the boy will be fine. So, come and have a drink while we talk about Rose, Julia, and your Victoria."

#

A pair of crows bounced across the roof of the barn in the early morning light. Beneath their feet, Ried stuffed his clothes in two saddlebags outside Devils stall and prepared another animal as a packhorse. Before saddling Devil, he winched open the safe door and went inside.

At the foot of the steps, he glanced over where they found Gemma with Rose and the girls. His fist balled from muted frustration. *I will either put this right or die in the fucking process.*

Ried collected his gear and surveyed the room again. *Wait...* "What the hell?"

The room was clean, with everything returned and in place. Ried shook his head. *Nicholas is too self-centred to care about his father's stuff, and Jack was busy with Rose's funeral...* "Bloody hell," he said in hushed admiration. "Is there anything Molly and Will won't do for Dom?"

With his bags in hand, Ried put his foot on the first tread and noticed a thin, rectangular line etched in the wall beyond the steps. *Come on, Ried. It's none of your business.* But the oddity of the line got the better of him. Dropping the bags on the stair, Ried walked around to inspect the wall.

Resting his palms on the surface, he discovered two small concealed covers over inset lever handles. He tested the two handles, but they would neither push up nor down.

Wrapping both hands around the lowest bar, Ried leaned on it with all his weight. When nothing happened, he braced his feet and pulled the handle up. He gritted his jaw, re-gripped the handle and repeated the process. With a gunshot crack, the handle snapped up on his third attempt.

"Okay, if the bottom one goes up let's see if the top one goes down." An artery in Ried's neck pulsed and bulged threatening to tear apart.

A second gunshot rewarded his efforts when the lever jerked down. With a hand on each lever, Ried pulled until the tendons in his wrist and shoulders threatened to snap, but the door refused his attempt to open.

Letting go of the handles, Ried took another deep breath and put his left foot flat against the wall for leverage. He grabbed the handles again and pulled until he thought the strain would snap his tendons from the bone.

At first, the shift was gradual, but then with progressive, stiff movements, the door crept open until a soft whoosh and whistle of air rushed through the enlarging crack.

Ried's arm muscles sang out in distress, and his back muscles joined the inner agony going on as Ried continued to pull until the door popped open.

"Okay, why the hell would Dom keep an airtight room beneath his barn?" Ried shook his arms to return the circulation in his overworked muscles, and stepped into the deep charcoal darkness, groping the walls for a light switch.

Two banks of fluorescent light flickered to life, and Ried then exhaled through a long, soft whistle.

"Fuck me…" Ried stood at the threshold in awe. Illuminated by the twin banks of lights was a well-stocked armoury. Back on his Earth, the weapons lining the racks were items often found in private collections and or museums.

What was the old bugger up too? Lost in his reverie, Ried didn't hear the shout from above. The next call carried more urgency to it.

"Down here," he called back

"Get your arse up here. We need to talk," Jack shouted down from the barn.

"Bugger that. You need to get down here and check this out."

Jack's heavy footfalls rang on the metal stairs and paused at the bottom finding an empty room. "Ben?"

"In here."

Jack strolled up to the armouries door frame which he ran his eye over before spotting Ried cradling an M-16 like an archaeologist who held Excalibur.

"Bloody hell." Jack let out a long, soft whistle. "Dom and his thieving Nomads have been more than a little busy in their games."

"Why would Dom have all this?" Ried ran his hand along a shelf of semi-automatic pistols, bayonets, and hunting knives.

Jack headed straight to a rack holding M-60 machine guns. He gaped in awe at the weapons. "I haven't a bloody clue." He lifted one from the shelf and cycled the action, pulled the trigger, and grinned when the hammer slid forward to stop with a solid, loud clack.

Returning the M-60, Jack let his gaze hover over the room filled with Roman carbines, sniper rifles, crates of ammunition, and grenades. "This lot must've taken years to collect. I wonder why he never told me."

"I reckon Dom used Gazza and his group to keep you safe at arm's length," Ried said, curious to see what else Dom may have hidden.

"From what?" Jack replaced the gun and followed Ried about the armoury while checking out the long reloading bench dominating the centre of the arsenal.

"Think about it," Ried said. "Even if the Romans found out Dom had this stuff, then you, theoretically, wouldn't be implicated." He saw Jack's eyes lose focus for a few moments. "What's the matter?"

"Protecting me? He's been bloody doing that more times than I can friggin' count." Jack wonder back out, sat on the metal steps and stroked his thick, red beard.

"It started when we lost Sydney and Orchid Hill back in '84. I was already pretty messed up from almost four years of fighting those Roman fuckers."

Ried raised a surprised eyebrow at Jack's last curse. Until then, he'd never heard the big man drop the F-bomb.

"I drank way too much, and I popped any drug or pill I could find to help me sleep and cope. I'd become a disastrous walking pile of shit.

"Hell, even though we were losing, my CO was ready to have me shot without a court-martial. The only thing saving my arse was the Romans beating the crap out of us in Sydney, and a desperate move, brigade pulled us back to the foot of the mountains near Penrith.

"Dom and his company had been dodging their artillery and flanking troops when he found me in the ruins of a house in Jordan Springs. I freaked out and nearly blew his head off." Jack hiccupped a mirthless laugh.

"Dom took one look at me and walked. Which was fine by me, except, the bastard came back, grabbed me by the collar, and threw me out into the street?" Jacks eye glinted with the memory.

"It had been a rough couple of weeks. I was scared, tired, and coming off a shitty high. From memory, I took offence at getting tossed out on my ear." Jack rocked his head back with a soft laugh. "Strewth, did we exchange some solid blows? And then, a stray mortar took out the rest of the house I'd been hiding in.

"When I sobered up, he put me under arrest and trotting beside a bunch of refugees. No one wanted to admit it, but we were lost and still behind enemy lines. Then a few days later, we ran into two Roman equites patrol. Outnumbered, Dom released me and gave me back my rifle.

"The bugger knew I wanted to shoot him, and we had words along those lines, but all he cared about was getting everyone out of there.

"Before we knew what happened, Dom's flank fell to pieces, and I charged in dragging his wounded butt to safety." Jack shrugged, "I guess we've been watching each other's backs ever since." He opened several wall lockers. "Let's see what else the old bugger's been stashing."

Inspecting the rest of the cupboards and draws, they found military fatigues, assorted civilian clothing, an assortment of webbing, pouches, water bottles, personal cooking equipment, and backpacks, while other cabinets overflowed with canned and dehydrated food. Each of the lower bunks held nothing but medical supplies.

"This is one hell of a collection." Ried lowered himself on the stairs and wondered at the armoury.

"It is that," Jack said, "just what were you doing down here, anyway?" Jack asked when he closed the last cupboard.

Ried grinned and headed over to his cases and luggage near the stairs. He lowered himself on his haunches and opened one of his locked cases.

When Ried turned around, he carried a smaller, blue, plastic case with the embossed words 'Smith and Wesson'.

Handing Jack, the case, Ried unlocked the padlock and raised the lid. With the ease of familiarity, Ried lifted out a stainless steel, six-shot, .357 calibre revolver and passed it to Jack.

"How much of this do you reckon we can carry?" Jack admired the pistol, testing the weight and balance. "Nice piece."

"Thanks. And what's this 'we'?"

351

"I should've been here to watch his back, and I wasn't."
Jack returned the revolver. "Which means I'm bloody well
going with you."

"Except I don't have a clue where to start."

Jack patted Ried's shoulder. "Time will tell, son. Time
will tell." Jack said walking back to the armoury.

CHAPTER TWO

On their third night in captivity, Dom wondered what motivated Gallio's actions; revenge, ransom or torture? Given the past and often awkward nature of his relationship with Gallio, Dom hedged his bets with the prime motivator being vengeance.

The sound of lithe footsteps crunching across the gravel, leaves and twigs silenced the nearby crickets. Dom rolled away from their pitiful fire peering into the bleak darkness as a silhouette emerged from the shadows to stand over Abbey.

Mettius tilted his head, inspecting Abbey in the fire's flickering light. The orange glow from the coals reflected in the black orbs of his eyes. He extended his hand to brush a strand of hair away from her bruised face.

Dom stiffened in impotent anger. He screamed at the Roman through the wad of cloth covering his mouth, his helpless outrage fermenting to a murderous, vengeful stare on Mettius who swivelled his neck to focus his unblinking eyes at Dom.

The sensation of Mettius's touch woke Abbey with a start. The sight of him so close sent her recoiling in fear. She kicked out her legs and shuffled backwards. Her eyes expanded with terror. Her cries muffled behind the thick gag over her mouth.

Mettius reached down, grabbed her shoulders and considered Abbey's frightened expression. He offered her a smile so cold the air around his face seemed to freeze. With his hand holding the nap of her neck, he let his other hand slip down her arm.

On impulse, driven by fear-tinged defiance, she lifted her knees to her stomach. The action producing a thick, rasping sound behind Mettius's wolfish smile.

The rasp evolved into a laugh. "If I wanted you, I would've taken you long before now." He moved her nearer to the fire. With slow, deliberate movements, Mettius leaned closer, stretched out his arm and gathered up a small log which he threw on the fire.

"The night is cold, and I am certain Gallio does not wish you to catch a chill." Mettius rose, looked down at Dom, and shoved him closer to the fire.

On impulse, Dom shrank back at the sight of Mettius's face in the firelight gleaming in those coal-black orbs. A cold reflection in a face paled by the fire's light gave Mettius the facade of a walking corpse. And the blood-soaked bandage over his right cheek and ear added to the illusion.

Mettius shifted his gaze to Marcus laying trussed and bound beside Dom. For a long, silent minute, Mettius contemplated Marcus before walking off into the darkness.

The next morning an acne-scarred man brought bowls containing their morning rations.

During the night, one of the Praetorian escorts belonging to Marcus had died – a result of injuries sustained in an earlier unprovoked beating. Scar-face swung his foot in a savage kick that landed between the dead man's shoulder blades. When the body rocked and made no sound, the thug spat a wet ball of phlegm at the dead Roman.

"Here." He dropped the dead man's bowl of rations between Dom and Marcus. "You can thank old mate for a bonus meal." Not caring if anyone commented, he trudged back to the rest of Gallio's renegades.

A few minutes later, three other men came over to the Praetorian's lifeless body.

In mortified disgust, Abbey looked on while two of Gallio's men stripped the dead man of his clothes and armour, tossing the items into a disarrayed pile. When they finished, they dragged the naked body through the dry undergrowth and, with callous disregard, threw the corpse into a small gully.

"Aren't they going to at least bury him?" Abbey asked.

"Why bother with a grave when the animals would only dig it up?" Gallio approached them – brimming with casual arrogance – and sat on his haunches and helped himself to some dried fruit and old cheese in Dom's bowl.

"What do you want?" Hissed Dom

"What do I want?" Gallio gave the question a long pause of consideration. "Oh, Dominic, I desire a lot. The slow death of you and Bennett, for a start." He rose and paced around the smouldering fire. "Something that should have happened back on your farm."

Gallio picked up a long stick and poked at the fire. "You two have been a constant irritant during my governorship. 'The great heroes of 'The War'." Gallio's voice lowered an octave, "do you have any idea what humiliation I endured? My authority continually placated by the town elders who sought your council at every juncture?"

"Did you ever ask why they came to me?"

Gallio waved the tip of the smouldering stick at Dom. "Every decision I made was for the good of all and not just the weak liberal minded fools such as yourselves."

Before Dom replied, Gallio moved over to Marcus. "And you... helping humans to build and grow things." He kicked the proconsul, his voice savage. "We are their masters! Not their allies. We rule by domination, and they build for us."

Like a petulant child, Gallio whipped Marcus with the stick. "But, what support do I get from you? Nothing. You strip me of my rank. You humiliate me, by making him – a human." Gallio gave Dom a look filled with hate, fire and ice, "a non-Roman – the governor!" Gallio crouched down, shifted his attention back on Marcus and jerked him onto his knees. "Know this, traitor. I will march upon Toowoomba and show your weak brethren the path to a better future. One in which the Romans will be the rightful rulers of this pathetic race." He shoved Marcus back and prowled around the proconsul. "I will take pleasure in killing you." Stretching out his arms, Gallio danced in a slow circle before placing his face a breath away from Marcus. "Then, I will burn away the infection created by you all."

During Gallio's fervent rantings, his men, Roman and human alike, waved and throwing their arms in the air, cheering and calling out his name.

With all eyes focused on Gallio during his fevered rant, Dom measured and weighed up each man and Roman. Some part of him felt sorry for those of non-Roman blood within the group. *The stupid bastards don't have a clue Gallio will toss them aside like bags of dog shit if he gets his way.*

At the back of the vocal renegades, Dom spotted two Praetorians, who saluted, but otherwise stood in stoic silence away from the others.

Marcus also reacted to the speech. His head whiplashed back and forward driving his forehead into the bridge of Gallio's nose.

Crying out in pain and disbelief from the lightning-fast headbutt, Gallio tumbled and rolled across the edge of the fire scattering a few hot coals. With the speed of a serpent, Gallio swivelled around in a crouch.

He rocked back on his haunches and wiped at the blood oozing from the split skin on his nose. For thirty seconds Gallio stared, through watering eyes at the dark smear across his fingers and palm.

If Gallio's earlier expressions smouldered with betrayal, his body language now burned from the fires of hatred.

Marcus's face showed no fear or concern with Gallio's move. Instead, he held a look of bitter disappointment. The expression a father shows a rebellious, willful, self-destructive teenager.

Gallio lifted out his gladius and rested the tip of the sword in the fire. He then reached out with his blood-stained hand and rubbed across Marcus's toga.

No one spoke or moved. The fire crackled in ignorance while Dom frowned at Gallios actions. Everyone fell quiet, and even the sounds of nature fell into a hushed silence.

Marcus willed himself to move. Yet every muscle and tendon held firm by a superglue made of rising fear. His eyes danced between the sword resting in the fire and Gallio's damaged face.

Tilting his head, Gallio's face morphed into an expressionless, blood-stained mask.

A Currawong cawed in a nearby gum. The bird's cry did nothing to reset the palpable tension around the fire.

Gallio lifted the sword and studied the iridescent point.

Marcus focused on the white-hot tip of the sword. From terror and anticipation, beads of perspiration tumbled over themselves to trickle down his neck and chest.

Using his bloody hand, Gallio wiped the sweat from Marcus's brow and cheek, leaving behind a thin, sticky red film. In a sudden move, Gallio grabbed a handful of Marcus's hair.

Then, with a vicious snap of his wrist, he pulled Marcus's head to the right to further expose his shoulder. Locking eyes with Marcus, his lips twisted into a malicious grin of unadulterated evil.

Trapped in Mettius's solid grip, powerless, and hypnotised by the surrounding scene, Marcus fell into the surreal, morbid horror of the moment.

The blades super-heated metal scorched, blistered and then melted the skin and flesh of Marcus's exposed shoulder.

In a brief interlude of surprise, Marcus's skin went cold from the first touch of the sword. In an instant, the surprise transitioned into something beyond comprehension when the pain receptors awoke.

Marcus flinched and wriggled from a sensation so intense, it allowed nothing but one long, terrified, primal scream.

The bitter, rancid stench of burning flesh filled the morning air.

A man in the group turned to hurl his breakfast in a stream of vomit.

Abbey cried and hid her face in her lap.

Dom spun himself around and lashed out with his legs catching Gallio by surprise. The sword fell from Gallios hand to land in the dirt hissing and smouldering on the dry leaves.

Marcus gaped at his burned shoulder and then collapsed.

Abbey screamed when somebody dragged her back.

Dom twisted toward Abbey and slid sideways in a shroud of darkness when a brilliant flash exploded inside his head.

#

The following day, Jack headed toward the tray of an old, beaten-up Land Cruiser ute. Slung over his shoulder, he carried the last long, thick canvas bag from the back of Dom's house.

"Strewth. I reckon this last bugger is the heaviest," he groaned after tossing the bag alongside similar bundles, crates and metal cases.

"Christ, I hope this shit heap drives better than it looks."

"Settle down." Jack rubbed his hand along the tray's side in mock pain and sorrow. "Nicholas ran his eye over her," he stepped forward and slapped the hood, "he reckons old man Gilchrist did a brilliant piece of engineering on the old girl."

"All right. Let's say the thing stays in one piece, and we make it to where Gallio's hiding," Ried said, "and they're not there, or worse, we walk into a trap."

"What, you don't trust your Nomads?"

"That's not what I said," replied Ried.

Jack reached through the Ute's passenger window to retrieve a map. "As long as old Gazza hasn't gone completely feral against the world, then I'm willing to put a little faith in what he gave us." Jack waved the folded chart.

Ried walked around to take the item in question from Jack's grasp. He unfolded the faded, tissue-thin tourist map and traced the roads marked on the paper, unsure which would be the best route to follow.

"Why would Gallio head so far away instead of finding a closer place to fortify and set up camp?"

"Did you say something?" Jack asked from behind the ute.

"How accurate is this map?"

"As good as we'll ever get." Jack came up and slid the chart from under Ried's hands and folded the paper along the well-worn creases. "Why?"

"Well, going by the map and what info Gazza gave us about the roads, we're in for a long drive."

"If you're asking whether we have enough fuel to get there and home again." He leaned back through the window. "I'll put your mind at rest." Jack twisted the glove-box latch. "Assuming we find them, rescue them, and we all survive," Jack shrugged his wide shoulders, "it's gonna be a bloody long walk home."

"What about bartering for extra fuel along the way?"

"With the methane plant reduced to nothing but a big hole," Jack gave Ried a consolatory pat on the shoulder, "I doubt any bugger's gonna give up what gas they have left." He walked toward his daughters, who came outside carrying an overloaded basket of food for the trip.

Ried left Jack with his family while he readjusted the ropes holding everything down on the ute's timber tray.

Over the last few days, Ried had gotten to know the girls a little better. The eldest, Stephanie, could hold a decent conversation with most adults. Her sister Emily, however, preferred her own company and wore her heart on her sleeve, with quick outbursts of emotions.

Jack stood and held their hands, stepping aside so Ried could collect the basket, and then wrapped his arms around his daughters to drag them in for a long hug.

Stephanie took her father's hand when he let them go as Emma sobbed aloud and ran back to the house. Jack stayed on his knees in front of Stephanie, who She wiped away a tear tracking a course through her freckles and brushed her auburn hair back from her face.

"Don't worry, Daddy. We'll be okay with Aunty Gemma and Uncle Nicholas."

"I know you will, princess."

Stephanie was about to follow her sister, but she stopped and threw her arms around her father's neck. When she let go, she wiped away her tears. "You make sure the man who hurt Mummy never hurts anyone else."

"Honey, we're going to rescue Aunty Abbey and her dad."

"Yes, I know that, Daddy. Just promise, for Emily and for Mummy." Stephanie shook all over but held herself high as she went to join her sister.

Jack stayed on his knees, too dumbstruck for words.

The approaching sound of vehicles coming up the drive saved Ried from adding any further comment. He dropped the basket on the passenger seat as Jack returned.

The driveway filled with a small convoy, led by two Roman war bikes followed by the vet's truck. Next came a faded, light-blue Holden station wagon, in front of a yellow Toyota four-wheel-drive.

Ried and Jack glanced at each other with bemused faces.

Hearing the small convoy, Nicholas, Gemma, the twins, Molly and William came out to the patio.

Ried glanced up at Jack. "Something you wanna tell me?"

"Nope. This isn't my doing."

When the vehicles came stopped, thirty men and boys climbed out to mill around the cars. At the head of the group stood Dr Mitchum, Michael Donaldson and Cassius wearing civilian clothing.

Dr Mitchum stepped forward when Jack and Ried approached.

"G'day, Doc," Jack eyed the group gathering behind Mitchum. "You wanna explain?"

"I would have thought it obvious."

"We're going with you." Michael came up from behind the doctor.

Jack's forehead creased from his raised eyebrows. "Strewth, Doc. Aren't you getting a bit long in the tooth for this?" He asked with crossed arms.

Mitchum lit a cigar. "Old I may be, but I can still drink you under the table." He puffed a cloud of blue-grey smoke in Jack's direction. "And if Dom or Abbey are injured, are you trained to deal with that? No, you're not. So, like it or not, you need me."

"Come on Doc. This ain't a drinking game."

Ried's own thoughts differed little from Jack's, but he conceded to the doctor's logic. He looked at Jack with a deep frown and long silent sigh.

Christ. I knew we should've left before sunrise.

He checked his watch and spotted Nicholas heading over to the crowd. "Bloody hell?" Ried ran to Nicholas and led him aside by the elbow. "What the hell are you doing?"

"Joining them."

Ried picked up on the 'them', rather than 'you'. "C'mon, mate. Stay with Gemma."

"Why?" Nicholas raised himself to his full height, contorted in pain while holding his side and wincing from the effort.

"That's why." Ried glanced over Nicholas's shoulder to catch Gemma's expression of confusion. "And what if we–"

"Don't you dare fucking say 'if.'" He scowled at Ried, his tone caustic. "All right, 'mate.' I'll stay behind, but you better bloody well bring them back." Nicholas gave Ried another of his frustrated, petulant looks, before marching back to Gemma.

"Christ almighty." Ried's shoulders fell under an audible sigh. Other than Jack, he hadn't counted on others joining the rescue mission, let alone be responsible for their lives.

Ashamed of his thoughts, he slipped his hands into his pockets and turned away from the group of men to stand against the rail at the far end of the veranda.

Jack, Mitchum and Cassius, led the group in a protracted discussion. Going by their body language and how everybody gesticulated, Ried gathered the conversation had gone beyond a simple 'we're coming' talk.

The discussion went on for over an hour before they reached an agreement. When the words and arguments concluded, the station wagon and yellow four-wheel- drive left with more than half of those who came.

The only vehicles left were Jacks Toyota ute, the two war bikes, and Lester Jennings's truck. The vet chose not to stay but left his lorry behind in his stead.

Ried surveyed the remaining fifteen men. "How do you reckon Cassius will react when we pull out the stash from Dom's armoury?" He asked Jack when they returned to the four-by-four.

"Dunno. I reckon we'll tell him you brought 'em with you." Jack patted Ried's shoulder with a broad grin under his beard.

"You were quiet before," Mitchum said, coming up to lean against the ute beside Ried, who readjusted the ropes and bags on the vehicles tray.

"I'm an outsider, Dr Mitchum." He finished readjusting the last knot. "It's not my place to tell them what they can or can't do." Ried turned to Mitchum. "I know why I'm doing this." He pointed to Cassius and the others. "I suppose they're here out of loyalty for Jack and Dom."

"Yes, loyalty to Dom and Jack is a factor, but that's not their only reason for coming."

"I guess they've also got scores to settle," Ried replied turning back to concentrate on the Ute's cargo.

Mitchum smiled. "You don't see it, do you?"

"See what?"

"They also came to follow you."

Ried's shoulders sagged, and he shook his head.

"The Doc's right. I didn't want to tell you, but your deeds have spread through the old grapevine." Jack joined them and leaned against the ute beside Ried. "It seems, you've become a bit of a hero."

After an elephantine, pregnant pause, Ried peered over his shoulder at the group. "I can't help what they think." He pushed himself off the ute. "It's getting late, and we need to get moving."

Ried knew to voice his own concerns and thoughts would fall on deaf ears so, he helped load the last of the men's belongings into the truck. When he asked about the stack of boxes tied in the corner, the young man from the pub, named Eddy, explained how Cassius liberated a few carbines, pistols and ammunition.

Ried looked over at Cassius.

Cassius replied. "Since no one here has any real weapons, I… borrowed them."

"Ah… Good idea." Ried scratched his ear, shooting Jack a questioning glance. "What about your absence from the barracks?"

"I've resigned my commission to help find Mr Harris and his daughter."

"I've never heard of you lot leaving the service," Jack interjected.

"Nor have I," Cassius replied.

"Jack tells me you can shed more info on what we know already." Ried jumped out from the truck.

Cassius shrugged. "Assuming what we've been told is correct, then Gallio is most likely heading for the Aquilae Nidus."

"Which is what?"

"Sorry. I believe in your tongue, you'd call it an eagle's nest. To be honest, I thought the place was just a myth left over from The Wars."

"It ain't a myth." The statement came from Gazza walking up from the back of Dom's house.

"Jesus." Ried spun around, "You really have to stop doing that."

"Being quiet has kept me alive. So, I ain't about to change." On either side of Gazza stood four other Nomads, carrying packs, hunting bows and spears. "I've decided to give you a hand."

A voice called out from the men grouped nearby. "I thought you people didn't like involving yourselves in our business."

Gazza rolled his pack from his shoulder to thump in the dirt when he swung his L1A1 rifle around to rest in his crossed arms. He took three steps toward the man who spoke. "Nobody fuckin' asked you." He took another step forward and shifted his rifle. "And if you were on fire, I wouldn't waste my piss to put it out."

"Then bugger off back to whatever bush you crawled out of."

"Best be careful, you scrawny piece of dried dog shit–"

"OI! Back off the lot of you." Jack's voice boomed across the fields, as he marched between the townspeople and the Nomads, and turned on the heckler. "Smithy pull your flamin' head in. This is about rescuing Dom and Abbey."

"Fuckin townies." Gazza strode away to collect his pack before heading back from where he came.

Ried ran after the Nomads. "Gazza hold up…"

"Look, boy, it took a lot to convince my people this was a good fuckin' idea. But it seems pretty fuckin' clear those wankers don't want us."

"Don't worry about them," Ried said. "Why did you say this Nidus place isn't a myth?"

"Cause my old man was a contractor who worked on it. Back before The Wars, some rich old nutter started building himself a castle on a mountain near the old border."

"I'm guessing it's not in ruins."

"Nope…" Gazza saw Ried's questioning face. "Shit. Go get the map."

Ried trotted back to the ute, retrieved the map, ran back and unfolded the map on the ground. The two men crouched, and Gazza pointed to an intersection near a mountain.

"We'll meet you here in two days. If you ain't there by then, you lot are all on your own."

"Fair enough." Ried shook hands with Gazza before he studied where Gazza indicated. "Huh."

367

The name of the mountain read Mount Hooker. Yet, back on his Earth, Ried knew the mountain in question as Mount Lindesay, and he knew first hand, no castle existed on its summit. Ried folded up the map and went back to Jack's new ute. "All right, everyone, mount up."

CHAPTER THREE

Panic and fear clawed their way upward within Dom. The weight of Abbey's unresponsive body lay against him.

The four-wheel drive, Gallio's men, stole, bounced, and swayed along a rutted, weather-worn dirt road.

Dom didn't care what became of him, but the fear for what might lay ahead for Abbey pooled between his lashes. His head fell against the rust-stained paint.

The more he tried to blink his tears away, the more his eyes filled with the sting of their replacements along with a dark cloud of vengeance brewing within him.

The vehicle lurched and bucked the hapless passengers in the rear after striking a cavernous washout in the road.

"Bloody hell, Gibbons. Watch where you're fuckin' driving," the scar-faced thug said.

"Go fuck yourself, Dwayne," the driver rebuked. "This piece of shit steers like a drunk fuckin' cow, and this track ain't what you'd call a fuckin' road either."

Dom tried his best to brace himself against the vehicles erratic pitching as Abbey rolled hard against the vehicle's rear door and moaned. Dom's heart wanted to explode with joy at her response.

Marcus lay at Dom's feet, still unconscious and flopping around like a rag doll. The proconsul's ragged breathing whistled through his dry lips, and his skin glistened from fevered perspiration around the weeping open wound on his shoulder.

With a sudden lurch, the vehicle stopped, and the two men climbed out, slammed the doors, and walked along the four-wheel drive.

The back doors opened to reveal Dwayne, who gave Abbey her black eye back at the farm. The thug surveyed the prisoners before growling instructions to get out. After Abbey and Dom shuffled out of the vehicle, the man climbed in, slid his hands under Marcus's armpits, and dragged him out to drop him at Dom's and Abbey's feet.

"You can untie them," Gallio instructed as he walked back from beside a nearby creek.

With her bonds removed, Abbey rushed across Marcus.

Dwayne gave Dom a look of disdain as he shoved him around to cut away the ropes. He sheathed the knife and pushed Dom down beside Abbey and Marcus.

The instant Dwayne turned his back, Dom attacked. He raised his left arm and plunged his elbow down hard between the unsuspecting man's shoulder blades.

Dwayne crumpled to his knees bellowing in pain from a fractured vertebra.

Dom moved over Dwayne snatching the knife from his belt and grabbing a handful of the man's hair. With a vicious jerk, Dom pulled back the moaning man's head to stare at Dwayne's face. He kept twisting the man's head forcing him to his knees.

Dwayne grunted when his left knee rolled from a sharp rock. He scratched at Dom's hand clenching his hair as Dom pressed a foot down on his calf. Dwayne's actions grew desperate from the sharp, burning pain in his neck muscles meant.

Ignoring the desperate man's exertions, Dom plunged the knife into the side of Dwayne's neck, slicing and tearing through tissue and sinew, until the hilt stopped against the skin. Bracing his knee against Dwayne's back, Dom punched his knife hand forward.

With sadistic pride, Dwaine believed in keeping a polished, sharp blade, and now this obsession made slicing through his own neck muscles, external carotid artery and jugular vein an easy task for Dom.

Dom stepped back and kicked the man forward amidst the ebbing geyser of blood.

In desperation, Dwaine tried to push himself up with a guttural blood-filled gasp through a severed windpipe, his body spasmed and he fell with his eyes locked open. His brain now bled dry, ceased to function.

From Dom's right came a vengeful cry. Overhead, leaves and branches shuddered when birds squawked and fled from the baleful vocal disturbance.

Dom moved to the side, crouched and faced Gibbons, the driver of Jack's four-wheel drive. Dom, waited for his new attacker to get closer, before launching himself at the man's legs.

Surprised, Gibbons fell forward, his head and shoulder striking the ground, knocking the wind out of him. Dazed, the man rolled onto his back and grunted when Dom's double fist thumped against his chest.

Gibbons bucked and twisted his hip to dislodge Dom, only to see the knife's handle jutting out above his heart. His bewilderment morphed into distress.

He clutched the leather-bound handle, but the blade stuck fast between his ribs. Gibbon's face contorted from the pressure and painful sting in his chest.

Under the sternum, his dissected heart went into fibrillation before drowning from the influx of blood surging into the pericardial sac. With a cough, Gibbons died.

Without hesitation, Dom reached for the knife's handle and clutched empty air as his own head jerked back. The chilling touch of steel caressed his exposed throat.

"Wait!" Gallio's command echoed through the small valley. The Roman commander marched over to Mettius and clutched the hand holding a Pugio against Dom's throat. "I don't want him dead yet. Not until I've shown him the body of Bennett. Then, you can kill him."

The warmth of blood trickling down his neck made Dom wonder if Mettius would ignore the command.

After a few tense seconds, Mettius removed his knife and lifted Dom by the hair to face him. The Centurion's expression twisted into a scowl before he catapulted Dom to land at Abbey's feet. Then with incredible agility, Mettius moved to stand over Dom and lift his chin with the Pugio's tip.

Dom locked eyes with Mettius, and in a slow defiant move he tipped his head back and palmed away the Romans knife hand.

"Stand down, Centurion," Gallio whispered the order into Mettius's bandaged ear.

Mettius tilted his head only a centimetre toward Gallio and then back to Dom. He gave a curt nod, sheathed his dagger and stalked away.

"I'm impressed, Dominic. Having your bonds cut, killing two men, and Mettius holding his Pugio against your throat all in less than two minutes," Gallio complimented Dom. "I see now why our intelligence considered you more than a modest threat to us, and it appears age has done little to diminish your abilities."

Gallio stood with his hands clasped behind his back. He raised his head to gaze across the clearing at the returning flock of pink and grey galahs scratching in the grass.

"I had you untied so you could freshen up in the stream." Gallio indicated the creek bank where his men were collecting water and refreshing themselves. "But now..." he spread his hands with mock sadness. "I hope you'll enjoy the company of the men you dispatched. Because they'll be resting here with you tonight."

"Where's the other one?" Asked Abbey.

"The other one?" Gallio feigned brief ignorance before he replied. "Ah, yes. It seems the Praetorian you refer to accidentally rolled out of his vehicle earlier in the day," Gallio's smiled and offered an unsympathetic shrug before he inspected Marcus's wound, offered a tut-tut, and walked over to a brooding Mettius.

Dom scanned the surrounding valley. A vertical cliff stretched skyward beyond the creek. Above the thinning trees, ran the rugged mountain carpeted in dense forest broken by more sloping cliffs.

A green and brown layer of bracken fern spread outward from the creek bank around the weathered, grey hulks of the fallen trees until the undergrowth gave way to grass and weeds near the edge of the glade.

"Why bring us here?" Dom mused aloud.

"Do you know where we are?" Abbey asked.

"I think we're somewhere near the old border." Dom knelt beside Marcus to inspect the proconsul's shoulder. The area where Gallio rested the hot sword tip went deep into the muscle and fat layers. White waxen skin surrounded with small chunks of curled, charred, and blackened flesh.

Inflamed reddish and butter-coloured blisters amid blood, thickening lymphatic fluid filled the open wound. A scarlet rash radiated outward over the tight swollen skin of Marcus's shoulder.

"Is it worse than the look on your face?" He asked.

"I'm not going to lie," Dom said. "If you don't get medical help soon, the infection will probably kill you."

"You do know I would have accepted a lie," Marcus replied with forced humour.

The acrid tang of eucalyptus-tainted smoke drifted through the glade to dirty the twilight and blend with the noises and smells of the coming night.

One of those more pungent odours made Marcus's face twist in repugnance.

Dom smiled at the proconsul's reaction while off in the trees, they heard the purring snarl of male possums.

In sudden contrast to the possum's growls, the twilight air vibrated with a series of long rumbling barks.

The sound gave Dom and Abbey overlapping goosebumps and prickled the hairs on the back of their necks. Even Gallio and his men moved closer to the fires, except for Mettius, who stood to scan the area. He smiled when another series of roars rolled down the valley, bouncing back from the cliff.

Abbey tugged her father's sleeve and pointing out a small, grassy ridge to the east, across the road.

Illuminated by the dying sun's light, a pride of lionesses walked with their cubs. The adult females tan fur glowed auburn from the setting sun.

Together, all three prisoners looked toward the dead men nearby.

"Dad?"

Dom gave his daughter a grin filled with confidence. "Don't worry. They won't bother us."

"What makes you so sure?" whispered his daughter.

"Because we're downwind." Dom studied the rustling leaves.

Another series of bellows rolled into the clearing. The thicker, bass growl raised an air of terror in human and Roman. The lead lioness stopped to face west and growled in return before her, and the pride disappeared over the ridge.

Mettius spoke to Gallio and pointed at the two dead men covered in clouds of feeding insects.

Within a minute of the pride dropping out of sight, Gallio's men hurried over to carry the bodies several hundred metres downwind.

With a carbine held at the ready, Mettius, along with another armed Vigiles, patrolled the perimeter, while two other men built a small bonfire for the prisoners, and then several larger ones for themselves.

"It seems our captors don't like the idea of being the Lions' next dinner date," Dom mused.

"I don't blame them," Abbey said with furtive quick glances into the encroaching night. "They were lions, right?"

"Yes."

"But they're not native? Are they?"

"No, you can blame his lot," Dom pointed at Marcus.

"I can assure you they did not arrive because of us."

"Well, maybe you didn't bring them, but those big cats and others like them are out there because of you lot."

Marcus gave Dom a quizzical look.

"Come on, Marcus. Think about it. How many zoos and safari parks were left abandoned after The Wars?" Dom sat by the fire. "And I used to think the stories I heard from the gypsies was a bunch of malarkey." Dom peered at the dark shape of the ridge.

When the rising sun broke over what Abbey called 'The Lion's Ridge,' Dom noted with some pleasure that their captors looked as drawn and tired as himself, Abbey and Marcus.

"I reckon none of us slept well last night," he said when two of Gallio's goons ushered them into the four-wheel drive.

"What about breakfast?" Asked Abbey.

"I don't think there is any," Dom said.

#

Two nights after leaving the Harris farm, Ried, Jack and Mitchum sat near a sizable fire. On their right, Michael and Cassius worked with the other rescuers doing basic weapons drills; dropping out an empty magazine and reloading a new one, clearing a jam, and how to best use the carbine in self-defence.

After studying the group, Ried wrote out a list of names he believed best handled a rifle, a pistol and the carbine in a close-quarter scenario.

He tossed the dregs of his coffee in the fire before taking the map from his pocket. He marked a cross on the outside edge of a red line Cassius drew showing the extent of Toowoomba's reach.

Back on his world, the trip from Kingaroy to the mysterious castle would have been a four-to-six-hour drive. However, in this world, with broken roads, washout bridges, and the vehicles in their convoy, the group averaged twenty kilometres of road distance per two to three hours.

The two bikes were each capable of straight-line speeds over one hundred kilometres per hour, but it came at a cost to stored battery life.

"Christ. I'd kill for just one UAV," Ried sighed, "or at least some satellite pictures."

"What's a… UAV?" Mitchum asked.

"It's an unmanned reconnaissance vehicle, a bit like a radio-controlled plane. Some bugger sitting in a tent would fly the UAVs over a target zone, taking real-time footage of the troops, support vehicles and the terrain."

"Lucky bastards," Jack retorted.

Ried tried to explain how the conflicts in his world relied on greater stealth technology and satellite data. But it didn't mean any battle or conflict ended with a faster resolution.

After completing the drills, Cassius, Michael and the others joined Ried, Jack and Mitchum. Everyone seemed relaxed during the meal. They chatted, shared a bottle of wine, and laughed at their own jokes. Of course, with the wine came the alcohol-fuelled boasts.

One person in the group nagged at Ried. Nothing definite or forthright, but Ried's inner voices told him the older man they called Smithy shouldn't be here.

Then, Cassius laughed and joined the jokes about abandoning Marcus, and for the moment, Ried forgot about Smithy and enjoyed the Vigiles captains bantering. *I suppose, even in an alternate universe, some soldiers diss their superiors.*

Leaving them to enjoy their pre-battle nerves and gallows humour, Ried went over to the ute where he rechecked his gear. He smiled when he overheard Eddy finishing a dirty joke, sending everyone into fits of laughter.

Jack came up behind him and leaned on the front guard. "That kid can tell the best jokes when he's pissed."

"They are good."

"You okay?"

"Back at the firebase, I always got scared shitless the night before a job or a patrol." Ried retied the ropes, leaned on the closest pack, and stared into the dark, green-black of the scrub. "Now, I don't feel much of anything, which worries the hell out of me."

"You'll be scared out of your bloody skin soon enough."

"I guess so."

"C'mon. You'd better fill them in on your plans."

Ried hesitated.

"What?"

"I dunno. When the CO gave us a briefing, it was all there ready for us."

"You've lost me."

For starters, the ops board was full of pictures, maps, and satellite shots of our target zones and copies of those were given to each platoon leader, so we all knew the what, where, when and how."

"Did all that stuff help?"

"Not always." Ried massaged the scar on his shoulder, "and now I've got a plan drawn up from an old tourist map and second-hand ancient intel." He gave Jack an earnest look. "What if I get it wrong or the plans shit?"

"Bloody hell." Jack pushed himself off the vehicle. "Dom used to ask me the same question before a mission."

"So, what did you tell him?"

"Time will tell."

"That's the most bullshit answer I've ever heard," Ried said to Jack's receding back.

In the cold, grey light of dawn the next day, Ried knelt by the hot coals of the fire, reviewing a folded section of the map.

"Bloody hell, son. Stop second-guessing yourself," Jack said. "Your plan's a good one." He reached over and poured them fresh coffee.

Ried accepted the drink and went back to the table to continue studying the map. Nearby, the others were waking up and had gathered around the fire to reheat breakfast and more coffee. He watched them gather in groups to eat and chat.

Eddie and Michael made a joke at the digital Auscams Ried wore, and Smithy made sure the whole camp heard his comments about Ried's combat attire.

"Don't listen to that old fool," Jack said.

"It's not just the plan or my camos." Ried kicked at a dead branch watching the group gathered around the fire.

Jack glanced over at Mitchum who raised his eyebrow and gave a small shrug. With a grunt, Jack stood beside Ried while Mitchum went for more coffee. "I thought as much," Jack said. "The doc told me what you said to him."

Ried ignored Jack to study the map.

"So what if you're not from here, and this ain't your world or your home?" Jack acknowledged Ried's unspoken sentiment. "I'll tell you this. Right here and now, I wouldn't have anybody else by my side to get Dom and Abbey back."

Jack's candid compliment stirred the blood in Ried's cheeks. At that moment Ried knew Jack was more than a mentor and more than a friend. He lifted his hand to Jack but found the action finished with his hand resting on the map.

Jack walked over to the fire and poured himself fresh coffee, calling the others to join him. When they were all gathered around the table, Ried drew their attention to the map.

"Dr Mitchum and Michael, here's a hand-drawn sketch of where to start the bushfires on the north-west side of the valley, and finish with the last one at the base of the north-east cliff."

"Remember, you lot," Jack chimed in. "After lighting the last fire, Michael and the Doc will move around the cliff and work their way back to the south behind us. So, no nervous trigger fingers."

"Surely Gallio would know the fires were a feint, and prepare for an assault via the road," Cassius said.

"That's what I'm hoping," Ried responded. "Like I said last night, Gallio's got the tactical advantage of the high ground." *Christ. Even a bunch of monkeys using rocks and sticks would knock our arse off the mountain.* "So, we need to meet him on similar grounds." Ried stepped around the table, drew a dirt map of the mountain, and added three crosses, "which is why the three assault squads must be in position by nightfall, long before Michael and the doctor light the fires."

"Yeah, well, I still don't get why we can't take out the bastards who come down for a look." Smithy sneered.

"Because you'd risk bringing the whole bloody lot down on us," Jack snapped back. "Ben's right. We let them pass and booby-trap the road, before making our way up the hill."

"What if he doesn't come down?" Smithy asked with a trace of smugness in his voice.

"Then we adapt and improvise." Ried held the other man's glare.

"Have you got a better plan?" Eddy confronted Smithy and then fixed his gaze on everyone else at the table. "Anyone else? No." He gave Ried a wink. "Then your plan it is, boss."

"All right, you lot get this place sorted, and your gear stowed," Jack looked at his watch, "you've got… ten minutes before we hit the road." He walked back beside Ried. "Adapt and improvise." Jack slapped Ried's shoulder, "and you reckon my answer was bullshit?"

"Time will tell." Ried shot back with a wink walking off as Jack laughed.

CHAPTER FOUR

With the campsite cleared and the vehicles loaded, Ried hefted a shovel and went back to bury the fire. Using the same technique as he did for filling sandbags Ried ploughed the dirt with the shovel.

Through the dry grass on his far right, Ried caught the slow, ponderous movement of an oversized goanna walking nearby. Ried always found something in the way the reptiles walked a little comical, and this bigger one no less odd.

"Strewth, you're a big one." He watched the reptile, with its loose dark grey hide studded with hundreds of small bumps of mottled algae green and pale brown.

"Jesus Christ," he whispered. "Where the hell did you come from?"

The giant lizard paused amidst the grass in a patch of sunlight beneath the canopy of forest reds. Its fleshy, salmon-coloured, forked tongue flicked in and out from its broad, rounded mouth. The reptile's head swung in Ried's direction and took several slow steps toward him.

Without moving, Ried tilted his head. "Whoever's behind me, just stop, and for Christ's sake, don't make any sudden moves."

"Why? Is everything all right?"

"On your right, Eddy."

"Holy shit!"

"Keep your voice down," Ried said as he tracked back with exaggerated slowness.

"That's one big goanna."

"I don't think our scaly friend is a goanna, it looks more like a Komodo dragon, or your version at least."

"Is it dangerous?"

In one last cautious step, he stopped alongside Eddy. "I'm going to go with... yes."

Ried watched the giant lizard move up beside the hot coals of the fire. A puff of wind dusted the reptile's head and shoulders in warm ash. The creature emitted a rasping hiss before lumbering off into the undergrowth.

"What about the fire?"

"You want to make sure the damn fire's out? Then here," Ried passed over the shovel, "be my guest."

The Komodo dragon halted from Ried's and Eddy's talking. Its tail swept the ground, and it bent around to fix its gaze at the two men.

"Nah, it's all good," Eddie said in exaggerated hushed tones as he kept pace with Ried.

"What the hell are you pair playing at?" Jack peered past the two younger men walking with their backs to him.

"I'll explain later," Ried said as they turned and jogged over to Jack.

"Where's Cassius?" Asked Ried when he and Eddy regained their composure after a bout of nervous laughter.

"I sent him ahead to do some scouting," Jack said. He pulled out the map. "I told him to meet us at this junction."

"That's where we meet up with the Nomads."

"Well, let's hope Gazza doesn't shoot them by mistake," Jack said behind his grin

.

By midday, the convoy pulled over beside the junction. Jack pointed out the circle of small bonfires in the nearby glade. Finches, sashaying leaves and the gurgling splash from the creek serenaded the rescue party.

Ried, Jack, and Mitchum made their way across to the nearest fire pit. Jack poked the pile of black coal, white ash, and the remains of an unburned stump.

"Can't be more than a day old," stated Jack.

"So, we must be close," replied Ried

A little way up the creek, they heard a shout. The three men made their way through the glade to where Eddy stood near the disturbed shallow grave of two bodies.

"Well, well," remarked Mitchum, bending over the corpses.

"I reckon we pull out the guns," Jack suggested, crouching beside the doctor, scrutinising the dead men and then the terrain.

"What's got you spooked?" Asked Mitchum.

"Apart from Cassius not being here and us standing in a perfect ambush zone. Nothing." Jack said.

"Any thoughts on who or what killed them, Dr Mitchum?" Asked Ried

"For God's sake, son. Only my nurses or patients call me Dr Mitchum," he growled. "If you can't manage Tom, then use Doctor."

"Or Doc," quipped Jack.

Mitchum said nothing and moved to the second body. With a small branch, he brushed away the leaves and ground litter covering the corpse.

"I'd say these two died no more than a day or two ago." Mitchum scooped away more of the loose soil over the bodies. "This one was stabbed in the heart, and his friend…" The doctor used the branch to poke, prod, and move the pale, torn skin around the corpse's eviscerated throat. "If I had to guess, I'd say somebody did a bloody good job at cutting this one's throat from the spine forward…"

"How the hell can you tell that?" Eddy grimaced at how Mitchum prodded the open wound.

"Ignoring where animals have gnawed the flesh." Mitchum pointed the stick. "You can see this area shows a clean cut."

Eddy went back to get help in digging a better grave while Ried and the two older men headed toward the vehicles.

"The question we should be bloody asking is why and how they got friggin' knifed." Jack stopped and crouched down to inspect the ground near one of the fire pits.

He rose and pointed out the tire tracks, and over to the right, they could see the signs of a heavy scuffle amongst the dry compost and leaf litter.

"Somebody had a blue all right. And the way the grounds all tossed about, I'd say it was a short fight."

Ried followed Jack and scanned the clearing and valley. "You reckon Dom tried to make a break for it?"

"If those two got careless, then he might've," Jack said. "But he wouldn't do it without Abbey or Marcus."

Ried crouched beside the cold ashes, and rolled an unburned piece of hardwood over, revealing dry, obsidian scales of charcoal.

The ash under the half-burned stump felt warm, and the small breeze ignited the exposed cinders to a brief flicker of crimson-gold life, filling the air with the smoky scent of burning eucalyptus oils.

Those aromas brought Ried's thoughts back to the night he and Abbey had dinner by a fire.

Along the road came the whining noise of the approaching electric motorbikes roused Ried to the present. He jogged back to Jack's ute and remove the ropes around his bags and told Eddy to break out the other weapons.

When Cassius rode around the bend, he and Michael skidded to a stop at the site of armed men blocking the road.

"For a second, I thought you forgot whose side I was on," Cassius said with a nervous laugh as he parked the bike.

"Sorry about that." Ried lowered his rifle and stepped toward the startled riders. "I suppose I'm a little spooked."

Jack's eyebrows lifted. "Must be something in the air."

Cassius's brow creased in suspicion at the comment and at the sight of the M-16 and M-60 carried by Ried and Jack.

Without hesitation, Ried explained the weapons belonged to him from his pastime in the army.

Diverting further questions on the contraband weapons, Jack asked Cassius what he'd found out.

"Not all that much, I am afraid." Cassius shrugged. "There was a patrol, so we had to hide for a while."

Before Ried could respond, Eddy tapped him on the shoulder and pointed towards the creek. Emerging from the shrubs and bracken came Gazza and the other Nomads.

"I'd just about given up on you lot," Gazza growled.

"I suppose you've been here a while then?" Asked Jack.

"Long enough to have a good look around and listen to you noisy bastards."

"So, can you tell us anything?" Ried asked.

"Yep. I can tell you hiking up the side of that mountain will be a bitch." Gazza studied the rescue group over from man to man. "Apart from the road leading up to the place, there's only one other approach you could try." He lit a thick homemade cigar. "The problem is, it's on the southeast side, and you'd be exposed all the way up the slope."

"Why am I sensing that's not all?" Ried said waving away the cloud of smoke Gazza exhaled.

"Cause it ain't all." Gazza puffed in thought. "At the base of the hill is an outpost and twenty or so of his fuckin' Vigiles." He pointed towards Cassius.

"Hence the patrol we encountered," Cassius said. "By the way, they are not mine." He reiterated to Gazza.

"No shit." The big nomad shook his head and puffed on his cigar. "Fuckin Romans." He turned to Ried. "It'll be dark in about five or six hours, and you're gonna need to be inside the place before then."

"Fair enough," Ried said.

"Don't get too excited." Gazza grinned chewing the butt of his stogie. "Cause you'll have to leave your vehicles here and hump the rest of the way."

"Why?"

"I don't know what's goin' on up there, but apart from them patrols, there's been gypsy wagons comin' and goin' through yesterday and this morning. So, your little convoy won't get within a bee's dick of the place, before your busted." Gazza bent down and drew in the dirt.

"You need to follow the creek for a few klicks and then head off to the east until the jungle thins out. About here." He stabbed the dirt. "That'll put you just under a klick from the base of the hill." Gazza stood and held out his hand, which Ried accepted.

"Do you want a signal when we get there?"

"Nope. I'll know where you're at." Gazza turned to leave, but then stopped and led Ried away from the others. "I know you and the Major can handle yourselves, but if you plan on takin' old men and boys into the place, you'd better keep your bloody wits about you. The place is a fuckin' fortress." Gazza slapped Ried's shoulder. "We'll still hit the outpost at sunset even if you get busted." He gave a wink. "At least, we'll get to kill some Romans and steal some booty."

"You know some of them aren't Romans," Ried said.

"Nor were the ones you shot at my camp," Gazza stated. "I'll give you a tip. If the bloke is shootin' at ya or wearin' the uniform, then he's Roman." With a nod, Gazza signalled his men and melted into the bush.

Ried ran his hand through his hair as Jack approached.

"He's right."

"Yeah, I know…"

"Did he happen to mention anything about the local wildlife?"

"Why do I feel you're not talking about a bull or a big stag?"

"Good guess." Jack frowned at the drawings in the dirt. "Michael reckons he spotted a bloody great lion sunning himself."

"Where the hell would lions come from?" Ried's mind reeled. Vicious aliens, giant Komodo dragons, tarantulas larger than a dinner plate, and now Lions. *Christ. Around every bloody corner of this world, there's something new and just as terrifying.*

#

An hour later, the seventeen men marched beneath an awning of eucalyptus, woven together by an inextricable lacework of vines, creating a dark-green and brown living cave.

Twice during their hike, they needed to go around areas where the light streamed in through gaping scars in the canopy created by a falling tree. Those sections of sun-drenched undergrowth proved an impassable mass of tangled ferns, vines, grasses, and saplings – all fighting to be the first to feed on the sunlight.

Once past those open areas, the men found the going slow, as they plodded through an ankle-deep carpet of humid compost. Ried wondered if everybody had the same concerns about carnivores wandering the shadow-filled rainforest.

The most pressing concern for Ried was the plight of Abbey and Dom which outweighed any fear of giant cats. He rechecked his watch and saw they'd been on the march for two hours. Satisfied with their progress, he called for a ten-minute rest.

"Did you do that on your patrols?"

"Do what?"

"Keep checking your watch."

"Sorry. This idea of going into a hot zone with no tactical background data isn't what I'm used to," Ried explained. "Besides, I don't want us taking too long to get there and discover that we have to spend another night in the bush."

"We've got plenty of daylight left. So, put the bloody thing away," Jack admonished. "Your checking the damn watch every few minutes isn't helping everyone's nerves."

"Fair enough." Ried took off his watch, and slipped the timepiece into his shirt pocket, and understood what sort of leaders the big man and Dom would have been during The Wars.

"Come on. Let's get 'em moving."

"Has it been ten minutes?"

"Nope, but they don't know that."

Ried scanned the dark forest from the undergrowth to the canopy. "I suppose, sitting in this place with the thought of lions roaming around isn't helping their mood."

Within the hour, the dense scrub thinned, and the composting floor filled with coarse ferns and knee-high grass. When Ried spotted a long, low-lying ridge.

Ried got the men to stop while he and Jack went to the edge of the clearing to check their bearings. He tapped the map with his pencil and recalled Gazza's directions drawn in the dirt.

"This looks about right, and we've made good time." Ried scanned the area ahead and rechecked the map. "But I reckon we're too close to the road."

"Righto, I'll move the boys down," Jack said before he waded back into the undergrowth.

Ried crouched behind the ridge and moved to his right where he poked his head over the top. Happy with his position, he pulled out a pair of field glasses from Dom's armoury, checked the sun's angle, and then shifted under a nearby tree's shadow to help keep the sun reflecting off the glass lenses.

He scanned the base of the mountain and roadway. There was no sign of the outpost Gazza mentioned, but he spotted several Roman soldiers standing near a boom gate.

He lifted the binoculars to track up the mountain. When the castle came into focus Ried settled down to study his objective and the two-tiered mountain.

He shifted his viewing angle and panned the binoculars along the cliff faces, which created steep natural ramparts.

Whoever built the old castle combined natural stone and concrete blocks to construct a continuous rampart on the second plateau.

Ried adjusted the focus until the rust stains, and cracked timbers on two large double doors in the lower wall section came into focus.

If there are doors, then there must be a road or path around the building.

High, arched windows decorated the stone and concrete walls, many of them either broken or boarded up from the inside. The top of the wall finished with traditional tooth-shaped parapets running around its edge. At each end of the walls, watchtowers rose above the parapet.

Behind the main rampart, Ried could make out the roof structure of an inner building, which also had two towers on the eastern end of the structure.

Searchlights, machine guns, and what looked like a rocket launcher made up the defences of each outer wall towers, along with three armed soldiers.

Ried panned the field glasses between each tower. "Damn it. Even if we managed to scale the cliff, we'd have to be invisible to scale the wall, or break in through the windows and doors." *Shit. Gazza wasn't kidding. The place is a fucking fortress.*

Ried shifted his gaze back to the bottom terrace, then to the longer steep slope, traversed by covered wagons passing through men stationed on picket duty. Back up the mountain, at the bottom of the castle's wall, people and covered wagons disappeared and reappeared.

Checking the sun's position, Ried guessed they had two, maybe three hours before sunset and Gazza's diversion. Rolling on his back, he drummed his fingers against the binoculars lying on his chest. He pursed his lips to consider their next move.

The towers had an unobstructed view of the valley below, which would make getting the Doctor and Michael into position more interesting. *They'll need to head out earlier than planned. Not to mention the pride of lions somewhere out there.*

Jack came up beside Ried and took the binoculars. Two or three minutes later, he handed them back. "Strewth, Gazza wasn't joking."

"Yep, plan A is rooted," Ried said.

"So, what's Plan B?"

"Honestly, I have no fucking idea."

"Okay, let's bloody well keep that to ourselves."

"I'm sorry," Ried snapped, "you did see the same thing through those as I did, right?" He shifted his position and pointed toward the fortified building. "That's not some old castle Gallio's sitting in. The damn thing's a bloody great fortress." He rose to head back under the trees.

"Okay, it might be a bloody fortress," Jack dropped a meaty hand on Ried's shoulder and whirled him around, "but that's where he's got, Dom and Abbey."

"Really, I wasn't–" Ried sniffed the air. "You smell that?"

Both men stared at the edge of the forest where they saw a billowing column of soft, grey smoke rising to the north-east.

"Shit!" Jack shook his head and ran toward the base of the pale-grey plume.

Ried shifted his gaze between the smoke and the castle before he bolted after Jack. When he reached the other men, Jack was already smothering a small fire with dirt.

Before anyone could say anything, Smithy poured water over the soil and coals. The now wet soil and compost worsened the problem, creating more smoke.

In mid-stride, Ried pulled out a blanket from under one man and threw it over the billowing cloud to diffuse the smoke.

"Which of you bloody idiots lit the fire?" demanded Jack.

"I did, and watch who you're calling an idiot," barked Smithy.

Ried pushed past Jack to grab Smithy's collar, dragging the surprised older man to the top of the small rise.

"You see that?" Ried dug his fingers into the man's greasy, salt-and-pepper hair to twist his head around. "You see that fortress? It's full of Romans who have Dom and Abbey." He dragged Smithy closer to him and snarled, "Gallio and all those soldiers suspect we're coming." Ried gripped the man's shirt in a quiet rage. "Well, thanks to you, they'll bloody well know–"

Smithy's fist sent Ried reeling. "Don't you dare speak to me like that, you murdering, little prick."

Before Ried recovered, he felt a thin rope cut into his throat. Reflex alone brought his hand which was then pinned against his neck.

"I'm gonna choke the life out of you… real slow." He dodged Ried's other backward swinging fist. "Then, you'll know what it's like to die slowly, just like my nephew did at that fucking nomad camp." Smithy pushed his knee deeper into Ried's back. "They told me he died screaming for his mother after you shot his liver out."

The pressure behind Ried's eyes threatened to pop them from his skull. He twisted his hand around to grip the garrotte and pull it away, enough to let a rush of air surge past his crushed windpipe and into his burning lungs.

The fresh oxygen gave Ried a surge of strength. With his trapped hand, he pulled the thin twine cutting into his flesh.

With a savage jerk, Smithy pulled back.

The next thing Ried knew was him landing on top of an unconscious Smithy.

With the pressure of the thin rope released, Ried jerked himself around and kneeled wheezing and coughing beside the would-be assassin now bleeding from a head wound.

Jack dropped a thick tree branch and hoisted Ried on his feet. "You okay?"

Ried nodded between gasps and coughs.

Dr Mitchum ran up to inspect Smithy and then checked the red welt around Ried's neck and his cut fingers.

"What the hell was that about?" Jack asked.

"His nephew… I think…" Ried wheezed, "… I think he might have been one of the Vigiles I shot helping Gazza." He coughed.

"I should have known something was odd when he volunteered." Jack turned toward Eddy. "Get some rope to tie the mad old bastard up."

"Screw that. Just cut the old prick's throat and let him bleed out." Eddy kicked the unconscious Smithy.

"No. Do what Jack said. Besides, there'll be plenty more bloodshed soon enough." Ried walked through the trees toward the road.

"Jack, what about the smoke from the fire?" Mitchum asked, following Jack, who followed Ried.

"Don't fret, doc. If we don't hear any shooting, we may be okay."

Behind them, Michael and Eddy hauled the limp body of Smithy down to the extinguished fire, where they gagged and tied him to a small tree.

Hearing Jack and the doctor stomping through the undergrowth behind him, Ried stopped and faced the two men.

Jack baulked, "Jesus. Dom used to give me the same look."

"Oh, you mean the 'you are a pain in the arse' look. Or maybe it's the 'your mates are friggin' wankers' look?" Ried quipped before walking farther into the trees.

"This isn't just about the fire, is it?" Mitchum asked. "I have a feeling the Smithy thing has changed our young friend's plans."

"Yes and no," Jack replied, squatting on his haunches to study Ried, who was sitting beside a tree near the road.

"Yes and no?" Mitchum shook his head. "Could you be any less vague?"

"Strewth, Doc. No, you and Michael will not be lighting any fires, and yes, I believe Ben still intends to rescue Dom and Abbey."

Mitchum looked from Ried to Jack. "Well, at least I'm not being offered up as lion food."

For the next few minutes, none of the three men spoke. The doctor picked his teeth with a blade of grass while Jack walked up beside Ried.

"You did what you did. So, crawling into yourself ain't gonna bring back the man's nephew."

"It's not just Smithy and his dead nephew. Well, it is, sort of. It's also the fort on that mountain." Ried gave Jack an almost pleading look. "I don't know if I can be responsible for more deaths."

"You're not telling me you're giving up?"

"What? NO. No, I'm not giving up…" Ried rose and rubbed his temples. His attention shifted between the castle and where the others hid in the scrub.

"Don't even bloody think about doing this on your bloody own."

Ried glanced in the castle's direction. "I'm not… I just need time to think about what we're going to do next."

Jack started speaking when Ried put up his hand and tilted his head. He closed his eyes and slowed his breathing. Then with the speed of a startled rabbit, he darted into the canopy and out of sight, sprinting along the road.

Jack sighed, shook his head in confusion, and ran after Ried. About a hundred metres through the thick bracken fern, Ried stopped and crept a little closer to the edge of the road where he crouched, listening.

Again, without warning, he turned, and with the same urgency, ran past Jack on the way back to the men.

Jack slid to a stop in the composting undergrowth, frowning at Ried's odd behaviour. Tipping his head back, he stared at a patch of blue sky beyond the leafy shroud of the rainforest.

With a moan, Jack complained about being too old before turning to follow Ried, again. He paused mid-stride when the younger man ran back, dragging Cassius with him, followed by the rest of the group.

Jack shrugged his shoulders, and went after the manic Ried, to find his young friend and a confused Cassius crouched near the edge of the forest.

CHAPTER FIVE

A draught horse plodded out of the canopy's shadows hauling a gypsy wagon with Eddy holding the reins and fidgeting from his ill-fitting clothes.

Inside the wagon, Michael, Jack, Ried and Mitchum sat with the wagon owner, who shivered under the blanket wrapped around his naked body.

The gypsy squirmed and pulled the blanket closer, mouthing a mute curse to his captors and his luck.

Ried shifted the barrel of the M-16, so the rifle rested on the man's shoulder. "Okay, let's keep absolutely still back here."

A sudden jolt rocked the passengers when Eddy reined the horse to a halt. Inside, everyone jumped. Jack slipped out his hunting knife and shimmied toward the wagon's door.

The door creaked open, and a gruff voice preceded the face of Gazza's lieutenant. "Don't none of you buggers do anything stupid."

Ried motioned for Jack to stand down. "Where's Gazza?"

"Close by." The nomad, in an oversized Roman soldier's uniform, climbed up to inspect the wagon. "The guvnor said you'd be clever enough to use one of these." He nodded with a near-toothless smile at the men inside. "He's got a plan to keep any more of these buggers from headin' up the hill." The nomad locked eyes with Ried. "But he says don't fuck around. Get in an' get out." Which is also what the nomad did.

Jack re-latched the door, sheathed his knife, raised an eyebrow toward Ried, and picked up the M-60. "I'll be buggered... Alright, Eddy, let's get up that bloody track."

Ried allowed himself a wry smile.

A hundred metres along the rutted path, the horse faltered. Eddy swore when the animal lost traction on the steep gradient. He worked the reins and foot brake to control the wagon and horse.

A worried frown crossed Ried's forehead. He hadn't considered if the wagons going up to the fort were empty. Unlike theirs, now loaded with the extra weight of the five men in the back.

Jack told Eddy to steer them to the side of the track and out of the smooth, well-worn ruts. Once on the less-travelled ground, the horse's shod hooves found better traction and picked up a steady pace.

"Let's hope none of them noticed the animal's little dance," Jack said.

With their ride gathering speed and no sign of unwanted attention, Ried let his thoughts drift. He recalled something his CO told him when he received his corporal stripes: *"No matter what, never let the men under your command see anything else but reassurance and confidence."* So, with a grin, Ried gave Jack a quick wink and a pat on his shoulder.

Once the horse settled into a steady walk, Ried quizzed the gypsy on the layout of the fort.

"How the hell do I know? We're not allowed out of the warehouse." He adjusted the blanket. "They make sure we stay with our wagon while they load the cargo, feed us, and then send us on our way."

"Just what do you transport?" Asked Mitchum.

"Mostly Enlightenment." The gypsy gave a small dry laugh at his captor's faces. "What? You didn't know this is where they make the stuff?"

"No. We only knew Gallio got the shit from another region." Michael's tone held more than mere disgust.

"Not just Gallio," the gypsy clarified. "There are also deliveries to four other regional governors between here and the Blue Mountains."

"So, who runs the operation?" Ried asked.

"I dunno." The man's face paled, and a soft, mewing whimper escaped his lips when the muzzles of three rifles pointed in his direction. "I dunno… I really dunno. I'm just a courier. All I know is the place belongs to some Roman nob who calls himself Neg… Negru Cerberus or something."

Ried tilted his head and raised an eyebrow at both Jack and Mitchum. "Really? I wonder who that could be."

"Come on. The man might be many things, but a big drug lord?"

"Maybe, maybe not. All I know is something about Marcus is off," Ried replied.

"I agree he's ambitious and can be a prick," Jack said. "Anyway, he and Dom practically rebuilt the bloody region,"

An audible "ouch" from the gypsy interrupted Ried's further cynicism. He whipped his head around and caught the driver staring in surprise at Mitchum before he slumped to the floor.

"It's an anaesthetic." Mitchum pouted when he saw Ried's face.

"Oi, boss. We're heading under the castle, into some sort of cave." Eddie's hushed voice came through the curtain.

Ried peered through the split canvas flap. "Park us as far back as you can."

When Eddy brought the cart and horse to a stop, he dismounted and leaned against the sideboard, trying to look like a gypsy rather than a nervous, would-be infiltrator.

Two Vigiles marched toward the wagon. The first waved his arm at Eddy. "Hey, you get back on that box and take your fucking nag over to where you supposed too."

Ignoring the approaching Vigiles, Eddy pretended to inspect one of the front wheels.

Infuriated by Eddy's disobedience, the Vigiles pulled out his pistol, and then shoved a nightstick into Eddy's shoulder. Eddy smiled and walked along, checking the sideboards and canvas cover, bumping into the guard to force him to the rear of the wagon.

The Vigiles frowned at Eddy's silent rebuttal. "Are you fucking deaf? I said get back on your flea trap and–"

Eddy stopped and stood to his full height. "Who are you to call my home a flea trap?" He slapped the nightstick aside and shoved the Vigiles until they were both out of sight behind the wagon.

Before the infuriated man and his partner could turn on their Taser's switch, the barrel of Jack's M-60 and Ried's M-16 pressed against each man's temple. Eddy gave the two men a wink and relieved them of their weapons.

The first Vigiles eyed Ried from head to toe. He opened his mouth to voice his objections, but before he could, he jerked around when the sting from a needle in his arm drew his attention to Dr Mitchum.

Ried smiled at the second man and motioned him to be quiet.

The second Vigiles also flinched and rubbed his neck before he collapsed in front of Mitchum holding an empty hypodermic.

While Jack stowed the guards into the wagon, Ried surveyed the cavern which covered an area about the size of two Olympic swimming pools sitting side by side. The light in the cavern came from four banks of double-domed lights.

A spider web of patched and filled cracks decorated the ceiling with dozens of steel plates held tight by fist-sized nuts on the threaded rods.

Twenty columns of reinforced concrete topped with sections of rust coated I-beams supported the caverns patched and bolstered ceiling

Jesus, this place looks like it's held together by Araldite and spit.

Lining one of the walls ran a series of control boxes with rows of dials and pimpled with bright green, red, blue and orange lights and illuminated gauges. Snaking out of the unit's lower panels were conduits and cables, which disappeared into the cement-rendered rock walls.

Ried nudged Jack's shoulder and pointed across the cavern to Dom's flatbed and an old four by four beside a half dozen horse stalls. "It looks like they are here all right."

Next to the stables was the forts motor pool and a workshop where a handful of mechanics worked on the small collection of bikes and trucks. The only other people Ried spotted were two Vigiles and some other men milling around the entrance.

Jack pointed at one of two spiral, metal stairs beneath wooden platforms leading to timber trapdoors in the ceiling.

A man in a different uniform climbed out from one of the trapdoors and onto the stairs to join the others by the door.

"I reckon they lead to the watchtowers," Jack said.

"Can you see any other doors or another set of stairs?" Asked Ried.

"Nope. Just some weird Roman art piece by the wall." Jack replied pointing toward a stack of crates, a metal cradle and an octagonal ring inlaid with eight soccer ball sized crystal tetrahedrons.

Ried shifted around the back of the wagon. *There must be another way in...* He edged farther back and found a riveted steel door hidden from view behind a column and a few crates.

"Bingo."

From a tactical perspective, apart from one pillar between the wagon and the door, they didn't have much cover, but at a push, and in a pinch, Ried decided, if things got awkward, the stack of boxes and the wagon would form a reasonable defence.

At that moment, the soldiers, gypsies, and workers stopped what they were doing and ran through from the cavern when they heard the distant, faint crack of gunfire rolled through the opening.

"Sounds like your nomad mates have kicked off the party," Jack said.

Ried glanced at the heavy door, expecting to see an army stream into the cavern. Two men in grey overalls ran out of the workshop and stopped a few metres in front of the horse. Ried swore while Jack, Michael and Eddy raised their weapons as Mitchum crept behind Jack.

"Wonder what all the shooting is about," the taller of the two men said to his companion.

"Probably a nomad raiding party." He spat on the floor. "You'd think the dumb bastards would learn by now." The man hawked up another ball of phlegm to spit at the base of a nearby column. "C'mon, leave the soldiers to do their job." He jabbed his friend's rib and gave him a lurid grin. "There's better and safer things to do inside."

"You don't think we should help?"

"What the fuck for? They get paid to be shot at. I get paid to fix old clunkers and load the wagons." The man pulled out a dark block of tobacco biting off a chunk as he sauntered off with his friend in tow.

When the men disappeared, Eddy made his way to the front, near the horse, "All clear."

"Eddy, you and the doctor stay with the wagon." Ried turned to Michael, "you're with Jack and me."

"What if you need me?" Mitchum protested.

"Sorry, but the fewer people running around back there, the better." Ried pointed to the wagon. "Besides you might need to put the two sleeping beauties back to sleep."

Mitchum turned to Jack for any kind of support. However, Jack patted the doctor on the shoulder and handed him the pistol taken from the guard, before he followed Ried and Michael at a crouch through the door.

Stopping inside the door, Ried thought aloud, "I never considered the fact there'd be other Nomads here as well."

"Yep, and a few klicks south-west is the free people's region." Jack closed the door. "Don't really know much about them, but if someone rallied all the nomad clans…" Jack shrugged and raised a lopsided eyebrow, "then the Romans would really have a problem."

A short way down the man-made tunnel, light reflected from a tarnished brass plaque screwed into the wall. Jack wiped away the dust and read out the words engraved in French. "*Pour ceux qui trouvent ce message. Faites attention à vos âmes. Ce fête Du Château et de la montagne sur la Mort.*"

"You speak French?" Ried asked with a surprised tone and face.

"Top of my class in high-school French, I was." Jack gave Ried a hurt look. "I'm not just a corn farmer you know."

"What does it mean?" interrupted Michael.

"The gist of it is…" Jack's brow puckered from concentration, "the castle and the mountain will bring you death… No, they feed on death. *"*

"Hopefully, not ours," Michael mumbled.

The deeper they walked into the tunnel, the more Ried understood the decision to abandon further construction. He was no geologist, but he knew enough to realise the foundations of the mountain were at best, shit.

Why would any architect or builder consider building on a fractured and decayed rock was a good idea?

405

A point highlighted by the number of reinforced steel pillars steel and timber lining the surrounding corridor. All showing the passage of time and the effects of extreme weather conditions after The Wars. The moist air tasted of old rock and dirt, which stuck to their tongues.

Leprous lumps of oxidised metal blistered under the paintwork of the tunnel's ceiling joists and beams. Many of those blisters had ruptured, weeping dried tears of walnut and coffee-hued stains streaking the dirty, white paint.

Stretched between the beams were lengths of galvanised chain wire; a metal net to ensnare the loose, crumbling rock. Wispy threads of spider silk, dusted in dark-brown, covered the wire net, hanging like dried, unkempt mistletoe.

Behind Ried, Jack swore when he walked into a nest of the greasy strands.

Ried shuddered from the idea of spiders dropping from above. "Now's not the time to worry about spiders," Ried admonished himself in a hushed tone.

"What'd you say?" Asked Jack, while combing the last piece of the web from his beard.

"Nothing."

Jack reached out and pulled Ried back milliseconds after the hallway filled with light. On their right, a metal door opened at right angles.

From behind the door, a woman in grey overalls stepped into the corridor and walked away from the trio. From inside the opening came a brief discussion between two men about having too much work left to do. A second later, the back of a Roman Centurion stepped into view.

"Instead of complaining, use the energy to finish your job. Cerberus wants the place cleared by tomorrow morning," he barked over his shoulder before jogging down the corridor and disappearing around a corner.

"Yes, sir," a voice replied behind the closing door.

The three men exchanged looks at the close call. They moved up to flank the pale-green door, while Ried inched his head up to a rectangular window in the top half of the door.

Beyond the glass stood at least two one-metre-wide, long, metal-framed benches with stainless steel tops. Scattered in haphazard piles on the top of the closest bench were several boxes and crates. Next to those were bundles of files and documents.

Ried reached out and rested his hand on the door's lever handle.

Jack snapped his hand over Ried's forearm. "Leave it," he said in an urgent whisper. "We've got to keep going."

"No, we need to check every room, unless you know for sure where Dom and Abbey are…"

"Fair point," Jack conceded. "Michael, you stay here," he ordered before he and Ried slipped into the room.

Once inside, they moved to the nearest wall beside a bank of filing cabinets and wooden crates. Ried directed his eyes around the room lit by large bright domed lights.

The second they walked through the door, Ried's skin erupted in goosebumps from the colder air belching from the air-conditioning ducts overhead.

He eased his head around the corner and discovered he and Jack stood in the foyer of a functioning laboratory, complete with white-cloaked technicians. Less than a meter away, a bored soldier leaned on a third stainless steel bench, toying with a piece of equipment.

Beyond the guard, several men in white lab coats were busy filling more crates with instruments, and smaller metal boxes with wireframes holding little glass vials filled with a honey-coloured liquid.

Against the back wall, two more guards came out of a room trailing fog. Mounted to the wall beside the door, stood four tall, thin gas cylinders crusted in frost.

A little farther around the walls, piled high in open metal crates, were glass bottles filled with a pale-green liquid and marked with a burning flame.

Ried drew in a quick breath and counted down from three. When he reached one, he stepped out from behind the boxes with the M-16 tucked into his shoulder. Jack followed Ried with the M-60 braced against his right hip, and a meter-long section of bullets draped over his arm.

A female technician dropped the box she carried when she walked around the corner, seeing the two men.

The first lazy guard dropped whatever he was playing with, and fumbled for his pistol, only to put his hands toward the ceiling when Ried waved the muzzle of his rifle at the soldier's face.

"Guns on the floor. Uh-ah, do it nice and slow." Ried kept a careful eye on the nervous actions of the other guard. "You too. Now's no time to play the hero."

From the corner of his eye, he caught a glimpse of Jack moving forward half a step. Ried allowed himself a small smile at the soldier's reaction to Jack's impressive bulk, dressed in green combat fatigues, covering everyone in the lab with the M-60. If anyone thought to cross Jack then, by Ried's account they were more stupid than brave.

With fumbling, nervous actions, they undid their pistol and sword belts and dropped them at their feet along with the carbines.

Ried, with a flick of the M-16, motioned everyone down along the wall and then kicked the pile of weapons out of reach.

Seizing the opportunity, one of the freezer guards charged Ried. And then stumbled against a wall clutching his thigh. He gasped in stunned disbelief at the bleeding hole in his leg.

The female technician reacted to the ear-destroying bark of Ried's rifle by screaming and dropping the wire basket she carried. Her assistant fell against the wall, and he began crying from shock.

With his ears ringing from the concussive sound, Jack mouthed a curse at Ried and darted over to the laboratory's door, peering through the thick glass, expecting to find Michael under assault. Instead, the young man threw him a concerned stare. Jack gave him a quick, okay signal, and marched back giving Ried a "don't do that again" look.

Ried ignored Jack's glare and stepped out into the area between the benches.

"You two, pick up your mate and take him in there." Using the barrel of the rifle, Ried herded them toward the cold storage room. "And the rest of you, in you go." They all jumped at his snapped commands.

When everybody was inside, he showed them a grenade. After shutting the door, Ried barricaded it with crates containing assorted glass jars.

He did a rapid search of the room and returned with a spool of wire to tie the door handle to the ring pull of a grenade which he jammed behind the frost-covered gas bottles.

Ried then darted over to a bench and rifled through the piles of paperwork and folders.

"What are you doing?" Asked Jack. "We're supposed to be rescuing Dom and Abbey. Not file a bloody report."

"I was hoping to find out who's in charge."

With an angry grunt, Ried flicked the papers on the floor but stopped mid-step when one of the documents caught his eye. Without hesitation, he stuffed the papers down his shirt and turned to leave when Jack stopped him.

"Hang about. You're not seriously gonna leave that grenade like that?"

"Why the hell not?" Ried pointed to the box the female technician dropped. "How many people have died because of that shit?"

Jack walked over to reset the grenade and adjusted the pin and picked up the spool of wire, tied the loose end to the pin of a second grenade which he jammed into crates of chemicals marked flammable. Then, he fed the wire around one of the bench legs and back to the storeroom door handle.

"The first rule of sabotage," Jack smiled, "is always have a backup." He walked past Ried and tapped on the door before he stepped out into the hall.

CHAPTER SIX

Back in the hall, Jack took the lead and stopped without warning when another door swung open and knocked him against the wall.

Behind the blocked door stepped another Vigiles guard doing up his trousers while shuffling his shoulders to keep the equipment belt draped across them from falling.

"Watch where you're going," the man cursed, kicked the door closed, and fumbled with his fly. "What the–"

The barrel and folded bipod of Jack's M-60 plunged into the surprised man's midriff. In a rapid follow through, Jack swung his right arm to bat the short butt of the machine gun against the man's head.

Ried opened the door as Jack dragged the unconscious man through the opening followed by Michael and himself. When Ried crossed the doorway, he expected to walk into a barracks toilet.

Instead, they found themselves in a long, broad room lit with soft mood lighting, and lined with a dozen curtained booths. The air reeked of incense, and faint melodies of instrumental music came from speakers mounted on each wall.

"Jesus. These people need to learn the top forty," Ried complained.

"That's what passes for Roman music," said Michael closing the door while Jack hid the unconscious Roman behind a curtained booth

"Is this one of their dorms?"

"No, Michael. This looks like the castle's cat house," Jack said. "But, there's no time to play."

A whiny voice called out from behind a nearby curtain which parted to reveal a chubby man dressed in a bright, aqua-green toga. "You know services are closing. So, come back at seven–"

He stopped mid-step at the sight of two men in strange uniforms pointing guns at him.

With a confused expression, the plump Roman stiffened and gave a small squeak, when a third man came up behind him, covered his mouth, and held a knife to his exposed right nipple.

"Be quiet now, or you'll be breathing through a new hole in your chest." Ried eased his hand away from the terrified Roman's mouth. "How many more?"

"T… T… Two at the end on the right."

Jack and Michael went to check behind the last curtained booth. Inside, they found the two men from the cavern, both naked and surrounded by two teenage girls also devoid of any clothing.

"Come back here, girl," the tobacco-chewing man grabbed the arm of a petite brunette. "I'm not done yet."

"No," Jack said. "I reckon you're finished." He rested the muzzle of his gun between the man's shoulder blades.

The other naked Roman slapped the second girl's head away from between his thighs. "Who the f–" He froze to gawk, cross-eyed, at Michael's carbine, two centimetres from the bridge of his nose.

"Okay, ladies. Out ya get." Jack tried his best to sound paternal and reassuring.

The two teenagers sat on the bed. Their eyes held a glazed, curious expression, along with dull-witted smiles.

"Shit, they're high," Michael said. He gathered blankets and sheets to cover the young women and then escorted them past Jack, who used the threat of the M-60 to keep the two men in check.

Michael guided the two girls through a nearby doorway opposite the bunks. Behind him came shuffling sounds, followed by the noises of a quick, one-sided fight.

Looking over his shoulder, Michael saw the first naked Roman flop to the floor, unconscious, and bleeding from his mouth and nose. A few seconds later, his friend slipped from the bed after receiving a none-too-gentle tap on the forehead from the butt of Jack's gun.

"Sleep tight, boys," Jack said with a satisfied smirk before following Michael.

A few minutes later Ried came through the door where Michael escorted the two girls "Jack, Michael, we need to go." Ried stopped mid-stride when he walked into a combined dormitory, kitchen and infirmary.

Beyond an assortment of disarrayed furniture, and gathered together in a corner, stood a group of women.

A tall, auburn-haired woman, aged in her late thirties, tended to the two teenagers Michael had brought in. Some of the women stared in fright at Ried, Jack and Michael. Four of them glared with defiance at the men while the rest focused on the grey concrete floor.

Ried flicked the rifle's sling over his shoulder to hold the weapon across his back at the sight of the women crowded into a corner. *Shit.* "Ladies, we're not here to hurt you. We are just he–"

"Ben, they're scared, and we should help them."
Michael came to stand by Ried. "Let me take them back to
the wagon."

"Christ, Michael. It'll be hard enough getting us, Dom,
and Abbey out," Ried said, "let alone take care of them."

"But we can't leave them," Michael pleaded.

"I can, and I will. I came here for Abbey and Dom, so –
"

Jack opened his mouth to speak and froze when a
familiar voice called out.

"So, you can take them with us."

"Abbey?" Ried sprang forward when the speaker
brushed past the women to run over to him.

Their bodies collided in a mutual and longing embrace,
with neither speaking for a full minute.

In her arms, Ried inhaled her scent. For those long
seconds, he forgot the world around him.

Abbey head against Ried's chest, wetting his shirt with
her tears. "When we heard the noises and voices outside,
they tried to protect me," Abbey said. "Then, Michael
came in with Bonnie and Raelene." Abbey pulled away
and held Ried's eyes. "I thought I was dreaming, but when
Uncle Jack walked in before you…" They kissed. "I knew
you'd come." She repeated the last words over and over,
hugging him, and burying her head in his shoulders.

"I'm sorry I'm late," he said, reaching down and lifting
her face. He leaned in to kiss her when a soft cough broke
the moment. Ried kissed her again even though he
understood Jack's concern. The longer they lingered, the
shorter their luck would hold out. "Where is your dad?"

"Gallio took him upstairs. He kept going on about
waiting for Uncle Jack so he could kill them both
together."

"Looks like he holds a grudge," Jack said. "But we need to shake a leg."

A red-haired woman in a light-blue caftan approached Abbey and Ried. "Abbey, the girls and I will be okay–"

"No, you're coming with us," Abbey told her.

"Abbey, love, Ben's right. It'll be tough enough to get our backsides off this rock–"

"Tell them we're leaving," Ried heard himself say to the redhead, and then to Jack. "All of us."

"good, because I wasn't going without them," Abbey told him.

With Abbey's help, convincing the others took under a minute. Less than five minutes later, the women stood together wearing a change of clothes and nothing else.

"Where is Rufus?" the redhead asked when they had all gathered near the door leading into the corridor.

"Who's Rufus?" Ried asked.

"He was brought here last week for this fat pig Titus." She walked past Ried and into the brothel.

Jack noticed a long slit in one of Ried's trouser legs stained with blood and a curved knife in his belt. Jack moved across and opened the curtain, Titus lay on the floor amidst his own urine and a slow-moving puddle of blood from his crushed nose and a gash under the temple.

"What happened?"

Ried flicked his head at the unconscious fat Roman on the floor. "We had a disagreement."

Jack raised an eyebrow at Ried after spotting the obese form of the pimp

"What?" Ried said moving out into the hall with a dark expression.

The two men stepped aside when the redheaded woman brushed past the curtain. "Rufus? It's all right. Come with me." The red-haired woman stepped out carrying a boy wrapped in a blanket, whose eyes were wide with fear.

Ried stopped in the hall with his hand gripping the brothel's door handle. "That boy is how old?" He looked hard at Jack and rested the M-16 against the wall before he drew his revolver. "I'll bet he's only eight or nine at the most…" His thumb levered back the pistol's hammer, and his fingers flexed around the rosewood grip.

Jack blocked the door, conscious of where Ried waved the barrel of the big pistol. "And we rescued him, so let's go."

Ried glowered into the room past Jack. "I don't give a rat's arse if he fucks a dog, but not a…" He swallowed, unable to finish.

"Now's not the time, son." Jack lowered his hand over the revolver, blocking the hammer with the web of his thumb.

Without a word, the redhead handed the small boy to Abbey. She then leaned across and slipped the curved knife from Ried's belt before going back into the brothel.

Several minutes later, when they reached the door leading into the cavern, Ried accepted the knife in silence from the redhead. Nobody commented on the dark stains on her dress, or the crimson smear on her face as she took Rufus from Abbey.

Ried stepped past everyone to sneak through the door and waved everybody back giving Jack a concerned look.

Jack crept up to Ried and crouched with the machine gun slung over his shoulder and drew his pistol. "What's up?"

"It's quiet." Ried pointed toward the gypsy wagons and motor pool, which showed no signs of movement around them. "It's too quiet."

They both eased past the door and across to the nearest column where Jack nodded toward three soldiers who stood to face outward at the entrance to the cavern. "I don't reckon our blokes made it up–"

"Jack," the doctor cried out in relief from behind the wagon, waving toward the two men.

"Strewth, Doc. Keep your bloody voice down." Both Jack and Ried tensed with their weapons raised and ready, expecting a hail of gunfire to rain in on them from the three figures who turned and jogged toward them.

Ried looked confused beyond words until the silhouette of the approaching soldier stepped into the light. "Cassius? What the hell?" Ried shook hands with the Roman and the doctor. "What happened to your face?"

"Your friend Smithy's desire for revenge proved greater than we anticipated," Cassius replied. "He freed himself not long after you disappeared into the cavern."

"That explains the gunfire," Jack said.

"Not the diversion your nomad friends planned, I'm afraid," Cassius said in a dry tone. "I tried to tackle him, but he broke free, and continued his efforts to warn the guards about you. Then, the guards from the watch-house attacked. The Nomads came in behind the soldiers, and well… let's say they are more than proficient with guns and knives than all our intelligence indicated."

"What about Smithy?" Asked Jack.

"Someone killed him in the crossfire."

Jack studied Cassius, but the Roman dropped no other hints or offered a clue who shot Smithy. He gave a slight shrug and dismissed any further questions. After all, things happen in the fog of battle.

"Okay, but how did you get up here so fast?" Ried asked.

"Luck and God's favour. During the fight, one man discovered a small cave with a stone and cement staircase leading through the mountain, to outside the wall on the south-west side." Cassius shrugged. "The rest we accomplished with stealth and surprise."

"Are any of you hurt?" Asked Mitchum.

"Two of us and a few Nomads," Cassius said, "they are all in the valley."

Near the wagon, Mitchum, with the help of the redhead gathered the woman and girls to examine each in turn. While he waited for the doctor, Ried toured the cavern and returned to the hall where he checked the lab door and paced back and forth. Eager to resume the search for Dom and then get the hell off the mountain.

He lifted the file from under his shirt and flicked through the pages and stopping on the pages with lithographed schematics. He frowned at one image and marched back to the cavern where he held up the papers on the diagram and looked past it to the giant stone ring. With a grunt, he closed the folder and marched across to the doctor. "How are the women and the boy?"

"Women," Mitchum fired out the word. "For the love of god, they are mostly girls in their teens. However, apart from a little malnutrition and mild trauma. they are fine." Mitchum's sharp steel-blue eyes glossed with sadness. "As for the boy," Mitchum shrugged. "He seems well fed, but the emotional scars will take far longer to heal than his physical bruises."

Jack and Cassius joined Mitchum and Ried. "Cassius, you help the doctor." Ried said, "I want everybody down the cave and stairs." He stepped inside the gypsy wagon. "Where's Eddy?"

"He took a bullet in the leg," Mitchum said. "A clean through-and-through in his thigh. He's down in the valley with the others."

Ried handed Cassius the papers he found. "Cassius, can you go through this stuff and get back to me with what it says?"

Cassius accepted the documents with a nod and placed them under his shirt.

Ried left the group and jogged outside to inspect the trapdoor hidden under an overhang beneath the wall. Without wanting to jinx himself, Ried wondered how much longer their luck would hold out.

Abbey stood with Ried under the overhanging cliff. "We'll be down when we find your dad." He held Abbey's hand. "What's the matter?"

"Dr Mitchum told me about Rose." Abbey looked at her father's friend. "I should go and say something."

Ried cupped her elbow in his palm and steered her toward the open trapdoor. "Tell him later. Now's not the time," he said in a hushed voice, glancing over at Jack who crouched on over-watch near the entrance of the cavern.

"What about you?" She asked.

"What about me?"

"I saw your face when Loretta found the boy."

"So?"

Abbey paused for a few seconds and reached for Ried's hand. "Would you really have killed him?"

"It doesn't matter. The man's dead and the boy is safe." Ried shrugged and thought Abbey would continue the debate, but instead, she nodded and stepped onto the stairs.

After watching Abbey's torchlight disappear, Ried closed the hatch and made his way with Jack and Michael back through the empty cavern into the hall.

They stopped at the brothel so Jack could check on the two Romans they found with the girls. The familiar metallic and piss smell told Jack his concerns were unfounded. He stood in the brothels walkway looking at the dark congealed pool of blood glistening on the tiled floor. When he came back into the hallway, he shook his head. "I reckon the redhead had a grievance or two with those other blokes as well."

When they rounded a corner past the lab and slave brothel, the three men stopped beside a long narrow room sectioned off by metal gates and wire mesh.

Ried raised an eyebrow at the sight of the castle's armoury, with its rows of shelving and crated ammunition.

Opposite the armoury, they saw two steel doors. Curiosity got the better of Jack, and he eased open the nearest door.

From inside came two men completing a debate.

"Why are we standing down?"

"You heard the guardhouse. It was just a couple of Nomads chasing one of their nutters. So, relax and finish the game."

Jack entered the room as though he walked on eggshells. A few seconds later he hurried back out.

"By the looks, I reckon it's their barracks," Jack said.

"How many?" Asked Ried.

"Around two dozen, and going by the bottles on the table, I'd say they were well and truly off duty."

"Probably explains why they didn't rush out to help the pickets." Ried felt a little bemused. "Beats me how this lot conquered your world."

Jack pointed to the steel door. "This lot couldn't invade a sandbox," he retorted. "And what you've seen ain't anything like the invading forces."

Ried and Michael left Jack to keep an eye on the barracks doors, while they inspected the hallway and nearby circular stairwell for materials to help construct a hasty barricade.

After several minutes, they scrounged up two slabs of hardwood, and a length of rusted steel rod and some wire cables, which they used to jam the doors closed.

Jack moved across the hall to the armoury cage and set about rigging four hand grenades in the caged walls near the floor and out of sight, before running a wire from each grenade to the gates.

"Hang about. This is our escape route," Michael said. "If that goes up, then we're stuck."

"If this lot goes off, we can use one of the towers on the south side to escape into the cavern," Ried assured him.

"You don't sound too convinced," Michael said.

"Come on," Ried said.

At the end of the hall and with exaggerated stealth, they climbed the spiral staircase to the next level and stepped off into another hallway.

They crouched to get their bearings seconds before a muffled thud, and several more definite bangs of more massive explosions sent shock waves through the floorboards and sifted dust down from the cracked plaster ceiling.

Before the cloud of fine dirt cleared, Jack ran back down the stairs like a ferret down a rabbit hole. Ried told the anxious Michael to keep an eye on the hallway as he stepped back and peered upward where the dark stairwell ended in the dull glow of a small, illuminated anti-chamber.

"I guess the blokes in the lab's fridge got cold and took a chance," Jack said when he returned. "The lab door looked a little buckled, but the main passageway is still passable."

"The barracks?" Michael asked.

"One of the beams came loose and fell across the doors with a pile of rocks from the roof." Both Michael and Ried sighed with relief. "Don't get too relaxed. The bastards are awake and hammering their way out. So, whatever we do next, we need to do it ASAP."

The hallway ended in a T-Junction with one arm continuing off to the left, and the right opening out into a spacious room filled with tables and couches, and a bar. In each corner, a wrought-iron staircase cast a skeletal shadow on the adjoining walls. Ried closed his eyes to conjure a mental image of the castle.

"Those two stairs must lead to the small, mid-level towers I spotted." Ried gave the room a quick scan before he turned to look at the ceiling behind them. "If Dom's not here, then they'll have him upstairs." He shrugged his shoulder and offered his two companions an apologetic look. "Here's the thing. There are at least three men in each of the larger towers on the bastion walls." He pointed toward a pair of double timber doors in the room's eastern wall. "So, we might be in for a scrap if they decide to investigate."

"About bloody time cause I've gotten bored with all our skulking about," Jack said.

"Bloody hell," Michael looked mortified. "You're serious."

"Did you think we'd just wander in, find Dom and Abbey, and stroll out again?" Jack replied in a flat, dark tone.

Before Ried could answer, one of the double doors creaked open. *Christ.* "Jack, cover us while we head down the hall."

Jack nodded with a wink and gave one of his cheeky grins.

Michael did not smile. Instead, he wiped the beads of sweat from his brow and followed Ried.

Pieces of the old, fallen plaster wall dotted the floor and crunched under their boots. They jogged past by windows on the halls outer wall. The inside wall held four doors.

The first two they passed were either broken or left ajar, leading to rooms full of rotten floorboards, decayed furnishings, and homes to various birds. Michael turned to cast more than a nervous look back down the hall and bumped against Ried who stopped in front of the third door.

"What's the matter?" Asked Michael.

Ried pointed the barrel of his rifle at the door. "The others are all open on broken hinges or rotten frames. Yet, this is the only one closed and in good nick, with a new lock." He leaned against the door. "Mr Harris?"

"Who's there?"

"It's me, Ben—"

Bullets snapped and whizzed past Michael and Ried, and the cracks of gunfire echoed along the hallway, drowning out any response from Dom.

The resonating staccato burst of the M-60 thundered down the hall, as Ried and Michael darted back to help Jack.

With comfortable ease, Jack braced the machine gun under his arm to unleash a storm of brass-jacketed lead in the timber door's direction. When the tail of the empty ammunition belt slipped from the breach, Jack swung back into cover.

With a twitch and a flick of his shoulder and wrist, he tossed the pack from his back and rested the gun on his thigh. He unsnapped the cover plate and pulled out a fresh strip of ammunition which he layered in the cartridge tray before closing the open breach and re-cocking the gun.

While Jack reloaded, Ried took shelter behind the bar made of thick timber slats, impressed by Jack's ability with the big gun. While next to him, Michael unleashed bullets into the room with indiscriminate fire.

"Michael, sight, and shoot in controlled bursts! We don't have enough ammo to spray and pray," Ried snapped. "Like this."

Wild-eyed, Michael nodded and tried to copy Ried's firm yet fluid movements when he returned fire. An incoming round ricocheted near his foot, causing Michael to fumble and drop back.

Jack grabbed a handful of Michael's shirt and dragged him forward to push the hyperventilating younger man flat.

"Breath, son, and keep yourself small," Jack told him, "or those pricks will put a hole in you."

They concentrated on the door frame, watching the shadows crossing the opening. The tower guards chanced on blind luck when they poked their rifles through the openings and fired random shots into the room.

The tactic worked in pinning down the three men. Ried swore when he ducked from the incoming rounds and loaded a grenade into the launcher under the M-16's barrel.

"Jack! Fire in the hole."

The older man nodded and tipped his head with his mouth ajar. Michael ignored Ried and kept shooting with his jaw locked in grim concentration, only to fall back on his butt when the grenade's explosion shattered the inside cinder block and plaster, exposing the outer block work.

Ried hauled the stunned younger man up. "When someone yells out like that, tilt your head and open your mouth."

Through the dust, two men dashed into the room stumbling a falling from the machine gun's bullets tearing through flesh and bone. Another of the guards poked his arms around the broken door jamb and fired in a blind semicircle.

Before the smoke cleared, Ried launched another grenade. The resulting detonation blew out the sidewall and most of the left door and frame.

Above them came the noise of fireworks cracking and booming. With a large section of the foundation removed, the tower collapsed and imploded, tearing away part of the wall and toppling into the courtyard beyond.

The crumbling structure sent clouds of choking dust into the room, along with shards of stone, concrete and timber.

Bright, orange flashes erupted behind the thinning dust from outside. Hot tracers lanced across the room. Bursting through the door from a wall tower, two Vigiles charged forward, shooting blind, they sprayed the room in an angry swarm of bullets for cover as they attempt to cross the courtyard and pin down their attackers. The tactic should have worked, except the men stopped, crouched and reloaded their empty guns

For those men, their lack of experience proved a mistake. For Jack, aided by surging adrenaline, reacted with instinct and experience. He braced the machine gun's butt under his right arm and raised himself to his knee. Then, he squeezed the trigger in a series of three-second bursts at the wraith-like shadows in the smoke and dust.

When he ceased shooting, Jack dropped and rolled across the rubble into the hallway, leaning against the hall door to watch a third figure rush past the shattered entrance and lose several rounds in Jack's earlier position.

Two more three-second bursts from Jack decimated the man from the chest upward. He pitched forward and drowned the cobblestones in a red, oozing puddle. When the dead man thumped the ground, Jack went over to the rubble-strewn opening, swung the machine gun around his shoulders, drew his pistol, and made his way into the night beyond.

426

Michael stumbled over the broken rock, concrete blocks and timber, and stood over the three bodies. He fell to his knees, dropped his carbine, and vomited until his stomach was empty. His eyes burned with tears and airborne grit.

A billowing wave of dust and grit filled the hall. Trailing dust, Ried bolted back down the corridor and yelled for Dom to move away from the door, he followed the instruction by raising the muzzle of his rifle and firing three rounds.

The timber of the door and frame splintered from the bullets as Ried, in one fluid motion, dropped the muzzle and fired another three shots on the lower hinge and then leaned back with his right foot raised and drove his foot against the door. The door swung on the lock's bolt before twisting free to tumble into Dom's cell.

Dom wasted no time in leaping from the room. "Abbey?"

"She's safe at the bottom of the hill with Doc Mitchum and some others." Ried patted his shoulder, almost pushing him down the hall. "C'mon, you blokes. Time to go."

CHAPTER SEVEN

Earlier that afternoon, Marcus, dressed in ill-fitting fatigues of the Vigiles, marched into a library on the top floor of the castle.

"Marcus?" Gallio gave a small start when the proconsul entered the room. "I do not recall asking for you."

Marcus eyed the opulence of the room and smiled. "No, you did not."

Dominating the centre of the room was an ornate tapestry rug on which stood several chairs, a two-metre-long oval table, and a desk of matching polished mahogany, where Gallio sat in a high-back, leather-bound chair.

Marcus stood before the table contemplating Gallio, who sat drinking wine and helping himself to dried fruits, cheese, and bread. Layers of dishevelled papers and platters of food covered the tablecloth.

"An impressive room." Marcus wandered around the table. "Is this table cover silk?"

"Brought in from Tharassia."

"Tharassia. I remember that campaign. They were a formidable race," Marcus held his gaze on Gallio for a few seconds, "but with little honour."

Gallio dismissed Marcus's barb. "The former commander had expensive tastes." He leaned across the table and steepled his hands over the plate of fruit, meat, and cheese. "I'm sorry, why are you here?" Gallio studied Marcus.

"A rather redundant question," Marcus responded.

"I meant in this room."

"I assumed, by not being detained in a locked room, I would be able to… explore." Marcus finished by spreading his arms.

"You assumed wrong," Gallio said in a blunt, dismissive tone. "Allowing the apothecaries to treat your shoulder was a difficult enough decision. However, since the former commander ensured the facilities here lacked for nothing, I saw no need not to use those resources."

"Former commander?" Marcus gazed around the room. "So, what have you done with the 'former commander'?"

"Nothing yet." Gallio twisted his lip in a cruel smile. "He is unaware of my little coup."

"I see," Marcus tipped his head. "That will prove to be an interesting conversation."

"No doubt," Gallio replied, "but why make it your concern?"

"Forgive me, I am just making conversation."

Gallio refilled his glass. "This is a good claret." He inhaled the liquid's bouquet. "Conversation…" Gallio took a sip and raised his eyes to the ceiling. "All right. How is your shoulder? Is it still painful?"

Marcus ignored Gallio's patronising tone and manner. Instead, he roamed the room exploring the floor to ceiling bookcases and the tomes filling them.

His attention was drawn to a broken Scutum above ivory and gold-handled Scimitar and Gladius. The shield and swords rested against a plush orange felt backing. All mounted in a transparent case separating two of the bookshelf cabinets. While gazing at the swords, he flexed his shoulder.

"The analgesics help with the pain. However, the synthetic flesh patch and dermal regenerator repaired most–"

Gallio offered Marcus a dismissive wave. "Never mind. I only asked out of 'conversation.'" He gestured for the two guards. "Take him back to his room."

Marcus ignored the implied threat of the approaching soldiers, who paused at his raised hand. He walked away from the books and sat opposite Gallio. Without asking, he slid the plate of food closer and sampled its contents and poured himself a glass of wine.

Gallio waved the two soldiers away, retrieved the platter, and shared a brief smile with Marcus. "Do not misunderstand your position here."

"My apologies." Marcus stood up and brushed away some crumbs of meat from his lap. "Although, I am relieved there is no sword or hot coals in the fireplace."

Marcus surveyed the room again, walking over to a section of the bookcase to study its contents. He perused the shelves, contemplated several books before selecting one, and wandered to the western windows to gaze into the beginnings of a twilight sky.

The sky faded into a pale silver decorated by high clouds. The clouds top edges glowed white above undersides of deep, blue-greys, and were lanced by shafts of platinum sunlight washed in gold. In the distance, the shadowed tops of the border ranges jutted above the bastion wall resembling a crumpled layer of rough cloth.

"It is a great pity the surrounding walls hide the view of the setting sun."

"I prefer the dawn."

"Do you? I find the sunsets on this planet quite remarkable."

"Enough, Marcus," Gallio said. "If you want a book, take one. And I don't care for your opinion of the sunset."

Marcus sat down and raised the corner of his mouth in a wry smile at Gallio's outburst.

The two Romans held each other's gaze. In silence, they measured their will and strength over the other.

Relaxing into the chair, Marcus raised his glass. "To the new commander and his fortress." Marcus offered a beguiling expression with the salute.

"Oh…" Caution clouded Gallio's acceptance of the compliment. "I plan for this castle and garrison to be much more than a mere fort. It will be the centre of power."

"Power?" Marcus relaxed back in the chair. "True power will come at a cost."

"Yes, for you and the Senate—"

"I meant for you," Marcus said, "or have you forgotten about abducting Dominic, Abbey, and myself?" Marcus continued. "It would make sense to keep me for ransom. However, Dominic and his daughter will be the most expensive part of your dream."

"I don't see either of them costing much. Harris will die, and the girl, I will sell at auction, or she can join her father. Either choice works."

"What of Jack Bennett?"

"Bennett is an old dog with rotten teeth and past his time." Gallio lent back and drank more wine. "When we find him, and we will, he will enjoy the same fate as Harris."

Marcus sipped and savoured the wine's bouquet. "And what of our guest, Benjamin? He will be your greatest cost." He peered over his wine glass. "You do understand he will come for them, and when he does–"

"He will also die," interrupted Gallio. "I'll admit this Ried has proved to be an inconvenience." He pushed the chair across the rug and rose to pace the room. "He is an abnormality upon this blighted world, and he has yet to feel the full vengeful might of the Empire."

"Benjamin is unique, not abnormal, and we believe he is well skilled in the art of soldiering. As his actions during the failed assault on the Nomads revealed."

Gallio stopped his pacing and stiffened. "I studied the report from Mettius. We agreed his unpredicted actions gave him the advantage."

"That advantage allowed Benjamin to survive against your pet. Not something many have achieved."

Gallio cast a betrayed look at Marcus. "You told me his involvement was inconclusive."

"Gallio, you are, on the whole, a good general, but I am afraid you lack certain political skills," Marcus took on a parental, mollifying tone. "The information was deemed classified because the science division and I wanted Benjamin brought to Toowoomba. It would have been the ideal opportunity for us to learn and study him. More so after his accidental involvement in our experiment–"

"Accidental involvement?" Gallio shook his head. "Decius confirmed the off-worlder and his vehicle turned up in an unknown cosmic event. Although, his belief in–" Gallio stopped and marched back to the table to lean over Marcus. "You're responsible for this dimensional tunnel and storm?"

"Yes, and the unusual weather was an unforeseen by-product." Marcus picked more meat from the plate. "Almost two centuries ago, our forward scouts learned the location of this planet and its relation to the galaxy's position was an ideal location."

"An ideal location." Gallio spat out a laugh. "To go past this planet, you end up in the void between this galaxy and the next."

Marcus exhaled in pity. "As I said this planet and its location are ideal for our continued multidimensional experiments."

"Is not the galaxy enough for our Emperor?" Scoffed Gallio.

The tenor of Marcus's voice dipped. "Indeed. However, we aimed to find a way back to the world of our ancestor's birth."

Gallio sat back in his chair offering Marcus a bored expression.

"For centuries," Marcus continued. "The closest we came was the creation of tiny fissures. Many of which formed in the vacuum of space and disappeared within minutes." Marcus poured himself another wine. "Eventually, the scientists, using lasers and amplified radiogenic particles, developed an annular targeting device. One which proved successful enough for them to locate and target solid space bodies." He sat back with a slight shrug.

"Through determination, the Emperors will and a measure of the god's favour, they discovered another dimension and planet believed to be the source of our ancestors."

Marcus rolled his wine glass between his hands. "As you know, our efforts to conquer this planet went awry, and most of the scientists involved died when the human's nuclear weapons destroyed our science vessels.

"Those who survived took the past twenty years to restart the experiments. Then in January, we were ready. However, they did not consider a simultaneous planetary alignment within the two systems." Marcus fixed his attention on a guard behind Gallio.

"The resulting changes in solar winds, gravimetric distortions, and magnetic flux caused the portal's opening to lose its coherent frequencies…" Marcus noticed Gallio's dull expression. "In short, Benjamin was in the wrong place at the wrong time."

"The wrong place at the wrong time?" Gallio shook his head with a forlorn expression. Suspicion soon replaced his look of disbelief. "Why are you telling me this?"

Marcus raised an eyebrow and shrugged. "I see no harm in you knowing about particular facts."

"Particular facts," Gallio spat the words back at Marcus. He leaned across the table stabbing a finger at Marcus. "Under my rule, there will be no more useless experiments. The only thing to take precedence will be Roman survival." His passion resounded across the room. "Which begins here, today."

"Would that also include the continued supply of Enlightenment?"

"It would, but not here," Gallio boasted with grand gestures. "However, we will continue to manufacture the drug and expand the supply, which will bring about the final demise of the human race's freedom."

"It is a rather clever name… Enlightenment… Do you know what the idea was for its introduction into their society?"

"Of course, unless you wish to enlighten me with your understanding." Gallio poured himself another drink enjoying his pun.

Marcus bowed in acknowledgement. "The drug with its alluring delights would, over time, render the user into a state of carefree ecstasy. This would pave a path of accepting our total domination."

Gallio frowned at Marcus's statement, putting down the bottle of wine.

"Oh, do not look so shocked."

"I suppose, being the proconsul, you'd have had access to the secure reports and scrolls from Senate investigations."

"Naturally." Marcus savoured the dark, plum-coloured alcohol in his glass. Then, with a casual flick of the wrist, he tossed the book he held across the table. "The drug did start showing encouraging signs in many of those addicted, but after a time, a different side effect appeared. Those with long-term addictions suffered a variety of psychosis, paranoia, and delusional anger."

Marcus took another mouthful of wine along with a handful of fruits before he continued. "What we failed to understand is the psyche of this race. You see, this species is incapable of accepting any long-term thoughts or desires for a peaceful utopia." He crossed his legs and lifted his shirt to inspect the layer of synthetic flesh below his neck.

"Naturally, you would have known this if you had read the latest and final reports issued to the cabal."

"Report? Cabal?"

"The one in the bottom, left-hand draw?" Marcus stared at Gallio, who studied the desk.

Despite himself, Gallio pushed the blank face of the cabinet.

"Forgive me. I forgot to mention there is a biometric lock. One that can only be opened by the commander of this castle."

Gallio abandoned his efforts to open the elusive draw when the faint pop of gunfire echoed from beyond the castle walls. He rose and went to a wall mounted intercom, thumbed a button and lowered his face to the oval metal grill. "Report."

"Nomads are attacking."

Gallio's faced flushed. "Damn Nomad filth." He thumbed the button again. "Can you contain the situation?"

"Yes, sir." Distorted gunfire echoed from the grill. "There's only a handful."

"When you're done place their heads on spikes along the road."

The speakers hissed for several seconds. "Um… on spikes… yes, sir."

"Somewhat extreme and barbaric."

"The start of many new lessons."

"And if it is a rescue party?" Marcus asked. "Do you not understand there is more than simple coincidence at work here?"

"Let them come." Gallio returned to his chair. "They will soon realise they face trained centurions and over a dozen armed Vigiles." His face darkened. "Now as for ransoming you…" Gallio rose, walked over to one of the windows facing south, and listened to the muffled gunfire before he returned to the table.

He lifted his glass to toast Marcus with a voice steeped in hatred. "I plan to lock you away with enough food and water to keep breath in your lungs. Then, when the time is right, I will have your starved carcass crucified in front of your precious Senate!"

"Your arrogance and perpetual stupidity astound me," Marcus said in a pitiless tone layered in sadness. "Do you not remember how this race almost destroyed themselves and the planet to prevent subjection by us?"

"But they failed. On both counts," Gallio rebuked. "And it will be no different for any pathetic rescue attempt by the off-worlder." He leaned over the table, his tone fell to a savage whisper, "because none of them shall leave this mountain alive."

"A common thread indeed." Marcus gave Gallio his best political smile.

"We have nothing in common," said Gallio.

He sat back down and reached for the book Marcus had thrown on the table, and with an air of casual indifference, he scanned the first few pages.

His other hand, holding the full glass, stopped halfway to his mouth, spilling some of its contents down his tunic.

Gallio placed the book on the table, his hand holding open the page with a hand-written inscription. The wine glass shaking in his other hand almost missed the table when he put it down.

"Do be careful. And that, by the way, is a sixty-year-old merlot, not a claret."

"You?"

"Yes."

"You're... Negru Cerberus?" In a sudden blind rage, Gallio pushed himself away from the table, knocking over the high-backed chair, and spilling the bottle of wine and unsheathed his Pugio.

In the same move, an odd burning sensation rose from his stomach, and he dropped the dagger as bile clawed in his throat.

The burning became a twitch, and he felt something pressed hard against his back. His confusion turned to shock when he looked down at the ten centimetres of a Praetorian Gladius cutting through his tunic.

Gallio stared in morbid fascination at the growing stain in the cloth around the sword. His hands reached down to the double-edged blade in slow revelation.

He coughed a bubble of blood and fought the urge to collapse after the Praetorian withdrew his sword, slicing Gallio's hand in the process.

The same hand, oozing a continuous flow of blood, Gallio pointed at Marcus mouthing the proconsul's code name.

Marcus rose. "Being the commander of the garrison and this facility," Marcus replied, walking around the table, "I denounce your coup."

Bending down, Marcus picked up the chair and slid it under Gallio before manoeuvring himself around to face the dying Roman.

Fear and panic knotted Gallio's brow. He tried to pinch his sliced abdomen closed, but his fingers kept slipping on his blood-slicked skin. He glared at the proconsul, his dread veiled by anger and disbelief.

"I am so disappointed in you, my friend," Marcus said and leaned over Gallio. "I sent you to the northern region to govern and covertly spread the Enlightenment. Instead, you embezzle the monies needed to fund the portal experiments while nurturing those ridiculous endeavours to create yourself a criminal empire." Marcus knelt, watching Gallio's contorting face. "You damaged the relationship I had with the people." He pushed his index finger against Gallio's forehead.

"Then, in an insane sense of your own worth, you abduct a well-known and revered member of their community."

Marcus cupped the dying man's chin and jerked his hand upward. "But worse still, your stupidity brings them here. And for what?" Marcus slapped Gallio's pale face. "A selfish, misguided desire for revenge, and the belief you can resurrect a new empire from this world and its cold and radioactive ashes."

Clenching a handful of Gallio's hair, Marcus pointed across the room. "Now this Benjamin Ried, whom you arrogantly misjudged, is here to rescue them – and no doubt believes our rule is a terrible wrong he must right!"

Gallio tried to speak, but slumped in the chair, coughing blood and bile.

"Do not die yet." Marcus wrestled Gallio back into a seating position. "There is something you should know. So, pay attention." Marcus in a warm smiled at Gallio's murderous stare. "The very day the humans showed their final retaliation with nuclear weapons…" His voice mellowed into bitterness, "our beloved empire tasted defeat, and abandoned us to die on this rotten, polluted world."

Marcus shook his victim. "Pay attention. This is important… After years of countless skirmishes amidst those devastating winters and summers, the last two high tribunes and I devised a plan. We would work with these people to rebuild a growing civilisation under a veiled banner of truce while rekindling the experiments.

"Since then, we gained their trust and established a working government in what is already a new Roman Empire."

Marcus slapped Gallio harder across the face, sending droplets of red saliva across his robes. "But now, your greed and lack of intuitive foresight have jeopardised it all." He stepped back, turning his back on Gallio.

Gallio's face twisted through his pain when he tried to stand, before stumbling against the table. He tried picking up a carving knife near the food platter, but it slipped through his unresponsive hand to bounce on the rug.

With both hands braced on the table, Gallio fought the growing weakness spreading through his body. His breath rattled in his chest, perspiration flooded from every pore and lead weights replaced the muscles in his legs, while around him, darkness enveloped the room.

Moving around the table, Marcus collected his wine and went towards the intercom giving Gallio a dispassionate gaze, laced with casual indifference.

As Marcus raised his hand toward the intercom, the floor shuddered with a series of muted thuds sounding beneath his feet.

It appears they may have entered the warehouse. Marcus sipped his wine. *Still, I doubt they will make it any farther.* He continued to watch Gallio die.

Gallio's body convulsed with each cough, spraying dark red spittle over the food platter and tablecloth. On the fringes of his darkening sight and hearing, he focused on a shadow walking through the open double door.

Marcus faltered from the sudden sound of gunfire coming from the floor below and the sight of Mettius in the door.

Mettius also paused, he drew his pistol and retraced his steps until a hoarse voice called his name.

Gallio leaned on the table, his waxen face pleading for help, his bloody hand pointing at Marcus.

In an instant, Mettius activated his shield boss, milliseconds before the praetorians opened fire on him.

Below them came the crump and boom from Ried's grenades.

The voices of rock and concrete breaking and dying resonated through the library seconds before the room heaved.

Decades of dust cascaded from rattling chandeliers and exposed beams. The hooks supporting a battle-scene tapestry tore free and dragged the cloth into a crumpled heap.

One of the bookshelves rocked, tipping books from the shelves. A window fractured before shattering, spilling shards of glass across the room.

Gallio's lifeless body, supported by his arms locked in death, collapsed on the table with a thud – before toppling to the carpet where his blood and gastric juices flooded the intricate, woven patterns.

Marcus dived across the floor to avoid a falling bookcase. The two praetorians swayed, planting their feet apart and tried keeping their balance.

Unlike the two guards wobbling in the open, Mettius fell against the door jamb and used the solid wooden fixture to balance his stance. He raised his pistol and fired, putting three bullets into the heart of the closest Praetorian.

Before the second guard could recover his senses, Mettius deactivated his shield and launched himself over the table. When his feet hit the carpet, his shield sprang to life, humming with power.

Mettius held his stance staring at the remaining Praetorian through the shimmering energy field and plumes of disintegrating bullets.

The Praetorian emptied the magazines of his pistol and carbine against the shield as Mettius charged. In a blind panic, the frightened soldier raised his arms as the energy field pressed against him.

Mettius shunted the soldier backwards. The crackling pale blue energy of the shield burning through the Praetorian's clothes, scorching his skin.

Mettius herded the Praetorian under the chandelier where he shot the light fitting until the supporting chain and cables snapped.

The tiered crystals tinkled when the chandelier's weight proved too much for the damaged, last link which gave off a sharp crack as it snapped, Mettius dived sideways as he switched off the shield.

The chandeliers crushed the Praetorian. His shrill scream lost amidst the grinding tinkle of falling crystal, brass rings, and chain.

Mettius climbed to his feet, giving only a cursory glance at the Praetorian's burnt, crushed, and lacerated body.

Horrified at the manner and speed by which Mettius dispatched the second guard, Marcus fled through the door amidst splinters, dust and ricocheting bullets.

With his ammunition spent, Mettius knelt beside the body of Gallio. In the flash of seconds, his stoic constant expression slipped. His pistol and shield boss fell from his grip.

Mettius lifted Gallios head and in a slow tender move wiped his fingers across Gallio's unseeing eyes. Then, with the same gentleness a mother uses to carry her sleeping child to bed, Mettius carried the body of his mentor, commander, and the only brother of his long-dead mother from the room.

CHAPTER EIGHT

Ried, Jack, Michael, and Dom, all raised their eyes when the sound of gunshots echoed down the stairwell.

"Before you ask, it's just us," Ried said when he caught Dom's silent glance.

"Did you find Marcus?"

Ried shook his head, knowing the question from Dom also came as a request. He thought about passing on his suspicions to Dom, but Jack's subtle shake of his head suggested otherwise.

Dom took the carbine from Michael; whose ashen face and shirt carried the stains of fresh vomit.

"What are you doing?" Asked Ried.

"I'm going with you."

"Like hell. You need to go to Abbey. I'll find Marcus."

Dom conceded, and tipped a nod to Ried, before following Michael and Jack.

As the three men's footsteps receded, Ried loaded a new magazine into his rifle and ran up the stairs. Upon reaching the top, he tucked the butt of his M-16 against his shoulder, dropped into a semi-crouch, and headed toward a double door on his left.

On entering the room, he checked the wall on either side of the door with a lightning-fast pivot at the hip.

When nothing moved or shot back, Ried made his way along a wall-length bookcase – with his knees bent, keeping his steps short, quick, and steady, the rifle tight against his shoulder, and his arms tucked. Every direction he faced, the muzzle of the weapon also pointed.

Three metres past the door, the body of a Praetorian lay beside a fallen bookcase. Ried didn't bother checking for a pulse. The three holes in the man's chest and his open, lifeless eyes, told him the man posed no further threat.

Ried skirted the table, and with his toe, he nudged the empty pistol and shield boss near a sticky puddle of red-black on the rug. He did another careful sweep around the dark room before he knelt and dragged his finger through the wet patch.

"Still warm…"

He dodged the chair to make his way over to the eviscerated remains of a second Praetorian. The quiet of the room heightened his hearing, his breath sounded like waves in a tunnel. The acrid, metallic odour hung thicker in the air the closer he got to the dead man.

"Whose side is who on around here? Ried gave the corpse – blanketed in shattered glass, and twisted metal – a quick frown before skirting the lagoon of congealed blood.

The two bodies did nothing to ease his tension as he did another visual sweep of the room and the hall beyond a floor-to-wall window. Whatever happened, those involved had left. He lowered his rifle and made his way back to the library.

When he passed the table, Ried inspected what lay scattered across the surface. He ignored the plate of food, to thumb through the first few pages of the book Marcus took from the shelves.

"Holy shit. A second edition." On a whim, he pocketed the book in his shirt and picked up the bottle of wine lying beside the platter. But then, something switched on his internal klaxons. In a swift, fluid movement, he pirouetted and raised the M-16.

The cause of his alarm came from a tapestry flapping in the breeze through the broken window. Ried continued his surveillance of the library cursing his heightened nerves.

Shaking his head, he lowered his gun when the flash of movement through the windows overlooking the hallway caught his attention. He darted from the room.

When he reached a T intersection, Ried braced his rifle against his shoulder and twisted to his right. Instead of finding soldiers or people, the corridor ending in a jagged hole from the collapsed tower with a draught gusting through the missing section of the building, creating small dust devils along the hall.

Abandoning the right branch of the hallway, Ried turned left, trotting past three renovated doors on his right, toward a door that opened onto a fire escape. Beneath the escapes landing was a paved courtyard, the battlements, and the curved wall of the north-west watchtower.

Across the courtyard, a figure scrambled through a hatch at the base of the tower.

"Marcus." Called Ried.

Marcus looked up through the shadowed light at the last moment before he disappeared down the interior stairway of the tower.

Ried shrugged. By his reckoning, Marcus had rescued himself. He turned his back on the escaping Proconsul and threw himself along the hall when a stream of bullets ruptured the door frame.

Behind his right, the storm of bullets tore through the hallway ceiling and shattered the inside windows of the library.

Ried scurried away from the chaos on all fours against the wall with the doors. Once more, the world slowed. Every sound around him played out on a separate track and each bullet hitting the walls imitated the sound of corn popping in hot oil.

A splinter of wood dragged along his cheek. The stinging pain tossed Ried from his slow world into the loud, chaotic one of real time.

He rose into a running crouch and threw himself around the T intersection and out of range from the tower's gun.

"Enough with the fucking time shifts?" Ried said in a hoarse, unnerved whisper.

Catching his breath, Ried took cover behind the library door frame. Down the hallway, sections of plaster fell from the wall, and the air filled with powdered and pulverised timber, plaster and stone.

Ried peered around the door frame as part of the library's roof collapsed. A fresh barrage of gunfire lacerated the timber door frame and the wall around Ried.

"Fuck." Ried threw himself down, rolled around, and fired the M-16 toward the source of incoming assault.

In response, the end of the hall flared in bursts of tangerine.

Pressing himself down on the floor Ried sighted down his rifle, he squeezed off three controlled bursts at his attacker's muzzle flashes.

With quick, and efficient hands, he loaded his last grenade and launched it down the hallway. The explosion tore away the closest corner of the hall's junction in a ball of flame and shrapnel.

Caught in the concussive shock wave slapped at Ried's senses, but he still recognised his attacker emerging from the cloud of dust: Mettius.

Then the Roman Centurion shifted his position to duck from view.

Two men in Vigiles equites uniforms replaced Mettius with their carbines raised.

"What is this, a fucking tag team?" Ried shimmied backwards on his stomach.

The first one knelt, flicked the carbine's firing lever too automatic, and pulled the trigger. The ten rounds spat from the gun shredding the floorboards within centimetres of Ried's arms and chest.

"For fuck's sake!"

Through the dust and smoke, the first man reloaded while the second Vigiles knelt to fire his carbine on full auto, miscalculating the fast, shuddering recoil and sending all ten rounds in a zig-zagging line along the wall above Ried.

Ried paused his reversed crawl and returned fire.

Now reloaded, the first shooter levelled his gun and snapped off two shots before the side of his head vanished in a cloud of blood, bone, and torn flesh.

The second Vigiles flinched from the other's grey matter spraying across his cheek and shoulder and then collapsed beside his companion in a fountain of his own arterial spray.

Ried hurried in a backward crouch toward the spiral staircase, pursued by Mettius, who had turned the corner squeezing off double taps from his carbine.

Ried's rifle breech locked open on an empty magazine.

Mettius grinned in triumph and took advantage of Ried reloading his weapon. He snatched up another gun from the closest dead Vigiles, and marched down the hall, his back straight, carrying a carbine in each hand.

"You're bloody kidding." Ried stumbled into the circular stairwell. "Who does he think he is? The fucking Terminator?" Ried slapped home a fresh magazine and abandoned his rifle discipline let lose blind wild shots toward the Roman.

Ignoring the swarm of bullets, Mettius's fingers danced on his carbine's triggers. The ensuing double stream of bullets decimated the walls of the stairwell.

Two found their mark on Ried – one punched through his sleeve, and the other near his waist, singeing his skin.

The closeness of the shots gave Ried all the desire he needed to be somewhere else. Without hesitation, he bounded down the staircase, as ricocheting bullets, and fractured, plaster rained down on him.

By the time Ried reached the hallway below him, he had tossed the empty magazine aside to reload a fresh one. But before he could turn to cover his retreat, Mettius loosed another full clip down the stairwell.

Ried stepped into the hall for cover and then twisted up and around firing back up the stairwell. Beneath him came shouts and cries from Dom and Jack as he rolled into the hall.

He took a cautious step onto the stairs and snapped off the last round in the magazine. "Give me a fucking break…"

When the bolt locked open over an empty mag, Ried flung the weapon around his shoulders and drew his revolver to fire three rounds before another volley of shots slammed the mesh stair tread, spraying hot shards of lead and steel.

"Christ all-fucking-mighty." He holstered the pistol, ejected the empty magazine of his rifle, and slammed the last one in place.

The instant Mettius stopped shooting, Ried stepped back with his M-16 pointed upward. He dropped to his knee and froze when a metallic clatter echoed through the mesh stairway.

"OH shit." Instinct catapulted Ried from the stairs, seconds before the grenade detonated.

The resulting concussion bounced him off the nearest wall to land in a winded heap with his ears ringing and the dust and cordite fumes burning his eyes. He rolled on his back, spitting out dirt and plaster. His head ached, a shrill whistle sounded behind the cotton wool smothering his bruised eardrums.

Ried blinked away the dirt and grit to peer through the clearing smoke at his non-existent escape route. He forced himself to move with a sense of urgency toward the destroyed recreation room.

Behind him, the compromised stairway creaked and groaned under Mettius's weight.

Mettius's feet thumped on the floor seconds before the fractured bolts, and brackets snapped, sending the twisted steel shrieking in metallic death toward the bottom of the stairwell.

The Roman soldier glanced back over his shoulder into the empty space, his face shaped by an arrogant smirk. Reloading a fresh magazine, Mettius glimpsed his prey's shadow, as it flicked out of sight.

Ried scrambled over the mound of shattered blocks and stone of the wall and tower. With a final lunge, he threw himself over the top and cried out when his shoulder flared in white-hot pain. The shock of the bullet's graze and his haste to escape sent Ried tumbling down the slope losing his rifle.

To the east, above the bastion wall's edge and the pale glow of fixed Sulphur bulbs came the blue-white flashes of an electrical storm.

In his efforts to stand, Ried's hand pushed aside a sheathed gladius from the rubble. He reached down to pick up the sword but recoiled when he held the original owner's hand still clamped on the blade's grooved hilt.

Prying the disembodied hand loose, Reid drew the blade free from its scabbard. He lifted the sword to test the weight when the blade's sheath slammed against his chest with a brutal thump.

The impact came like a mule's kick and sent him crashing onto the paved courtyard. Ried rolled onto his hands and knees coughing and wheezing to re-inflate his left lung.

At his feet lay the sword's sheath with a hole punched through the metal and leather case.

"Holy shit…" He leaned back on his haunches and ran his hand over his bruised ribs and lifted out the book he found. The bullet, after piercing the scabbard, had buried itself in the novel to mushroom out in the last dozen pages.

"Jesus bloody Christ." His fixation on the lifesaving novel halted when a series of booming cracks rolled around the enclosed courtyard. Ried dropped the book when he dived forward and crawled up to the pile of rubble from the fallen tower.

Silhouetted against the grey block wall, he saw Mettius fire another round at the back of a fleeing figure, before approaching a second man kneeling with his left hand clamped around the opposite bicep.

Without a single spoken word, Mettius raised his sword and plunged the double-edged blade into the man's lungs through the base of his neck.

"Off-worlder, it's just us now," Mettius said. "OFF-WORLDER… I know you're alive."

A shrill voice in Ried's head urged him to run, which, considering the circumstances, he took as advice. The second voice in his head argued run where? You know you are trapped.

He jogged around the hall to see a door leading into the south-west corner tower and smiled. *Trapped my arse.*

His moment of relief disappeared at the soft footfall of Mettius's boots on the courtyard's paving. Ried whirled around with the sword raised and parried the downward arc of Mettius's blade.

The force of the impacting swords caused Ried to falter, almost tripping over his own feet. In his efforts to defend himself he swung the sword in wild, desperate arcs.

Ried's education in swordplay came fast and hard.

Mettius preferred quick thrusts with subtle flicks of his wrist, keeping the point of his sword within reach of his opponent's body.

When one of Mettius's forward strokes came millimetres away from slicing through Ried's neck, everything again fell into slow motion.

Ried rolled his head to the side and ducked under Mettius's passing blade. He was learning to work with the slow-moving world around him.

A laugh slipped past his lips at how he could almost predict Mettius's every move. With his confidence, inflated Ried countered his attacker.

When Mettius thrust, Ried parried. Small sparks flashed as their swords clashed. Unfortunately for Ried, Mettius didn't take long to adapt to Ried's pre-emptive assaults, which cut away Ried's fresh flower of confidence.

The perspiration from Mettius's nose and chin arced through the air, landing on the ground in tiny, expanding puffs of dust. Around their feet, the dirt exploded outward with each stomp of their boots.

Ried wavered, and his arms grew heavy; his muscles burned from lactose, and his shoulder throbbed from the deep graze of Mettius's bullet.

Ried's growing agony and weariness drove home the understanding, even in his heightened state, he lacked the stamina for a continued melee.

In a desperate move, Ried fell to his knees, bending he arched his back under one of Mettius's sweeping strokes. He could almost count every chip and scratch along the edge of his opponent's sword slicing the air above his face.

Ried swung out his left arm to grab and push Mettius's sword arm away and down. He continued in a rolling motion which unbalance the Roman.

However, with decades of experience in hand-to-hand combat, Mettius pivoted his wrist, rolled and ran his sword along Ried's right bicep.

The adrenaline fuelling Ried's body overrode the pain as he kept rolling to the side and dragging the edge of his sword across the back of Mettius's thigh.

Caught off-guard, Mettius grunted and stumbled when the blade sliced into his muscle.

With teeth clenched, Ried twisted and followed through by raking his sword up and carving a long gash into Mettius's shoulders between his body armour and the plated shoulder manica.

When Mettius cried out and fell back, the slow-motion sensation ceased and catapulted Ried into real time.

He stumbled for a few disorientated steps, but the movements of Mettius increased Ried's recovery, and he ran toward the south ramparts.

Ried threw his weight against the wooden door of the closest tower. The impact ignited the pain in his arm, but the door held fast. In desperation, he pulled on the metal ring, but the door refused to yield.

He sprinted back to the other tower and found the first guard Mettius had shot, crumpled against the closed door. He took a handful of the man's collar and rolled him away. Ried went to clamp both hands around the doorknob and jerked back from the splinters impaling his knuckles.

The shots Mettius fired smashed the lock and jammed the door.

"Fuck!" Ried searched for the dead man's fallen carbine, but all he found was a pistol with an empty magazine. He kicked the body in frustration. "Who the fuck would join a gun fight with no bloody bullets?"

He twisted and brought up his sword when a series of diffused, slow flashes cast eerie shadows around his surroundings.

Ried spared a brief look eastward into the night sky. *Fan-fucking-tastic. A thunderstorm.* He doubted his clumsy sword skill would hold out in a repeated round against Mettius. So, he hunted around the tiled courtyard for his M-16.

The Sulphur lamps along the wall revealed nothing other than weeds, and grass sprouting between the dislodged and cracked paving stones. He ignored the two-storey building in the courtyard's centre with its broken semi-circular garden beds nestled between boarded windows.

Between the watchtowers, the curtain wall stood fast, stained with algae, moss and grime. Not even the accumulated composting leaves and dirt showed any promise of a weakened wall.

A closer flash of lightning lit the paving stones at Ried's feet, revealing something which gave him a sense of hope. A tangled cluster of vines and creepers from a garden bed clawed their way over the southern rampart.

"Face it, Ried. All that's keeping you alive is sheer fucking luck."

A mad thought flashed through his growing fears. He rushed over, grabbed a handful of the stringy plant, braced his feet, and pulled back. Under his weight, the green, rubbery vine stretched and tore away, leaving him on his backside, and cursing the useless vegetation in his hand.

Ried hacked at the creeper in frustration.

What the fuck are you doing? Even if you got away, Abbey and Dom would never be safe with that fucking freak still alive.

He took a long breath, which escaped his lips in a slow sigh of resignation.

All right, Ried – Live or die – That prick never leaves this fucking rock.

"I assume, Off-Worlder, you found the old man and girl?"

Ried hauled himself up and brandishing his sword toward the Roman found something new to spur his confidence.

A rough, blood-soaked tourniquet wrapped above Mettius's knee and the trailing of cloth stuck to the side of his armour with more blood.

Look at that... The bastard does bleed.

CHAPTER NINE

"With Marcus doing the bolt, and you standing there, I'm guessing the blood downstairs is Gallio's," Ried said.

"You are right." A dark shadow crossed Mettius's face. "Gallio is dead, along with his plans." Mettius fixed his black gaze on Ried. "But mine are not," he raised his sword arm, "you are an abomination, and do not belong on this world."

At first, Ried squinted with a look of disbelief, but the set jawline and look of disgust on Mettius gave him a slight pause. "Christ. You're serious, aren't you?" Ried spread his arms. "News flash, Mettius. This isn't our world. Neither of us belongs here."

"No!" Mettius took one step forward with his Gladius pointed at Ried and the index figure f his left hand stabbing downward. "This world belongs to the Empire because these humans lost the courage to keep fighting for it."

Ried's knuckles turned white with the increased grip on the sword.

Time to end the debate.

He stepped away from the wall and hesitated when the paving stones beneath his feet buckled and dipped in rippling waves.

The Armoury.

The castle's rampart walls and towers convulsed and cracked. Ried jumped to his right when several terracotta tiles from the hall's roof, shattered on the stones beside him.

A grumbling cough and bass rasp behind his right shoulder announced the top section of the south tower sheared itself from the main structure.

The waterfalling tower sent Ried in a frantic dive and roll through a billowing cloud of rock, bricks and concrete dust as a basketball-size rock bounced over his head and break apart against the wall.

Beneath their feet, the castle belched a throaty growl before the eastern side of the courtyard rose in an expanding bubble of broken cobblestones and rock, thrown skyward under a mushrooming ball of flame and debris.

Ried stood transfixed by the chaos around him. *Okay, now this slow-motion shit is getting annoying.*

The dust and smoke billowed outward in an infinite calm, streaked by flames coloured in hues of amber, bronze, and blue.

The hall's remaining corner tower swayed from the shock waves and twisted on itself to collapse inwards amidst popping mortar and concrete blocks.

The towers impact released an expanding cloud of flame skyward, howling in freedom, followed by another explosion, which sent up a rolling ball of viscous, bright, orange fire and smoke. The resulting cloud raining lethal debris across the torn courtyard past the perimeter of the dying castle.

Another quake heaved the courtyard, fracturing the base of the bastion wall. Ried scrambled away, a prisoner to the sluggish world around him.

The hot cinders and powder seared his lungs and throat. Ried blinked away stinging grit through watery eyes as he blundered his way around a maelstrom of destruction.

Then, beneath his feet, the stones shifted, and a new sound assaulted his battered eardrums. A slow, crackling, rat-a-tat scrape. The slow passing of the lightning's flare revealed a meter-wide crevice snaking its way toward him.

The growing crevasse breathed with a drawn-out whoosh, followed by dozens of double slaps and whacks as the foundations of the courtyard succumbed to the destruction below.

With a stomach-turning lurch, Ried launched himself in a desperate dive over the widening black-brown chasm. He hit the opposite sides edge with an awkward landing. His legs flayed and kicked as he rolled away and thereby avoided falling into the abyss.

Behind him came more warbling snaps of masonry and rock. The north-west tower now collapsed in on itself, falling sideways and tearing away part of the northern rampart with it.

Ried lost his footing from the added shockwave and fell into the depths below. With frantic, wild swings, his hands caught a mass of the tangled creepers, which, stretched and flexed like bundles of woven elastic bands.

His laboured breath echoed and hissed in his ears like a charging bull, and his arm muscles – gorged on lactose – cried out against his efforts to claw his way along the vines as he tried to scramble out of the crevice.

His hand clawed amidst the vine at the edge of the courtyard when the plant broke free under his weight. With a cry, Ried clutched the broken tiles and dragged himself back on the courtyard.

A flash of Lightning revealed a mountain of rubble a few metres below the edge of the courtyard's foundations.

Another flash of lightning silhouetted Mettius looking at Ried across the chasm. Beyond the castle, angry clouds filled the horizon, along with the quick bursts of more lightning. Only minutes before, the night sky was clear, but it seemed the explosions pulled the distant storm toward the castle.

Ried's heart dropped into the pit of his stomach at the thought of what might come.

The lightning streaked groundward beyond the crumbling rampart walls, cracking the air as if Thor's hammer struck an iron plate.

Despite being blinded and concussed, a staggering and profound sense of relief washed over him, when he understood this was nothing more than a simple thunderstorm.

Ried stood, gasping to replace the air in his winded and dust-choked lungs. His efforts faltered from the numbness in his left thigh, which slammed against the jagged rock under the pavers when he swung on the vines.

He shifted his footing to keep most of the weight on his good leg and looked over at Mettius, whose soulless, black-on-black eyes above a thin smile reflected the flashing lightning and background fires.

Strewth. A corpse has a warmer bloody smile.

Standing there, Ried broke the staring contest in search of his fallen sword. The numbness in his leg faded, and his breathing became less ragged.

The blade, however, seemed lost, and his only consolation was the curved knife he had taken from the pimp, lying near his feet.

"A knife's better than nothing," Ried uttered and then proved his mettle against the Roman's hard glare by making a deliberate show of retrieving the blade.

A lightning bolt struck the devastated courtyard behind Mettius. The flash cast everything in a blue-white halo. The impact flung razor-sharp shards of stone outward within the deafening crack of its shock wave.

Ried covered his face from the harsh glare and stumbled backwards. His hearing drowned by a high-pitched ringing.

Mettius jerked forward raising an arm across his eyes.

When Ried turned his head, his right hand brushed against his revolver, still resting in its holster. In his escape and fear of Mettius, he forgot about the gun on his hip. A tiny flicker of hope sparked in his thoughts as he slipped the knife into his belt at the small of his back.

When another lightning bolt flashed overhead, Mettius glanced skyward at the billowing storm clouds.

Go on. It's now or not at all. When Mettius returned his gaze, Ried pretended to falter on his bruised thigh and unclipped the retaining strap on the holster.

"Your bravery does you credit," Mettius said with a slight tilt of his head.

"A compliment?"

"The truth."

"Fuck you." Ried knew the words were cliché, but somehow, right then, they seemed right.

The Roman raised his voice over the wind to shout at Ried. "When I first saw you at the nomad camp, I understood you, Off-Worlder," Mettius continued, "and the business with the Harris boy and his prostitute confirmed it."

"Is this your plan? Talk me to death?"

461

Mettius sighed. "You want to set the world right." He stared at Ried. "Except you can't." Mettius took another step toward the edge and paused when another bolt illuminated the clouds above.

Ried blinked when the world around him decelerated again. The rope-like twists of lightning ambled overhead as Mettius jumped over the crevasse.

The brilliant flash silhouetted the slow-moving Mettius, revealing the Centurion's every fold of clothing, which shifted between his armour and the passing glow shadowed Mettius's face. A flesh and blood gargoyle of hatred.

With casual slowness, Ried raised his .357 and squeezed the trigger. The Magnum's hammer rocked back and fell. The hot gas flared out between the cylinder and the barrel with each strike of the hammer.

Mettius landed on his knees, in front of Ried, frowning at the smoking revolver in Ried's hand. He stood up with a backward step and poked his finger into one of the three holes across his chest armour.

With Mettius distracted, Ried snapped open the cylinder and ejected the spent cartridges. His hands felt numb, and his fingers seemed uncoordinated.

Around him time reverted to normal. Ried fumbled a speed loader from its pouch. He fought to stay calm and keep his hands steady while he loaded the cylinder with six fresh rounds.

By the time Mettius raised his eyes, Ried stood braced with the loaded pistol and the empty loader bouncing on the cracked pavers.

Mettius spat a wad of blood and pointed at his midriff. "This is where my heart is, human–" For the second time that night, a look of genuine surprise flashed across Mettius's face when his legs crumbled.

462

Ried's smile broadened, and he called back over the wind. "Yeah, but your spine's in the same place."

Mettius squared his shoulders and shouted a curse in his native tongue. However, the cry faltered when he staggered from the super-heated sensation of another three bullets punching through his body, tearing apart his lungs and intestines.

A fourth one shattered the Roman's right shoulder blade before his face twitched from two more slugs puncturing his skin.

The hollow points mushroomed after hitting the bone and cartilage in Mettius's skull. The two expanded bullets tore away the back of Mettius's head. Shards of bone, flesh and matted hair blossomed outward amidst grey matter, blood and cranial fluid.

In soulless defiance to his death, Mettius sat back on his haunches for several seconds. With one black-on-black eye nothing more than a blood-filled hole the other stared at Ried.

Ried tried focusing through eyes seared from the bright chamber and muzzle flashes as the billowing wind nudged Mettius into the cavern.

The Romans body fell past the mound of rubble and slammed with a hollow wet thud on the floor below.

The yellow and white flashes on Ried's retinas faded to points of white as he studied the spot where Mettius fell. Exhaustion washed over him, he limped over to where Mettius's gladius had dropped from his lifeless hand. For several minutes, he stood under the storm clouds, studying the sword.

Above him, the storm released the rain in torrential sheets. Stepping over the sword, Ried jumped, and half climbed, half fell down the mountain of rubble.

On reaching the bottom, Ried sat on a rain-soaked chunk of rock. He glanced at the crumpled body of Mettius and wondered why he felt no joy or remorse for winning the day.

After regaining some strength, he sloshed through the spreading water on the cavern's floor. By the time he walked from the cavern, the collective effects of weariness and emotion caught up with Ried. He slumped against the plateau's cliff face while the rain continued to fall, blown about by the wind squalls.

Around him, the broken wall's exposed reinforcing bars became lightning rods. When the lightning struck the steel bars, the explosive energy sent chunks of earth and concrete to pepper the sodden ground.

Stunned by the barrage of lightning and falling debris, Ried staggered back into the cavern.

A hand reached out of the dark drawing Ried into the shadows.

"I see you survived." Marcus leaned closer so Ried could hear him over the storm.

"And you, but only just by the looks of it," Ried shouted back, referring to Marcus's dirt-smeared clothing, dishevelled hair, and battered bleeding face and arms.

Marcus blinked through the blood oozing from a deep cut below his hairline. "Perhaps we should leave here before this all collapses on us."

"I reckon we–"

In a sudden move, Marcus clenched both hands around Ried's throat, lifted him from the ground, and slammed him against the wall of the cavern. "I told that idiot Gallio what you are capable of." With each word spoken, Marcus thumped Ried's head against the rough concrete. "Do not think for an instant that killing Mettius will keep your new family safe." Marcus moved his face within centimetres of Ried's. "I will ensure they all die. Except for Abbey. Her, I will keep for myself."

Ried's warm blood matted his hair from the blows tearing his skin. His cheeks puffed in and out like bellows trying to suck air past his restricted windpipe.

Ried dug his nails into Marcus's hands and kicked at his legs in a desperate attempt to loosen the larger man's constricting hold.

Pulsating white dots exploded across Ried's vision as he started losing focus. His lungs burned from a lack of oxygen, and his heart started beating so fast it lost all rhythm.

The sound in his ears drummed the tune of impending death. His withered adrenal gland pumped out the last millilitre of the hormone.

Marcus sensed Ried's struggles weakening. However, this only increased his anger. "Everything you touched will burn… Your existence will be erased from the history of this world."

A short while ago, Ried hadn't cared if he lived or died. His defeat of Mettius meant he had saved his friends. But now, his oxygen-depleted brain understood that Mettius and Gallio had been brutal soldiers. Marcus, Ried realised, was something different and a much greater threat.

Ried reached behind him, twisting against the choking grip. In response, the proconsul stopped his thrashing of Ried and lifted him higher.

Marcus offered his victim a sinister sneer dripping with dark arrogance and hatred. Then, with casual ease, the proconsul loosened one hand from the younger man's throat to grab Ried's belt. In a herculean move, Marcus lifted Ried and hurled the battered human across the cavern floor.

Stunned and almost choked to death, Ried tried to roll away from the approaching Roman, who drove a boot into Ried's chest, cracking a rib, and sending him sliding through a stream of muddy water. The point of the curved dagger digging into his hip.

Marcus strode over and clamped his hands around Ried's head to lift him upright.

"When I found out about you, I believed you could have been an asset." With a contorted face, the proconsul squeezed harder.

Dangling in the proconsul's grip, Ried rolled his shoulders and twisted an arm behind his back. He fought the urge to claw at Marcus's hands crushing his skull.

Instead, Ried wrapped his hand around the scimitar's handle. The pressure of Marcus's grip intensified, and the knife handle slipped from Ried's fingers.

Marcus drew Ried closer.

The closeness of Marcus and the gleam of triumph in his eyes reignited Ried's focus. With the last remaining trickle of adrenaline, Ried folded his fingers around the knife's handle as he twisted and swung his arm and the blade around and up.

Marcus jerked and dropped Ried.

The two men collapsed to their knees, falling toward each other. A growing pool of black, crimson spread between them. The Roman's head fell against Ried's shoulder.

"You… you came here by our doing…" The dying breath of the proconsul hissed against Ried's ear. "We tried to open…" he coughed when he pulled the knife from his chest, "…and leave this world… Instead… you arrived… destroyed it all…" With a final sigh, Marcus's hand dropped the instrument of his death and flopped sideways – dead.

Ried sat down and stared at Marcus, trying to understand what he had said.

The flare of lightning flashing from outside and above through the broken roof, along with the thump and crackle of dislodged rocks boosted Ried's tired body into action.

He staggered out of the imploding cavern where after half a dozen steps, he fell face first in the mud while above him, the storm broke apart after spending the last of its energy. The clouds grew thin and parted in the high winds to reveal a black sky dotted with faint stars.

"Over here!"

Ried opened his eyes and saw a large shadow standing over him. "Jack," he whispered through his bruised larynx and windpipe. "G'day, mate."

"Bloody hell, son." Jack tilted Ried's head back to inspect the myriad of cuts and grazes on his young friend's face, neck, and scalp. He tore Ried's sleeve away and wrapped the long gash on the younger man's bicep.

From behind Jack, another figure moved up in the flickering darkness to kneel beside Ried.

"How is he?" Gazza asked.

"Lucky to be alive, I reckon," Jack replied.

Ried's weak fingers held Jacks arm. "Abbey?"

"Down below with the colonel," Gazza said.

Ried pointed into the cavern, "Marcus…"

"Easy, son. I'll go and get him."

Ried grabbed Jack's arm and winced from the cracked rib. "No… He's dead..."

Around them, the cavern's ruptured integrity failed. The rhyolite and basalt broke apart. Sharp cracks pierced the damp night. Hollow thumps went with the shriek of twisting steel. Avalanches of stone, brick, and gravel bulldozed through the trees.

"I reckon it's time we got our arses off this fuckin' mountain." Gazza flicked his head around to peer over his shoulder as a table-size boulder buried itself in the mud near the entrance of the tunnel.

"Shit. Here, take this." Jack passed Gazza his torch, and then hoisted Ried over his shoulder.

With each step, the big farmer took, black fire exploded in Ried's chest and head.

Once they reached the road, the avalanches subsided apart from the occasional echoing thwacks of rocks bouncing against the trees. With each step, the big farmer took, black fire exploded in Ried's chest and head. He patted his friends back.

"Jack… for Christ sake, let me walk." Begged Ried

When Jack knelt, Ried would have fainted were it not for Gazza coming over to support him.

With a nod, Ried pushed himself free from the two men and held his hand out to Gazza, who, after accepting the gesture, turned, and made his way towards his people sitting some distance away around a fire.

"Not big on goodbyes, is he?"

"I can't say if he ever was," Jack replied.

468

Ried did a slow turn from watching Gazza and walked over to three covered bodies.

Abbey left the warmth of the fire to walk towards Ried, but Dom grabbed her elbow and sat her back down when he saw Ried's expression.

"Leave him be for a minute."

"Why?"

"Trust your father, Abbey," Dr Mitchum said, putting the blanket back around her shoulders.

"Who are they?" Ried's larynx grated with his whisper when Dom stepped up to him.

"Bill Henderson and his son," Dom told him. "Jack told me about Smithy and his nephew." He rested his hand on Ried's shoulder. "But by the look on your face, it's something else."

At first, Ried hesitated, but then found himself wanting to tell Dom.

"I should have died with my squad. Christ. For months after, that was all I wanted." His gaze shifted back in time. "We were out on patrol when a couple of IEDs took out their Bushmasters." He sighed. "I was scouting the road ahead in a LAM. When we saw the explosions, I told my driver to turn around. That's when they attacked." He paused to massage the scar on his shoulder. "We took two RPG hits, wounding my turret gunner and my driver. I got Simmo out… but the bastards killed him before we got to cover and then hit my LAM with another RPG…"

Dom waited for Ried to continue.

"I joined the army because I wanted to make a difference…" Ried knelt beside Smithy's corpse. "Everybody, from my CO to the troop's Padre and the shrinks told me it wasn't my fault. When I got home… I avoided everyone… I was too ashamed… too guilty…"

"Because you were alive, and they weren't."

"More than that... I felt like I had somehow failed everyone, and I guess I was angry at myself..." Ried looked over his shoulder toward Abbey. "I had the same feelings after you and Abbey were taken."

"And now?"

"Now?" Ried stood and offered Dom a bittersweet smile. "If I told you, I feel like I made a difference, would that sound crazy?"

"Oh, I reckon you've made a difference," Dom said.

"Can I ask a question?" Ried turned to stare at the mountaintop peppered with faint orange glows.

"Sure."

"Do you believe in irony?"

"Irony." Dom shrugged. "I suppose so. Why?"

"I don't know... Something Marcus said before he died." Ried shrugged and held Abbey in his gaze for a long minute as she talked with Eddy and Dr Mitchum.

"Marcus is dead?" Dom's tone held genuine sorrow.

"Yes," Ried said.

"How?"

"In the cavern on the way out."

"Do you know how?"

"Does it matter?"

"I suppose not."

Ried lowered his eyes back to the covered bodies. "This is gonna cause a lot of waves..."

"You're not wrong there."

EPILOGUE

The following morning Ried stood alone staring at the remains of the castle and broken mountain top. He didn't sleep well because his bruised body objected to every move he made.

Bird song echoed through the valley and the previous night's storm brought out the full bouquet of the surrounding scrub. All this went unnoticed by Ried who watched the steam and dark grey smoke being pulled southwest from the remaining fires still smouldering amongst the rubble and ruin on the mountain top

Dom patted Ried's shoulder and handed him a mug of tea. Ried took a sip. The brew was strong and sweet.

"You look like shit," said Dom.

"Cheers." Ried's reply held no mirth. He didn't need a mirror to know Dom spoke the truth. Also, he felt like shit.

Dom followed a mouthful of biscuit with his tea. He ate and drank in silence beside Ried until the younger man drained his mug. When he took Ried's empty cup, he gestured toward Eddy and a group of men moving around under the tree's shadows.

"The lads saved some horses and gear from the stables. We'll kit out the best looking two for riding and then one for a packhorse."

"Why two?" Asked Ried.

He tipped his head down the road. "Eddy told me he is going with you." Dom rested his hand on Ried's shoulder. "After you've both rested, head west, stay on the move and avoid any small towns or settlements cause the Senate will be out for your blood."

Ried gave a weak smile and nodded toward Abbey. "This will break her heart." His own heart turned to cracked porcelain. Each beat sending a razor-edged sliver of pain against his cracked rib.

"Not as much as seeing you hanging on a cross with your throat cut." Dom's eyes glinted with a father's sympathy within a face of stern understanding. "Because that's what'll happen if you stay."

Ried shrugged. He watched Abbey sitting by a fire and thumbed away a small drop in the corner of his eye. The night's past actions now faded under the weight of telling Abbey he couldn't go back.

Dom shifted to watch three men and Cassius lower a shrouded corpse in the last of five graves. He released his own long sigh. "We'll be heading off in the next half an hour." Dom headed back to the main group loading up the vehicles.

Ried followed alongside. "Where's Jack?"

"He headed off with Gazza at first light."

Ried nodded with a small, sad pout before walking over to Abbey.

I was right... The hero never drives off with the girl.

The End...

Authors notes.

Over the centuries there has been considerable conjecture on what happened to the Roman Empire's Ninth Legion. Many speculated the legion perished in battle against the Caledonians in ancient Britain.

However, in the latter half of the last century evidence arose to suggest the Legion simply fell shy on numbers during campaigns in northern Europe and as a result, it was disbanded and no longer recorded on the military records.

I think being swallowed by a rip in the continuum and ending up in an alternate universe to become a new empire is a much more fitting scenario.

Why? Because the Ninth Legion or Legio IX Hispania were badass in every sense of the word. They were one of the four legions inherited by Julius Caesar and went on to participate in a long history of successful campaigns many of which were in Roman Britain.

I have, for a long time, held a fascination regarding the missing Ninth which is why, for me, they were the perfect choice as the founders of my Roman Galactic Empire.

Lucius Neratius Marcellus did govern Roman Britain between 101 to 104 AD, and during this period the Roman Emperor Trajan requested Roman soldiers from Britain's legions to help with the First Dacian War in Europe.

This reduction of troops in Britain spurred the Caledonians from the north, what we now call Scotland, into acts of rebellion.

Despite this, Marcellus did bring stability and later withdrew his troops back from the Antonine Wall. Later known as Hadrian's Wall.

The town of Eboracum, during its prime, was the largest town in northern Britain and a provincial capital.

The original settlement was founded in 71 AD when the Ninth Legion constructed a military fortress on flat ground above the River Ouse near its junction with the River Foss. Then after the fall of the Roman Empire, the town evolved into what we know as York.

The poor soldier who died of his wounds in the prologue was, as Marcellus pointed out, the Ninth Legions Imaginer. A legionnaire who carried the banner and battle standard of the Legion and his name was indeed Lucious Duccius Rufinus.

This little nugget of history, I found during some research when I read an article regarding a stone tablet discovered in 1864 in the area of York which bore inscriptions saying it was the headstone of Lucious Duccius Rufinus who died at the age of Twenty-Eight.

However, nothing on the inscription explains his manner of death. So, this lack of information left it open for a little dramatic and creative license on behalf of the author.

***

Thank you for purchasing the first book in the Off-Worlder series. I hope you enjoyed it.

Regards,

AJ. Adsett